Bill James

is a former journalist who worked for the *Western Mail* and *South Wales Echo*, *The Daily Mirror* and the *Sunday Times*. He is the author of eighteen crime novels in the Harpur & Iles series, which are published all over the world. *Protection*, the fourth in the series, was televised by BBC 1 as *Harpur & Iles*, starring Hywel Bennett. Hollywood is currently negotiating for *Halo Parade*, number three.

James also writes under the name David Craig, most recently a series set around Cardiff docks, where he grew up. The Warner Brothers film, *The Squeeze*, with Stacy Keach, Edward Fox and Carol White was adapted from the David Craig novel, *Whose Little Girl Are You?*

Middleman saw James tackle development corruption in his native Cardiff.

Bill James is married with four children. He still lives in his native South Wales and divides his time between his home near Cardiff and a caravan on the Pembrokeshire coast.

Books by Bill James, published by The Do-Not Press:

Split
Middleman

D0569268

First published in Great Britain in 2003 by
The Do-Not Press Limited
16 The Woodlands
London SE13 6TY
www.thedonotpress.com
email: ame@thedonotpress.com

Copyright © 2003 by Bill James
The right of Bill James to be identified as the Author of this work
has been asserted by him in accordance with the Copyright,
Designs & Patents Act 1988.

Casebound edition: ISBN 1 904316 20 4
C-format trade paperback: ISBN 1 904316 21 2

British Library Cataloguing in Publication Data. A catalogue
record for this book is available from the British Library.

All rights reserved. No part of this publication may be repro-
duced, transmitted or stored in a retrieval system, in any form or
by any means without the express permission in writing of The
Do-Not Press Limited having first been obtained.

This book is sold on the condition that it shall not, by way of
trade or otherwise, be lent, resold or hired out or otherwise circulated without the publisher's prior consent in any form of binding
or cover other than that in which it is published and without a
similar condition being imposed on the subsequent purchaser.

1 3 5 7 9 10 8 6 4 2

A
Man's
Enemies

by

Bill James

MORAY COUNCIL LIBRARIES & INFO.SERVICES	
2O 1O 54 79	
Askews	
F	

BOOK ONE

Chapter 1

'Because, because, because, Simon, you know about deaths in the Service.'

'So do you. So do most of us.'

'So I do. So we do,' Latimer said. 'But what you know is… oh, call it *particular*. Yes, that. Unique to you. Personal to you.'

'Don't see it.'

'Of course you see it. You know about deaths in the Service, which would admittedly be routine enough, and would probably be so in any country's Intelligence Service. But, more important, you know about deaths in this Service *brought about by people in this Service*. And, to focus tighter, you know about deaths in *this Section* of the Service, brought about by people in *this Section* of the Service – in the Outfit, as we lovingly call our Section. Such knowledge is special. Now, surely you'd admit that. In-house deaths. 1997. Those terrible days when the terrible, terrible spring-cleaning happened.

'But so do you know about them. So do most of us,' Abelard replied.

'So I do. So we do. But you, Simon, were close to these killings. Remarkably close.'

'Just close. To some of them.'

'Remarkably close. And to the most important ones. You're our expert on colleague snuffing colleague. Oh, on other facets of Intelligence operations, also, but above all on the appalling hates and rivalries that can arise in our Section of Her Majesty's Intelligence and Security Services.'

'A long time ago.'

'A while ago.'

'And an accident.'

'What?' Latimer asked. 'Not the death, deaths? You're not saying those deaths – Julian Bowling, Verdun Cadwallader – were an—?'

'No. An accident that I was close to.'

'I thought... I thought...' Turkey Latimer let laughter give him a truly disabling time for a minute, his face gorgeously merry, his body mildly convulsed... 'I thought you were saying the death, deaths, themselves should be regarded as accidents. That would be some claim, now wouldn't it? In the circs.'

'I meant it was a fluke I happened to be close.'

'Remarkably close.'

'But an accident,' Abelard replied.

'Oh, certainly. Would I say otherwise – or allow anyone else to say otherwise about you? No imputation of *involvement* in the death, deaths. Nothing like that. I would definitely fight anyone who said that about you.'

'Thanks.'

Latimer worked at some precision: 'I wouldn't call it so much an accident as brilliantly fortunate chance. Does that sound callous? I suppose it might. Look, Simon, I don't refer to the deaths themselves, Bowling's, Cadwallader's, as fortunate chance. Obviously. These were colleagues, after all, and in some very real sense, friends. I hope I'd never speak casually of the slaughter of such folk, no matter what the usefulness might have been to the Outfit and us *in* and *of* the Outfit. Remember that kindly phrase they had in the Indian army, "He was of use"– meaning a man had died actually on the battle field? Empire understatement. Sublime. But forgive a digression, do. No, no, I was saying only that your closeness to these awful events was a fortunate chance, Simon. It *qualifies* you, you see, is *enabling*. You are bound to have unique insights, supremely valuable insights, given the new situation. This bloody book situation.'

'In which very real sense were the deads friends?' Abelard replied.

'Yes, friends. I feel you wouldn't argue with that. Colleagues one had worked with for quite long periods and in some senses trusted and admired. I certainly don't believe "friends" is too personal a term, do you?'

'In which senses were they trusted and admired?'

'People removed so – there's bound to be a gap, isn't there, Simon? Oh, that was generally feared, I'm sure. Well, we recovered, didn't we? The grief faded, as grief will, and the Outfit survived, as the Outfit does. August 2001 and we look as settled and fit as any Section can, these thin and purposeless days. But now... now the rather awkward possibility of a revisit to those bad, internecine times. Why I refer to you rather briskly, perhaps, as an expert. Brisk or not, we do *need* an expert, Simon. None of us wants the unpleasantnesses of that era given a foul re-airing in print, I know. You wouldn't wish this yourself, I'm convinced. My impression, and not merely mine – several of us – yes, we do believe you're the one to stop this damn book. And probably the only one.'

'Which several?'

'Oh, I'd call it a consensus. Nothing less. I don't see that as an exaggeration. There's a warm, all-round faith in your delicacy, tact and yet forcefulness as a considerable Outfit officer.'

'Which of those?'

'Which of those what?' Latimer said.

'Which of delicacy, tact and forcefulness is a matter for their all-round faith?'

'All of them. Or permutations. Everyone in the Outfit shares a truly heartening certainty, Simon, that, with your beautifully developed flair and unwavering regard for what is right or rightish you can truly shut this fucking shithouse down double quick or sooner.'

'In what sense shut this fucking shithouse down?'

'Exactly. Shut him down. It's brilliant and comforting how you hit on a phrase.'

'Which we is this?'

'Which we in what context?' Latimer replied.

'Which we share the heartening certainty I can do it?'

'Exactly. Yes, shut him down. It's a comfort that I can report back you're so ready to handle this, Simon. But, then, nobody would expect less of you.'

'Report back where?'

'People will be delighted to hear you came up with the phrase for this operation: "shut him down." Shows an instant, indeed *instinctive*, mastery of what's wanted.'

'Did I?'

'Grand.'

'Will I get back-up?' Abelard replied.

'And, you see, if this works all right, it should convince others not to try a similar literary thing. That's the real objective. Alleged exposé volumes coming out in clumps, like May violets. Do we want this kind of damaging crud across the Press every couple of months, for God's sake? Damned rough, obscenely well-informed questions in the Commons about our command structure and budget and *raison de* fucking *être*'.

'When I say back-up, he's bound to realise he's vulnerable. He might have bought himself protection. He'd probably have money for that now. Might be a condition of the contract with his publishers. I'd make the approach to him solo at first, probably.'

'Best.'

'I'll be wide open. So, some discreet back-up?' Abelard said.

'We don't want him scared, stampeded, by a bicep crew descending. Those lovely assets of yours already mentioned – delicacy, tact – wouldn't have a fair run if you were operating with a batch of our Outfit heavies – estimable folk, yes, but heavies. That's how we see it.'

'Which we is that?'

'I heard no dissent at all, as it happens.'

'But back-up on call?'

'It's not for me to tell you how to talk to him,' Latimer replied. He had another laugh, now at the preposterousness of this idea. 'That would be in contradiction of everything we've spoken about. It's *you* who have the delicacy and tact, and you must clearly be left to exercise these as you, personally, decide. Could I instruct you in the nitty gritty, for heaven's sake!' He chuckled a little more. 'Just this, though, Si – he needs to understand – he and his fucking intellectualising wife – they both need to pick up unmistakably from what you in your delicate, tactful way tell him – they need to cotton on that not everyone in the Outfit or the rest of the Service is like yourself, like *my*self, and able to behave with decent restraint and control, despite the damn purple threat to many – oh, yes, many – in the prospect of this book. All our people have certainly been *trained* in decent restraint and control, but situations may arrive where, for some – I say *some* – for some that decent restraint and control can collapse. Their reactions may then become vivid and extreme, and entirely unforgiving. The fact that decent restraint and control *have* to be trained into them – have to be trained into *us*, I don't deny – the fact that we have to be trained in these qualities indicates doesn't it, that they are not necessarily natural? Under provocation some people can revert. This is the hazard they should be made to see.'

'Threaten him, them, that some of our frontline boys might get ungovernably wild? Poor reflection on leadership, isn't it?'

Abelard asked. 'You'd give them the quiet nod to do him
because of a book?'

'The pen can be shiteier than the sword. Let them know
how much we'd hate it if they turned themselves into targets
for the sake of a bit of scribbling.'

'He must have considered all this and still decided to
proceed with the book,' Abelard replied.

'We feel that a cogently phrased warning from someone
like you would have a notable impact,' Latimer said.

'What's it mean, someone like me?'

'The delicacy and tact, plus forcefulness – forcefulness
when necessary. If a really fucking terrifying warning to
someone comes out of a conversation notable otherwise only
for delicacy and tact, this can be wonderfully telling, not just
because of the shock element, but because this delicacy and
tact will have shown that you are a sensitive person, Simon,
and seek only the improvement of Mankind. He'd know that,
anyway, from past acquaintance, but your behaviour now
would confirm this. It makes the harshness of the underlying
message so much more acceptable, so much more credible, so
much more, yes, forceful.'

'He might have been put up to writing the book by all sorts
of enemies wanting to damage the Outfit. These enemies could
have units around, looking after him. That's standard, isn't it?
I feel I should be able to call on immediate help if things go
bandy.'

'Plus, another considerable plus is your blackness,' Latimer
replied.

'How does that come into it.'

'Many people seem to think that a black speaking with
sincerity sounds more sincere than a white speaking with
sincerity – like Paul Robeson singing *Ole Man River*. I don't
say I agree. It sounds racist to me – anti-white. But it *is* the
view of some, so we would be dim to ignore this.'

'Which we is that?'
'Oh, you and I, Simon.'

Chapter 2

Revelation – so much the fashion now. Pity the Scriptures got there first. All sorts these days could have stuck that title on their literary work, or *Revelations*, as so many wrongly called the Bible's final book. Abelard thought of Peter Wright with his *Spycatcher*, Richard Tomlinson and *The Big Breach*, Shayler with *his* Press disclosures, Dame Stella Rimington's, ex chief of MI5, due soon. All in the revelations game – the I Was A Spy game.

And now, Oliver Basil Horton. Abelard must prepare some conversation rich in delicacy and tact for Olly, as Latimer recommended, yet, also as Latimer recommended, forceful. Horton was in a cottage somewhere or a library or computer caff or even at home, word processing his biography as an Intelligence officer. He had resigned from the Outfit six months ago. You'd think the shops couldn't handle *another* ex-spy memoir. But, apparently, Olly was sitting on a publisher's commission, a deadline, good funding and the promise of more. So, had Horton convinced the editors he would come up with something wholly fresh on the Intelligence services, something to make all previous exposes look pale? This was what frightened Turkey Latimer, and those beyond Latimer. What Turkey might term a *consenus* fright. On the whole, it was wisest not to scare Latimer, let alone those beyond Latimer. People beyond Latimer could be especially malign. After all, they got beyond Latimer by being able to cope not only with fairly minor figures like Olly, but also with Latimer.

Olly had been working under Turkey when that terrible, in-house murder session he'd mentioned took place. Spring cleaning, to go back again to a Latimer term. Although Horton was never as much caught up in it as Abelard, Olly had been near enough. Some of what happened then he could probably recount or write about from direct knowledge. And some of it he could describe from what he'd heard, read, sensed, imagined, intuited. It would fail in a law court, but this was not a law court, it was another lid-off book perhaps capable of fucking up much. That is, it might if Abelard and/or others failed to cajole and sweet-talk Olly out of doing it. Was this what Latimer meant by 'shutting him down'? Was it? Maybe not. Turkey used that phrase and then claimed it was Abelard's. Why? Because, in any aftermath, RCV Latimer, the Outfit's Assistant Director Research and Co-ordination, must be able to deny he had suggested physical moves against Olly Horton and possibly his wife, Kate. Victor Latimer, often known as Turkey because of his eating style, was famously brilliant at foreseeing aftermaths and at keeping himself out of them if likely to be harmful to Victor Latimer.

As a tale, British Intelligence officers killed by other British Intelligence officers would probably rate a readership, even among the present welter of spy recollections. So, what was it Horton had to sell? What might he have heard, read, sensed, intuited? In those late 1990s days, there were two Outfit deaths. Julian Bowling had been a very talented officer, who found his spy career meaningless after the Berlin Wall came down, and deftly transformed the espionage techniques he had learned into the skills of international drugs trading. His behaviour, of course, sickened many in the Service and when Bowling was shot dead in a still unsolved murder there were plenty of reasons to decide he had been seen off by someone as high as you could get in the Outfit, Verdun Cadwallader. A while after this, Cadwallader himself disappeared and was

succeeded as head of Section by Judith Stewart, who Abelard
and others sometimes or continuously thought, might have
had Cadwallader violently removed: spring cleaning, in
Turkey's words, and information that should be kept out of
the best-seller lists. Judith still led the Section.

The thing was, Horton's book might set off similar dark
episodes, now with himself as the spy targeted – yet another
Latimer word – or, at least, *ex*-spy. A sombre, contradictory
logic operated: someone threatens to describe dodgy incidents in
a book and so brings on to himself another dodgy incident to
ensure the previous dodgy incidents are not described in a book.
Abelard had heard the lit crit doctrine which preached 'the
author is dead' – meaning the reader was supreme and could
make what s/he liked of a text. In Olly's case, though, it would
be not only the author dead, and deeply unmourned by former
colleagues, but also his book, and possibly his wife.

Olly was certain to change the names of those featured in
his volume, of course. All spies-turned-writers showed that
much loyalty to the Service and its men and women in the
field. Plus, there was fear of the libel laws, though security
personnel tended not to sue. Simon Abelard wondered what
re-christening he might get. And his lovely American girl
friends of that time, Lucy McIver, would probably rate an
appearance under another name, too, if Horton's research
discovered her. As Latimer had implied, Abelard was certain
to appear in anything Horton wrote. A pain, but it also
reached Abelard's vanity. This he accepted. He considered he
deserved at least a chapter in any book about those appalling,
formative times. He had unquestionably been a feature,
possibly even a principal feature. Maybe a star, and with
blood on his jacket. Turkey was right to say Abelard had been
very close to some of those events, especially the death of
Julian Bowling. Abelard and Lucy watched that happen, tried
hopelessly to save him.

It did not matter now very much that Abelard's name would be coded in Olly's book. *He* would recognise himself, and so would others. Didn't this sneaky career make aliases routine? Abelard had never felt there was anything holy or unique about a name. In fact, he occasionally met people in the trade who thought 'Abelard' itself was a doled-out, concocted label from the Outfit's New Identity barrel. They assumed it echoed that tragic tale of Peter Abelard, the twelfth century castrated monk, and his pre- and post-castration teenage love and later wife, Héloise. Wasn't this the eternal, dismal fact about taking a career in secrets and deception: people's hold on the real, the true and the genuine got badly loosened, or slipped altogether? They were so used to putting on a cover, they took *everything* as cover and forgot how to look underneath at what was real or true or genuine. Eric Knotte, number three in the Outfit's Operational Supplies Suite, was a born, eternally-non-Nobel poet, and recently circulated these lines about all field operatives:

> This guy's
> disguise
> became
> this guy.
> So what's
> the name
> behind
> the mask?
> Don't ask.

There was an Eric footnote pointing out the ambiguity in 'became'. It could mean 'suited' or 'took over.' Ambiguity was big with Outfit operatives, as well as Outfit poets.

Abelard recalled periods when Olly himself was Mr Lionel David Ivens for a period in Lebanon, and Neville Thane when at our Embassy in Beijing. The Chinese had liked the name

Thane, thinking he must be a Scottish laird, or was pretending
to be. For his own appearance in Olly's book, Abelard fancied
something solid and ordinary, like Maitland or Kemp, and an
ordinary first name also: Frank or Clifford or George, no Ivo
or Rory, suggesting curls, audacity and the standard ditched
degree course at Durham.

Abelard's duty was, though, to stop the sodding book
rather than quibble over how it named him. The duty pressed
a bit, not because Abelard was bothered all that much about
what perilous confidentialities Olly might sprinkle through his
volume; but he did fret over Olly's chances of staying whole
and unshot or unknifed or ungarotted or unpoisoned or unhit
by a car, or cars, or something – or some *things* – bigger if he
refused to quit the quit-and-tell project immediately, and so
continued to bring Victor Latimer unease, and those beyond
Latimer. After all, Olly had once been a good and reliable
colleague-friend and Abelard would prefer him kept intact.
Olly was bright and brave.

Of course, he did know about self-protection. Mr Lionel
Leonard Ivens had proved that with undetected hard flair in
the Lebanon. The trouble was, though, Turkey Latimer knew
– and those beyond Turkey knew – *they* knew all Olly knew
about self-protection, and Turkey would know, and those
beyond Turkey would know, how to counter, negate and then
trample on everything in this line Horton knew. It was
possible, in fact, that everything Olly knew, Turkey had taught
him. And Turkey was the kind who would prudently keep
back a few details of what he knew in case of a time like this
when what a pupil knew could be a fucking dangerous
obstacle unless he – that's Turkey – knew more, and knew
how to get inside what Olly knew and nullify it and him,
virtually before he knew it – that's nullify Olly before Olly
knew it. Turkey had his own flair, and not just at the head
back, neck stretched feeding mode that brought his nick name.

Olly was at home. He picked up the phone immediately, in person and live, not even a sentry answering machine. Sharp, Olly. This all suggested he had no need to hide, and was intended to suggest it. He had been trained that breaking wrists was only one way to disarm. Perhaps, in addition, he believed the famed 'new openness' really meant something, made him and his potential book part of an admirable, liberating trend and, in consequence, more than safe, a trail blazer. But surely Horton must be too big in the brain to swallow that.

'So, you're the boy, are you, Simon. You've been elected capital-v Visitor by Turkey and those beyond?'

'I *would* like to come around.'

'More or less any time,' Olly replied. 'We'd love to see you. I'm glad they've picked *you*. Honestly. In the role. Kate will be, too, I know.'

Abelard quite liked the term, capital-v, Visitor. Had Horton thought of it just like that, as they spoke? Smart. Creative. But, then Olly was due to become a creative artist, unless Abelard could convince him he'd really be better off totally *un*creative. The term Visitor had friendliness and dignity, it had small-v vagueness about purpose, and no suggestion of small-v violence or victimisation. Didn't some universities keep a Visitor on the governing staff, a mightily responsible outsider summoned to settle big disputes? Abelard would be responsible, too, and informed. He must pull out of the archive all reports on episodes in Olly's career he might choose to cover in his book. Obviously, such archive reports would be judicious, sanitised, incomplete. Hell, they were written for the eyes of a Minister. Abelard would be able to add the harsh extras, though, using memory and/or hearsay. Even from a logic and politeness point of view, if you were going to Visit a lad to try to stop him writing something, you ought to know what it was you were going to try to stop him writing by your visit. *Oh, listen to me, Oliver, Kate, or you'll get a different kind of visitation.*

Chapter 3

In the Outfit building, there was a Closed Library, where secrecy and security prevailed as far as they could, and, of course, an Open Library. The Open Library contained, for instance, dictionaries of fifty or sixty languages; Who's Who type volumes from every country that published them; atlases; encyclopedias; transport information for the world; restaurant information for the world, so that expenses money and entertaining/facilitating money could be efficiently spent; guides to comparatively hygienic and otherwise safe girl bars and boy bars and male-escort bars and women-only bars and so on for the world, including Carlisle; lists of churches, chapels, mosques in all major cities of the world; files giving all principal newspaper and media headquarters, and some less than principal. Other files listed gymnasiums, weights centres, public gun ranges, horse riding facilities, competent hairdressers, tailors – reach-me-down and made-to-measure – for all major cities in the world; street maps offered directions to hospitals in all major cities in the world, and some not so major, those with accident units asterisked, those with unusual mortality rates marked l.d.o., 'life or death only'. Addresses of embassies, consulates and British Council centres were also available.

Inevitably, Olly's reports were in the Closed Library, like the reports of all field officers. Its proper designation was Operatives' Secure Archive, but people found that rosy and melodramatic, and so the blander alternative. Olly featured quite big in the OSA. Some of his stuff was on paper, some on disk. He was industrious and capable, and Latimer and others had given him plenty of classified work.

The Closed Library ran its own name code system based mainly on numbers. Olly had been 19-481-H.C. Probably there was some 'meaning' to the figures and letters. They might indicate year of recruitment; grade and salary; category and amount of insurance allocated – life and disability; physical fitness standard; number of dependants. The H could signify the level of operation regarded by Latimer and those beyond Latimer as in Olly's range; or his mental stability rating; or his financial condition, as known. Abelard was not told how to interpret 19-481-H.C., just provided with the formula by Turkey to access the Horton narratives – the Horton narratives as spruced up and given due tact, in case they were called for one day by people at the Ministry of Defence or Foreign Office. Abelard did know what the C signified. It stood for Ceased. That is, Olly had left the Outfit. Sometimes C could mean more than that. It could indicate Deceased. This was not Olly yet.

The Closed Library had Attended Service. You could not browse through bins or shelves, not even someone of Abelard's rank. You filled up and signed a request form – authentic name, of course – giving the numbers and letters key, and an OSA officer brought the asked for items – and only those – to a lockable booth, sometimes using a kind of shopping trolley when there was a load of paper and folders. Most of Olley's was disk and arrived in two wire baskets. Each booth had an individual computer to read disks. You were confined to your booth with the material.

Up to three people could use a booth at once for joint examination of reports and simultaneous discussion. Abelard had never heard of definite monkey business when there were two or three locked in, but, then, nobody would hear of it, would they? This Operatives' Archive was Secure. The booths had quite decent heavy-duty carpeting, which might be reasonably easy on exposed skin. Although the booths were probably not absolutely sound-proofed, an astutely silent fuck in government time could be sweeter than none at all. Or possibly fucks, if a threesome. At the end of a booth stint you pressed a button and were released. It would obviously be important not to hit that accidentally if there were uninhibited capering, and with three this risk could be high. Normally, people would have time to tidy up clothes and check each other for smudges and foolish, above-the-collar bites and so on. Almost certainly there were no concealed cameras. Concealment would have had to be exceptional to fool the kind of trained folk who utilised the library, either for genuine work or intimacies, or a happy combination. They'd had been schooled and schooled to spot honey-traps.

Naturally, Abelard looked first in the Horton collection for records of work areas he was somehow involved in himself, for instance, the death of Julian Bowling. If any material harmful to the Outfit was due to be carried in Olly's book, it would most likely start with Julian's end. Oh, God, that had been so messy and terrible. Abelard and Lucy McIver were the only ones with him when he died, in a chic little cottage he'd rented up near Brompton Oratory, Knightsbridge, London SW3, a fine district. He had been shot elsewhere – Abelard never found out where – but somehow managed to get back to the cottage. Lucy and Abelard could not report the death. Or had chosen not to. It was a secret, maverick project, secret to just those two. They had left the body and Olly Horton officially discovered it a day after. Olly could not have known Lucy and Abelard had been there, and could not know it even now.

Alone in a Closed Library cubicle, Abelard might find out what Olly *did* know about that killing and what followed, though there might have been some editing: reports and information were obviously crucial to any effective organisation, but not stupidly full reports and information. He'd give himself a maximum of three days in the library, with an opening call on the Hortons at home on afternoon two, as a small break-out from the screen and paper and rest for his eyes.

Chapter 4

Horton said: 'All right, this is going to seem phoney to you, Simon, and self-serving, of course, I do realise that, but ultimately I see my book – when it's done – so much work yet! – I'm finding out I'm not one of your born writers... not so far, anyway... but when it's done, I say it will be no betrayal at all. The opposite.'

'You know how Oliver is,' Kate said. 'There'd be nothing casual about a decision like this – to leave and do the book. We really talked. Have I ever, ever, been in such talks!'

'Think of it this way, Simon: isn't there a case for a rebuttal of all the cheap stuff that's been published lately by ex-officers?' Horton asked. 'Now, be fair, isn't there?'

'That's how Oliver sees the purpose of his writing,' Kate said. 'Only that'.

'Positive,' Horton said. 'Entirely'.

'Well, of course. Would Oliver set out simply to smear and destroy?' Kate asked. 'Is that his nature, Simon?'

'The Outfit can't reply to all this derogatory printed tripe for itself, can it?' Horton said. 'I don't underestimate what words on a page can do. Of course I don't – that's why I want to get some of my own words out there for public viewing, to put another side of things, *our* side, Simon.'

Kate said: 'Can it be reasonable that some whole area of experience – the work place experience... because that's all it is, after all, the Outfit... yes, I admit, obviously, a work place with certain special conditions... but, then, doesn't almost every work place have its special conditions and confidentialities... can it be reasonable or even wholesome... can it be reasonable to bar some whole area of experience as fit subject for literary examination? So... well, nugatory.'

'"Literary" might be overstating a bit,' Horton said, 'but you'll see Kate's point, Simon.'

'Literary as to do with letters, that's all – to do with writing,' Kate replied. 'Just a label.'

'Right,' Horton said.

'Look, have you come alone, Simon? Is there backup out there? Are there heavies – I mean heavies as well as a heavy like you? Oliver says you would never be a party to anything like that, some ambush or entrapment, not you, not Simon Abelard. All right, that's what he says, and I listen. But in my time with him I've learned a bit about how operators operate in your game and... Ultimately, you're from the Outfit. That's the nub of it. You belong to them. You have your uncrackable loyalties. So, then, have you come alone? Posse?'

'You mustn't ask, shouldn't ask, Kate,' Horton said. 'It's a slight. For God's sake, we don't physically attack one another, whatever the intellectual differences between us.'

'Which we, which us?' Kate replied.

Horton said: 'Simply because I've left the job doesn't mean that I'm—'

'You're not part of them any more, Oliver,' Kate said. 'There's no "simply" about leaving that job. You've left it and to them you're just another outsider now. Or no, not just another outsider. No. You're an outsider but with a lot of dicey knowledge – dicey for them.'

'But it's still crazy to think of physical moves against me,' Horton said. 'The lawyers might come after us, but "heavies"? Oh, come on, Kate.'

'What happened to Julian Bowling?' she replied.

'Mystery,' Horton said.

'Yes?' Kate replied.

'No comparison with me at all,' Horton said.

'Simon, we don't have any special safety measures here because... well, because we don't want to – despise that damned hunted, guilt-infected mentality,' Kate said.

'I'm with Kate on this,' Horton said.

'I mean, are we Salman Rushdie?' she asked.

'We're insignificant, and it's how we want to stay,' Horton said.

'But even if you *thought* you were coming alone there could be tails with you – unknown, I mean, couldn't there?' Kate asked. 'Some of these people are so smart. And heavy.'

'Alone,' Abelard replied. 'Latimer wanted it like that.'

'Of course,' Horton said.

'Simon's an explorer?'

'I think Simon's a friend.'

'Yes, certainly,' Abelard replied. 'What else?'

'And Turkey Latimer sends him as a friend,' Horton said.

Kate said: 'Is Turkey the one who—?'

'There'll be threats, naturally,' Horton said. 'It would never come to actual violence, I'm sure of that, but Turkey knows how to lean on people, how to growl. What did he say, Simon – that you and he wished, so fervently wished to behave like friends, real friends to me, even now, but there were others in the Outfit who might not be easy to hold back? He'd like you to tell me just that – no actual strong-arm yet, just a nice, dark warning? Let slip the dogs of war stuff? Turkey would frown with concern and ask how could he be responsible for what angry subordinates choose to do in their own time? It's make-believe, yes, but chilly make-believe.'

'Sort of sly and ruthless, is that Latimer? How you described him once, Oliver?' Kate asked. 'But, Christ, you can all be that, can't you? It's part of the job spec, like chorus girls need legs, arse and tits.'

'Turkey has some of the cleanest hands in the Outfit, and

allegedly some of the direst mates. He likes to suggest they have to be pointed the right way, that's all, like missiles,' Horton replied.

'And mightn't it be true?' Kate asked.

'It's diplomacy, rough diplomacy. Bluff,' Horton replied.

'For instance, Simon, Oliver would never publish anything that endangered people in the field,' Kate said. 'He couldn't. His feelings would not allow that. Yes, his loyalties. You're not the only one. We're certainly unafraid of the word. Oliver's loyalties haven't just expired because he's bought a word processor, you know.'

'Of course, Latimer would probably tell you, Kate, that at my level I couldn't fully know what might expose people in the field,' Horton replied. 'According to him, I wouldn't be able to appreciate all ramifications. It's the standard argument.'

'That's mad. You're not sloppy or dim,' Kate said. 'Anyway, which field, for God's sake? There's no Cold War, not even much in Northern Ireland at the moment. All right people worry about the Mid-East, Afghanistan and terrorism, but for now at any rate everything seems—'

'There's still a field,' Horton replied. 'I do accept that. And, yes, it might sound mad, but what Latimer would say, isn't it, Simon, is that something I include innocently, or even something I leave out, might tell a clever spook the whole Outfit programme?'

'Absurd,' Kate said. 'Anyway, *is* there a programme beyond internal war?'

'Latimer would say all this to make sure nothing, but nothing, is published,' Horton said. 'How Latimer is. How those above him are.'

'Well, they're too late on that,' Kate replied.

'To make sure nothing *more* is published, and especially nothing more that's special to me, Oliver Basil Horton and to

the Outfit,' Olly said. 'They're scared I'll produce something
new and devastating.'

'Kate's mentioned the death of Julian Bowling,' Abelard
replied. 'So let's take that. Will you be dealing with it in the
book?'

'In a way Bowling's the absolute essence of what I want to
show,' Horton said.

Kate said: 'The Outfit was sick. The Outfit has utterly
recovered. As I understand it, this is Oliver's whole theme.'

'Positive, you see,' Horton said.

'You're worried about the Bowling episode, Simon?' Kate
asked. 'Why? Were you close to all that – how he got it,
etcetera? And wasn't Lucy McIver tied in with him somehow
at one stage – I mean, a work contact?'

'Kate says sick, but I don't necessarily see it like this,'
Horton said. 'Bowling was sick, sure – morally sick, loot-
lusting sick. I don't consider the Outfit could have prevented
that, except possibly by better personnel selection a long time
ago. I'm sure this has been put right now – although I suppose
Turkey would wonder. How did *I* get in, for instance, and the
others who've turned author? You're Personnel, Simon, so
you'd know if recruitment screening has been tightened. But at
the time, Julian must have looked all right – education fine,
parents rich and fine, class impeccable and fine, and class
mattered a bit more when he was recruited than now. What
happened to Bowling was sick, too – the execution.'

'That has to be the word,' Kate said.

'And some of this all-round malaise was bound to touch
the Outfit as an entity, I'll concede that,' Horton said. 'Julian
was a staffer, yes. That's my message. What I want to show is
that the Outfit managed to continue its proper work even
through the bad Bowling period and then, after him, conduct
its activities unimpaired, uncompromised. Surely this is a
triumph? Positive.'

'Do you see the objective now, Simon?'

'You'll have been down to the Closed Library, won't you, and had one-to-one commune with 19-481-H.C.'s account of his discovery of Julian Bowling, renegade officer, dead? After all, this is information in the public domain, Simon. The police were told, the Press had a story.'

'Yes, they had a story,' Abelard replied.

'He was named,' Horton said.

'Yes, he was named,' Abelard said. 'But there wasn't much more than that.'

'Am I going to say much more than that in the book?' Horton asked.

'Are you?' Abelard replied.

'You saw the Closed Library account. You know how it was.'

'I'm talking about a book for the public libraries.'

'Why are you so concerned about Julian Bowling?' Kate asked. 'You weren't actually involved in that, were you, Simon? The death – the... yes... execution? His business network? Or maybe through Lucy?'

'My reports – you know how it was, Simon.'

Chapter 5

How it was. Yes, Abelard did know how it was. Yes, he had been 'close to all that,' and so knew how it really was. And, of course, Lucy knew, too.

And, yes, from time spent in his chaste booth at OSA, he did also know how it was according to the reports of 19-481-H.C. Two of these described discovery of Bowling. One was PRE-OPERATION and said how Horton became involved. The second dealt with the actual find.

PRE-OPERATION REPORT

I received an invitation to meet Julian Bowling at 33, Home Place, London SW3.

The invitation: an eight-line (58 word), handwritten letter delivered to my home by normal First Class postal service, the envelope likewise addressed by hand to me as OB Horton, Strictly Addressee Only. Envelope and letter are included with this report as Enclosures A and B.

NB: I refer to Bowling In Clear because media coverage of the death and finding of the body has already appeared and published his name, and address and family background.

The letter required certain considerations:

1. At the time of delivery, Bowling was categorised as an Officer in Breach of Contract (OBC) and had been so to my knowledge for more than six months. Efforts to locate and recover him had failed. The offer of a meeting was therefore unexpected and potentially advantageous. Reportedly, since becoming OBC, Bowling had secured some as yet undefined part, but possibly 'boardroom', in the large-scale trafficking of recreational drugs in Britain, Europe, the United States and Canada, while still utilising his Service credentials when they could assist his purpose. His activities were regarded as deeply harmful to the reputation of the Service; as well as illegal in most of the countries concerned.

2. The apparent approach to me was especially surprising because, although a colleague of Bowling for a period of years, the contact between us had been entirely formal.

3. It was necessary to examine several possibilities:

a. The letter was not genuine: that is, it did not come from Bowling; or, the meeting had some other purpose than the 'one-to-one private little chin-wag' as offered in the letter.

b. The letter was genuine and indicated a wish in Bowling to re-establish departmental contact, possibly with the aim of negotiating an end to his OBC status and assessing his legal position. As a comparatively inexperienced and unauthoritative colleague this officer might have been chosen by Bowling to serve as go-between. That could perhaps be inferred from the request in the letter, 'for now, Oliver, I know I can rely on you to disclose nothing of this note or projected meeting.' It appeared reasonable to read the phrase 'for now' as signifying Bowling expected matters to develop. He might have felt that a younger officer would be flattered to receive the letter and more likely to accept conditions of secrecy and, so, possible individual credit for having reached Bowling.

However, I immediately informed Assistant Director, Research and Coordination, (ADRC), my department head who examined the letter and envelope. On comparison with file examples of Bowling's handwriting, and consultation with

Calligraphy Suite, it was decided the letter and envelope should be presumed genuine until there was contrary information. The slang locutions 'private little chin-wag' and 'how's about showing' were considered in keeping with Bowling's informal manner. Accordingly, I was ordered to comply with the arrangements suggested in the letter and call at 33, Home Place that evening at 18.30, behaving as if alone. The house would be put under immediate, continuous, covert surveillance.

It was recognised that, as a trained former officer (still nominally a serving officer) familiar with standard procedures and current technology, Bowling would not necessarily expect me to observe his request for confidentiality and would be alert to the possibility of exterior surveillance. It was therefore stressed that this should be of maximum discreetness.

1. To ensure no personnel might be recognised by Bowling, surveillance would be conducted by officers with less than six months' attachment to headquarters (ie, who arrived after Bowling's withdrawal), and/or by occasional officers or agents from the Casual Register whose Assignments Record showed no operational contact with Bowling before he became OBC.

2. Similarly, vehicles used should be unknown to Bowling. 'Lurk' vans with one way glass in the rear compartment were NOT suitable because Bowling would recognise the type, if not the actual van.

3. Other set patterns of surveillance should be avoided, since Bowling would be familiar with these as well, eg, young mother with perambulator passing back and forth in front of house; road repair/telephone engineers/gas leak team; battery-failed car; Jehovah's Witnesses on call with tracts; student augmenting income as door-to-door sales person of magazines or brushes, dusters and chamois leathers.

4. NO early attempt to penetrate and place hidden listening devices would be made because it was unclear

*whether Bowling might already be in the property. He would
be alert to this method of surveillance also. A long-distance
electronic 'snoop' would be attempted, but traffic noise could
make this inefficient. There would be separate surveillance and
support units.*

*It was regarded as probable that, when the visit occurred,
Bowling would suspect use of a hidden transmission device
and insist on a body search at the outset. Accordingly, it was
decided that I should conduct the visit without sound
equipment and unarmed; objective, to provide Bowling with
unhostile circumstances for an explanatory statement and
possible negotiations. This officer's orders were 'to be
accommodating but unspecifically accommodating' to
Bowling: ie, to encourage him to speak about his absence – its
cause and his activities and locations during the period – while
offering no undertaking as to departmental response beyond
the assurance that any statement or request would be relayed
through proper channels. Unless there were visible or auditory
evidence of an emergency, the support unit would allow one
hour for interchange between Bowling and me before entering
the house, if necessary by force. Some members of the support
unit would carry pistols, but these were not to be drawn
except in case of an armed challenge by Bowling or Bowling
and others. It was recognised that he might not be alone for
this meeting. Accordingly, the support party should be twelve,
plus ADRC. The surveillance party would be twenty and have
positions in front and at the back of the house.*

*Street maps showed it as a terraced property with rear lane
entrance to the walled garden as well as a street door. ADRC
to head the operation from Control Vehicle, Azure Neddy,
and, because known to Bowling, would remain concealed
until he (Bowling) was taken. It would be assumed only one
letter had been sent. All members of the surveillance and
support parties should be explicitly instructed not to discuss*

this project before joining their group: despite his withdrawal
and subsequent activities as reported, Bowling might have
sympathisers and friends within the Service who could attempt
to warn him against the rendezvous.

EXHIBIT A

OB Horton, Strictly Addressee Only,
23A Paling Yard,
London NW15.

EXHIBIT B

My dear Oliver,
I've been wondering whether you'd fancy a one-to-one
private little chin-wag about this and that. If so, how's about
showing at 33 Home Place, SW3 at 6.30 this evening? Near
the Oratory. Please, for now, Oliver, I know I can rely on you
to disclose nothing of this note or projected meeting.

Best,
Julian

OPERATION REPORT

Daylight. Sunny. I arrived by taxi at 33 Home Place at
18.30 and took time paying off the driver in case Bowling
were observing from the house: he would have opportunity to
see I was alone. I wore a summer jacket and slacks. A trained
eye might detect I had no holster or firearm. The intent was to
allay suspicion of an onslaught. I opened the street gate and
walked a few paces to the front door and rang the bell.
Nobody responded. I rang again. There was a small, leaded
bay window to my right but the curtains were across. The

front door was solid and I could see nothing interior. I waited several minutes and then rang the bell again.

Procedures for this stage of the visit had been laid down in pre-briefings. If there were no answer, I should wait and continue to ring periodically. It was thought likely Bowling would not cease from checking for back-up. He might be in the house or observing from somewhere outside. After fifteen minutes, as agreed, I left the front garden and walked to the end of Home Place and back down the rear lane. I tried the garden door but this was locked or bolted. I returned to the front door and rang twice more. I crouched, opened the letter box and called Bowling's name twice in full, ie, 'Julian Theobald Bowling.' I heard no answer.

Accordingly, and as earlier agreed, I returned to the lane entrance, scaled the stone wall and entered the small garden. The house door into the garden was solid and locked. A ground floor window was uncurtained and I could see a kitchen. I smashed the glass, opened the catch and climbed in. The house remained silent. I moved from the kitchen to a small living room and found Julian Bowling. He was lying face down on a Persian rug in the middle of the room. He was still and I heard no breathing. I assumed he was dead. I went forward and confirmed this and Bowling's identity. He had at least one bullet wound in the upper chest. Blood had run down both arms and coated his hands. The blood was dry and I deduced he had been dead for some time. His shirt had been partly torn from him and a blood soaked piece of it lay near the body. It appeared to have been used as a bandage or pad in a failed attempt to stop bleeding. There were several thin lines of blood on one wall. Possibly he had tried to clasp the wall for support before falling. I made a cursory, security search of the rest of the house, then opened the front door as an agreed signal for when the interview had ended. Members of the support group arrived immediately. I ensured they did not disturb the room where Bowling lay. ADRC arrived soon afterwards. He assumed control.

Chapter 6

'Well, yes, your reports – I know how it was,' Abelard said.

Kate said: 'I want to expand my argument, feel entitled to do that, Simon. I ask again, can there be any defensible reason why the death of someone... someone comparatively young and – whatever we might think of him now – someone very, very gifted... any defensible reason the death of someone... well, someone so, yes, golden, the death of someone like that in such circumstances should be treated as a subject forever off-limits? I mean forever? This was a significant death, surely, and... also surely... surely this significance can be responsibly examined in print? Can be, ought to be. If not, I mean – where are we? Where? What was the purpose of great declarations in our history clarioning the freedom to write... I mean, I'm thinking of something so... well, central, yes central to our traditions, as Milton's *Areopagitica*, so noble, so brave, so fucking seminal. Ask any half-way-to-decent scholar about the *Areopagitica* and she/he'll say "fucking seminal". All right, Oliver's not Milton, but I see him as in a line from Milton. Anyone who insists on writing awkward truths is in that magnificent, radical line.'

Abelard decided he'd prefer not to be distracted from this amazing gush by taking account of how she looked or how Olly looked or how the room of their flat looked. They were factors that would let in too much definition and sense. He wanted to let the talk bubble around him and maintain its high lunacy and scholarship. It probably had its own crazy shape, this outpouring, and if he let it go on without trying to fix any workaday distractions on it in his head, such as her features or their wallpaper, the shape might eventually show itself, at least for a second or two.

'Simon, I'm not naïve,' she said, 'and I know there could be... well, political, tactical... yes, genuine security considerations making some events in your and Oliver's game special. Of course, of course, of course. Can the spy trade ever be totally transparent, fully open to public examination? No. Absolutely not. The terms are uncomfortable with each other, in fact deny each other, defy each other – spying, transparency. Only a fool would say otherwise, even in an era when at least some barricades and secrecy drapes are happily coming down. But this need for some basic security cannot dictate that every aspect of the work should be permanently unknown and unknowable, surely. Every aspect? Forever?

'Oh, you're going to say... I know you're going to say... you're going to say that some aspects of Julian Bowling's death *have* been publicised. A death from shooting in a bijou cottage alongside the Oratory is a strong media story, and it was given the treatment Presswise and broadcasting wise. All right. Conceded. But given the treatment only to a point. There was a cut-off, wasn't there? How exactly did it go in the news reports? Like this – "Julian Theobald Bowling, scion of a wealthy industrialist, and believed to have worked for the Intelligence services was found dead with gunshot wounds in one of the smartest districts of London where neighbours include this pop singer, this Cabinet Minister, this clothes designer, this race horse owner." And that was the lot. Nothing truly investigative ever appeared. Not even in the *Guardian*. Your friend Latimer did a lovely little wrap-up job there. What is it you call him? Not Turkey – the office plaque initials.'

'ADRC,' Horton replied.

Abelard felt forced to speak, but still did not want to intrude too much from outside – from outside Kate and her superb, empowered ramblings. He said: 'The difficulty is, we still don't know very much beyond what the media had. The shortage of additional fact is not to do with Latimer.'

'No?' Kate replied.

'He's as baffled as the rest of us,' Abelard said.

'Yes?' Kate replied.

'Obviously we're working on it. And so are the police,' Abelard said.

'Yes?' Kate replied.

'I don't know how you'd approach this in a book, Olly,' Abelard said, 'but unsubstantiated material could be very harmful.'

'Alternatively, a book and the publicity around it might provoke new information,' Kate said.

'What information?' Abelard asked.

'Information to help find as proven fact who killed him, naturally,' Kate said. 'Isn't that what you want? It is, isn't it?'

'The book wouldn't be out for months, maybe longer,' Abelard replied. 'I'd hope we've concluded things by then.'

'I had the idea you'd already concluded them,' Kate said. 'Not solved anything or caught anyone, just concluded things.'

'Kate's a bit tougher on all this than I am, Simon, but I do agree with her that there has to be a case for ending arbitrary and pointless secrecy at a time when—'

'You didn't really answer, Simon, but were you close to what happened, in ways that haven't come out? Perhaps you don't want a book that could trigger off more revelations, more awkward speculation. I even wonder if Lucy might be pulled in to it, too. That scares you… in your nice, protective way?'

'Well, I certainly knew Julian,' Abelard replied. 'Had worked with him two or three times. I don't think it's breaking the Secrets Act to tell you that.'

'The events?' Kate said. 'Home Place – number 33.'

'I feel Olly had it right in the reports about that,' Abelard replied.

'Right how?' Kate said.

'Bowling's hopes for the meeting. And the reason he approached Olly, rather than someone more senior.'

'That's not what I'm asking you,' Kate replied.

'Oh?' Abelard said.

'It's always seemed to me you might have been tied up in it somehow – not just pals with Julian Bowling, but tied up in what went on,' Kate replied. 'Yes, the actual events.'

'This is Kate's view of things and only Kate's,' Horton said. 'I shalln't mention you at all in the chapter on finding Julian. How could I? It's me, personally, who's the "centre of consciousness" of this book. That's the jargon phrase for it, I gather. I write about what *I've* seen, nothing else. My eye is sovereign. That's another thing they call the centre of consciousness in telling a story – the eye. Here's what will give my book its force and, all right, I'll use the big term, its integrity. I'm showing only what this eye saw for itself. Sure, I've heard rumours of this and that.'

'Everyone's heard them,' Kate said. 'That's what I mean.'

'Which?' Abelard asked. So, was it over, her blurb talk? Sharp question and answer now? Should he start systematically describing for himself where he was, whom he was with and how they seemed today?

'Oh, *which*?' Kate replied. 'You know which rumours, Simon.'

'But rumours are what I must do without, thanks,' Horton said.

'For instance, I mean,' Kate said, 'would Julian have been strong enough in his state to rip a bit of his shirt off to make a plug?' That could be womanly, couldn't it? Couldn't it? But have we heard of any woman present? Have we?'

'A possibility – a possibility – of at least one other person

in the house around the death time. I've heard this suggestion,'
Horton said.

'Everyone's heard it,' Kate replied.

'Detective theory based on I'm not sure what,' Horton said.
'And definitely useless to me, because I can't personally
authenticate it.'

'You see what I mean about Lucy?' Kate asked. 'You *do*
see, don't you, Simon, although you play dazed and lost?'

'I think I'd like to know if I feature in the book,' Abelard
said.

Horton said: 'Well, naturally, Simon, I'll have to cover the
whole chase aspect, the hunt for Julian – it's essential to what
I'm trying to put over and—'

'I believe you *want* to feature, Simon,' Kate yelled.

Abelard said: 'I suppose that anyone—'

'Your fifteen minutes or fifteen pages of glory!' Kate
replied. 'That's what you're after, isn't it? Don't you realise
this confirms entirely what we're saying, Oliver and I – that
there's an actual human appetite, an entirely legitimate need,
for publication, and that this is a wholesome, irrepressible
impulse, the fine lust for truth?' Kate's pace and volume
gloriously rose to what they had been earlier. 'It's one of the
bases of Christian practice, surely – "Go ye into all the world
and preach the gospel" – in other words, "publish, publish,
publish." Clearly, it's also the raison d'être of great literature. I
ask you to consider that famous Spenser sonnet:

"One day I wrote her name upon the strand;
But came the waves and washed it away…"

'Yet Spenser does not surrender, does he? He fails to give
her perpetuity by beach writing but he can in the very poem
which is about the beach writing, you see:

'"My verse your virtues rare shall eternize."'

'Kate can put everything into the bigger, even universal,
context,' Horton said. Abelard would never contradict this.

'Then again, "Publish and be damned," Kate said. 'That's the Duke of Wellington, but picked up by Hugh Cudlipp and embraced as title for his book about the old-style, risk-taking *Daily Mirror*. There's always been a glorious inevitability about publication, you see. You *do* see, don't you, Simon. It's simple. Publication is its own justification. The medium is the message and the message says, "I must be read."'

Horton said: 'I don't know whether I'd actually claim to be—'

'So have you actually written some of the book, Olly?' Abelard replied.

'You're here to vet?' Kate asked. 'Not a raid, you and a team – not at present – but a glance over the stuff to see where the damage might be done. Then report back to Turkey, for the next move? That it, Simon? Oh, Simon, really!'

'Kate, I thought you've been telling me there can't *be* any damage,' Abelard said. Oh God, was it right to argue with her? Was it humane to ask for consistency?

'Hemingway would never show work in progress,' Kate replied. 'A kind of superstition? I feel so, I really do. A dread of cheeking fate through hubris? He felt no other form but the final form was valid.'

'By then it's too late,' Abelard replied.

'Late for what?' Kate asked.

'Corrections,' Abelard said.

'You want to censor?' Kate asked.

'For accuracy,' Abelard said. The word sounded harsh and spiky.

'Oliver's told you – he'll only write about what he knows. First hand knows. He first-hand knows nothing about Lucy, for instance, so as things stand she's off limits. And, listen, Simon, realise this, will you, will you – no point you and a team coming around here on the q.t. to break in and confiscate or destroy what's already done? We put a copy disk of every chapter as it's finished into the bank and the publisher banks another.'

'Kate, Kate, Simon would never be a party to anything like that. We're friends.'

'All right, it would be easy to burgle, it's true – no special security,' Kate replied, 'but if it's suppression of Oliver's material you're after you'll fail. Of course, if it's suppression of Oliver himself you want—'

'Kate, don't,' Horton said. 'A disgusting allegation. Courts, injunctions – that kind of thing, maybe. But not what you're hinting.'

'Bowling didn't get taken to court. What *did* happen to him?' Kate replied.

'We don't know what happened to him,' Horton said.

'We know he got himself fucking killed,' Kate replied. 'We know he got half his shirt ripped off him somehow when he must have been as feeble as feeble through loss of blood.' After the roaring blah the bright, awkward insights. This was a stupendously complicated woman, no matter what she looked like. Actually, she was pretty, Abelard thought, in a delicate way.

'Julian Bowling did a runner with millions of dollars that belonged to a world-wide drugs syndicate,' Horton said. 'Julian Bowling had enemies everywhere.'

'You've got enemies,' Kate said. 'All sorts now. What about the money, anyway? Where is it? Millions of dollars, yes? The book's not going to tell us where it finished up, is it, Oliver?'

'And then there's the disappearance, likely death, of Verdun Cadwallader,' Abelard said. 'How will you treat this, Olly?'

'Cadwallader?' Kate said. 'Verdun Cadwallader, Welsh and named after the First War battle where many of the Welsh were killed, right? Someone not just above you two, but above Latimer, yes?' Kate asked. 'And he gets to drop out of sight no

time at all after Julian Bowling? This the character? The body
never turns up, if there is one. Someone of that rank!... Oh,
look, how the hell did I get into this kind of life, anyway? I
could be living with a... well, a university administrator or
fashionable chef. And you really tell me, Simon, you think
none of that with Bowling and Cadwallader deserves a public
explanation? Or a public explanation as far as it can be given
– not all the way, I'm sure.'

'God, yes, Cadwallader. Maybe another terrible death,'
Horton replied.

'Could be,' Abelard said. 'No report by you on it in the
archive – or not as far as I've got – so I take it you know
nothing about this, nothing direct. You couldn't have
witnessed any of that personally. You're the eye of your book,
but the eye didn't see anything. How can you include it? And,
yet, if you don't is your tale complete?'

'Who *did* see anything?' Kate asked. 'Where were you
when this with Cadwallader happened, Simon?' Kate asked.

'Abroad then, with Lucy and my mother. A sabbatical,'
Abelard said.

'That right?' Kate said.

'An appalling end for Verdun, most probably,' Horton
replied.

'But why do you mention Cadwallader at all, Simon? Why?
Why? Why? A bit more rough diplomacy? You're trying to
scare Oliver, scare us, silence him, silence us? Like, "Look
what happened to Bowling. Look what happened to
Cadwallader." People had better not try anything like that
with Oliver. With us. I've told you, the discs already finished
and safe would point to the likelies.'

'Which likelies?' Abelard asked.

'Yes, all, all the likelies,' she replied.

'But, look, Simon, we haven't offered you even a cup of
tea, a drink,' Horton said.

'Yes, drinks,' Kate replied. 'Get glasses, Oliver, there's a love. Horton went out of the room. Quietly, she said: 'Simon, maybe I should see you alone somewhere. Not your place.'

'The Carlton Club, noon tomorrow.'

'Carlton Club? The Carlton Club! The Tory party haunt?'

'Outside in St James's Street, of course. They're not going to let us in, are they? We'll move on to somewhere.'

'God, you had that ready fast.'

'I've used it before. It's a useful spot. I wouldn't think you'd see anyone you know there, and I won't.'

'Ah, I get it – an Outfit procedure: all meetings in two stages, and don't disclose the second until you've sussed the first.'

'Olly tells you many things.'

'Listen, Simon, did you expect me to ask to see you?'

'The spiel was a bit large and glittering, wasn't it? You're not really sure what he's doing is right, are you – so buckets of further-education theorising to convince yourself first, then him, and possibly me last?'

'Oliver needs to hear it.'

'Hear it from you,' Abelard replied.

'Of course. I'm his strength. So, it didn't convince you? Or is this hindsight?'

'My God, all that Milton and Spenser fog, and the Duke of Wellington.'

'Sorry. Very impromptu. The Spenser quote was accurate, though. But as references – well, not completely irrelevant and stupid.'

'I was neutralised,' Abelard replied.

'Condescending shit,' she said.

Horton came back and poured three beers. 'So you'll be able to brief Turkey in quite reassuring terms, you see, Simon,' he said.

Chapter 7

'Carl Briers, *The Sunday Post*.'

'Yes, of course.' Abelard knew him, liked his work, had liked it since he – Abelard – was a teenager, beginning to worry about the world and trawl for causes. Briers had done some of the sparkiest journalism there was on the old renegades: Philby, Blake, Cairncross, even a few bright retrospectives on Burgess and Maclean, with one or two slivers of new information, new to Abelard, at any rate: that is, new to him *now*, a professional harvester of murkish points, not just as a kid. Briers had been to Moscow a few times to see Philby, brought back some of his jokes and samples of lousy charm and general wrynesses for *Post* subscribers. If you read Briers and Phillip Knightley you knew close to the lot about Philby, and not necessarily just what Philby had wanted you to know.

'We met, didn't we?' Abelard said. 'One of those Outfit parties, when we began to open some doors and get cwtchy with the media.' Briers must be past sixty-five. His feet didn't seem all that good and his shave abattoir standard, pre humane killer. People lost interest in their faces as they aged and didn't want to stay long at the mirror. His eyes had a look of haunted, vain astonishment, as though he felt odd to be handling a smart job still. The paper would keep him on. He was a name and had credibility in a field of Press work otherwise famed for imagination. He believed in traditional suits. Abelard remembered Briers wore something dark and magnificent at that frat party. And this morning he had on something even darker and just as magnificent: single-breasted, three-piece, Abdication-year style but replicated not more than a year ago judging by the wool's lovely glow. This was a suit that said bohemianism and beguiling racketiness, but bohemianism and beguiling racketiness under necessary wraps. The buttons were very black and looked the sort that never came off. This suit said appearance meant more or less everything, a happy touch when your realm was spies. Somehow his lapels had no blood stains. God, why didn't he get an electric razor to keep his chin as slick as the clothes?

Briers said: 'I'm really sorry this turns out to be a confrontation in the street. Discourteous. Not at all what I intended. I was going to call at your home.'

'Bollocks, Carl,' Abelard said. 'Doorstep me? You wouldn't want a front door banged on you, not a man of your distinction, and loose teeth.'

'You wouldn't bang a door on anyone, not a man of your tact and acumen. You'd always be ready to hear how the other fellow sees things.'

'Which other fellow – someone I might meet in the street?' Abelard said.

'It's about an Outfit colleague, ex-colleague: Oliver Horton.'

'How did you know where I live? We're more open, yes, but the office doesn't give addresses. And I'm not in *Who's Who* yet.'

'I haven't spoken to Horton,' Briers replied. 'I thought you first – Personnel Director, and so on. There's a breakfast caff in Daviot street.'

'Yes, I go there sometimes,' Abelard said. 'But you know that. You've been doing research, Carl? Thoroughness – that's one of your things, isn't it?'

'Despite all the changes, heavy papers still love espionage,' Briers said. 'I wanted to switch to Property Correspondent but they said I must stay Our Man In Spookland. They want to hang on to people with the knowledge. They think they hear serious rumblings from Afghanistan way. Do you folk pay enough attention to Bin Laden, I wonder."

'Oliver? I hear he's turning author,' Abelard replied.

'Is that right? Another?'

'That's why you're here, is it?' Abelard replied.

'This trouble you?'

'What?'

'Horton writing,' Briers said.

'Does it trouble *you*, Carl? There'll be nothing left for journalists to say soon.'

'Or Turkey? Is he bothered? Or even above Turkey?'

'Above Turkey. Gee!'

'It troubles you?' Brier asked. 'Or them? Have you been to see Horton? I mean, you as Personnel.'

Plainly, this was not a question Abelard could give an answer to, because Briers might already know it. Research. Briers had poor feet, but he could probably tail by car all right. Or more than all right. Abelard had not spotted Briers – supposing he followed him to Paling Yard. Perhaps Philby taught Carl skills around the streets of Moscow. If Abelard said he had *not* visited Horton at home and Briers knew he had, it would indicate nerviness about the book. If Abelard said he *had* visited Horton at home and Briers knew he had, or didn't know he had, it would indicate nerviness about the book.

Abelard lived these days between Spitalfields and Whitechapel and they walked down Whitechapel High Street towards Aldgate Underground station, Abelard keeping his pace moderate, to accommodate Carl's shuffle. Abelard did consider inventing an early morning conference. He could reasonably speed off towards the station then and ditch the second breakfast and the breakfast talk. But Carl was too venerable, doddery and gorgeously dressed for that sort of harsh brush-off, wasn't he? Lesè-majesté. It might be only respectful to discover what he had, or thought he had.

They turned into Daviot Street and found a window table at the All Day Breakfast. Window tables were generally disrecommended, but Abelard wanted no impression of furtiveness. He ordered a mixed grill and tea. If you took a second breakfast it needed weight to push the other one down. Briers asked for fruit. He had travelled and knew the world's natural plenty. Between the slabs of conversation he drank lime juice in vast gulps. It was like a reformed ale alco convincing himself his need was simply liquid, any liquid. Twice he called for more. Abelard thought his own social rating would rise now the caff management saw the kind of wrecked, white, parched old dandy who didn't mind his company. He might have learned all that thirst in hot countries with the Colonial Service.

Briers said: 'He's been distributing stage-by-stage discs of his book, for safety.'

'Is that right?'

'You knew, did you? He's told you, face to face? You're a kind of friend, yet he still has to warn you not to try anything, because it can't work. Or the woman has to. She can be tough, I'd imagine. Your friendship with Horton – that wouldn't matter to her. I've come across a lot like this: class, education, will. Intransigent, full of vocab and fucking vile, talented perception.'

'She's not someone I'd have much contact with, except the odd social get-together.'

'Is that right?' Briers replied. 'We see the discs, as he deposits them.'

'Who sees them?'

'The paper. We might serialise. Horton sends a copy to the publishers, among others, and the publishers give us an

unofficial glimpse. They want an early bid – sight unseen of
the rest of it. Yes, they wonder whether there've been too
many spy books already. A good serial rights sale before
completion would boost their morale and coffers – recover
some of the advance.'

'You advise? Like Lord Dacre with the goofball Hitler
Diaries.'

'Horton's stuff is dull,' Briers replied.

'And have you been told to spice it?'

'Expand it. The deaths,' Briers said.

'Which?'

'Bowling. Cadwallader. Cadwallader, assumed. Horton's
hopeless, vacuous, on them. You heard of lacunae, Abelard,
meaning gaps? This boy should get the Nobel for lacunae.'

'They're baffling, the deaths,' Abelard replied.

'I don't know whether it's fear and some sort of lingering
esprit de corps with him or ignorance.'

'There's a lot of ignorance about.'

'Ignorance doesn't sell serial rights,' Briers said.
Cadwallader's end is so crucial.'

'*The Post* will bow out of making an offer?'

'Of course you'd love that.'

'I'd hate seeing one of our great newspapers give big space
to material that's obviously inadequate – inadequate in a
different fashion from the Hitler Diaries, but equally self-
damaging. We all need our serious Press to preserve its
credibility. Helps keep the country stable. The *Sunday Times*
will never get over the Diaries.'

'Fuck the Diaries. Fuck piss-taking big thoughts on the
Press,' Briers replied.

'I ought to get along. Breakfast's my treat. It's been
fascinating. Thanks.'

'I need some guidance,' Briers said. Humility might be one
of his techniques. His voice had softened for pleafulness. This

was someone with not long to go. Abelard almost wanted to be kindly. Briers pulled at the lime juice and then touched a face wound. 'So, you'll ask, why do I approach *you*? Why would you want to help me get this sort of material published? Oh, I can see it would seem strange. You'd prefer silence. The thing is, though, Abelard, the book's going to come out regardless. The contract's signed. And it would be absurd to try to stop it – stop it through all that court carry-on again – the useless, would-be repressive injunctions. Turkey has other ways in mind? My job's only to make sure it's accurate – accurate and readable – worth what we'd have to pay for it. Now, you wouldn't like the book to appear with errors and flagrant holes, surely? Or do I sound naïve?'

'Carl Briers naïve?'

'All right, all right. Naturally, I can see the possibility that you and Turkey, and, yes, even those above Turkey, would prefer some holes in the story. There are the rumours and more than rumours, aren't there?'

'Which?'

'Oh, first, Bowling nursing a quiver of filched drugs trade money, say around $9 million or even up to $13m – and he an Intelligences Services officer! Second, that Bowling was not alone when he toppled at 33 Home Place, although he'd certainly been shot somewhere else. Third, Cadwallader's disappearance and likely death linked to Bowling's? An appalling power fight inside the Outfit, maybe? I'm still nowhere near clear on how the present leadership got there. Carl Briers naïve? More like Carl Briers without a fucking light.' His head was bent down towards the table and his figs. Abelard considered it wrong for anyone in his sort of suit to sound abject. Briers said: 'If word's around that Horton's writing – and it is, it is around – have you thought the people looking for their loot stolen by Bowling might wonder whether Olly has discovered hints to its whereabouts and visit

him? Really visit him. Certainly you've thought of it. Has
Horton thought of it, or his woman? To me their place doesn't
look at all secure. Does anywhere look secure when aggrieved
folk hunt heavy dollars?'

'You've done a recce in Paling Yard, have you?' Abelard
got the bill.

Latimer said: 'Look, I have a little idea. Simon's assessment of
Olly Horton as at present is brilliantly helpful. Helpful above
all as to tone. Tone, certainly. And of what does that tone
comprise? I'd say it certainly comprises a measure of
arrogance and stubbornness in Olly, but also a genuine faith
in his elected purpose. There is, to be fair, a kind of decency
about him, even a kind of honour. This is what I hear when
Simon tells of the meeting. And, of course, it ought not to
surprise us. After all, we did select him. We did until very
recently find him to be an admirable colleague.'

'Have you really considered – I mean itemised it – have you
properly set out, paragraphs and sub-paragraphs, the damage
this sod can do us, Turkey? And will do us if we dawdle,' Roger
Link-Mite replied. 'Verdun Cadwallader's death – I call it that
because that's what it is, even without a body – this book is
bound to spill a ream on this. Cadwallader! Never mind
Bowling for a minute, though all that's harmful enough, Christ
knows – but Cadwallader. This kind of revelation could shake
the whole Outfit, maybe finish the Outfit as the Outfit is now.'

'But Simon has told us, hasn't he, Roger, that Horton will
write about only what he knows first hand? I don't believe this
could cover Verdun Cadwallader's... well, fate. Very few have
first hand knowledge of that, I'd say. And even when we come
to Bowling the role of Olly is not more than discovery of the
corpse. I think this is right, isn't it, Simon – the bounds Olly
has set himself?'

The three of them were in easy chairs around Latimer's

office in the Outfit building. 'He'll write from first-hand experience only,' Abelard replied.

'Oh, that's what the sod tells you, Simon,' Link-Mite said, 'but is it believable, even half-way believable? No criticism, Simon – you've simply told us what he said.' Small, lean, bony-faced, Link-Mite was the Outfit's interrogation expert and looked it, sounded it.

'It's what I was trying to put originally about tone,' Latimer replied. He gave Link-Mite some blue-eyed stare.

'Tone is arseholes,' Link-Mite said. 'Tone is seminars. What we've got is a fucking predicament.'

'The tone of this encounter with Simon, as I read it in Simon's words, the tone was one of remarkable frankness on Horton's part, a friend talking to a friend, despite the dodgy circumstances. I do believe it's... well, do believe it's believable.' There were times when Turkey and Link-Mite put on together a standard friendly-fierce performance, but Turkey was genuinely gentler, perhaps more constructive. He never claimed to be an originator, only a gifted developer of other people's ideas.

'The dodgy circumstances are that Horton has to satisfy a publisher and a market – possibly a newspaper if his publisher is looking for serial, and, of course, his publisher is looking for serial,' Link-Mite answered. 'Naturally, you'll both remember Trollope in his *Autobiography* on the pressures of publication in serial episodes. The tale has to be strong, strong, strong – something special for the reader in every instalment. Horton will need to give them a powerful tale, and a powerful new tale. Quit-and-tell spy books are everywhere. Why would editors buy another – and why would the public buy another – why would anyone, unless this is a spy book that offers something fresh and unique? What's fresh and unique, among other things, is a former head of the Outfit removed and destroyed, by who knows who? Turkey, do you

imagine the risk-takers who'll print and market this book
haven't been promised by dear Olly that he'll provide some
intelligent hints about how Verdun might have been – oh, yes,
only might have been – but might well have been butchered in
the filthy interests of some internecine vendetta and jockeying?
This was 1997, and Olly will be suggesting violent Outfit new-
broomism came in good time for the millennium.'

Latimer said: 'Roger, are you really implying that we have
at our head now a—?'

'You're sure about this room, are you, Turkey? You get it
swept? Link-Mite asked.'

'Routinely cleared, like every other,' Latimer replied.

'You talk so sweet and amenable I wondered whether
you're performing for the mikes,' Link-Mite said.

'I don't consider I was talking sweet and amenable. I was
talking reason,' Latimer replied.

Link-Mite said: 'If Horton refuses to write that sort of lid-
off material himself, they'll get someone to ghost it and insist
it's added – a ghost ghosting on spooks. A newspaper thinking
about serial might send its own people to do some digging,
expand and sauce up the material, given a pointer from Olly.
I'm surprised none of us has been accosted by someone so-
called "investigative" from the serious Press already. I take it
none of us has?'

'When I use the word tone,' Latimer replied, 'I'm thinking
above all of—'

'And always there's the money side,' Link-Mite said.
'Newspapers can understand money. They're dim on
espionage, except for someone like Briers, but they know how
to count cash. They like millions of dollars in a headline.
Millions and dollars together are as sexy as tit and bum. Extra
drama. People out there looking for those dollars – riled,
ungentle people. Might they move on Horton before the book
appears if they think his researches show something?

Alternatively, could the book and any serialisation articles suggest people out there might move on Horton? That gives a true flavour of peril and suspense. Journalistically this is prime stuff. Did Horton suggest you might know something about the money, Simon? Or did his woman? Kate, is it? She sees much, that one, I've been told. Does she mention Lucy? It would be some juicy tale, wouldn't it – the only black in the Outfit to reach any rank and now maybe involved in a mighty drugs swag conundrum and under bloody threat because of it?'

'When I speak of tone,' Latimer said, 'I'm referring also to what I perceive as this sort of openness in Olly Horton, as described by Simon. A commendable willingness to discuss – to put his views and perhaps to consider ours. He's not scared of intellectual scrutiny of his intentions, even invites it. I feel that if we proposed to send someone else from the Outfit to see him he would agree. Yes, openness. Now, this is not a reflection on how Simon conducted that first meeting – or it is a reflection, but entirely positive. Simon's interview with him has, in fact, provided the circumstances for the second one.'

'Horton has to be fucking silenced, hasn't he?' Link-Mite replied.

'It would certainly be better if he were silenced, Roger,' Latimer said, 'but what is to be our method?'

'Not many options as to that, I'd say,' Link-Mite replied. 'What we have to—'

'To consider or propose any sort of violence is surely preposterous,' Latimer said. 'I did ask Simon to point out that some of our more extreme people might be precipitate – and not at all hinting at you and your eternal malevolence, Roger. Obviously. I'm told this warning did not seem to impress Olly. Simon informs us that some parts of the book are already distributed in disk form and not recoverable. We could guess where some of them might be, but not all. In any case, can we really contemplate burgling a publisher's office, a newspaper office, a bank deposit? This would be as gross and doomed as that 1970s episode in the States. Remember? People broke in to that doctor's place hunting psychiatric notes on a Nixon enemy – Ellsberg – the Pentagon papers business? But even apart from such practical objections, I'm sure we are all conscious that the heavy techniques of the past are no longer acceptable in the new climate, except as the most final of last resorts.'

'That's exactly where we're fucking at,' Link-Mite replied. 'I just read the station name as the train pulled in: Final Last Resort. All change. Simon has done his intelligent sweet-hearting and has been told by Horton and his girl to piss off. I endorse what you say, Turkey – that Simon's approach and tenacity could not have been improved on. We've exhausted the persuasive bit. Now we—'

'My little project is to send one of our newest recruited people to talk to Olly,' Turkey Latimer replied. 'I wonder if you can see my thinking, Rog, Simon?'

'Well don't sodding wonder,' Link-Mite replied, 'because we can't – I'll speak for Simon, too. We've got a predicament here that three hairy arsed old experts don't see a way out of and you're talking about putting some rookie on to it.'

'My thinking being that someone new and fresh might, without being aware of it, remind Horton what he, too, was like when he first joined. That is – possessed of a wonderful enthusiasm for the career and for the Outfit – a justified gratitude at having been chosen from among the crowds who apply – a certain idealism – no I don't, do not think we should fear such absolute, wholesome terms – an instinct for loyalty – an instinct for endeavour, even for gallantry. My impression – admittedly only an impression, an instinct – my guess is that Horton might respond to such an oblique yet potent approach. He would be compelled to wonder at the decline that has come upon him since those early months. Perhaps he will feel overwhelming regret, dark shame. Perhaps he will suddenly wish to return to the condition of those times. Perhaps he will abandon the book, recall his discs. We could perhaps find room for him if he asked us to take him back. We are not strangers to quid pro quo. The practicalities of my idea are these: we often send recruits out on initiative tests and it would be simple to brief one of them to prepare a profile of Mr Oliver Horton of 23A Paling Yard. There would be no need to tell our emissary what Horton is or has been. That is for her/him to unearth.'

'Are you fucking joking, Turkey?' Link-Mite asked. 'Do you think her/him wouldn't have heard the name of Olly Horton around the Outfit, no matter how recently her/him joined? Olly resigned to whistle-blow. That's a very gossipable topic and one thing the Outfit excels at is insider gossip.'

'Absolutely irrelevant,' Latimer said. 'He/she just gets on with the test profile. Obviously, we are not even marginally interested in this. We know everything about Horton. What we *are* interested in is the impact on Olly of a bright, questing, committed personality. This might get to him, better even than Simon's priceless intercession as a friend. It would be a yearning from within Horton for his own original happy – and, yes, to some degree innocent sense of rightness in the Outfit. For of such is the kingdom of heaven. You, Simon, and you, Roger, perhaps more so, may think I drool and dream. Yet I feel this could – just could be a goer. And how else?'

'Turkey, you know I detest hearing the Scriptures used flippantly,' Link-Mite replied.

Chapter 8

Kate arrived in St James's street a little after midday by taxi. She did not get out but opened the rear door and called to him reassuringly, like a teacher to a child: 'Come.'

'Where?'

'Come,' she said. 'I can't neglect my jewellery.'

'No. Right. Of course not.' He climbed in and the taxi pulled away from outside the Carlton Club.

'Friday's always a big, big day.'

'Right.'

'It's in Oliver's dossier, is it?'

'What?' he asked.

'My jewellery stall. The importance of Friday business.'

He chuckled a bit, a rounded, poised kind of chuckle, right for the back of a cab in a fine neighbourhood, and as lead-in to some attempted lies that he knew wouldn't work. 'Kate, you really imagine Oliver's dossier would have an entry on yourself?'

'Of course, of course,' she said.

'And do you think we'd bother to profile every officer's wife or husband, partner, lover, mother, father, granny, for heaven's sake?

'Naturally. They're crucial. I'm *extremely* crucial.'

He gave it up. 'Right. You're described there as a part-time market trader,' he replied. 'Bibelots.'

'I considered university teaching. I might have tried for a media job.' She spoke deadpan, no grandiosity. Deadpan was not often her style. 'But I needed something I could run as I wished,' she said.

'You know jewellery?'

'I've learned. Am learning. Antique stuff mainly. Some crap, to use Mr Ratner's word, that supremely frank British jeweller. It sells best. Crap always sells best, whatever we're talking about, doesn't it – food, clothes, films, tv, cars, art—'

'Books?'

'Oliver's book won't be crap. Anyway, books are different. Given time, good books will do better than crap. They go on and on. Consider Second Kings or Winnie-the-Pooh. Historians will want Oliver's book. It puts light on a system, a whole political and social system. In the widest sense. System in the sense of a whole national culture, an inculcated mood.' She turned and stared from the rear window. It was a sunny, slightly misty, late August day. 'Have we got a tail? Did you hide a stand-by team there in case I tried something like this – the unscheduled pick-up by taxi? You people plan for the unplanned, even if you did miss Burgess and Maclean.'

'I'm acting alone.'

'Oh, yes?' she said.

'I'm not afraid to be in a taxi by myself with you.'

'I've heard Oliver say your only fault as an agent was a dislike of going solo.'

'We don't call ourselves agents. That's the FBI.'

'Pardon me, do. What then?'

'Officer. And, yes, 'I do dislike working alone,' Abelard replied. 'I'm a team boy.'

'Well?'

'But now and then I do it. Now.'

She gave up looking for a shadow car behind. The taxi man obviously knew where they were going and drove down Pall Mall, through Cockspur street and into the thick Whitehall traffic. Anyone trying to tail unseen would have to be talented. Abelard had certainly not organised any follow-up. Nobody in the Outfit knew he revered the Carlton's approaches as meeting spot. At least, he hoped not.

He checked the cab partition was properly shut. 'So, could you take Oliver into the jewellery business, Kate?' he asked.

'Why?'

'If needed.'

'What's that mean?'

'If needed,' he said.

'Oh, I see: the Outfit would add capital to expand things as long as he forgets the book?'

'We sometimes look after people who have to leave and find another occupation,' he said. 'It can include a new i.d. if an ex looks to be in danger.'

'He didn't have to leave. He left.'

'The cause of quitting is sometimes open to argument and negotiation. You know – whether a resignation was enforced: that kind of imprecise area. The Service can be reasonable. We regard it as an absolute obligation to resettle our ex-people well.'

'I like to hear you talk official. You can sound damn credible.'

'It's on my Personal Assessment form: "Can sound damn credible. Executive potential."'

'This taxi and the trip to my stall – I wanted to show you I can take control,' she replied.

'Yes, I got that.'

'I pay the fare.'

'Certainly.'

'You said – or gave the order – "Meet me at such-and-such and then we'll go on to such-and-such," a standard Outfit two stage encounter drill. I decided, Wreck this procedure, so you'd know you weren't handling a push-over.'

'Yes, I got that. I knew already, anyway.'

'What?'

'I wasn't handling a push-over.'

'Did you expect it – me arriving that way?' she said.

'Not a bit.'

'It seemed a weird spot for a venue – crawling with power people, or at least Opposition people, but crawling. As if you wanted to wrong-foot me, brow beat me from the outset.'

'No. I told you, I don't *belong* to the club. Could I? It's just a bit of easily findable street,' he replied.

'That's all?'

More or less. Perhaps there was something else: Abelard did find rendezvousing there medicinal. If he had to wait, he could gently pace and think in peace about his soul's sick instabilities. Because the Carlton was so exclusive, he liked to believe he despised the men who did not have to hang about outside, but went righteously in on their burnished footwear as members: no training shoes. He longed to feel he would noisily reject membership of the Carlton even if the whole committee blubberingly rushed out and implored him to join: 'Oh, be one of us, one of us, do, Si-boy, pleeeeeease.' 'Never, ever, you lucred, landed clique!'

But then, awed by the indisputable quality of the un-dog-fouled pavement, he'd ask himself, how sane was this fucking high-minded rattiness. After all, hadn't Abelard's whole adult experience been a smug, schemed, accelerating move away from his childhood's social category in what used to be Tiger Bay, around Cardiff docks? Oxford, the Intelligence Services – they magicked him pretty fast into a different life league, didn't they? He had never really objected. Objected? He'd sought it, loved it. Hadn't his parents and the neighbours *expected* him to seek it, and understood and approved when he did? If you could pass an exam or two and swing an interview, you had a holy duty to rise and rise. What else was education for? How about giving himself a second forename, Meritocracy? 'Our Simon's got a CAREER, you know.'

So, if you were climbing, why not climb as high as you could? Where did the conscience quibbles suddenly pop out from, and what sense to pretend contempt for a supremely polished set-up like the Carlton? Nerve gone? Why balk at joining the club: that is, balk in his daft imagination because no offer would ever come, of course, not even the kind of token black concession that got him into the Outfit? Waiting surly at the kerbside like a tramp or a tart, he could detest the men sauntering in, for their politics and possessions and ritual avoidance of denim on club premises. And he could detest himself for thinking badly of what he couldn't have, and thinking badly of it *because* he couldn't have it. His coat of arms should show sour grapes verts, when he got one. Yes, when, when, when. He was jumped up. He was a small bit jumped up and hopelessly stuck at where he'd jumped to. This was what really angered him, wasn't it, not fine scorn for Rightism and wealth and the accessories of wealth? After all, he had some wealth, a real heap thanks to Jules Bowling, preposterously dead by the Oratory a while ago in half a shirt.

'All right,' Kate said as they crossed Westminster Bridge, 'so it's not working.'

'What?'

'Oh, *what*! Come on, Simon.'

'The writing project?'

'I talk loud for Oliver when he's present, naturally – that's loyalty. And I do believe in the book. But I can see how things are. He's cut in two.' She looked all right yet sounded as if she might sob.

Abelard said: 'I'm really—'

'Mentally, psychologically split. It's close to a pathological state,' she said.

'Ah. Naturally you'd be worried.' But Abelard realised he,

himself, might be psychologically split, too. What he knew was lacking in him – and what the Carlton Club had plenty of – was old-fashioned, elusive, solid class. He loathed that kind of class, and intensely fancied it. Abelard suspected all in that class, and continually wondered how to join them. He knew he was as mixed up as a Socialist Lord or leching nun. Possibly he chose the St James's meeting spot to help lure out from his sub-conscious all those slimy contradictions, and that fart-arseing man-o'-the-people stuff, to where they were visible and could be given a true kicking. The Carlton was probably too politically explicit for anyone in the Service to belong, though Turkey certainly had the custom-made shoes and that marquistic, eternally indifferent, blue-eyed stare. Although Abelard persisted in using the Carlton pavement, he always feared to be seen loitering there by leadership people from the Outfit. Wouldn't he look helplessly, everlastingly prole? That thought always brought a savagely reproachful cry inside his head: Oh, Abelard, why do you deny yourself? He had an answer, though: CAREER, IN THE CAUSE OF HER MAJESTY. He recognised it was always a disgusting betrayal to turn your back on your upbringing, but didn't Abelard's upbringing say, and say often: 'Soar, Simon, and turn your back on your upbringing?'

The taxi pulled in soon at a three-storey, red-brick building on the corner of Trace Street and Sinclair Square in Walworth. This was the Antiques Market. Kate had a stall on the second floor. She unlocked and raised a metal roller blind and they sat behind the display stands on two wooden dining chairs like partners. He glanced at the jewellery display and wondered whether the security blind was necessary. As she'd said, most items were twinkling rubbish. There probably wasn't one livelihood here, and certainly not two. But, obviously, that might be quickly changed with a slab of extra backing. However, would she know how to buy good stuff to sell, and would it sell here? Turkey might be willing to find some funds, as long as he judged this worthwhile: if the business died, Olly was liable to turn author again in the search for earnings, and all the Outfit agonies would be revived. Although supervision of the Section's budget was vague – had to be because of all the secrecy, even now – it would detect really flagrant, barmy waste and make a fuss. This could mess up Turkey's progress towards his eve-of-retirement coronet. In any case, Turkey's taste and snobbery might be offended if he were asked to subsidise a tat depot. And, another element: for any business arrangement of this sort, the Outfit would provide cash to buy Olly out of his present publishing contract and repay the advance. Abelard had heard the newspaper maxim, 'Comment is free, facts expensive.' But eliminating facts could be expensive, too. Silence was golden because gold bought it. Turkey would require the promise of infinite silence. *Investors are advised that the value of their stake can disappear altogether, as well as just go down.* Turkey was not the kind of investor to need this warning.

'You're afraid for Olly's mind, Kate?' Abelard asked.

'So don't come over so fucking pleased about it.'

'This stall – not what you'd call sound-proof. You've got neighbours on both sides, plus the public.'

'I lack that built-in, trained-in taste for furtiveness,' she replied.

'Oliver might not want to have the condition of his mind discussed where all sorts can—'

'So OK, we talk low.'

'Well, very.'

'As a matter of fact,' she said, 'I wondered if you'd bug the stall. You might look at my dossier profile – it saying caution, wilfulness, wiliness – and guess I'd insist any meeting happened on my own patch.'

'You're scared Oliver's brain might be starting to—?'

'So, again, don't come over so fucking pleased about it.' Now absolutely no deadpan.

'We agreed to talk low,' Abelard said.

She whispered, but sharpening up the savage s and f sounds to compensate for dropped volume on the third use: 'So don't come over so fucking pleased about it.' And she leaned closer to him, got it smack into his right ear like a potted pool ball. He could glimpse her fine, square back teeth, undarkened by fillings.

'Do you want him to stop doing the book, even though you think it would be great?' he replied.

'That's what I mean. You talk as though you've won, you and Turkey and the rest. No, I don't want him to stop it. NO. That would be bad, a loss to future scholars, and yes, a loss to the precious concept and fact of Truth itself, Truth with a capital T. If that sounds frothy, too bad. But I don't want Oliver into breakdown, either.'

'I've known this happen to people. Disintegration.'

'Yes, you would.'

'Tragic.'

'Of course, the Russians sent people to asylums when they questioned the State. Simple logic, wasn't it: if you doubted perfect dogma it had to mean you were disturbed? Scepticism equalled lunacy. I think therefore I'm mad. Are you coming around to viewing difficult friends like that?'

'I've heard some of our own officers splintered mentally when their loyalties wobbled. And CIA folk.'

'Because the apprenticeship's shaped to colonise your minds,' she said. 'To have a private idea is treachery, so guilt moves in. And, Simon, what happened to the people you knew who came apart like that? I suppose they were led back to faith, were they, by someone considerate and smart, such as you, and then, suddenly, they're at full health again? Or they committed suicide. Alleged.'

'Oliver could probably come back into the Outfit,' Abelard replied. 'At times, Latimer is surprisingly positive. He recognises that if the Service insists on recruiting only thoughtful, intelligent people, it may not always be able to control the thoughtfulness and intelligence. He'll tolerate some apparently subversive independence.'

'Oliver doesn't want to come back. I don't want him to go back.'

'When someone leaves, often that may be final as far as the Service is concerned,' Abelard replied. 'Leaving is taken to signify more than simple need for a career change. Resignation can be regarded as – well, as disowning the Outfit and its reason for existence. For instance, it might be on account of a newly developed doctrinal objection in the officer – something deep, not easily reparable, and therefore dangerous. So, future exclusion is total, unnegotiable. "Goodbye laddy, lady, we both made an error." But Latimer might not see Oliver like this. Although he'd probably have to do another probationary stretch in non-sensitive duties for a while, there'd be no molten lead tipped on him if he tried to re-enter. I think I can be sure of that.'

'*Think* you can be sure – you're talking gibberish. People do that when they hand out bullshit,' she said.

OK, that seemed fair.

A fat white man in a tan cape and white bobble hat pulled hard down over his ears was crouched at a tray of items and Kate went to serve him. He wanted a brooch to give his cape a 'focus point' and take people's eyes away from the age lines in his neck. He explained that the one trouble with capes was they left the neck at the front unpleasantly visible. This was not enough to destroy the appeal of capes – or why would he be wearing one, for heaven's sake? – but it had to be taken into account. Kate replied that she would never have noticed those lines and did not even think they could be called lines, but confirmed that brooches on capes were all the thing these days in circles where fashion really zinged.

'You, sir,' he said to Abelard, 'absolutely no disrespect, I hope, but why do I never see a black in a cape, its shade immaterial?'

'Many's the time I've asked myself this,' Abelard replied.

'But do you, you personally, have a cape, sir?'

'Three. All enlivened by jewellery, of course. A cape is not really a cape without that.'

'I refuse to abandon capes. That would be a surrender to ageism.'

'You don't look to me the kind who would surrender to anything,' Abelard replied.

'Beauty – an affection for beauty and style. This is what counts. Capes are just an item in that, yet a notable one.'

Kate sold the man a large, brilliant, mock silver brooch in which a cow jumped over the moon. She pinned it on the cape for him at a point where it should divert all attention from his neck, then returned to her chair alongside Abelard. 'Oliver left because of what happened to Verdun Cadwallader,' she said. 'That destroyed all his belief in the Outfit, and his belief until then had been virtually total, wholehearted, unshakable.'

'Verdun, yes. A continuing mystery.'

'Oh, yes?'

'Many would like to know the truth of that, Kate.'

She eyed him, then laughed. It was contemptuous, it was despairing. She seemed aware of being blocked by a brick wall, loathed the brick wall for blocking her, but knew a lot about brick walls through marriage to someone in the Outfit, and realised she probably couldn't get around it. She repeated his words nice and slowly, nice and derisively. They were stupid and false-formal, reeking with pretended ignorance. 'Many would like to know the truth of that, Kate,' she said. He used to think when he met her socially with Oliver that she always made a point of looking aggressively intelligent: a kind of continuous half frown in sharp concentration, turquoise

eyes fierce with focus – the sort of woman who would
obviously know the *Areopagitica* and would also expect
others to know it and wish to talk about it in reasonably
offhand style, or why was she bothering with them? Now,
though, he saw real anxiety in Kate, as well as that standard
wish to browbeat, probably picked up in a damn good school.
She was small, very slight, pretty going on beautiful in a
miniature way, and she did not look right for the degree of
trouble and responsibility she obviously carried. Christ, she
was taking on the Outfit and people like Turkey, even Link-
Mite. Abelard felt a bit ashamed at having to get it across in
reasonably oblique language that things for Olly and possibly
her might turn grave. He had always liked Kate, despite the
gabble and the learning. She could relax, but not now. He did
understand that. She had called the meeting and, presumably,
wanted something from Abelard and was tensely working
towards asking for it. 'Is the cape man somebody?' she said.

'He is now, with one of your brooches.'

'Why do you get someone to appear here like that?'

'Exactly,' Abelard said. 'Why would I?'

'Part of the terrorising ploy? Everything I do, everywhere I
go is logged? A threat. "We know where you live." Will the
brooch be on his expenses? I should have jacked up the price.'

'I'm not being snooty about market stalls, but with some
financial help you might be able to move to a main street shop
premises,' Abelard said. 'You'd probably know more about
the trade than Olly, so you could look after the valuable
antique pieces – selling and buying – and he'd take the more
popular, mass produced side. Real prospects for an outlet like
that. It might seem a trifle sedate for Olly after the Outfit
work, but as he came to know more about jewellery perhaps
the shop could go upmarket, and there'd be the excitement of
dealing with really beautiful items and very big sums. I can
imagine Olly squinting at a lovely diamond through a

jewellers' magnifying glass, can't you, Kate? That concentration he's famed for.'

'I'm used to doing deals,' she replied.

'That's what I'm saying. You could handle the buying of the more important things and—'

'I'm here to do a deal *now*,' she said.

'Like with the brooch? Go ahead. I'll watch. Where's the customer?'

'Don't act fucking thick, Simon. You know what I'm saying: a deal with *you*.'

'Olly sent you to do a deal?'

'Oliver doesn't know about this meeting and should never be told about it.'

'Right.'

'I believe I know his thinking.'

'I'm sure.'

'What are you saying – you're sure I believe I know it, or you're sure I know it?

'Shouldn't he be present at any attempt at a "deal", as you call it?' Abelard asked.

'I see these as very preliminary talks, defining where we're at.'

'Right.'

'Where we're at is this, Simon: I know he won't do any further digging into your role in the death of Julian Bowling, or into what happened to the money.'

'Role?'

'Yes, you know – role.'

'Do you mean role in the investigation of his death?' Abelard said. 'That's a job for the police.'

'No, before and up to his killing. That role.'

'I'm—'

'The money – this is millions we're talking about here, isn't it? God, aren't you scared people will come looking for that –

very rough people, the kind of people Julian worked with, maybe stole from, after he quit the Outfit? They chased him, didn't they? Don't you think they might chase *you*? And chase Lucy, wherever she is? They'd imagine they're entitled, wouldn't they – their profits hijacked?'

'Ah. Do you think, then, that Julian was killed for money by crooked people he'd worked with,' Abelard replied.

'Do I? I'm not sure.'

'It's tricky,' Abelard said. 'Obscure.'

'What I'm sure about is that *you* know who killed him, and who did whatever was done to Cadwallader.'

'One obvious and simple way out of all this acute worry is to submit Olly's book for vetting under the Secrets Act,' Abelard replied. 'Like Dame Stella's.'

'Which acute worry?'

'Oh, the worry and stress that make you imagine one of your own customers in a cape might be planted.'

'Was he?

'What – employed by the Outfit, with neck age lines like that?'

'Oliver would leave the Bowling episode at what he experienced and saw. Nothing more.'

'I thought he said it would all be like that. The centre of consciousness stuff.'

'He did say it. But I ask you, Simon, who'd believe him? Did you? Would someone like Link-Mite? Oliver had to fend you off, get more time, maybe. The book would be impossibly flat if he stuck to those limits. The publishers could reasonably back out and ask for the return of their cash. He hasn't seen enough – not direct. And he hasn't seen anything at all about what he really longs to write about – what happened to Cadwallader. He believes the disappearance of Cadwallader reveals the whole rottenness of things. It typifies the dominating culture, the established mood. These made him resign from an organisation that could countenance them, an organisation he previously worshipped. He believes now he has an obligation to reveal such circumstances. But, of course, he doesn't actually *know* the circumstances. We think you do, Simon. That's why I speak about a deal, and that's why I sought this meeting. Oh, I can turn on the Milton flam and the Spenser flam when I wish, but I also know how business arrangements are come to. One such arrangement is what I'm trying for now with you. We believe Bowling's death is certainly significant and would be dramatic and, yes, meaningful if described well in a book, plus the matter of his money. But none of this is so significant, so shatteringly symbolic of entrenched evil, as the death of Verdun. *Institutionalised* evil, to borrow a one-time buzz word.'

'One day everything about that terrible sequence will be known,' Abelard replied. 'I'm convinced of this.'

'You know about it, Simon, know about it now. I'm certain. Oliver is certain, though he'd never be able to say so to you. Pals, and so on, weren't you? Well, because you're a pal, he will seek to resist any pressure from the publishers to say nothing about Bowling's death that might point to you or Lucy McIver. And then, because you're a pal, I know he'd like you to tell him the lot on Cadwallader. This is what would make his work enduringly important. He sees an authentic writing future for himself if he can begin with a book that is gripping but also serious and deep. Something that portrays the dirty *fin de siècle zeitgeist*.'

'It's like being abroad, I don't know where,' Abelard replied. 'Here are two more heavies come to terrorise you.' A couple of girls around about eleven or twelve and probably mitching school were studying a spread of very cheap pieces. Kate went to them and chatted nicely. The girls tried on a variety of rings. Kate held a small mirror for them to get the full impact. Eventually they went off delighted and noisy, wearing a ring each. As far as Abelard could see, Kate did not charge them. When she came back she said: 'You can't be satisfied with how things went – the death of Verdun, then the succession. Was he killed from inside?'

'Inside what?'

'OK. Play thick again. Inside the Outfit.'

'Kill one of our own main people? You're playing thick – and naïve – aren't you?' Abelard said.

'Remember that *Godfather* scene where Michael Corleone tells his respectable wife, Kay, that his father is just like other powerful men: say a senator or president? And Kay replies that this is – your word, Simon – says this is naïve because senators and presidents don't have men killed. Michael says: "Who's being naïve, Kate?" I think Oliver's amazed you've stayed in an organisation that can live with... live with what it can apparently live with. He'd expect better, though, again, he'd never tell you that. God, you can't need the wages now, Simon.'

Abelard stood. He'd only lately had a discussion with Carl Briers on naïveté and didn't feel like a re-run.

She said: 'Naturally, I can see that Oliver will be in danger if he's going to suggest Verdun's death was an in-house killing.'

'He would be, were there the smallest possibility that what he seems to believe is true.'

'And what *I* believe.'

Abelard said: 'Kate, as we've been toying with foreign languages just now, have you ever heard the phrase *folie à deux,* meaning two people thinking together can get things more than twice as wrong as someone on their own?'

'And is there that smallest possibility?'

'Obviously, if so, you could be in danger yourself, Kate. You're telling me, the book will suggest there's someone around in the Outfit – still around in the Outfit – who'd—'

'Not just *around* in the Outfit. High. Highest?'

'Someone who'd kill whenever it suits, and it could clearly suit to remove Olly and shut him up. It might also suit to remove anyone he's confided in.'

'Thanks for that comfort, Simon.'

'You'd thought of it already.'

'Let's stick with *you*,' she replied. 'We haven't mentioned Bowling's mum and dad. Wouldn't they feel entitled to some of the cash, crooked and filched or not? Suppose they come after you – come after Lucy, too, if they can find her – maybe using hired odd-job men. Tons of pros for hire these days, aren't there? I'd say you'd be damned exposed, Simon, if Oliver felt he had to plump out the Bowling death in his book and speculate about who's nesting the golden eggs.'

'I can understand that Olly might not want to come back in. Pride. Genuine dissatisfaction. Well, all right. A number of folk quite legitimately look for a job switch these days. Nothing has to be permanent. Commerce has a genuine pull for many and so has the artistic creative life. The Outfit would definitely recognise this.'

'So, what do you say, Simon? I won't inform Oliver about this discussion, but I want to be able to tell him I think, I sense, I intuit, that if there could be another meeting of the three of us you'd probably be willing to give him what he needs in exchange for supreme tact on Bowling and the money.'

'Right away I could get our research people to prepare a list of empty shop premises that might suit you both as jewellers,' Abelard replied.

Chapter 9

In his bright effort to prevent rougher treatment of Olly Horton, Turkey sent one of the Outfit's newest girls to see him. The decency and moderation of his scheme seemed to thrill Latimer and let him feel humane. That blue-eyed stare became warmer for a time and he looked the kind of person who might buy the Big Issue in aid of homeless folk without being harangued, and who would be generally unopposed to charity. Abelard could believe a genuine sensitiveness had moved in on him, and that this was beyond the soft role he sometimes deliberately played to Link-Mite's toughie. Latimer was certainly not dangerously squeamish but he did have these occasional manic lurches into restraint.

The girl's task was to radiate in an oblique way real love of her career and loyalty to it, in the hope that Olly would recall when he, too, was like this, and might be made to hunger for such glorious simplicities again. She would prepare a profile of Horton if she could get him to see her and co-operate. Apparently, Turkey still hadn't told her who Olly was, but she would know, of course, just as Link-Mite had said. You could not work in the Outfit even for a few days without hearing Horton's name as part of dubious current folklore. People speculated non-stop on why he had left, what he might publish, what the Outfit would do to counter him. For now, this girl, Iris Insole, aged twenty-five with an honours degree in Theology, was what the Outfit would do to counter him. Yes, for now.

Because of Roger Link-Mite, Turkey had apparently

instructed her that he wanted nothing written down or disked. Whatever was written down or disked, Link-Mite often somehow got to find and read. If you were a spy or had been a spy you spied. Occasionally, Roger would immediately reveal he had found and read whatever it was and little damage might be caused. At other times, though, he said nothing at once, but stored the knowledge until it could be used best to get him ahead, and possibly wreck a few colleagues. Obviously, these two aims generally overlapped plenty.

So, from Iris Insole, Turkey wanted a verbal report only. He asked Abelard, as Personnel, to sit in on the interview when she presented her Olly profile. This probably meant he was afraid Link-Mite would telepathise the existence of their meeting, perhaps even barge into the room while it was on. Abelard's presence should then make things look official and proper: routine. Because the session was intended to be totally secret from Roger Link-Mite, Turkey would hate Link-Mite to discover it regardless, in circumstances that showed this session was intended to be totally secret from him. If it failed to stay totally secret, Link-Mite was sure to glory in the failure, move into a longish period of blatant smirk around the office and clubs, and Turkey would be humiliated. Wearing fine shoes like his off a personal last, Turkey could not contemplate humiliation. He warned the girl and Abelard that nothing should be said about the proceedings. Although Link-Mite did, of course, know Turkey had proposed this little operation as a means of avoiding or postponing outright physical harshness to Olly, and possibly Kate, he was not told of its implementation, and quite possibly need not be told. The operation had been only a Turkey notion and not all of Turkey's notions went anywhere much. Turkey was a synthesiser and coordinator, hardly ever an ideas font.

'All the time I was with him I felt he knew,' Iris Insole said. They had an armchair each in Turkey's room for delivery of the profile. During one part of his career he'd lived for several years in the USA and kept on his walls several framed photographs of famous baseball players pitching or striking, including de Maggio.

The girl said: 'I had my cover tale – an in-depth, door-to-door multi-point consumer survey – and it seemed to stand up all right – I mean, he answered the questions seriously and thought about some of them for quite a time, po-faced – but I felt he might be playing along.'

Abelard saw this girl could be a very sharp, perceptive addition to the Outfit, and was glad he had been on one of the boards that picked her. He had liked the Theology aspect: they needed an expert on worldwide beliefs. Yes, almost certainly Olly would have seen through Iris, as she sensed. And almost certainly Kate would have seen through her, too. They would both be expecting a visitor, visitors, who were not necessarily what they said they were. Olly had been well-trained to spot people who were not what they said they were and deconstruct them. Kate was not trained but had probably osmosised some of the skills from Olly and, in any case, had her own strong, natural, sceptical talent. Of course, in Turkey's healing scheme, Olly was definitely meant to know where Iris actually came from, though she could not be informed of this. Olly had to recognise and respond to her enthusiasm for the job. Neither could come at all clean with the other. 'Would you define what made you think he had you sussed?' Abelard asked.

'An impression,' she said.

'But run it slowly through your head – run the encounter with him slowly through your head, and see if you can select the moment when you began to wonder.'

'I've done that. I've done it so many times, believe me,' she replied. 'I knew I could learn from it.'

'Please, Iris,' Abelard said. 'Once more. Absolutely no rush.'

'This is not to question your efficiency in the cover role,' Turkey said.

'It sounds an excellent front,' Abelard said.

'I suppose obvious,' she replied. 'But, if you want to get into someone's house, how else, other than burgle or pretend to be Gas Safety?'

With quite a grin, Turkey remarked: 'So true. You could scarcely sound a clarion and expect the walls of his home to fall down for you.'

'What?' she answered. 'Clarion?'

'Like the walls of Jericho when Joshua, son of Nun, had the trumpets of rams' horns blown by the priests for seven days,' Turkey said. He and Link-Mite both knew the Bible, Old and New Testaments, and Turkey would like to get on to a footing with Iris and her Theology degree. The Book of Micah was Turkey's favourite. Abelard often heard him recite from it and could remember bits of the verses Turkey declaimed most: 'Trust ye not in a friend: keep the doors of thy mouth from her that lieth in thy bosom. A man's enemies are the men of his own house.'

Iris had it right and commercial surveys were a fairly standard means of entry. Olly would be familiar with it, might even have used it himself. 'Did you do some of the neighbours, for credibility – in case they chat?' Abelard asked.

'Of course.'

'Mock i.d. card? Abelard said. What did it matter? His questions were a game, a cloud, and not a very good game, not a very thick cloud. No ploys would have worked on Olly and Kate. It was not a mystery that Iris had been rumbled. The Turkey script expected it, required it. 'I made myself one,' she said, 'knowing that Mr Latimer wouldn't want Documents section to learn of the project.'

'One purpose of the exercise is to test all round secrecy and that would mean secrecy even from other parts of the office,'

Turkey replied. 'This is necessary now and then in our work –
the For Your Eyes Only rigmarole. You did well there, Iris.' *A
man's enemies are the men of his own house.*

'Have you got the i.d?' Abelard asked.

She produced a plastic covered card from a pocket in her
tan suede blouson and passed it to Abelard. There was a head
and shoulders photograph of herself on a blue and silver
backing, plus some large, mysterious initials at the top
signifying the supposed name of the research organisation she
represented. The print work was good, the colouring tasteful.
Abelard considered this a remarkably skilled computer
product. He passed it to Turkey. Although the card was
brilliant, it would not fool Olly, because, even if Olly were
not so sharp, he would be keyed up, waiting for some kind of
approach, possibly bogus, possibly brutal, possibly both,
possibly about now. But Abelard thought if someone had
called on him, personally, at home with this kind of i.d. and
the patter to go with it he could have been taken in. The
thing was, Abelard always loved being surveyed at length as a
consumer, and he'd *want* any caller to be genuine. This wish
might affect his judgement. Continually it delighted him to
manufacture an utterly new yet consistent being for himself
by giving wholesale false answers for such a questionnaire. It
was a kind of escapism, a kind of low level creativity, the
only kind he could manage. Deception thrilled him. He was
in the right job. Abelard delighted being data-based as
somebody else. This knocked the supposed autocracy of data,
made data as ludicrous and shaky as most of life. After all,
someone had to fuck up their knowledgeable stats. Too much
information, too much truth, always destabilised. His father
would not have agreed or understood. This was something
Abelard had learned when out on his own.

'Fellow-feeling,' Iris said suddenly. 'Horton seemed to relay
that.' Perhaps while Abelard and Turkey studied the i.d. card

she had been doing what Abelard asked and re-reviewing in her head the session with Olly.

'This made you think the encounter was not... well, not what?' Abelard asked.

'I detected a kind of sympathetic attitude towards me,' she replied. 'Or that's what I felt.'

'Would this be because of the work you were doing?' Abelard said.

'Yes, I suppose so.'

'Ah,' Turkey said. He would like this. The plan.

'Did you sense this man might have done around-the-houses commercial surveys himself and knew the difficulties of doorstepping?' Abelard asked. For now the game persisted.

She gave a small, exasperated groan. 'Oh, come on,' she said, 'we all know he's no around-the-houses commercial surveys operator, don't we? He was in the Outfit. This is Oliver Basil Horton. Remember?' She looked pissed off but also a little deferential. After all, Turkey was Turkey and AORC at the last count. This was a turkey that could fly and might go even higher. This turkey would last beyond Christmas, probably.

'I'm really interested in those words "sympathetic attitude" towards you,' Latimer said. 'Might it be... Look, Iris, do you think, that he envied you?'

'Envied? Oh, I don't see that.'

'It probably isn't something you'd wish to suggest, Iris, not even to yourself, because it sounds arrogant,' Turkey said, 'damned arrogant, and its nice of you to draw back from it, but do ponder this for a few seconds: "sympathetic attitude", "envy" – they seem very distant from each other, I concede, yet might not the first arise from the second?'

'Envy what?' she asked.

'I'm sure you displayed a remarkable belief in the task you were doing,' Turkey replied, 'a conviction that it was wholly worthwhile. As, indeed, it was. Oh, indeed. And all this accompanied by a remarkable drive and ingenuity – enough to get you into Horton's home and persuade him to be interrogated at survey length. This must have seemed admirable to him. And, so, yes, he would be won over and wish to co-operate – would appear "sympathetic" – and at the same time might wish he still possessed similar qualities and "envy" you for them.' Latimer seemed to fit himself with a very cheery paroxysm – coughed and waved an arm excitedly for a while in his chair. They were drinking coffee from proper cups, but he had to put his on the floor to avoid tipping. 'No, no, damn it… no, I don't… will not consider this far-fetched. I see it as a formidable accomplishment by you, the kind of accomplishment we always hope the exercise will reveal, don't we, Simon?'

'Sympathetic in the sense that he saw I was play-acting and didn't want to do anything to show he knew I was play-acting,' she said. 'That could have been part from sympathy and kindness, couldn't it? It could also have been from a wish for me to go on talking, stay with it, so he had more time and material to assess what I was really up to. Well, naturally – he's trying to read in me what the Outfit's likely to do about him. He wouldn't think I'm the last word on the situation, would he? I'm just a novice. Cat's paw?' She was lightly built with a round face that could seem childlike at times and at other times ferociously grave. She wore spectacles in large black frames and this might account for the impression of girlishness – a form five pupil who thought of devoting herself to education and possibly the Church. Her hair was dark and almost to her shoulders, her eyes also dark, busy behind the glasses, suspicious and worldly, on the lookout for deceptions, heresies, slackness. This novice might have a Whatever Happened to the Inquisition poster on her wall.

Turkey said: 'My view… tentative at this point, certainly,

yet not insubstantial... not at all insubstantial, in fact... my view is that a rapport seems to have been established between you and Horton, Iris, and that this might be extremely fruitful.'

'Fruitful, how? May I say, I came to wonder why I was there?' she replied.

'Oh, to show you could get in,' Abelard said.

'Is that all – just the test?' she asked.

'And to achieve the profile,' Abelard replied.

'To what purpose?' she asked. 'The Outfit must have every aspect of him dossiered.'

'So that we can compare your instant profile of him with what we have,' Abelard said – 'judge how good on people you are.' It would be mad to go on denying Olly had been in the Outfit.

'As part of the test?' she asked.

'Right,' Abelard replied. 'To measure accuracy of first assessment of a notional target figure.

'And that's all?' she said.

'What else?' Abelard asked.

'I don't know what else. But *something* else.'

'We're running this sort of exercise all the time,' Abelard replied.

'So do you want me to give you my profile of him now, based on the survey questions and my observation?' she said. 'Only him. His wife wasn't present, though he spoke about her very fondly.' The voice hit something between a snarl and a sneer. She knew they longed above all to avoid getting dragged through the profile.

'When I say rapport I'm not implying anything sexual, Iris, I do hope you realise that... not in the least,' Latimer replied. 'There are other kinds of harmony between woman and man, I hope. Oh, certainly. What I do sense was achieved is the kind of understanding which might go quite a bit deeper in him than you, perhaps, would imagine – because it would be presumptuous, possibly, of you to imagine it. This is why I thought potentially fruitful. Yes. I'd say you've managed this test with... well, with rare aplomb. Wouldn't you say aplomb, Simon, rare aplomb?'

'Was I there to get him to return to the Outfit?' she replied. 'Shame him? Shake him – through his own sweet, freshman memories? Or was I supposed to notice the layout of the place and the security, for follow-up? But you'd have all that, wouldn't you?'

'I don't see how Simon could record other than a Maximum on your R 17 for this work,' Turkey answered.

'The profile,' she said. 'Shall I begin? You really want it?' Again the tone expected the answer, 'No, thank you very much, not just now.'

Turkey said: 'People think of our activities as run either by electronics or by street skills like tailing or document drops or... or, yes... I have to say it, by some skulduggery. Few realise the psychological finesse required for the sort of operation you've just brilliantly completed, Iris.'

'Completed? What have I completed?'

'The exercise test,' Abelard replied.

'You think he'll abandon the book because of me, come back asking for his job and forgiveness?' she said. 'Really?'

'Don't underplay yourself, Iris,' Turkey replied. 'By underplaying yourself you underplay us, too. We selected you for the Outfit. We selected you again for this assignment.'

'All right, when I was sent to see him I know I wasn't supposed to know, not know officially, who he is,' she said. 'But, of course, I did know. And I decided I wouldn't play ignorant.'

'I'd say that's in character, admirably in character,' Turkey replied.

'So, if I gave you my profile of him – was allowed to give

you my profile of him – it would mention the book and stress that he's not doing it just to cash in,' she said. 'Or even mainly to cash in. He's got a quite fierce truth mission – in fact, a truth compulsion.'

'It's because you have this kind of perceptiveness that we sent you to see him,' Turkey cried. 'This is where your theological flair comes in – the ability to spot the larger prospects. We find this observation heartening, don't we, Simon? Someone focused on money only would be appallingly difficult to shift, if shiftable at all. Money is such a narrow, concrete, inflexible ambition. But truth's another thing, isn't it? Here again your theology training would operate, because you're sure to recognise that truth is a variable. Think: the "true" version of God in the Old Testament is of a jealous, vengeful force: "I will repay, saith the Lord." But in the New Testament the "true" God is forgiving; the "true" God is love. Yet both notions inhabit the same Bible. And, of course, you'll recall that description of the pulpit in the de Vries novel, *The Mackerel Plaza*. It was made of four different kinds of wood to symbolise the four Gospels and their failure to harmonise. Truth is adjustable, ephemeral, seasonal. Oh, yes, if it's only truth he's after we have good hope. Through your radiant faith in and devotion to your duties, Iris, you may have persuaded him that truth is not some fly-by-night caprice of an individual. Truth is corporate, communal, multi-faceted, democratic.'

'Sounds like Beijing,' she said.

'China is never to be dismissed entirely.'

'Truth is the Outfit?' she asked.

'Your very person endorses that,' Turkey replied. 'And we believe Horton might have realised this, been moved by it.'

There was another one of those accidental meetings in the street with Carl Briers, *The Sunday Post* correspondent. This time it happened not far from the Outfit. Abelard was on his way home. Although, like everyone else in the buildings, Abelard could use one of four exits, varying them daily, Briers was old and full of knowledge, of course – familiar with these little procedures. Perhaps he'd waited for Abelard in the wrong spot a few evenings, but eventually he would click. Abelard saw Briers would obviously have liked another café sojourn, this time for tea, but Abelard kept walking hard. Carl wouldn't be able to sustain this for long. He said: 'I find that straight after Julian's death you and Lucy and your mother spent a time in Switzerland.'

'A sabbatical. I was researching "Business ethics: their range and limits".'

'Perfect.'

'There has to be some clear purpose to a sabbatical project, but not slavishly connected to one's routine work."

'Sure.'

'Lucy and my mother came as a holiday. Their part of it properly paid for. Not Government funded.'

'Anyway, Switzerland is a money place, isn't it?' Briers replied.

'A *beautiful* place. That's what they enjoyed.'

'Did Julian's beautiful leavings somehow end up in a Swiss bank?' Briers asked. 'One of those code-numbered, no-name accounts, trite but practical. You could draw on it somehow? Lucy could draw on it as his ex? Then you could draw on Lucy as her current. He'd fixed it before he died? Perhaps Lucy had actually to appear physically before the bankers to prove i.d., did she? Sole named beneficiary? Julian found some gallantry at the end, did he?'

Abelard slowed his pace, then stopped and faced Briers. 'Here's my station, Carl,' he said.

'Do you know what I thought then, when you halted and gave me a stare – that you were going to warn me?'

'You're getting nervy, are you?'

'Is it reasonable?'

'What?'

'For me to get nervy. Am I safe – still reasonably safe? Wasn't some journalist connection of yours who got caught up in Outfit matters killed? A kind of accident? New York? Hit by cars – that's *cars*, not *a* car. Tate? Charles Tate?'

'You'd have damn sharp instincts, Carl, after all these years at it.'

'I feel trouble from too many directions,' Briers replied.

'Yes, well, a lot of people seemed to target Julian. And anyone poking into his life and death now might still interest them. You folk are so obsessed about seeing your name big on a page, preferably the front. You sometimes take risks you're not trained for.'

'Ah, so, yes, the warning.'

'But I'm sure you're used to being all-round vigilant.'

'*You're* one,' Briers said.

'One what?'

'One of the directions I feel trouble from,' Briers replied.

'Yes, I think I got that.'

'Should I?'

'What?'

'See you as a direction to feel trouble from.'

'None of us can do anything about a journalist following his proper professional concerns.'

'Is that right?'

Chapter 10

Briers did not come with him into the Underground but stood on the pavement looking almost deferential, almost sympathetic, as Abelard gave a short wave and moved away. Perhaps there was something in Abelard's face that showed Carl he had said enough and more for now. Always, Abelard disliked thinking about Charlie Tate, but his mind often sneaked back to those episodes, despite his efforts to bury them. He disliked even more hearing Charlie's name and his slaughter chucked into a conversation as an 'Oh-by-the-way-old-son...'

But, of course, although it might have sounded like that, Briers did not just chuck Tate's name in. There was a newspaper story to lever or woo out of Abelard that might ginger up and top or tail Olly's half-cock disclosures for the paper, and Tate's mashing in a New York street could feature large there. There were headlines in that kind of death, and so Brier applied his techniques and strategy to net the material: high artisan skills. Briers would have been watching to see how Abelard responded. And, for fuck's sake, Abelard should not have responded at all. Hadn't training and time in the profession taught him by now how to keep his eyes blank and his skin twitchless, no matter what he heard? Generally he managed it. A sudden, unbidden recollection of Tate's death, though, or an unexpected reference to it like Briers', could stab Abelard hard and might get a give-away reaction. This was self-indulgent, sentimental shit really, he knew that. Someone had been killed through getting too brave and blind.

Too brave could be all right on its own: call it audacity. But too brave *and* too blind – that was only darkness. It could happen in this sort of work. Charlie had been a classically foolish journalistic prick, not a sacrifice. There were definitely times when Abelard could believe this. Then there were these other flabby, mawkish times.

Abelard continued into the station. Possibly Briers on his dodgy feet did not like the shoving and stairs of the Underground, anyway. Or he might regard it as poor form to pursue someone right into his bunk hole – a crude breach of the manhunting code. There was a mystical aura about the entrance to the Tube for some: it proclaimed we were all part of the multitude and that in the multitude a man ought to be safer, like a beast in a herd, a vote in a box. Perhaps Briers felt that. Reporters had their sensitivity, many of them. It might increase as they grew older. Briers had time to be considerate. People working on investigative stuff for Sunday papers were not harried by deadlines. Briers would ask around elsewhere for a while, almost certainly including the States, and then most likely stage another lucky street meeting with Abelard. Or if he thought he really had piled up all the stuff he needed, he might get to feel strong, brazen, impregnable, and appear at Abelard's front door, or even make a formal call at the Outfit to reveal what he'd got and announce that further secrecy about the past by the Outfit was ludicrous. 'So please cough the lot, would you?'

Turkey would be disturbed if he found out about it and, of course, he *would* find out about it. Roger Link-Mite would be disturbed and enraged if he found out about it and, of course, he *would* find out about it. Link-Mite's rages could be brilliantly constructive – in the special way a demolition firm's crash ball was. His rages made him strive to obliterate whatever or whoever caused them. Then he could build on the cleared site something he approved of, something helpful to his lovely future.

Briers and his interest in Tate troubled Abelard. The situation now might start imitating the events that preceded Charlie's death. But, Christ, must he start to get tender about Carl now, as well as Charlie Tate? Of course, Abelard did believe tragedy was often cyclic. One disaster set up procedures for the next. People jibbed at accepting this because it sounded like the worst determinism; and sometimes their hopefulness was right. Don't rely on it, mate. Look at 1939. Look at Sarajevo. Abelard hoped that if Briers did consider inquiries in New York necessary he would get the paper's resident correspondent there to do them for him: someone who might have a home-patch alertness to the perils, and be more aware than an outsider that any error could lead to another Press corps corpse.

Waiting in the ten-deep crowd on the Tube platform, Abelard found himself unable again to stop the replay in his head of how Charlie had become implicated in the pursuit of Julian, and how the hazards for Charlie had begun to stack up – because of that same naïve obsession with a story and a by-line now madly pushing old and very breakable Carl Briers.

But, of course, Abelard knew he, extremely personally, had begun it all. During that pursuit of Julian he came across the name of one of Julian's possible US drugs business contacts and had phoned Charlie, as an old Oxford friend, to ask him to do a little gentle backgrounding on JJ Ovalle, the American – nothing super-penetrative or aggressive or dangerous. Charlie had agreed, though at first was blatantly not very interested. Then he seemed to get positively gripped, thrilled. Scoop mania moved in, at least for a while. Later, in subsequent phone calls, Abelard noticed Tate was becoming jumpy: jumpiness came across with surprisingly fine and terrifying clarity via the satellite, stronger than in an interrogation suite. Tate's voice had scuttled up and down the scale, part fright, still part excitement. The fright interested

Abelard more and he had felt uselessly guilty about it, just as uselessly guilty then as it was now. He asked Charlie to back out at once, forget JJ Ovalle, return to his own standard, safer journalism: there would be other ways to Ovalle's profile, and someone paid by the Outfit and trained by the Outfit to handle chancy work could do it. But for Charlie the priorities reversed themselves: excitement somehow stayed more important than the fright. Abelard never knew all Tate had unearthed and was still unearthing at the end, but he seemed to have caught in Ovalle and those around Ovalle the whiff of a possible Pulitzer prize for flair-rich reporting.

He stuck with his investigations, despite Abelard's plea to quit. Next time Abelard rang he sounded more edgy still, but still adrenalised. He said his flat had been turned over. That did scare him, yes, and his voice by now was a frail jangle piping through space, but he claimed the break-in was also an encouragement. Didn't it mean he had been asking the kind of good questions that worried someone, getting into areas where he was not supposed to be – which signified, surely, surely, they were the right areas, the relevant areas, the smart, worthwhile questions? Abelard had recalled there was a famous rule of thumb for newspaper people: it said the Press only did its job right if fucking someone up. The rest, advertising.

A few days later, listening to the News on his car radio, Abelard heard that the prominent US-based British journalist, Charles Tate, had been killed when hit by at least two cars late at night in a New York street. There were police inquiries, obviously, but not much came out of them. Charlie had considerable drink in him, they reported, and drinkers did get hit by cars late at night in New York streets, yes, even by a succession of cars if the victim lay exposed. This was the Big Apple and pips in the Big Apple were sometimes crunched. To Abelard it sounded fairly pat and fairly final: JJ Ovalle might have some well-placed friends in law and order, as would be basic for the kind of prosperous stars of villainy Julian had been working with and against.

That had been a time when Lucy McIver, too, was close to very harsh, very bone-threatening trouble. Well, naturally. People – a lot of people, most of them intent on gains – these people knew she and Julian had been quite long time lovers and they were bound to wonder whether Lucy knew where he was: where *he* was and where the money was, money which some of them certainly had a crooked case for saying should be theirs, totally or a respectable share. They were also bound to wonder whether she held a portion of it herself, possibly access to all of it. Abelard had not been able to give her the sort of continuous, clued-up protection she needed, and while he was away one day she was snatched from the house – drugged and snatched and freighted to a hiding place to be rough questioned when she came round. In fact, she had not known where Julian was, nor did she have any of the money, not then, nor any route to it. Was that credible, though? Wouldn't they work on her, just to check she wasn't doing her loyalty piece, and her selfish piece? These questions had ripped at Abelard as he worked his way across London, trying to find her and bring her back then.

And now, this evening, he was working his way across London or trying to in a comparatively unanxious state after a day's work. His train pulled in, but only the first four or five ranks on the platform could get aboard. Stuck there, until at least the next, he let his mind jog on a stretch more in the past: Lucy curled and still three quarters knocked off in a gleaming supermarket shopping trolley, the fight to recover her from the pair who abducted her, then Lucy, finally, more or less safe in his car as the News came up on the radio and Charlie's destruction was announced. In what he half recognised as puerile fashion now, while he stood docile on the platform watching these mind pictures again, he felt a grand superiority to the people around him. His head could screen for him a private, real, no-messing playlet in which a woman might have been at least brutalised and possibly killed if they had grown impatient and angry with her and forgotten for a second that she had to stay alive to lead them to Julian and the funds, or what remained of them. And they had been counting on plenty remaining. They were also counting on settling with Julian, that is, *settle* with him, regardless of how much of the profits they retrieved. Perhaps settle with Lucy, also.

Abelard still enjoyed the memory of how he handled that rescue. It could have been a young man's exploit. It had required speed and force. He treated himself to a small smile. Often among crowds he would become very aware of his distinctness: the rich slabs of drama he had starred in, his cheeky stratagems, his off-on coolness. These all had to remain secret, despite folk like Olly. Abelard did not mind the secrecy. The glow from his legend was more intense through not being spread everywhere. He could warm himself in it.

A middle aged woman who might be Vietnamese stood jammed alongside him in the station crowd. Much shorter than Abelard, she never looked up at him and gazed blank faced towards the tunnel, peering for the train. Although she could not have seen Abelard's smile, he suddenly felt ashamed. Wasn't it arrogance, an early senility symptom, to imagine he was the only one here who had seen some tension, beaten an enemy? Who knew what kind of reminiscences this woman could call up if she went into the kind of futile self-loving doze favoured by Abelard? They might not be the sort to make her smile. Her impassivity unnerved him. No wonder the Americans lost that war.

He wanted to get out of the crowd here, as if leaving these people behind would help him leave behind also that stupid smugness over Lucy's rescue in the shopping trolley. What the fuck was he doing, earnestly filtering out for the good of his ego comfy bits of the past like that? Well, he knew what he was doing, didn't he? If he focussed on that farcical little triumph, he could exclude a rougher segment of the past, and his responsibility for it – the death of Charlie Tate. And, of course, what made this episode even rougher was that it might soon get a bloody repeat: yes, bloody. Briers was obsessively poking around in dangerous areas just as Charlie had obsessively poked around. All right, this time Abelard was not in the least responsible. He certainly had not asked Briers to start his inquiries. But he did know that Briers would try to push on, discounting risk. And with the memory of Tate back sharp and unforgiving in his mind, Abelard found he could not treat Briers as he probably deserved to be treated – could not just leave him to take his own risks, go his own dicey professional way.

What he recognised as a weird notion hit Abelard. He found himself thinking that, if Briers were a character in a novel, he would be the kind of figure any experienced reader would pick out as likely to get killed. He was faded and a bit pitiable, he was foolishly courageous and, in a sense, admirably devoted to his mission. He was on the edge of the plot: his murder would be dramatic and sad but not fatal; that is, not fatal to the yarn. Briers glowed with dispensability. Abelard yearned to prolong him.

As the train came in, Abelard turned abruptly and began to force himself towards the exit, against the shove of ranked commuters determined on reaching a carriage. They might think he was mad or incontinent. No, they wouldn't think about him at all. They thought trains, trains. They would not notice him forcing his way between them. It was possible, was it, that Briers on his bad feet might still be somewhere near the Tube entrance? Was it? And if it was, would he be locatable in the home-time mob up there? He might have found a caff so he could sit down and deal again with his dehydration. Abelard knew his thinking was junk, not thinking at all, probably, just desperate impulse, but he had to try somehow to reach Briers and get the warnings into him, really into him, really frighten him, and there was no other straightforward way. Briers was someone who appeared by deft accident on streets. Abelard had no private address for him, no phone numbers. Yes, trawling the pavements and coffee shops around the station might be a far-out, feeble chance. Abelard could start from there, though.

It was a start that produced nothing. As Abelard eventually came out from the Underground he realised something loony in him expected Briers to be still standing at the same spot on the pavement, as if knowing by telepathy or magic that Abelard would have to return. Now and then Abelard wondered whether he was getting a bit soft and fanciful for his kind of job. Briers a story book figure, for God's sake. Briers a mystic! Abelard did four nearby eateries and three pubs and walked about half a mile of pavements looking. It occurred to him that Briers might have followed him into the station after a little while and gone to a different platform, maybe even gone to the same platform: would Abelard, ravaged by panic, his eyes preoccupied with the Exit sign, have noticed him in that mob?

When he could not find the reporter, Abelard tried a call on his mobile to *The Sunday Post*. The News Desk recognised his name. 'Carl was due to see you, Mr Abelard.'

'I've seen him. I need to see him again.'

'He's not here now. This kind of story, he'd rarely come back to the office. Not until it's finished.'

'Which kind of story?' Abelard replied.

'Sort of complex. I think it's fair to say complex, don't you?'

'How do I contact him?'

'Mr Abelard, on this kind of story, Carl might have decided to act wary.'

'Which kind of story?'

'Sort of dangerous.'

'It's because he's in danger that I want to see him.'

'You're Mr Abelard of the... well, Outfit, as Carl calls it, correct? You're concerned with stopping the Oliver Horton... memoirs? You might look bad in them?'

'Olly Horton is a friend.'

'Well *was,* I'd say.'

'Olly wouldn't want to hurt me,' Abelard replied.

'I don't think we doubt that. But what Carl's probably thinking – I guess here, obviously – maybe I shouldn't, but I will – I've worked with him so often, I know how he's liable to see things – he'll be worried that if Olly's memoirs are harmless there'll be a lot of people who'll decide that Carl's the real menace, grubbing away in that style of his and adding discoveries of his own.'

'Are you saying I'd stalk him, to silence him.'

'A lot of very well trained people might decide he's the new menace you see, Mr Abelard. I mean, trained in quite rough skills. Carl might not want to be on a plate. He's done a lot of stories of this sort.'

'Which sort?'

'Where revelations could be awkward and more than awkward for powerful, well-trained people. He's worked out a personal safety programme. It's certainly not something anyone here would compromise.'

'I want to help him,' Abelard said.

'A good number of these investigative Press people are inclined to be elusive. You, in your career, can possibly understand that.'

'Yes, but I'm scared he won't be elusive *enough.*'

'Ah, you're thinking about that reporter in New York. Tate? That was bad. You were concerned somehow there, I think.'

'So if I can't get to Briers, you tell Briers to get to me,' Abelard replied.

'I'll tell him you would like him to get to you. He'll decide whether he'll come. Where are you, Mr Abelard?'

'In a very pretty shop doorway not far from the office.'

'I think I know it. A nicer class of litter blowing about there?'

'Perhaps it's absurd, this concern for his safety. Why should I feel like that?'

'*Do* you feel like that, though, Mr Abelard, or is the interest something other? I think Carl would be afraid of an arranged meeting with you. That's the real trouble. I hope this is not offensive. I don't think he would like an arranged meeting with many of the people in this kind of story. Now, you might ask, Which kind of story?'

'Why would I ask that?'

'By this kind of story I mean the kind of story where it would interest some participants to suppress specific episodes and even suppress those who try to get those episodes revealed. Yes, suppress. You see, folk aiming to do that sort of suppression would be able to get things sweetly lined up for it in advance, if there were a properly arranged meeting. Well, of course you see. That would be basic in your kind of work as much as in Carl's. In fact, we probably learned this kind of hygiene from an Outfit manual. I expect Carl had the fine luck to bump into you in the street, did he? You know the ploy.'

'Others might bump into *him* in the street.'

'I certainly will ask him if he wants to call you, or come to your niche – unlikely that.'

Abelard said: 'My mobile number is—.

'He'll have it and the others and so on. He'd feel very nannied if I offered him your number.'

After three minutes, while Abelard was still in the shop doorway, Briers rang: 'Here's how you can help me,' he said. 'Who's the lad in the cape who hangs about Kate Horton's jewellery stall at the Antiques Market? One of yours? One of the loot hunters?'

'That's not how I want to help you.'

'It's how *I* want you to help me. And the taxi driver who took you to the Market? Was he a real taxi driver, or what? You *did* arrive by taxi, the two of you, that right? I can't find the driver. I expect you've tried yourself.'

'Listen, Carl, journalists who—'

'You know, Abelard, I'm astonished – astonished someone like you, with your kind of grab-the-moment training should be so thralled by the past. I'm not Charlie Tate. Stop using me as an exercise for your baby-faced conscience. I reckon either you're enslaved by the past or your sub-conscious sees me like some marginal figure in a novel.'

'A *what?*

'A bit player touched by doom from an earlier death who can get bopped for a bit of drama, without hurting the tale. Relax. We're not in a book.'

'We shouldn't be blabbing like this on a mobile phone,' Abelard replied. 'I need to see you again.'

'Well, we're not blabbing on a mobile phone now.' He rang off.

Abelard gave up the idea of going home yet and returned to the office. Mobile phones were banned about the buildings, in case they upset sensitive machinery, but Abelard did not switch his off. He had the notion that if Briers wanted to call back he would attempt it through the mobile, even if he did have other numbers. In any case, he wouldn't expect Abelard to be at work again, because he had seemed to be on his way

home. He thought the true reason the office discouraged
mobiles was that people like Roger liked to monitor the calls
of anyone he felt curious about, and that was easiest if they
came via a switchboard. Abelard longed to believe Briers
hadn't deliberately broken the link to him but was cut off. Of
course, this was rubbish. What he'd said just before garotting
the call was unambiguous. It meant, Fuck off, Abelard, and
don't call me, because you can't.

In the next couple of hours Abelard built on the screen a
visual of the cape man as he remembered him, but leaving out
the cape. Capes could come and go, and his might have been
decoy. Perhaps Abelard should have asked the computers
about this lad earlier. He knew why he hadn't: Roger Link-
Mite. By his own electronic smart-arseness Roger was inclined
to discover who had approached the computers about what,
and it wasn't wise to give him pointers. On some inquiry a
while ago Abelard was warned by a police detective he
worked with briefly not to ask computers too many traceable
questions. They could give away as much as a placard. He
could not remember details of the case now, but he did recall
the detective's name: detective chief superintendent Colin
Harpur. It had stuck because he found it strange for such a
senior officer to be advising how to defeat the system. It stuck,
also, because Abelard had realised he should not need such
advice: wasn't he supposed to be an expert himself on security
and self-preservation and defeating the system?

But, now, Briers' question about Cape Man sharpened the
uncertainties and Abelard decided he must risk Link-Mite. He
got seventeen possibles when he finished the picture and asked
for i.d., none members of Her Majesty's Intelligence and
Security Services. This awkward plenty he would have
expected. He reckoned the likeness was not bad, but only not
bad. Four names had Britain in their listed operational areas,
three were predominantly US, five mainly Russia and former

satellites, one France, two Australia, one Israel. For another
hour and a half he did some unproductive digging into the
four with British orbits. A survey of the seventeen would mean
a lot of work and might still turn out useless. Naturally,
Abelard had noted the registration and permit number of the
taxi that took him and Kate to the Antiques Market, but had
done no check, also for fear Link-Mite would find out and
wonder things. Now, Abelard chanced this, too. He confirmed
Briers: the cab did not exist.

Turkey Latimer seemed also to be working very late. He often
did. Whatever people accused Turkey of, it was not laziness.
Maintaining and furthering himself required time. He could
not rely entirely on his suits, shoes and decorous style of
feeding. Abelard met him in the corridor. Turkey was on his
way upstairs. He carried a pale blue print-out, the colour
signifying middling security, middling urgency. Just the same,
Turkey appeared unsettled. 'Simon, something unpostponable
keeps you here?'

'Routine stuff I wanted out of the way – to clear things for
the, as it were, morrow. You know how it is.'

'That's a fact,' Turkey replied. 'Oh, this?' He waved the
piece of paper. 'The FBI tell the Yard, who tell us, as a kind of
courtesy, that Olly Horton has been in touch with a New York
bumper edition drugs man called JJ Ovalle.' He spelled out the
name. 'You'll have heard of him.'

'Charles Tate was looking into Ovalle when killed in the
street.'

'Yes. Horton must think Ovalle can tell him useful matters
for the book.'

'Christ, it's unsafe,' Abelard said.

'*Can* Ovalle tell him anything?'

'*Would* Ovalle tell him anything?'

'Ovalle and Julian Bowling had dealings?'

'How it looked,' Abelard replied.

'So Oliver, in his thorough way, would like to know details and blazon them on the page.'

'Christ, it's unsafe,' Abelard said.

'Is it the case, then, that the Outfit might come out of this seeming responsible for the exceptionally crude death of an American based, notable British journalist? It was you, unilaterally, who involved Tate, I think. No consultation here. Certainly no approval. Even Roger would see the perils in commissioning Tate. But it will be the Outfit as the Outfit, not you, personally, to catch the shit. Do I foresee Parliamentary questions? Do I hear further accusations of a "department out of hand?" Do I sense more demands for fucking *accountability* and further ungenerous questions re our funding?'

'I do worry about Olly,' Abelard replied.

'I'm afraid your mind inclines to the cyclic, Simon – the way kiddies need simple, rhyming repetitives like wee-wee and poo-poo.'

'Yes, cyclic. I've sometimes wondered if I see things that way. I've used the word to myself.'

'You're chained in history, pathetically mesmerised by supposed returns to the past.'

'And I've been told that before.'

'Yes? Are you in therapy? I'm not surprised. Don't let it get about. Roger sees anything like that as indicating lack of moral fibre. Do you know that fine old, unequivocating armed services phrase from fifty or sixty years ago?'

'Fifty or sixty years ago? Is Roger stuck in history?' Abelard replied. 'Are you?'

Turkey wagged the paper again to signify duties, and turned away to the stairs. Abelard's mobile rang as Turkey reached the first landing. Latimer did not stop or turn but started on the next flight and disappeared. Conceivably he had not heard. When Abelard answered the call, Briers said: 'Get here.'

'What's happened?

'Happening. Get here.' He gave an address in Lewisham. 'You armed, Abelard?'

'I need that?'

'You armed?'

'How many people?'

'Just get here.'

Abelard had the idea Briers' concentration was somewhere else, not on the talk, except the bare basics of the talk: get here, bring a gun. He might be watching out, listening out, trying to hide. From how many, for God's sake? Abelard would have liked to ask again. Should he take not just a weapon but a team? Perhaps Briers didn't know how many people – why he was watching and listening. Fuck using the time to speculate down the phone. Abelard ditched the question.

Of course, he preferred to go alone. A team meant all-round knowledge of what was happening, and his instincts and habit and guidance from detective chief superintendent Colin Harpur were never to offer all-round knowledge until it seemed vital. If he did not know how many people Briers felt troubled about, Abelard could not tell whether aid was vital. He would have to go unaccompanied, and this suited him. There also remained and remained the matter of compensating for what had happened to Charlie Tate, that other nobly nosy journalist. Abelard still realised this was a mad, deeply impossible objective for him: what Turkey had called chained in history, meaning skewered by the past. Training should have squashed long ago all weak, foolhardy inclinations to guilt. Just the same, guilt about Charlie tinted his thinking. It required him to get to Briers fast, possibly armed, best alone, because, as Turkey had also mentioned, it was Abelard solo who dragged Tate in, and, at a couple of removes, killed him.

Chapter 11

All right, Abelard did get there and got there at fair speed. At fair speed only. And he was not armed. Did Briers after all those years close to the spy game really suppose that someone at Abelard's level in a sweet, post-Wall world would keep a gun on him as routine? Would be allowed to? The James Bond myth must still be about and might confuse even an accomplished observer of our times like Briers. Yet Abelard could have drawn a weapon from the Outfit armoury without much delay even at this hour, and on his own authority. Abelard did not have a Bond 'licensed to kill' status, since there was no such thing, but he did have a glossy and adequate rank. He decided against a gun, though, and against rushing – as opposed to making that fair speed, or as fair a speed as was possible in evening traffic. No, he fell below any proper frenzy to reach Briers and to reach him tooled up, because Abelard knew it would be too late.

That was to simplify things. At the time he was not actually aware he *knew* Briers would be dead when he reached him, no matter how fast he reached him, and no matter what ordnance he had aboard. The revelation hit Abelard only later, *after,* he found Briers' body, unmaltreated, thank God, except, that is, for two head bullets. When he looked back to the final call from the journalist and to the Lewisham journey he saw... saw what? Saw that he had certainly acted urgently, but that he *could* have acted *more* urgently but didn't because intimations told him it was useless. Yes, that was it, intimations. He liked to think of himself as still sensitive enough, tuned enough, to be on the end of intimations, even deeply dark ones. His mother spoke sometimes of intimations: in their favour. She'd probably be pleased – proud – to hear Simon was prone to an intimation or two. But where the fuck did this smart, subliminal slab of forecasting come to him from? Had his dud, cyclic thinking – Christ, *thinking*? – had it started up again unnoticed by Abelard, bringing as ever those miserable, fated, production-line certainties? And, in any case, *was* it so dud, given how things turned out? A reporter killed. A reporter killed. Cyclic?

Alternatively, had Abelard been subconsciously taken over by that notion of Briers as character in a novel, just right for tactical disposal in the spinning of a tale, *existing* only for tactical disposal in the spinning of a tale? Did the narrative say it was time for a death and that Briers suited? Even hindsight couldn't show Abelard the answers clearly. But, yes, he had known, hadn't he? Hell, was he getting psychic as well as cyclic? Should he buy an Ouija board? This could give him the drop on Turkey, Roger. Probably Ouija, like mobile phones, was unbuggable.

Briers might have done better to dial 999. There was a police station not far from his flat. Perhaps he was too frightened for logic. Or did he think Abelard would certainly come, whereas the police might regard him as another nut with a phone and put him far down on their crowded priorities list, if anywhere at all? He was menaced by people he could not describe or quantify, if the call to Abelard was an indication. Police heard such manic cries for aid all the time from weirdos. They competed with the paper work, and lost.

Briers had, then, been right about the need to bring a gun. That's to say, he had been gunned himself, and one way to cope with people who shot people or meant to was to be able to shoot the people who shot people or meant to. If Abelard *had* turned up in time, how would he have coped with Briers' attackers – yelled, 'Halt: unarmed Government officer, so please, do, halt?'

Abelard had the notion some would call it 'a professional killing'. The term came from the finest law-and-order cliché chest, but he wondered what it meant. Did only professionals understand that if you wanted to be certain someone you shot died you put the bullets into the head or heart, not the elbow? Had Briers actually seen the armament when he called Abelard? Or had he seen the people, perhaps recognised them from his researches, and knew they would not be here at all unless they were armed and commissioned to finish him. Abelard found he automatically thought plural, although there'd been no answer when he asked and asked, 'How many?' These people would kill Briers because he might fill his paper with awkward disclosures about them. Olly Horton they might regard differently. He could be an inside knowledge man, couldn't he, with information about how to get to Julian Bowling's money? They would want Olly intact and able to converse, for now. Obviously, he would be due a visit, though.

This was a basement, garden flat, its views on to the street limited but all right and fine at the back. When Briers phoned he might easily have been watching someone, or more likely more than one, starting the approach. Abelard couldn't tell whether the head wounds were from the same gun or two. Suppose Briers *had* rung the police and told them he'd seen weapons coming for him. They might have treated it as serious despite their other pressures and sent a couple of cruising armed response vehicle – luridly painted, powerful cars rich in cannon and Lippitts Hill-trained SO 19 cannoneers, able to siren-bully their way through traffic much faster than Abelard's unmarked Outfit Vectra. But Briers didn't. He must have had true, exclusive faith in Abelard. Oh, shit, he'd run across that kind of fan fantasy before. It couldn't be lived up to. Surely someone who'd been in or near the trade as long as Briers knew about fallibility?

Abelard saw big complexities in this death. Obviously, these combined to make it impossible to report the find. Here was someone else who would not be dialling 999. Report it? Idiotic. In a way, this was disrespectful to the corpse. As far as Abelard could judge from the flat, Briers lived alone, so who knew when the body would be found if Abelard stayed mum? The reporter's paper should start missing him after a while and send someone to look. But, because Briers was secretive and autonomous, *The Post* might be used to long stretches when they didn't hear from him. Yes, it was bad to leave someone like this, but Abelard had to give his thinking width – what he meant by *big* complexities. It could be unwise to get enmeshed in a police investigation of Briers' death. Outfit people were not guaranteed understanding and sympathy from detectives. Occasionally, the Outfit looked as though it disdained the law, or could be made to look as though it did. Police grew pissy about that.

They might, for instance, wonder how Abelard happened to find the body. Perhaps they'd speculate that if the Outfit, or an individual in the Outfit, feared Briers was liable to come up with hurtful revelations there would be an Outfit's or individual's motive for destroying him. Police liked the word, 'individual.' It could be spoken official deadpan, but with a touch of snarl or sneer. Abelard did not want it stuck on him. After some evil formalities an individual could become 'the accused'.

As to now – immediately – he would need to search Briers and the flat, without the aid of, say, Turkey or a police Scenes of Crime team. There could be items on Briers, around his rooms, to show why somebody, or more than one, had considered he must be stopped. Had he managed to harvest stuff for publication that could damage some interested and

very interested parties, some interested and very interested
parties in addition to the Outfit and Abelard, as an individual?
These would be parties who felt that Briers and his efforts
might get in the way of recovering Julian Bowling's hijacked
loot, or what was left of it. Of course, such people would
know that the true route to Julian's hijacked loot was through
Lucy – and possibly Abelard himself. But they would not want
their names and project headlined in *The Post* before they'd
perfected a method of getting to Lucy – and possibly Abelard
himself. They must have deduced that Briers, with his old,
sensitive, nosy nose was more likely to discover and publicise
their names and project than was Olly Horton in his book.
That could be shrewd. *The Post*, too, had decided that Briers
had a better chance of finding lively, deadly stuff than Olly.

Lucy was not easily findable. No. Abelard had found her
once, knocked off by chloroform or something like and done a
rescue. Ah! for the simple days of closeness and lover status
and shopping trolleys – lover status in succession to Julian
Bowling. Abelard did not know how to locate her now. He,
like Horton, *was* easily findable, but Abelard might seem a
tricky element to get at: he was trained in self-preservation
and had the Outfit to help him. True, the Outfit would only
help him if Roger Link-Mite found it convenient. But people
outside might be ignorant of this and assumed wholehearted,
effective camaraderie between Outfit employees, unless an
employee fell into total corruption, like Julian, when
camaraderie was cancelled. However, camaraderie might be
cancelled, or at least suspended or reduced, for less extreme
reasons – reasons generally picked by Link-Mite, occasionally
by Turkey. This was not universally known, though. People
might even assume that Abelard, being exposed, had a minder.

Julian's will named Lucy as the only legatee. Abelard could
not have been more excluded. At the end, Julian regarded him
simply as an enemy implicated in his destruction, and

treacherous filcher of his former girl. The will had never been made public or probated because Julian's estate was criminal, but people might guess it had been Lucy solo who collected. They probably did *not* know that once Lucy received the money she decided on a share out, and that Abelard, as lover at the time, was main beneficiary, straight down the middle of the residue after other smallish handouts.

Despite the wealth, he had stayed in his job for a bucketful of reasons. First, his mother would have been disgusted if he'd gone for full time idleness. Money or no money, she would not be able to understand how a healthy, youngish man could choose to turn layabout, above all a healthy, youngish man produced and nurtured by her. He did not wish to be despised by his mother. Although not much given to despising, when she did despise she despised flat out. To be despised by Link-Mite was comparatively minor, and you were in good company.

Second, if Abelard *had* resigned from the Outfit, it would be fairly apparent that he had come into funds and Link-Mite would not be the only one who'd feel it a holy duty to discover where they came from. And where they came from was, of course, top-notch villainy. Booty. Link-Mite's reaction would be uncertain, possibly holy and dangerous.

Third, Abelard had wondered, and wondered right – had wondered painfully, sadly right – whether it would last with Lucy. If it did not, he had thought he should return as much of the cash as was still left and nominally his. He would have less of it left if he gave up his Outfit salary and started spending to fill the days. It had *not* lasted with Lucy – oh, God, a misery, that – and now he would give back the remainder when he could find her. Complicated, though. The money was in a joint account, on her insistence: she said she'd never live with a kept man. Could someone resign from a joint account as a means of giving all it contained to the other party? He might have to consider this. But he believed it was the kind of thing that should be done personally, if possible at a proper meeting, not just as an on-line transaction. In any case, he knew that if he handled it that way she would immediately send him back his share by cheque. She believed he had earned it in the long and dicey hunt for Julian. About money, they both had a strange decorum – at least about *this* money.

Abelard would need to explain to Lucy that it was hers and only hers, because this was what Julian wanted. When Abelard and Lucy were a unit, he had been prepared to ignore Julian's wishes, because *she* wanted to ignore them, and because then they were sort of one flesh, so what went to Lucy could reasonably be shared with Abelard, as everything else was shared. Couple economics.

He had been fond of the money and the wondrously bulging bank statements, no question, their columns burly with in-credit figures, like built-to-last-a- millennium architectural pillars. And he could have been fond of them again. But he knew that if he asked his mother about it – which would, of course, be the ripest fucking lunacy – but *if* he did, she would undoubtedly say he had to make the repayment. In fact, she would probably tell him he should not have accepted any of the money in the first place, and that he must make up to Lucy everything he had spent. She had come to be fond of Lucy while the three of them were together. His mother did not run Abelard, but she was an influence. And he knew his father would have said pretty much the same only louder had he been alive. He might come through on the Ouija board. Abelard found it hard to buck such imag-ined orders. Possibly, even without them he would have refused to dupe someone dead who was once a friend, although the friend had become the crook of crooks, and although the profits he left were entirely dirty and entirely lovely and nourishing.

Abelard began his search of Briers' clothes. There was a taught method and Abelard stuck to this. In fact, two taught methods existed. The first was basic, easy and official. You went through the subject's pockets and piled up the stuff, making a paper or tape note of where each article came from: now and then, which pocket held what mattered. But for a secret search things became harder: vital to leave no signs you'd trawled, and there were people very smart at spotting signs. Scanning Briers would have to be as imperceptible as Abelard could make it. In this kind of rummage, for instance, you might want to keep something from one of the pockets as a future help with inquiries. And loss of the something would perhaps get noted when the subsequent, official search was done.

Other practicalities could also give bother: to replace a tie or redo shoe laces as they had been before might be tricky, especially if blood was about and you were trying not to collect any or spread it. Normally in this kind of episode, blood *was* about, though, in fact, only minimally today. The shooting had been small calibre, possibly .22, and the wounds neat. Briers remained totally recognisable, his snide, pudgy, slightly sagging face still snide and pudgy and only marginally more sagging through death and the panic that preceded it. But even when scarce, blood *was* a pest and to be absolutely skirted. Blood rated high as a teller of awkward tales. Removing a tie might seem pedantic but an item could be hidden in the knot or under the collar fold. They said Edward VIII invented the big Windsor knot to carry a rubber in, while still only Prince of Wales and pre-Mrs Simpson, because girls *de bonne famille* doted on the sense of intrigue and back street, knee-trembler urgency this brought. While Edward talked to the titled smart set in West End haunts, there was the johnny, almost up those moneyed hooters, like the common cold germ. Apparently, he would giggle over this later when he took the tie and so on off and pulled the royal johnny on. Of course, Briers, a journalist, not an agent, would be unlikely to have microdot material in his tie, but Abelard's search procedure was ingrained and vertical: you began with the shoes and socks and moved up to the tie, mouth, ears and hat, if there was one. This method gave all-round respect to the corpse and its clothes by treating all parts as equally liable to produce something vital.

Anyone searching was vulnerable. The process usually involved crouching over the victim on the floor or in a chair and giving a lot of concentration to buttons, zips and linings, while keeping an exact, running log of discoveries. Abelard had, of course, done a quick tour of the whole flat as soon as he found Briers. He opened the three big built-in wardrobes in the two bedrooms and the kitchen broom cupboard, and looked under the beds. There seemed to be nobody here now, but he still felt exposed when working on him. Luckily, *rigor* had not started or the body might have been difficult to get cooperation from. Abelard knew it would take him fifteen minutes to complete the search and restore Briers and his clothes. He decided he should work in five minute periods. At the end of each, he would do another quick trip around the flat and carry out a spell of neighbourhood watch from the windows on to the street and back gardens. Obviously, the flat was not secure. How would he be inside, otherwise?

When he arrived, he had parked in a street parallel to Briers', then walked past the address once. It was a spacious old house, now in flats. Briers lived down steps. Abelard could see nothing significant, and you never walked past a target property twice for another look. Another look for you could be another look for them. He did not try the front door but moved around to the rear and found french windows on to the garden had been forced. After a minute listening and watching, he entered that way himself, wishing, as he'd sometimes wished before, that he had persuaded himself to bring a pistol. He had come to regard carrying a gun as gaudy and wrong for the flavour of the time. This he recognised as egomaniac, as if by going armed he, Simon Abelard, personally, might endanger the whole shaky post-Wall *entente*. In any case, the Wall was not an issue here.

He pulled the french windows to behind him, but they would need only a little push to let someone in. He did not search the garden. Whoever – singular or plural – did Briers might still be out there, possibly having noted Abelard casing the house and flat and grown jumpy. The killer, killers, could have withdrawn, but not very far. There was stacked timber near the back fence where a couple of men could have hidden, could have hidden and watched Abelard enter the house. Perhaps he should have looked. But was it sane to get confrontational when you were unarmed and they were not and cornered?

Because of how the body lay, Abelard's back was towards the study-type room where the break-in occurred. Perhaps he could have swung Briers around, but that would almost certainly produce blood skid marks and betray interference. And it might suggest flippancy. Briers was entitled to lie as he had fallen. This was someone venerable. For God's sake, he had talked to Philby.

After the first five minutes Abelard stood and did a spell at both main windows, front and rear, keeping to the side and, he hoped, concealed behind the folded back swathes of curtain. The front looked out mainly on to the steps down from ground level, though it was possible to see small sections of the street to the left and right by moving from one side of the window to the other. At the rear, he had a full view of the garden and, over low fencing, to some gardens of neighbouring houses. Abelard watched and saw nothing to perturb him. There was normal activity in the street – cars, children, pedestrians – and more children in a couple of the gardens, plus an elderly man at some weeding. Abelard

returned to Briers. He would allocate the first two five minute
stints to searching, the third to restoring Briers to how he had
been. Exactness about his appearance was probably not
crucial. Almost certainly, those who found him when he *was*
found would not know the details of how he had been
dressed. It would take a wife to detect differences, and there
seemed to be no wife, or not here, at least. Everything about
the flat said man alone. But Abelard had his drilled-in
methods of tidying after a search, as much as his drilled-in
methods of handling the search itself. He would have found it
hard to vary them. Although he was not all strict method, all
by-the-book – not all zombie star of the long-ago Outfit
training course – method did bring him comfort, in the way
that, as a Sunday School child, the plodding rhythm and
organisation of the Psalms used to, statement, then balancing
statement: 'The heavens declare the glory of God; and the
firmament showeth his handiwork.' His father used to recite
that Psalm and a few others. Turkey wasn't the only one who
knew the Bible. Abelard's father loved music and system. He
considered almost any system better than none, even the
system he'd lived under, though it did next to fuck all for him
– except getting his kid educated enough to move on.

His father would not have thought much of Abelard's
behaviour here, now. Almost certainly it was criminal, and
almost certainly his father would have recognised that
instantly and given a warning. The intruder, intruders, who
had killed Briers might be catchable if the police were told
quickly enough. They were not going to be told quickly
enough, or at all, by Abelard. He had his own purposes and
would follow them. Abelard himself might have termed it 'his
own agenda'. He knew he was fond of a bit of jargon. It made
him feel in touch with folk wisdom.

His tactics now sprang from the kind of arrogance that
made police eternally suspicious of the Outfit, and would have

made Abelard's father anxious and enraged. But sometimes you had to shift away at least a degree or two from courses advised by a parent. This was development. Or it was if you joined an outfit like the Outfit. Adjust to the moment. For instance, would anyone imagine Roger Link-Mite was such an all-time, snooping, scheming shit because his father had recommended it? This, surely, was Roger's own achievement, within the Outfit's ambience but from impulses special to his personal core. Surely? Abelard wavered. Perhaps Roger's father *had* pointed him towards that pinnacle of shittiness, and Roger was only following home guidance: after all, Link-Mite's family and Roger himself were in *Burke's Landed Gentry* and *Debrett's*, the lineage *Debrett's*, not that hanger-on volume, *Debrett's People of Today*.

Abelard brought Briers' trousers down a bit, just in case of a body belt worn under. That was enough, enough. Abelard had to keep reminding himself this was a member of the noble Fourth Estate not a spy, and unlikely to be geared up for secrecy. Occasionally, even now in Abelard's maturity, a few of those training course procedures could take over and become absurd. No body belt. Somehow, with his clothes pulled about and shoes and socks off, Briers looked much younger, a little like a schoolboy half re-dressed after a gym lesson. Often, you could get this with someone violently killed. The look of the body would seem to summarise – would *embody* – the whole good range of their life. Abelard might see waste and tragedy in the death then. To pick up that weird term used by Briers about himself, he did not seem dispensable in his present state, even if he had been dispensed with. Abelard found he could think of Briers mainly as a man who had progressed over the decades since his schooling to decent stardom in a passable profession. Yes, he had talked to Philby. Newspapers sent their most reliable people on that kind of job, people who could fashion adequate contempt for the subject of their writing, but without making the trip to Moscow for an interview look perverse. The fact that Briers had been such an intrusive fucking pain in the Olly Horton crisis could hardly signify his death was lucky or even negligible. Although Abelard would leave the murder unreported, this was tactics only, no slur on Brier's rating as a human.

Briers' feet when bare seemed especially youthful – slim and hard – not the kind of feet to produce the old reporter's arthritic slouch. Feet like these made claim to be noted. These feet would have given Briers distinction if nothing else had. As to his search, Abelard had found only them in the socks. *How beautiful upon the mountains are the feet of him that bringeth good tidings, that publisheth peace.* This was another Old Testament verse Abelard's father used to recite. What Briers was hoping to bring into the open might not have been very good tidings for the Outfit. What he'd meant to publish was meant to stir, not deliver peace.

'Are you alone in this, Simon?'

'In what?'

'I suppose I entered the same way as you.'

'I didn't hear you.'

'Thanks,' she said. 'I'm a spy, aren't, I? A novice spy, but a spy. Spies know how to fool other spies. And it's no big skill to enter quietly through unlocked french windows. Are you alone in this?' She stood in the room doorway, gazing down on Abelard and Briers.

'In what?'

'To a degree, I'm acting alone myself,' she replied.

'Well, yes you are.'

'Oh, look, I did the mock profile of Oliver Horton you and Turkey asked for, and I came to that weird debriefing, but it didn't seem the end of things, not a bit.'

'Which things.'

'The end of the test exercise you'd given me.'

'Latimer and I regarded it as the end, Iris. He considered you'd done admirably – wanted me to make sure this was reflected on your R 17, didn't he?'

Iris Insole grew excited and lost some hold on her verbals, or pretended to for emphasis: 'It seemed to me that the deliberate inconclusiveness of it all – God, neither of you would listen to even a fragment of the profile, not a bloody fragment – so it seemed to me, yes, that the way everything was just allowed to fade – it seemed to me, and still seems, that this was calculated – that it was subtle – so typically subtle – a subtle invitation from you and Turkey to hunt out new facts about Horton and the book. It was part of the test, wasn't it, isn't it? You wanted to find whether I had the initiative and drive to go on solo, trying to resolve things. Why I'm here.'

'No. You're out of order.' Abelard was on his knees alongside the body, with Briers' wallet opened out in his hand, five or six twenty pound notes pulled half clear so he could examine what might be concealed under them. He saw that Iris Insole spotted the quaintness of being told by someone pillaging a corpse in disarranged clothing that *she* was out of order. Iris did not laugh, though, just gave him a bit of a mild gaze through those large, heftily-framed spectacles.

After a while, she switched her eyes to Briers' wounds. 'Very small calibre weapon,' she said. 'What exactly?'

'Yes, probably small.'

'But what?'

'Could be a Smith and Wesson .22,' Abelard replied.

'That's not an Outfit weapon, is it?'

'Why?'

'It's not, is it. Where is it now, Simon?'

He saw that Iris, their gifted recruit, thought he had killed Briers. She put her good brain to the likelihoods and selected this one. He did sympathise. It was a credible reading in all kinds of ways. Iris wanted to make sure the gun could not be traced to him – that it wasn't a pistol he had drawn from the armoury, but something private, unregistered, ditchable, preferably already ditched. This gifted recruit considered Abelard could do with some lessons on post-crime security. He felt her give him an eye search, trying to work out where about him he might still have the gun. There was an astonishing, total matter-of-factness to her questions, as if she considered such a killing might be natural for the Outfit in a rough predicament, and, of course, Briers had brought, and actually *was*, a rough predicament. This was the kind of head-on, unconstrained career she had short-listed and finally picked for herself, in outright preference to one centred on theology. She'd accept it as it came. Had she once intended to take orders? Now, though, *I'm a spy, aren't I?* And spies had their own kind of behaviour, as long as they were not caught.

'Will it work?' she asked.

'What?'

'Does knocking over Briers mean no harsh revelations in the Press, on top of Horton's? Horton's are innocuous, are they? Old loyalties make him discreet? Your name will be kept clear now – no fuss about the money, and so on.'

'How do you know about Briers?' Abelard asked. 'How did you get the address?'

'I told you – I felt I was… well, like *required* to go on poking into things.'

'Yes, but how?'

'The basics were fairly easy to discover, weren't they?'

'Were they?'

'He's hanging about outside the building, isn't he? I've seen a picture alongside his by-line in *The Post*. I tailed him home one day. And then I thought I might unearth more if I could look at his place on the quiet.'

'And have you?'

'One of two things. And you – have *you* come across much? A nice leafy street for Lewisham, isn't it? Fine large Edwardian mansions, flatted, but flatted with taste, and the outsides expertly preserved.'

'What does that tell you?'

'Oh, that even major journalists who've hobnobbed with world figures like Philby want to come home to a tame slice of suburbia. Turned up anything much, Simon?'

'Can you re-dress him while I do the flat and gardens?' Abelard replied. 'Is this your first visit here?'

'How were the shoes,' she asked.

'Left over right laces and a double bow. But I doubt whether anyone but himself would know. I'm assuming he lives alone. Correct?'

'You're going to search the flat and garden? Listen, have you noticed that collection of wood out there? A platoon could hide in it. Have you still got the gun?'

'What gun?'

'Tie?' she asked.

'Burly triangular knot, a red stripe fronted. We don't notify the death.'

'Oh, really truly?'

Chapter 12

'Have I abandoned you, dear, dear Julian, have I, have I?' Pamela Bowling cried. It was loud yet intimate. 'This, as it were, corner of a foreign field – foreign, that is, to me, now, having with such selfishness deserted to Portugal. No, Simon, it's kind of you to object – I sense you mean to, sweet, sweet lad – but I will not withdraw that word, will not dodge *any* of those hard words: *abandoned, deserted, selfishness.*'

Abelard said: 'I know Julian would never accuse you of them, if he were—'

'Oh, certainly, I can return like this now and then – a little fleeting trip to look once more upon his resting place, and, of course, my thanks for accompanying me. It must be a right pain in the whatsit for you. An hysterical, absentee mummy intent on homage to her longed for, tainted yet precious, bullet-broken boy.'

Abelard said: 'In many ways a privilege, please believe me, Mrs Bowling. I'm grateful to have been asked to—'

'Nobody, nobody to visit him regularly, week-in, week-out. Death is a week-in, week-out business, isn't it, Simon? It does go on. Nobody to keep this grave decent. Would you suppose, for instance, that his lousy father would come out here, say every month or so, even less, bring flowers, concern himself with a modest jam jar for them, contemplate this eloquent though small mound, among so many other small mounds? *Would* you suppose that? I don't think so. 'She bent and readjusted five white and pink carnations in the jar. '*Some* flowers but not an excess. One can have a *grossness* of flowers – Princess Diana, a Kray. The flowers take over. The one they mourn is set aside.'

'Are you in touch with him?' Abelard said.

She was startled. 'Who?'

'Julian's father.'

'Don't take this as a reproach of yourself,' she answered.

'What?'

'I chide *Philip,* my husband, but this must not make *you* feel guilty. Why, why, should *you* come to his grave regularly? Why should you even know where his grave *is*, until I showed you now? He was your beloved friend at one time, yes, yes, but this cannot mean you have a duty to know where he lies, much less a duty to tend this spot, weep upon this spot. Oh, no! You, you had another duty, didn't you – a duty to damn well hunt him to his appalling end, and one you so devotedly carried out, despite that previous closeness? You – *you* had a career to think about, didn't you, didn't you – a reputation and the reputation of that indestructible, exclusive sect, the Outfit?'

Abelard had always known that Julian's mother would turn up in Britain again. Clearly, the line between a mother and her child could be unmatchably powerful and, in Christian teaching at least, sacred: more so when in-depth dollars were around to be cat fought for. Abelard had never believed she would stay happy with the fair but moderate fraction of the thirteen million Lucy had felt scared into doling her after Julian's death. Oh, yes, thirteen. In his clever, bustling way, Julian had stolen nine but turned it into thirteen by trading and speculation even while on the run. Flair. Push. Confidence. Julian was a true loss to commerce and could probably have advised Marks and Spencer in their bother if he had not been shot like that.

'Look, Mrs Bowling, I did know where his grave is,' Abelard replied.

'From some sodding Personnel dossier marked Dead and the date but not the full details I expect,' she said. 'You'd know which graveyard he's in because that's probably a notifiable bit of datum, the neat conclusion to what's called an operation, I imagine – one of those operations which would be considered a success although the patient died. Or *because* the patient died. But without me you would *not* know where in that graveyard the grave is – nothing to bring upon you the exactitudes of affection and grief or the awkward pulls of only faintly recollected friendship.'

'Nobody from the Outfit could attend Julian's funeral, Mrs Bowling.'

'*Could*? What, what, in God's name does that mean, Simon? You were all sick?'

'It was considered—'

'Inappropriate,' she said. 'Of course it was inappropriate. He's remorselessly stalked by you, then shot by one of your people – *executed* by one of your people, by one of your *chief* people, so it would be absurd for any of you to show and pretend to sorrow, wouldn't it, or even send a posy? What could the card have said? *In never fading memory of a dear friend, colleague and lovely target.*'

'Actually, it's general policy not to attend funerals of any Outfit field staff, Mrs Bowling. Simple security. Funerals are public matters. Some of our work isn't.'

'Plus, of course, you're shagging his woman by then and spending his money. How could you, I mean, you *personally*, appear at his interment? You wouldn't have been able to stop giggling, would you? More important, oh, so much more important, how could *she* have come? In fact, I see a kind of delicacy in your staying away, the both of you. You at least avoided a chance to crow. And yet I believe she is what would have been called his lover. His *lover*? Would you regard it as love, Simon, when a woman shuns the funeral of her man and is happy to stay ignorant of where he rests? All right, he is a discarded man, and she has craftily switched her love from the man touched by peril to another, whose behaviour has been so coyly conformist and predatory and malign and safe. Just the same, there are obligations. I hope I can display a different quality of love from hers, Simon.'

'Jules often spoke of you to us, always spoke well of you to us.'

'I wish to cry out over his grave words of regret and self-condemnation for permitting the waste of his death,' she said. 'Do you understand such an almost irresistible urge? Do you? Oh, do you? Do you understand my terrible need to be forgiven by him? Where was I, his mother and so on, when he was stalked and dragged down?'

'Mrs Bowling, as I understand the circumstances of Jules' death, you could not possibly have saved him. He had chosen a criminal life and that life always had the chance of violent death included in it. You mustn't—'

'You think I'm only over in this country for another nibble at the fucking moolah, don't you, Abelard?'

'Many say the fullness of grief doesn't always strike until long after the loss.'

'And then the death of this journalist, Briers,' she replied. 'When I read that in the continental *Telegraph*, plus the background, I naturally saw implications.'

'The police are looking very hard at it.'

'Well, of course.'

'It's a difficult one.'

'Yes? How?' she asked.

'It was some time before his body was found.'

'Yes?'

'Apparently he lived alone.'

'Yes?'

'That can make it tough for them,' Abelard replied.

'Yes? Oh, I expect so. All sorts must be swarming, Simon,' she said. 'Doesn't his murder prove that? Fear of disclosures, messing up the money pot. So, annihilate the journalist pest. Plus there's this damn book and the rumours around this damn book. Oliver Horton. That's going to bring in even more, angling for bits of the split. They damn well think they have a right. Do they give a shit about his mother? Oh, Julian, my lad, what a stew you've left for us. I hate talking funds over a grave like this, and especially *his* grave, but what can one do if one foresees a stampede? I feel Julian would sympathise with my attitude.'

'Was it hearing of Briers' murder and the fear outsiders could swallow the cream that brought you back?'

'In street cafés and Porto supermarkets I yearned to see again where my dear son lay, you see. I ask you, Simon – is this unnatural? Have you encountered the beggars in Portugal – beggars holding in their arms a child, to guarantee pity and contributions? Thus, continually there I am reminded of my Julian.'

'Was it hearing about Briers' murder and the fear outsiders could swallow the cream that brought you back?' Abelard replied.

'I know you have a mother, Simon, so you will easily comprehend how I cursed the distance I had put between us, Julian and self. You are right – grief may strengthen with time, make it impossible to rest.'

'Was it hearing about Briers' murder and the fear outsiders would swallow the cream that brought you back?'

'A kind of catharsis,' she replied. 'The inescapable hankering for catharsis. Do you know catharsis at all? Well, of course you do. All Outfit folk have schooling.'

'Things are still fairly cheap over there in the street cafés and supermarkets, aren't they?' Abelard replied.

'And where are you hiding the Yank cow now? I've no address for you, except the Outfit. She's with you? I expect you're careful about giving location. Happy chortling in some enseamed, de-luxe nest, the two of you, and good riddance to Julian? She still controls the account?'

'I wonder if you could profit from a financial adviser to help you budget and establish a comfortable and viable pattern out there. You and your husband had properties, didn't you – the London flat, a house in Wiltshire, a flat in the Vendée? Were they joint? Aren't you due for half the capital value?'

'I know you'll believe one never felt the smallest jealousy when I visualised Julian banging that Yank slag,' she answered. 'Never. And I frequently did visualise it – I mean, in motherly concern, almost entirely this. Oh, incessantly. Julian had to go his own way, even if his own way was that way. And now, you, too, go that way.'

The cemetery was nicely kept. Julian had a green headstone set on the small mound mentioned by Pamela. White capital lettering gave his full name, Julian Theobald Bowling and age, 'esteemed son of Philip and Pamela. Never forgotten.' Perhaps Pamela had done the ordering from Portugal. Or it could have been Philip. As Abelard remembered him – thin, full of leadership, calibre false teeth – he would have the terseness for that testimonial.

Apparently, the Pamela-Julian special closeness shut out her husband, Philip, Julian's father. Quite wisely she had loathed him. Abelard remembered her asking him once whether he had ever seen Philip Bowling cut up a fried egg at breakfast. In her case, God knew how many eggs and breakfasts.

A long time ago, while Julian was still alive and the search for him in hand, Pamela had more or less spelled out for Abelard the detail of her intimacy with her son during the boy's approach to manhood. What she'd called 'a bit of *Sons and Lovers,* plus.' Although that had left Abelard confused,

Lucy tended to store fragments of knowledge about many topics, including psychology, and suggested this childhood might explain why Julian joined the Outfit. For a son to be utilised by his mother if he did not want it, or want it as continually as she did, might destroy his faith in everything. Lucy argued that, even in the British upper middle class, learning to distrust your mother for sex reasons would make it tough to trust anyone afterwards. Result, he would pick a career where nobody *did* fully trust anyone, where duplicity was not just normal but a must-have, and where the individual officer intensely guarded his separateness because separateness might protect him from betrayal. *A man's enemies are the enemies of his own house.*

But Lucy had said that, although the Outfit might seem at first sight a good spot for lone souls, it was, of course, a system, had its ranks and order, was a machine, a piece of inter-locking State apparatus, a kind of army where everyone depended on everyone else, as in any army. This army happened to be a spook army, that was all, and spook discipline could be as real as any other. Outfit members did *not* in fact exercise absolute separateness. They belonged. Their pay was on a list and a Civil Service scale. They could qualify for sabbaticals, like Permanent Secretaries. And so, according to Lucy, Julian was destined after a time to drift clear of the Outfit's system and structure and into the comparatively ruthless self-centredness of crime. Wasn't crime the supreme private enterprise, *very* private?

Yet, even there, he might have found intolerable network bonds and calls on his constancy, Lucy said. After all, he was part of a trade syndicate, and members had to co-operate in crookedness and keep faith with one another, or no profits. Remember the Five-Families turf meeting in *The Godfather.* Lucy's theory was that, to escape this unmeetable demand for villain-to-villain honour, he had finally gone for *absolute* freedom, by thieving syndicate loot and doing a bunk with it, solo, solo, solo. She'd mentioned the poem, *I wandered lonely as a cloud*. That was Julian, she said. Wordsworth got there first, the way geniuses would, but then went towards daffodils. Julian's cloud had a very silver lining. Lucy diagnosed him as someone compelled to re-show through his own adult life what he had been cruelly forced to grasp as a child – that, regrettably, trust was for fools, a terrible frailty liable to exploitation. Once grown up, he exploited it.

Perhaps. Abelard thought psychology was a trade like politics, religion, law, medicine, history and the study of literature where you could prove whatever suited, depending on start point. Each of these jobs attracted people who had brilliant minds until they made them up, as someone said of Hitler. Whether Lucy was right or not, Abelard had known from the beginning that, once Pamela saw her handout from the thirteen million dwindle, she would tell herself, and go on telling herself, she was owed more: owed what she'd probably regard as a spouse share, as well as a mama's share – conceivably equal to Lucy's. If you could formulate a life plan from someone's treatment of fried eggs, consider what you could do with the scent of treasure.

To escape a threatened, awkward dispute over Julian's very contestable do-it-yourself will, Lucy had spat twice on the carpet in rage but then capitulated to their badgering and given Pamela and Philip Bowling a quarter of the total between them. Abelard's mother said at the time she could understand someone in a money rage spitting on the carpet but twice must be small-town US. Lucy did clean it up, though only after Abelard asked her. She felt hygiene compromised her protest.

Almost as soon as the Bowlings were paid, Pamela broke from her husband and went to live in Portugal, presumably with her eighth, just over a million and a half dollars. But she had grown used to an expensive life through Philip, no matter how much she detested and despised him. Although she was in her seventies, she had still been beautiful and active when Abelard last saw her, and there might be another man, other men, to keep now. Because of the EU, Portugal had come to know more about good wages, and male companionship was probably no longer cheap. Anyone would expect her to suffer gratitude shrinkage, as the treasure sank. Pamela had the need and greed and deviousness and balls to come looking for loot top-up – for at least that. She'd worry in case what was left of the fortune disappeared before she'd collected a second, heavier lump, in line with what she saw as her doubly special status. Pam might devise some impressive, surface reason for coming, but underneath it would be about pickings. She no doubt realised that Lucy and Abelard had others to make donations to, though not many of these payments was even near what the Bowlings received. Lucy hung on to about $9 million, insisting it should be in that joint account with Abelard.

At the end, Julian had recognised no bond with Pamela, regardless of what she imagined. His rejection of her seemed virtually total. Lucy said a wish to blot out a tormentor was likewise typical of the abused child later in life. *Necessary* to the abused child. For Abelard or Lucy to explain this to Pamela, though, would inevitably look like nothing but rotten self-interest, and the rotten determination to keep as much of Jules' rotten estate as they could. In fact, Bowling had wanted Lucy to take virtually all he left. This was really the only relationship he acknowledged finally in that messy SW3 death episode. Lucy was regarded by him as spouse, though they had never married, of course.

And then things had moved on and Lucy became spouse in that sense to Abelard. This would naturally sharpen up

Pamela's wariness. The fact that Lucy had moved on again since then would not change this wariness. Pamela might not have heard of the break-up, anyway.

Now, in the cemetery, Abelard waited for Mrs Bowling to complete her shady homage. Julian's grave, like all the others, was flat, apart from the head mound and stone, so a mechanised mower could do a brisk, uninterrupted run over the dead and keep the place neat for those above. The sun had good, bright power today and the lettering stood out bold, like a voucher. Mrs Abelard's topcoat was grey shantung, and she wore it unopened over a black, high-necked suit in the same material. Her hat was a dark cloche with two silver feathers on one side. None of these clothes came from an Oporto supermarket. He could see how the money might go. In her seventies or not, she was still brilliantly nimble around graves and brought true vim to her grief and suspicions.

Pamela said goodbye to Julian. It was restrained and heartfelt. Abelard, standing a little way behind, could believe in her then. He had feared she might throw herself on to the soil to be nearer, head towards the jam jar. There were other people about visiting graves and he had dreaded having to pull her up from the ground and steer her back towards the car. Some folk seeing a biggish half black man wrestling with an old white lady in shantung might revert to prejudice. He did not want anything like that in the local Press. Roger Link-Mite and possibly Turkey would regard it as unforgivably public and sloppy for him to have gone viewing a renegade's grave.

Mrs Bowling and Abelard walked slowly back to the car. 'What will you do now?' he asked her.

'I have a purpose.'

'You'll stay in this country?'

'Do you understand what I mean when I say a purpose?' she replied.

'Money.'

'That's meant to insult me, hurt me, is it?' Pamela sounded resigned, as though she had expected abuse from Abelard and would take it with dignity.

'I don't think it's going to work,' he said.

She turned, stopped and stared back toward's the grave, her profile fine. 'My purpose is to ensure that what I know would be Julian's wish as to the disposal of his estate is finally carried through. What I *know*.' Her voice became a fierce whisper: 'Yes, Julian I shall strive to put things right for you, my dear.' She looked ahead again and resumed walking. 'This, surely, is the duty of a mother. Even you, with your professional scepticism, can see that, concede that, can't you, Simon? Oh, can't you? If a mother thinks there has been a brutal perversion of her dead boy's sweet impulse to provide for her, she must act, must she not – not, not out of selfishness and greed but out of wholesome regard for *him*?'

'It's dangerous to be stalking funds here.'

'Regardless of threats,' she cried. Once more she paused and looked back at the grave. 'For your sake, Julian, mother will ignore all perils, will continue the quest.'

'How?'

'Yes, continue the quest. I see it as holy.'

'Continue the quest where?' Abelard asked.

They walked again. 'Never has Pamela Bowling shirked an obligation.'

'I don't understand where you can start.'

'I *have* started. I've started here with you and Julian today.'

'It would be wiser if you went back to Portugal. I'd make sure you are informed of anything important.'

Suddenly, she grabbed Abelard's arm and began to hurry him, as if they had been stupidly wasting time. Her voice was loud again and urgent now, hot-tailing it across the long corridors of smooth grass. 'Lucy's ditched you, hasn't she,

Simon? I can feel it. And predictable, anyway – that skip-about piece. You became surplus, as Julian became surplus before you. So, where do I find her, how so I collect what is plainly mine? There is such an item as natural justice, I believe. *You* don't know where she is, do you? I feel that, too. My God, so many will try to track her. Oh, hell, has *Philip* located her? Consider that. Oh, hell, do you think *Philip* has located her? That frail and pitiable child. The bastard will wring every drop from her. He's trained in this sort of work. Hasn't he been in boardrooms for decades? Yet, Simon, I can't go back to him, can't, no matter how much he corners. Would you? Would *you?*'

Chapter 13

Roger Link-Mite said: 'A matter like this death of the journalist, Briers, we all hear of – that kind of situation – in that kind of situation I'm not ashamed to admit I virtually always see it as our function actually to *help* the police.'

'Oh, certainly,' Turkey Latimer said.

'Help how?' Abelard said.

'It's an instinct with me,' Link-Mite replied.

'I always feel that such spontaneous impulses are superior to almost any other, and more authentic,' Turkey said.

'Help the police insofar as we can, that is,' Link-Mite said.

'Certainly,' Turkey replied. 'I'm sure Simon and Iris would go along with that. Simon? Iris? Yes, obviously agreed.'

'It's come out, of course, that Briers was interested in some of the areas *we* are interested in. Horton and so on. It's remarkable we hadn't come across him – come across him *again,* that is. He used to hang around the buildings looking for so-called "exclusives" in the old days, didn't he? Anyway, we might be able to put things in their way, you see, *useful* things,' Link-Mite said. 'I mean put things in the way of the police. Yes, useful things.'

'I would see this as virtually a duty – that's in addition to its being an instinct, in your personal, unique case, Roger – a duty, if, of course, we should have any such useful things,' Turkey replied.

'I asked for both you and Iris to be invited to this meeting, you see, Simon,' Link-Mite said.

'I gather the police have difficulties over Briers' killing,' Abelard said.

'They have, they have,' Turkey replied. 'The delay in discovering the body is a drawback. Days.'

'I heard this,' Iris Insole said.

'Yes,' Abelard said. 'That can make it tricky.'

'He lived alone, didn't he?' Iris said. 'I suppose he just lay there, shot, until either his landlady or his paper grew uneasy about the silence.'

'Obviously, police found evidence of entry but they wonder whether there was a subsequent visit by someone, or more than one, after the killing – using the already forced french windows, you see,' Turkey said. 'Someone, or more than one, who did not report what he, she, they found.'

'Well, of course they didn't fucking report it,' Link-Mite replied. 'This is a death with depths.'

'But come now, Roger, I think one could say that *any* murder is likely to have depths for *some* of those involved,' Turkey said.

'Sod what one could say,' Link-Mite replied. '*These* depths are what we can *really* call depths. This is resonances. This is overtones.'

'So, they suggest a visit to kill him and then another visit. With what purpose?' Iris asked.

'Not necessarily or even probably by the same person, people,' Turkey answered.

'It's why I say depths,' Link-Mite replied.

'All right, perhaps on reflection I can concede there are unique depths here,' Turkey replied.

'Fuck concede,' Roger said. 'People in and out of Briers' flat like Victoria station.'

'Roger, in his way, is taking an individualistic line on this,' Turkey said.

'Fuck individualistic,' Link-Mite said.

'I'm not saying quaint or wilful,' Turkey replied. 'You see, Iris, Simon, some people who regard Roger as an out-and-out shit, and they *do* exist – when they are asked to list his specific faults they will maintain he is quaint and/or wilful. As a start. I dissociate myself from such criticisms, and I don't say that merely because Roger is present.'

'Or perhaps it's just a... just a bit of guess by police that there was this second visit,' Iris said.

'Yes, a guess,' Abelard replied. 'Is there evidence, actual evidence?'

'I have my own reading of it,' Roger Link-Mite said. 'It's why I insisted Iris, particularly, should be here. Thank you Iris for showing. I say again, I'm not in the least ashamed that, when I encounter a situation like this, one of my first – yes, instincts, impulses – those *are* the words – these instinct, impulses tell me – *command* me, indeed – yes, command me to do everything to assist the police. Insofar as that is practical, obviously. After all, the police are law and order, I believe, and if we do not support law and order what *do* we support, for God's sake? We are paid to look after the realm, but what is the realm without law and order?' Roger stared somewhere between Turkey and Iris, cheerfully confident that this question did not need a reply. They were in Turkey's room at the Outfit, Roger standing, the other three on straight backed office chairs.

'Rectitude has always been one of your most refulgent aspects, Roger,' Turkey replied. 'And yet not sanctimonious with it.' He smiled confidingly at Iris and Abelard. 'I don't think I've ever heard anyone refer to Roger as sanctimonious, no matter what an out-and-out shit in other respects they might consider him.'

'You see, I think we can get that fucker Olly Horton done for this,' Roger said. 'It's a beautiful gift to our cause – Briers' death, I mean.'

'Get Horton for what?' Abelard asked. 'For the mysterious subsequent visit? But why would Olly want to nose in there, inviting risk at—?'

'Fuck subsequent visit,' Roger replied. 'For the Briers killing *per* sodding *se*.'

'The police suspect *Olly Horton*?' Abelard asked.

'This is my point, isn't it?' Link-Mite replied. 'They could be helped to. They need our guidance. We should not be lacking.'

'What Roger is arguing – suppose I have it right – and I do believe I have it right, oh, yes,' Turkey said, 'what Roger maintains is that, if we get Olly truly engrimed by suspicion in the Briers matter, the likelihood of his being able to go on with the book will diminish.'

'He'd be finished,' Link-Mite said.

'His credibility gone,' Turkey said. 'This is someone supposedly writing a work to expose violent malpractice in the Outfit and yet guilty of the worst kind of violent malpractice himself – murder of a distinguished reporter.'

'Extremely distinguished,' Link-Mite said. 'As I understand it, he spoke to Philby. Yet along comes this footling turncoat, Olly Horton, and not only does him in his own property, but leaves the corpse there, unnotified, for others to pick at. Base. A dear, dear old man, and credit to the Fourth Estate. No publisher's promotion of a book could counteract that behaviour.'

'This is how Roger sees matters and I don't regard his view as wholly untenable,' Turkey said.

'Yet, for all that, I'd prefer to have it done this way,' Roger said.

'Have what done?' Abelard replied.

'I don't want Olly slaughtered, not by our own people gone wild – understandably wild, but nonetheless wild – nor by people looking for the money, who might try to beat or burn out of him before death what he's discovered. This man was once a decent colleague. I've no wish to see him as a helpless, tortured prey.'

'Roger's feeling is that if we can get the police to do him for Briers, you see, it will be a kind of *protection* for Olly,' Turkey explained. 'Locked up he's pretty well unreachable. He'd be safe but magnificently discredited.'

'It's why I referred, and referred approvingly, to law and order. What we need to think about is whether the police have started with an entirely wrong reading of this death,' Link-Mite replied. 'Than myself, I hold there is no greater admirer of the police, but once they begin wrong they're liable to go on messing up from arsehole to breakfast time. Don't we owe it to them unstintingly to offer re-direction – to, in fact, assist them, hold their hands?'

'What kind of wrong reading?' Abelard asked.

'They'll know from his newspaper chiefs what Briers was doing,' Link-Mite said. 'His job, as I've been told it myself, was to ginger up, fatten up, what Horton hopes to publish in book form and serial. The police have assumed – as have many others, no doubt – that Briers was killed by people interested in the Bowling leavings and scared the reporter might get too efficient in his inquiries and expose them. The police don't look yet towards Olly Horton, and even less towards his wife.'

'Roger sees Olly's wife as equally implicated in the murder,' Turkey said.

'Clearly,' Roger replied. 'This is a smart, devoted piece. Would she expect Oliver to see off Briers alone? Oh, so unlikely. I don't want her still around, free, if we can get Olly convicted and locked up for Briers. A smart, devoted piece like that could instigate further mischief, couldn't she? It's in their nature – smart, devoted pieces of this sort. She'd have Olly's script and notes, wouldn't she? A smart, devoted piece might use material of that kind to go public and cause embarrassment. All right, Briers' newspaper considered the material not incendiary enough, and so they sent him to do some stoking. But this is only an editor's judgement. We know that Olly was in on enough Outfit incident to expose all kinds of things better left private. I'm entirely in favour of freedom of information, but that freedom must surely include the freedom on the part of those holding the information to refuse to disclose it. Freedom is very much an all-round concept, or where are we? Kate Horton runs a successful jewellery and knick-knacks trade. She's a woman who knows what selling's about. She'd turn that commercial brain to hawking Olly's stuff when he's jailed, and then all the effort getting him convicted and neutralised would be wasted. My impression is that someone familiar with the beauties of jewellery even at a cheapo level is likely to have a creative side. This is one reason I asked for Iris to be here today.' He smiled towards her and nodded his narrow head of dense fair hair.

Iris said: 'Oh? I'm not sure I—'

'You've been in touch with Horton more recently than any of us, most probably. I'd be interested to know whether, when you were profiling him, you picked up indications of his relationship with his wife – the nature of it, the way he can be led by her – that *creative* element in this interfering bitch. No, don't answer now. Not hastily. Let me tell you first how *I* see things, shall I? Good. This is a smart, devoted piece with a *creative* side. Do you get what I'm saying? I'm sure you do. And I'm certain you'll go along with it. But, so there can be no ambiguity, let me put it starkly what I believe about Mrs Kate Horton, shall I?'

'We're all conscious of a bonny mind at work here, Roger,' Turkey said. 'Yours. A formidable, clear, uncompromising mind. I know this is Iris's and Simon's view also. I don't think it's too much to say we are riveted.'

'Given someone smart, devoted, creative, what deductions are inescapable?' Link-Mite asked. 'Entirely inescapable.'

Abelard said: 'I don't think myself that Kate is—'

'Exactly,' Roger said. 'I'll tell you how we are bound to view things, how all of us are bound to view things.'

'Riveting and compelling,' Turkey said.

'View things thus: that, of course, *she*, not Olly himself produced the notion of, and – as to impulses – the *impulse* for this fucking treacherous book. Could Oliver Horton have built such an idea himself? Oliver? *Oliver?* Oliver Horton has certain virtues, I don't dispute it, but literary? Oh, please. No, this required a true, creative push. Creative. You see my thinking now? It's not difficult, is it – not vague or far-fetched? A woman like that would look at Horton's job in the Outfit – a fine and promising job by the standards of many, but, of course, she is *not* one of the many – she is smart and devoted and *creative*. She decides his job is not up to dear hubby's qualities. There could be a raft of reasons for her attitude. Some might be political. Perhaps she despises the whole Security Services structure – sees it only as the means of propping an authoritarian State.'

'Oh, so crude and clichéd,' Turkey cried.

'The training in violence and secrecy and subterfuge might offend her, as well as the occasional episode of violence and secrecy and subterfuge in the Outfit's actual operations,' Roger said.

'Women can be so blind and judgmental,' Turkey replied. 'Not all women, clearly, Iris, but an unthinking proportion.'

'Though, of course, she's willing to make use of his training in violence and secrecy and subterfuge when it comes to doing Briers,' Roger said.

'Such double vision is typical of some women, though, certainly, not all,' Turkey said.

'Or, perhaps she considered Olly's position too lowly – too

lowly for someone married to such a smart, devoted and *creative* woman as herself,' Roger replied.

'Vanity in a woman can be so destructive,' Turkey said.

'She suggests to Olly he resign from the Outfit and turn author instead,' Roger said. 'This is a role without political overtones, or at least without the kind of political overtones that offend her libertarian soul and her gross endorsement of the people's "right to know".'

'So ludicrous to flaunt such attitudes,' Turkey replied.

'Author is a role with glamour and prestige. Clean. It might be profitable,' Roger said. 'She could feel then that he's a fit partner for her. He'd be, "My husband, the writer," not, "My husband, the State snoop."'

'Although women are entitled to ambition and to an ego – few would deny this these days – distortion can result,' Turkey said.

'And now consider the kind of impact on her thinking, on *their* thinking, the sudden intrusion of Briers would have,' Roger Link-Mite replied. 'I know you'll see the almost irresistible motive for a killing this would bring. It's so clear, it's so *vivid* that we probably don't need, after all, to ask Iris for her interpretation of the Horton relationship. Why should I put her through that laborious carry-on? Forgive me, Iris, for dragging you into this session.'

Iris said: 'I'd be quite willing to give my—'

Turkey said: 'You mean, Roger, do you, that Briers would, in Kate Horton's view—?'

'This is a smart, devoted, creative woman,' Roger replied. 'Can she simply spectate while her husband is put at increased physical hazard and at the same time degraded by having Briers take over chunks of the author function? I'd say, No. And this is the kind of perception we must, I think, lead the police towards. An obligation, an urgent obligation. We do it subtly. We arrange it, of course, so the thick bastards can imagine *they* reached the notion themselves.'

Iris said: 'In my meeting with Olly Horton, I don't think I—'

'Increased physical hazard in this sense,' Link-Mite replied: 'Briers comes with his damned professional competence exposing more of the Julian Bowling situation than Olly on his own would ever have been able to bring off. Result? All sorts of loot hunters get anxious. They imagine Briers and Olly might be working together. Doesn't Briers come from the paper where Olly hopes to sell his serialisation? These loot hunters want their identities protected. As I see it, there is a double-pronged motive for Olly and Kate, one of those motives seemingly more concrete and compelling than the other. The obvious motive would be that the Hortons think Briers with his lousy, brilliant curiosity is going to endanger Olly as well as himself. So, the Olly-Kate answer is to knock Briers over before he can do any more provocation, hoping some of the risk to Olly dies with him. *Get out of our fucking territory, Briers.* Yes, this is the clearer, more banal reason he had to be seen off. But there's something more profound, too – on the face of it woollier, perhaps less easy to grasp, but in my view more potent. Crucial, indeed.'

Turkey said: 'One of Roger's special aptitudes is in bringing out from the seemingly abstract – often the dauntingly abstract and elusive – bringing out salient, solid themes and making them clear and comprehensible for the rest of us. Oh, yes. This is an astonishing skill. I've heard even people who regard Roger as an out-and-out shit admit this ability, not necessarily the same people I mentioned previously.'

'Kate wants status for her husband because status for her husband implies status for *her*,' Roger replied. 'Authorship can bring that status. But when Briers turns up and starts operating in the same area as Olly, what does it indicate? It indicates that

Olly as an author is just a couple of points up from fucking useless, and has to be helped out by an aged hack who, decades ago,
might have been enough of a star to talk to Philby, but who now
is good only for helping dud writers make their stuff mar-
ketable. Can you see how this would humiliate a smart, devoted, creative piece like Kate? It's not just that *Olly's* rating would
be lowered by the intrusion of Briers. So would her own, because she's married to him and demands a husband who's *wor-
thy* of her. Hence, Carl Briers must be removed. She is the kind of
smart, devoted, creative piece who would see matters as simply
and uncompromisingly as that. When I say "devoted" – this is
very much a conditional devotion. It can and will be withdrawn
if the object of it drops below a specified standard. Kate Horton
has specified that standard to herself. It requires Olly to be sen-
sational in his new profession and not obscured by the shadow
of Briers. Olly would know this and realise that, to keep her, he
must resurrect some of his discarded training in violence, secrecy and subterfuge and apply it to old man Briers.'

Iris said: 'Oh, surely, you can't believe two people like Olly
and Kate Horton would—'

'This is the kind of thesis – as with so many of Roger's
theses – a thesis which I know will grow more and more
irrefutable as one reconsiders and weighs it,' Turkey said.

'As to the practicalities of opening the eyes of the police to
the way things arc, I'm content to leave this to you,' Roger
replied.

'Thank you for that confidence,' Turkey replied.

'Olly as the actual executioner, Kate as accessory, though in
truth the instigator,' Link-Mite said.

'What I'm conscious of is a totally logical structure and
now a totally obvious structure, yet one which until your
exposition, Roger, none of us would have been able to
discern,' Turkey replied.

Iris gave something between a grin and a frown: 'All right,

this is somehow part of the exercise, isn't it, Mr Link-Mite?'
Iris asked. 'It's to see how I react, yes? You're role-playing, the
two of you.'

'Probably not, probably not, Iris,' Abelard answered. 'I
wouldn't say any more.'

'It has to be,' Iris said. 'Mr Link-Mite is putting up these
mad, arsehole theories because I suppose Outfit people – some
of Mr Link-Mite's people – killed Briers, and he's testing to see
if I spot how flimsy and far-out his diversion yarn is, before he
tries it on the cops. Real tossers' moonshine. Are we truly
meant to believe someone kills because his rating as a scribbler
suffers? Or because his wife thinks his rating as a scribbler
suffers?'

'In so many ways a quite tremendous hit,' Link-Mite
replied. 'As far as I can make out, there was absolutely
nothing left at Briers' place to incriminate either Olly or
Kate.'

'Are you in the charade as well, Simon?' Iris asked.

'If the death of an esteemed old man were not involved one
could even feel pride in how Olly Horton applied his combat
skills training,' Link-Mite replied.

'He did come out very near the top on the heavy areas of
his course I recall,' Turkey said.

'Although his wife might have done the intellectualising,
the, as it were, *strategy* of the slaughter, it was Olly who had
to manage the actual one-to-one bit. We can reluctantly
admire the efficiency, but also feel a dreadful, ineluctable duty
to act for law and order,' Roger Link-Mite said.

'I think that, disloyal wretch as he may be, Oliver Horton
would still see you are bound to prioritise what you so rightly
term your – indeed *our* – "dreadful duty," Roger,' Turkey said.
'Iris, Simon, many of those who regard Roger as a Titan
among shits nonetheless speak of his unwavering devotion to
right and justice.'

'So, do I come out of this knockabout scenario OK?' Iris replied. 'Look, Mr Link-Mite, because *I* see through the flim-flam it doesn't necessarily mean the police will. After all, I know you, don't I?'

Chapter 14

Abelard's mother said: 'Simon, you part of this?'

He knew what she meant. Just the same, there was a rigmarole for Outfit business. 'Part of what, ma?' They were having breakfast in the kitchen, smoked mackerel and tea for him, Sugarpops and milk for her. He always tried to sound patient and reasonable, but without telling her anything much, of course.

'Seen the papers?'

He *had* – had made sure of seeing them early, and especially *The Sunday Post*. What appeared had been well trailed in its daily stablemate, *This Morning*. TV ads had also fanfared. Plus, a *Sunday Post* call to the Outfit several days ago summarised what they intended printing as a posthumous tribute to Carl Briers and offered, in line with journalistic ethics and practice, an opportunity for the Outfit to comment, in publishable form. This offer was naturally ignored. The Outfit had its own ethics and practice. Even in the new era of glorious openness, these often entailed a fair amount of silence: an unspoken 'fuck off'. There was a lot unspoken. That's what silence meant. Abelard said: 'Which paper, ma?' They took three on a Sunday – *Post*, *Telegraph* and *Mirror*.

'Yes, they've been interfered with, but put back as if not. Didn't they teach you how to re-fold properly? What about if you were going through someone's classified documents? It says here... hang on... here... yes...' She passed a finger down the page of newsprint. 'It says "names have been changed for security reasons".'

'Ah, is this the *Post* piece about a shot journalist?'

'What else? And it's *pieces,* not just one piece. This was their own reporter, wasn't it? Big-time reporter. Like an obituary, but with extra. He knew the famous spy way, way back, the one with the girl's name. It's here somewhere.' She rattled the page, looking.

'Girl's name?'

'Kim Novak. Kim Bassinger.'

'Oh, Kim Philby. No, not always a girl's name. There was another male spy called Kim. Rudyard Kipling's.'

'They haven't changed Philby's name for security reasons.'

'Well, he's dead. And it's long ago. The journalist must be pretty old,' Abelard said.

'Have they changed *his* name for security reasons?'

'Whose?'

'The journalist's. But he's dead, too, so maybe they wouldn't. It says "By Carl Briers".'

'No, I think that's his real name.'

'You mean you don't know?'

'Probably he's been around a while.'

'Not now.'

'It's bad,' Abelard said.

'So, they only change the name of people still alive, do they – "for security reasons?"'

'The papers try to be careful. Sometimes.'

'So, you could be in this article, could you, but with a different name?' Mrs Abelard asked, 'you being still alive? Look, there's somebody here called Stanley Vermont, supposed to be. That sound right to you? I mean, *real?* I expect they'd just go to a map and pull out a name like Vermont. Pick a state. Same as Tennessee Williams and Mississippi Fats, but now it's surnames. Could have been Stanley Washington. I don't know where they got Stanley from. One of those old-school Hollywood film makers before

Quentin Tarantino? So, is this you, Simon – Stanley Vermont? They kept the S of your first name, did they, like a clue? They could have done two initials – Stanley Alabama. But perhaps they thought, too close.'

'Stanley Vermont? I'd feel like a totally different being if I was called Stanley Vermont.' He didn't mind the Stanley. All right, it was less solid than George, but had a nice ordinariness, despite Kubrick, Kramer, Donen. And, as to Tennessee Williams, there was that other Hollywood Stanley – Kowalski of *Streetcar*, strong and earthy in a singlet, played by Brando before he became Cameopart Fats. Stanleys had foursquareness.

'This totally different being, S Vermont, knew a lot about how Julian Bowling died. What it says here, anyway. The address where it happened. Blood. We get the whole tale. They don't change *his* name either, being dead. You knew Julian Bowling, so well, didn't you, Simon? I mean you... you, Simon as Simon, not Stanley Vermont. Julian was a friend, wasn't he, until he went adrift and then got gunned and died at that address?'

'A colleague, yes.'

She handed the paper to Abelard. 'Here, read about him. But you've read it. And, in any case, you knew about this already, didn't you? Maybe you were there when it happened. Stanley Vermont might have been there when it happened. Or that's what the dead Briers says.'

'When what happened, ma?' He would regard it as damn rude to shut down a conversation with his mother, but had to try to tire her.

'Oh, Lord, *when what happened?* Come on, Simon. When Julian Bowling died, of course – died of bullets, despite attempts to stop the blood. That you, with the torn shirt? Maybe you were there when he got shot.'

'These people – they guess and imagine.'

'Which people?'

'Journalists. They have to fill the paper. What they don't know – can't know – they fabricate. Famed for it.'

'So, this one must have really fabricated top-notch if he had to be killed to quell him. Did he fabricate the bits about Stanley Vermont?' She gave a small, stagey groan. 'Simon, ever notice how half my talk with you is questions, hopeless, pitiful questions, getting no real answers? Or, I keep on saying "So". That's because I'm trying to work out, puzzle out, what you're really telling me, if you're telling me anything at all, that is. Whenever I say "So" it's because I think for just a second I can see some clearness, some cause-effect in your conversation. Only for a second, mind – don't fret, you don't give anything away. You! You? "So" means I'm reaching out for some sense, like grabbing a life-line. You won't let me hold on, though, will you? Is this... well... *right* between a son and his mother? Remember those days when you were just a kid and could often speak the truth? You ashamed of that now?'

'I don't know any Stanley Vermont,' Abelard replied.

'No, I don't suppose so.'

'And, in any case, I need to read the article before trying to comment.'

'So – *so, so, so* – *t*here we go again – so, read. Again.' She handed Abelard the paper and went out of the room, expecting no sane or believable comment on it from him. His mother was smart. Mothers had to come to terms.

THE SUNDAY POST *is proud to publish today a report by one of our most famous and admired correspondents, Carl Briers. His name will be familiar to regular readers of the Sunday Post who, over the past three decades or more, have come to trust and value his dispatches from almost every part of the world: Viet Nam, South Africa, Moscow, other African countries,*

*India, Ireland, the United States, Iraq, Iran, Israel and main-
land Britain itself.*

*Important as those reports were in their time, we think the
one we print now surpasses even them. It is unique in several
respects. First, and tragically, it is the final piece of work Carl
Briers ever wrote for* The Sunday Post. *Less than twelve hours
after he filed this article, he was dead, murdered by some
person or persons terrified that Briers and* The Sunday Post
*would expose secrets they wanted desperately to remain
hidden. They knew of his reputation for scenting and finding
and revealing such material, and they feared him, and they
feared this newspaper and its reputation for upholding the
traditions of a free Press. In their search for the killer or killers
of Carl Briers, one question the police will repeatedly ask
themselves is, Who would have the strongest reason to quell
his voice?*

*And there are other reasons for the uniqueness of Carl
Briers' report. Details about the killing of the British
journalist, Charles Tate, in New York – a death with dark
similarities to Briers' own – have never before been published,
neither here nor in the United States. British security sources
have always refused to admit that Tate was somehow involved
in the case of the British Intelligence officer turned
international drugs dealer, Julian Bowling.*

*Nor was the amount Bowling is believed to have stolen
from the criminal syndicate he worked for generally known
before Briers' investigations. Readers will see he puts it at $9
million, possibly rising to $13 million. Such a sum – still
unrecovered – would explain why underworld interest in the
circumstances of Julian Bowling's death in 1997 persists so
strongly years after. Other criminals, beside Bowling's former
associates, might also be interested in the disposal of those
illegal funds. No will was ever registered in this country or
abroad.*

*But, as Briers suggests below, this does not necessarily
mean no will existed. Those benefiting might have privately
agreed to accept its terms, fearing confiscation of illegal drug-
trade profits if a dispute reached court. Briers' view that
someone – or possibly more than one – 'close to Bowling' may
have inherited the bulk of the millions opens many
possibilities. Briers was seeking to clarify these when
assassinated. Here again police may wish to examine his
findings for pointers to motive, and* The Sunday Post *will
naturally give them all the aid we can.*

*The unknown recipient, or recipients, of Bowling's evil
fortune would, of course, feel themselves threatened by Carl
Briers' work. Identification might make them a target of
Bowling's fellow syndicate members, who feel cheated; and of
the authorities determined to reclaim the proceeds of crime.
Drugs traders chasing this large sum would prefer to use their
own search methods, so as to corner the treasure whole;
whereas disclosure by Briers could produce a free-for-all,
likelihood of a damaging war and fragmentation of the prize.*

*There are many possible reasons for the removal of such a
dedicated, perceptive, brave reporter as Carl Briers. Those
reasons all have to do with greed, ruthless self-preservation
and brutal power-seeking, aims which Carl Briers always
sought to lay bare and counter through his work. He was not
alone among newspaper men and women in this, but he was
arguably the greatest and will be gravely missed.*

When Abelard first read the testimonial earlier this morning,
before his mother was up, he had found it lush: standard in-
house unction. *Our lad was great, our lad is dead, our lad has
earned some space.* Now, though, on a re-visit, the words
seemed about right. Briers probably deserved the eulogy. After
all, hadn't he spoken with Philby? In addition, he possessed an
undoubted ability to come to things which were already on

their way to getting well fucked up and fuck them up a good bit more. This was the higher journalism. Abelard did wish, though, that Charlie Tate could have been given the same class of printed farewell in 1997. Why? Was this a tremor of contemptible, half-baked sentimentality? Would a plump obituary compensate for getting Charlie killed? It might have made things worse, in fact: Abelard would have had to blame himself then for the destruction of someone eminent, someone rating a big post-mortem write up, not simply for the slaughter of a one-time friend.

Self-blame was a bit of a tic with Abelard. It could make him feel momentarily humble and righteous, and he had often tried to wipe it out. Blame was an item he had been brought up with. The household was much committed to rough extracts from the Old Testament like, 'be sure your sin will find you out.' These days they'd call it a *culture* of blame. *Then* they called it 'harking to the Good Book.' The Good Book expected you to be better, and if you weren't you had to sweat.

Tate's death in 1997 was not reported or commented on with anything like the fullness given Briers. Perhaps that was because – as the New York police insisted – this could have been an accident, an accident to a careless drunk in a busy night street. And foreign with it, though they never actually said this: another of those unspokens. Abelard had realised Tate might indeed have been careless, but not as the police thought – and did still.

Of course, journalists were used to dealing with dangerous material, but only some of the time. Now and then they covered Siamese twins and talking dolphins. They had not been trained to regard everyone as potentially destructive and their caution could slip. They might think more about deadlines than safety. Perhaps Charlie Tate was a little hurried and obvious in the inquiries he made for Abelard, and Abelard should have realised before approaching him that he might be. And so, blame. *Be sure your sin will find you out.* Clearly, the US police could not be told about any of this.

As a matter of fact, Briers seemed to have picked up some of the private knowledge by his own means, and this final article showed he most likely understood at the end why Tate got motored. In his last few weeks, Briers had done some remarkable digging. The trouble was, such intense inquiries were bound to make him noticed, just as Tate's had. You could not work in a vacuum if you put the kind of intelligent, intrusive questions he had been putting. As an Outfit maxim phrased it, *Ask and ye shall reveal.*

Briers had obviously managed a trip to New York in search of more about Tate's killing. Abelard knew this would have made the old reporter especially liable to attention and possible removal, again as Tate's original inquiries had made *him* liable to attention, and possible removal. Although the comparison brought Abelard big and fierce despair now, he was the kind who could never keep despair going for long. He knew he lacked the width of vision for that. In his banal little way he always scuttled back to quick recovery. As an adult he had taught himself escapism. If you were down, find a way of forgetting about it. This was his way of conforming to the Government's fashionable 'life-long learning' initiative. Learn how to put up with the unbearable. *Be sure your sin will find you out on the town dodging harsh memories.*

Abelard started now on Briers' own last article. It was headlined, WHO KILLED BRITISH RUNAWAY SPY, AND WHO BAGGED HIS LOOT? A strap line beneath read: EX-OFFICER BECAME DRUGS TYCOON AND SWINDLED CROOKED FIRM OF $9m. As Mrs Abelard said, the long feature carried his by-line. This was big and very black, like RIP on a headstone. Possibly the paper would have fed this material into Olly's serialised book if things had worked out

better, fattening it, heating it. Now, though, Briers' murder
gave an immediate drama to the revelations which no
newspaper would let slip. The Briers writing demanded
publication at once and Olly's stuff would have to stand on
its own when he finished – *if* he finished, if he was *allowed* to
finish, if he *lived* to finish. Stress was a great killer.

As originally schemed, perhaps Briers' name as a
contributor would have been withheld or disguised for safety
– 'Additional reporting by Caspar Maine? Clifford Delaware?
Briers could do without that now.

*A FORMER BRITISH Intelligence agent carried out one of
the cleverest and most ruthless robberies in the history of
major international drugs trading, securing for himself a
fortune of millions of dollars. But it was a fortune that cost
his life. Only now, more than four years after these
astonishing events, has this reporter been able to assemble
some of the details. Even today, the whereabouts of the money
remains unknown, except to those who have it.*

*Julian Bowling, Oxford graduate, former public schoolboy
and son of wealthy middle class parents, big-swindled the
illegal drugs syndicate he had joined after ditching his top-
flight security services career. As part of that career, he had
been instructed in all the black skills required to squash an
enemy. But Bowling's victims were not really his enemies at
all. If the business had been respectable they could have been
called colleagues. Since it was certainly not respectable the
term is associates or accomplices.*

*By brilliant scheming, Bowling was able for a time to
outwit some of the world's most formidable and dangerous
criminal minds. But then, perhaps this is understandable. He
was once a magnificently talented spy. It's just that he let his
superb, devious skills get perverted and lead him into
international crime.*

All intelligence agencies know that the training they offer recruits brings risk. If an officer turns renegade, such training can be used against those who gave it. In the past, though, this danger was always perceived as a matter of doctrine: that is, the renegade might change sides because his or her political views changed. There were Western spies who went Communist, and there were Communist spies who went Western.

Julian Bowling was something new. He did not defect from principle. He did not defect at all. He became a crook, the motive not social conscience but very heavy cash. In him some would see a symbol of Britain's continuously fading international role. From a favoured background he had been chosen for what was until recently one of the most élite security organisations in the world – the British secret service. Yet from inside this select force Bowling began a grossly criminal second career, a career that would lead in 1997 to his terrible, mysterious death.

It was as if, since the destruction of the Berlin Wall, and the régime that built and maintained it, almost all the great political and intellectual debates of the 20th century had become irrelevant. Much less relevant, too, was the influence of a small, Western democracy like Britain, and the clandestine guardians of its soul. Was it this final dwindling of status and purpose that pushed Julian Bowling into lawlessness? Only the prospect of wealth could motivate him now.

Julian Theobald Bowling was the son of prosperous factory owner Philip Bowling and his wife Pamela. The family owned Old Demesne – a sixteenth century manor house in Wiltshire – as well as a flat near Marble Arch and another in the Vendée region of France. Both in their seventies, Pamela and Philip Bowling have separated since the death of Julian, and Pamela now lives in Portugal. Family friends say that an exceptionally close bond existed between Julian and his mother.

After his time at the famous British public school, Harrow, (whose former pupils include nineteenth century famed novelist, Anthony Trollope, and outstanding statesman, Sir Winston Churchill), and at Magdalen College, Oxford (est 1458), where he took a languages degree, Julian Bowling spent some years travelling abroad, supporting himself in casual jobs. He appears to have kept in touch with several of the Oxford dons who taught him and it is probable one of these recommended him for employment with the security services – a traditional role for some Oxbridge staff. Bowling was recruited in 1989 at the age of 27. He is said to have settled quickly into a section referred to familiarly as the Outfit and was regarded as highly gifted. His responsibilities included liaison in Paris and Brussels with NATO allies on Middle Eastern security.

However, by late 1996 or early 1997 doubts about Bowling had begun to surface. It is possible he grew demoralised by the reduction in authentic espionage duties, first through removal of the Berlin Wall, then through subsequent entente with Cold War countries. I have been told that Bowling admitted he felt his career no longer had meaning. Almost certainly it was around this time that he came to realise his native aptitudes and training could be put to a different, very profitable purpose. He made his first gradual moves into drugs trafficking.

Not all stages of these early, immensely significant steps are clear. I have established, though, that Bowling travelled to New York early in 1997. The trip had nothing to do with his Outfit duties. During this visit, he was in contact with one of the world's biggest drug traders, JJ Cardinal (*changed name). Probably it was now that Bowling began to emerge as a major member in the distribution network.

It is possible that the Outfit, or – more likely – someone from the Outfit acting independently, had heard hints of this meeting with Cardinal and wanted to know more. A British journalist, Charles Tate, based in New York, may have been asked to do informal inquiries into this relationship. The security services will sometimes use overseas journalists for such basic work. There is evidence that Tate began the inquiries and had reasonable success. Not long after he started, though, he was killed, hit in a New York street by at least two vehicles. Police continue to regard the death as a road accident. Other, less routine explanations have been suggested. Was Tate deliberately wiped out?

None of the newspapers and journals to which he contributed had commissioned him to start a drugs trade investigation. And the Outfit officially denied any contact with or knowledge of Tate. This response, though, does not exclude the possibility that an officer who, perhaps, knew Tate personally asked him to give off-the-record help.

Later in 1997 the Outfit was forced to accept that Bowling had effectively broken from the organisation and turned professional villain. This was not something the Outfit could passively accept. One of their most trusted and formidable officers, Stanley Vermont (*changed name), was assigned to locate Julian and, if possible, bring him back. By now, Bowling's case had acquired a political aspect: Ministers saw that such a security failure had – at the least – damaging implications for Britain's image among her allies. It was the time when a new Government wanted to puff its régime as 'Cool Britannia'. Instead, Bowling had shown how to fool Britannia.

Vermont, a former colleague of Julian, began his search for him in Paris because, when still following his Outfit career there, Bowling had an affair with a young woman from the United States embassy, Lynne Martha Peterson (*changed name), ostensibly a clerk, but probably a CIA operative using embassy cover. Vermont was able to trace Julian Bowling via

Peterson but lost him somewhere in France, possibly following a car accident.

Vermont returned to Britain with Peterson and it is likely that a sexual relationship began soon afterwards between these two. Perhaps in search of Lynne Martha Peterson, Bowling later came back to Britain himself. He appears to have been detected very soon, then stalked and shot.

His body was found in a mews cottage he had rented at Home Place near Brompton Oratory in South West London. Nobody has been charged with the murder. It is not thought he was shot in the cottage. He had either been brought there and dumped or managed to reach the cottage on his own, despite fatal injuries. Although attempts had obviously been made by someone else to stop the bleeding from his wounds, it has never been ascertained who was present in the cottage as he died. Police believe at least two people were there.

I have discovered that at the time of his death, Bowling was on the run not just from Her Majesty's Intelligence and Security Services, but also from fellow drugs dealers. Through a remarkably subtle fraud on his associates, Bowling had been able to direct into a secret personal Swiss bank account $9 million (£6.5). He is believed to have increased this filched capital, by trading and currency deals, even while being hunted, to $13 million (£9.4 million). Some estimates even put the figure at $17million (£12.3). Former associates were sure to want revenge, and recovery of the money. Other criminals, also, would be interested in this spoil and might be ruthless with Bowling if he refused to supply it. Does this account for his execution?

Attempts to discover what happened to the dollars on Bowling's death have always been blocked. Notoriously, Swiss banks do not disclose information about clients, not even to the police – or especially not to the police! Illicit funds in a Swiss bank may sound like a cliché, but it is a cliché because these banks are so expert. Were criminals able to terrorise Bowling into making the dollars available before they killed him? Did he have time to pass the money somehow to Lynne Martha Peterson? Were she or Vermont or possibly both somewhere near when he died? Conceivably Bowling made a will which beneficiaries agreed to accept without probate, fearing the whole of Bowling's crooked estate might be sequestered if disclosed to the courts. It is very likely that one or two people close to Bowling at the end have cornered his money.

Where is Lynne Martha Peterson? The US embassy in Paris says she did work there in 1997 but has left. Further information is refused, and I have been unable to determine whether she is still employed by the US government. Bowling's parents decline to discuss either his death or the disposal of the fortune. Pamela Bowling says that the ending of her marriage and move to Portugal were not related to Julian's death or to any inheritance from him. It is known that Stanley Vermont remains in post at the Outfit. His present relationship with Lynne Martha Peterson and connection, if any, with the Julian Bowling profits is unclear. Both Peterson and Vermont could be at risk if they are holding the cash, or even if they are only thought to be holding the cash.

I've found that, some time between 1997 and 1999, one of the most prominent and influential figures in the Outfit, Vincent Morgan (*changed name) disappeared and has never been found. For a while there was speculation that it might have been Morgan who shot Bowling, punishment for soiling the Outfit's name: the violent, principled removal of a blot. But it is possible that Morgan was subsequently a victim to rivalries within the Intelligence and Security Services and himself did not survive. His post at the Outfit has been filled.

This, then, is the Julian Bowling narrative, as far as known. The tale has little to do with those seemingly outdated *qualities which once were standard in espionage sagas, real or fictional: competing national loyalties, competing political dogmas, agonised consciences. The motif now is money, for ever money. Revenge might also have a part. The next moves are almost certain to concern attempts to locate that $13 million, or what remains of it, and, if it is located, the probably violent efforts to collect. That once noble, though shady, game of State security has shrunk to the basest of quests, Find the Swag.*

Abelard agreed with a lot of this, though he could have done without the prêchi-prêcha tone and corny symbolism: Julian as the decay of Britain; as pollution of holy, timeless values; as collapse of the family; as the cosmic rush to materialism. He could also have done without the speculation about an officer in the Outfit who knew Tate personally and might have asked him to help. Link-Mite would nibble at that.

Abelard thought the name Stanley Vermont would grow on him if he gave Briers' piece a few more readings. The 'St' letters and the 'V' could be spoken with a real crackle and suggested push and decisiveness. He would want the 'Stanley' in full always. Stan Vermont sounded very much less: cheap rather than sterling, like a paper-tearing act down the bill in old music halls. That mighty dealer and probable murderer, JJ Ovalle in New York would naturally recognise himself as JJ Cardinal, if he saw *The Sunday Post* on the web or someone kindly sent him a clipping.

And Abelard also wondered what Lucy Mary McIver would make of *her* new name, Lynne Martha Peterson. Lynne was pleasant and, spelt like that, not gender-ambiguous. Martha contained admirable religious history, yes, but Lucy might regard it as heavy. That was one of her words, "heavy", as last word in criticism of a style. He had an idea that she came to regard *him* as heavy before she left. Fair? Probably. It

was a question of upbringing. Abelard knew he would slip
into worthiness now and then. His father had always insisted
he should make himself 'worth something' and Abelard had
listened, and would have gone on listening if his father had
still been about.

Briers was sharp to suggest Lynne Martha Peterson
possibly inherited Julian's money and to hint that Stanley
could also have grown lucky. The journalist was again right,
bleakly right, that she had become unfindable now,
unfindable even by Stanley Vermont and Simon Abelard
combined. And, yes, Vincent Morgan was unfindable, too.
Abelard had a fairly reliable notion of what had happened to
him, when his name was still Verdun Cadwallader. But what
had happened to him meant he would probably stay
eternally unfindable. Verdun, named after that terrible First
War battle where so many of his Welsh countrymen died,
had been a pretty reputable Outfit chieftain, yet with a
foolish, arrogant indifference about making enemies.
Perhaps if you were called Verdun all later hazards and
disasters looked minor. But, *A man's enemies are the enemies
of his own house.*

Abelard's mother came back into the room just after he
had finished reading. She sat down opposite and stared at him.
'"Trusted and formidable." That you? *Was* Stanley Vermont
there in the cottage by the Oratory when Julian died?
Cottage? I bet it's one of those bijou nests worth half a
million, plus. An Oratory view costs. And then that Charles
Tate. Did you know him personally, as well as Julian?'

'It's a real yarn, isn't it, ma?' Abelard replied.

'What's that mean?'

'A yarn.'

'Not true?'

'They have to get a yarn – for their editors.'

'This Briers doesn't get *yarns*. He knew Philby. That's why he can keep putting the capital I in his stuff. He's allowed an ego. Listen, Simon, did Stanley Vermont get a slice of the money? Dangerous? And listen again, I even wondered – just a tiny thought, no strength to it, I promise, just very, very brief – but I wondered whether… well, whether Stanley Vermont didn't only *find* Julian… but I thought maybe Stanley Vermont could have shot him. Purge? People like Stanley Vermont have been taught how to do that kind of filthy job when necessary, haven't they?'

'Which kind, ma?'

'Wasting.'

'That slang is so ancient.'

'Killing.'

'These names they've concocted!' Abelard replied. 'Some really far out.'

'That Lynne is Lucy? Same initial.'

'Probably the paper has a box of pseudonyms always ready for sensitive tales.'

'Where is she, Si? Is the paper right and she's got a lot of hazard?'

Yes, of course, the paper was right. 'So much of it is speculation, ma. It's not like the usual newspaper piece with quotations from folk to back what's being said.'

'I tell you, once you've talked to Philby you can write the way you want,' his mother replied. 'You're like a legend. What's Briers mean about Julian's special thing with his mother? A son *should* have a bond with his mother, surely. I heard some sons even talk to their mothers, and talk truth, no damn clouding of things. You ever heard that?'

BOOK TWO

Chapter 15

Iris Insole fancied herself at surveillance and especially tailing, by foot or car. Today, car. It was a private project, thought up by herself, no orders from Turkey Latham or Link-Mite or anyone else beyond or below. She was behind Kate Horton. She liked this plodding, old skill. Not everything had gone electronic yet, although, of course, there were electronic gadgets for tracking cars. She did not have the use of one. There was still a function for the internal combustion engine and low-level flair. This flair she reckoned she possessed and felt a proper gratitude.

Always the same nerve-battering difficulty when on a tail in a city, though: did you stick close and risk obviousness, or did you lie back for concealment and get separated by so much traffic you lost touch? She framed the question in her head like that, but actually there was no 'always' about the difficulty for her because this was the first time she'd ever tried to tag anyone, except in training. The 'always' came from her instructor then. He said clandestine central city tailing was dead difficult – 'always' – unless you had five or six vehicles to interchange at the close up position, and impossible if you were alone – like Iris. On a private project you went solo. She liked private projects. She reckoned she could handle them. If she hadn't reckoned she could handle them she would have reckoned she was not really up to working for the Outfit and she knew she was.

She planned to get to wherever Kate Horton was going, leave the car and do a bit of confrontation. *Mrs Horton, I believe.* This ought to scare her. Iris wanted her scared, and, if possible, terrified. It would make Kate feel her life and movements were charted. People knew how to find her. And if she was scared, terrified, she might be easier to talk at and persuade. She'd realise things were grave.

Iris's tailing technique was to keep at the most only two vehicles between her and Kate. As long as neither of these was a bus or furniture van, Iris could still see the Focus and follow if Kate turned off. Kate sat very upright and poised behind the wheel – like a fucking conqueror, Iris decided. That had to be changed before Iris could start work on her.

Iris believed the only way to cope with the whole current, dark situation at the Outfit was to have another go at Olly Horton. She *knew* the Outfit needed the freshness and clarity of her mind, and she would respond – was responding now, getting her wheels after Kate's. Iris did not think it wise to go direct at Olly. Do it through his woman. And so this motor trek, with a start at Paling Yard, London N15. It had to be from there because this was the only bit of geography for her Iris had. There were slightly dated pictures of Kate at the flat when Iris interviewed Oliver, enough for an identification now. Kate's car seemed to be in basement parking under their apartment building and, from where Iris waited, she had time to take a decent look as Kate appeared at the front door then walked to the side of the building and the basement entrance. She was short, thin, energetic, fair haired and, as far as Iris could tell at this distance, and from her memory of the photographs, pretty, even beautiful, in her damn prissy-featured, round-faced style. She had on a half-length, green, woollen jacket and dark skirt to her ankles. It might be working dress. This was the kind of woman Iris considered she could see off intellectually and in any tussle of wills.

Iris did not think anything really rough with her would be necessary: verbal rough, that is, psychological rough. She had to be leant on. With luck, it would come to nothing more than civilised argument, in which Kate could be flattened. Then, when she saw the point, *she* would lean on Olly and stop him publishing. Possibly, he had more material than Briers. Or, because Briers had disclosed so much, Olly and his book editors might now feel he'd better *find* more, to give his work something fresh and make it sellable. Olly would take to really intense digging, and that could be awkward. He had been very well trained to dig – not into his own organisation, it was true, but the methods were the same wherever you did it. Anything might come up, and anything could be disastrously damaging to the Outfit, and specifically to Simon Abelard. Iris worried about damage to the Outfit, but not as much as she worried about damage or worse to Simon. Kate had to convince Olly to give up, and Iris had to convince her she must.

Iris dismissed as the purist eyewash, didn't she, Roger Link-Mite's line that Olly and Kate killed Briers? Didn't she? That was either some extra test for Iris, or Link-Mite put this thesis around as a strategy for the long-term benefit of himself. At present, Iris could not see how it would work, though. She did not *expect* to see how every personal stratagem in the Outfit operated. Its staff were rarely transparent. She accepted this, adored it: these were the kind of people she had chosen to work with. They were layered, complex, devious, as, too, was life. If you wanted transparent mates, become a jelly fish. If Link-Mite ever did suggest to the police that Olly and Kate did Briers, there would no doubt be a stack of evidence to show they did not. The police would have a giggle at him – or wonder what scheme of his own he was pushing.

It had been obvious to Iris when interviewing Olly that he hugely valued Kate's judgment. She had not been present, but all his references to her views were deferential, reverential. Pathetic. Grand. Perhaps she would see the new death hazards a lot more sharply than someone who fancied himself as a whistle-blower, scourer of the body politic, and emergent contender for the Nobel Literature prize, the vain, stupid, treacherous prick. Briers' article in *The Sunday Post* convinced Iris that things had suddenly become very urgent. By 'things' she meant what might happen to Abelard if someone in the know and damn capable failed to act.

Who else was there in the know and damn capable but herself? Turkey? Roger? Those beyond Turkey and Roger? They might all be in the know and damn capable – were definitely in the know and damn capable – but was it certain they would wish to be damn capable of safeguarding Simon Abelard? Turkey, Roger and those beyond had their own objectives which she certainly could not itemise, but what she did feel was that they might be at variance with safeguarding Simon. Almost certainly they would be. The Outfit was no welfare home. But although Iris did not want to be on the staff of a welfare home, she could still look after someone she felt drawn to look after, especially if he did not realise he needed to be looked after: that lovely concept of the lost one hundredth sheep when all the rest were safe, as it came up in so many religions. Abelard was like this, most probably. Couldn't he understand how much *The Sunday Post* report endangered him? He had become blasé, cocky, inured to hazard. Men in big jobs and used to good breaks could get like that. Oh, God, how lucky he and the Outfit were to have her available, a neophyte but so brilliantly precocious. Iris did not see it as boastful to think like this: simply she had picked the right career and would excel. A natural, that was all.

Kate and the Focus seemed to be going south towards the Thames, possibly making for London Bridge. On the other side would be the Borough and Walworth. Did she have some interest there: an office, a lover, a shop? That's where the confrontation would have to take place. If Kate had the kind of judgment and brain Olly suggested, or even half that much, she must see how right Iris was once it had all been explained. With gifts like those, Kate would soon realise she was not the only one with judgment and a brain. Iris promised herself that some patient reasoning with Kate would do.

Yesterday and earlier this morning Iris had read and several times re-read the *Post* piece to confirm again how exposed Simon Abelard was now. When dealing with such material, Iris knew you should ask first who fed Briers stuff for the article, and fed it hoping for what. The actual words in any newspaper report – all those lovely *mots justes* and jolly headlines – these mattered so much less than where its ideas originally came from, who infiltrated them. Even a correspondent with as big a by-line as Carl Briers', and all that epic, olde-worlde Philby chit-chat – even Briers was likely to be nowhere near as significant as his source. Her view of journalism had been implanted very early in the Outfit's *Information Evaluation* course, and on the whole she thought it wise: Iris longed to shed naïveté, worked at it, worked at it. She would prefer to be thought vicious than naïve. Naïveté was dereliction. Had whoever freighted this lot to Briers also shot him? She admired sequence, but not obvious sequence. She had to find the hidden lines, the deliberately buried lines.

Iris knew her degree in theology was sweet training for the Outfit. Similarities teemed. Religions obviously suggested system, a unique system for each, but never a system simple to understand: few totally lucid connections between one bit and another. What were called 'leaps of faith' might be required to deal with the woozy bits – were *always* required. Think of Sir Tom Browne in the 17th century, a doctor and full of scientific exactitude, but crying out in his pamphlet, *Religion for Medics,* that he loved to lose himself in devotions which soared way, way above the rational, an *oh, altitudo!*

And in the same way, she felt pretty sure that some kind of system did operate in the Outfit, but for God's sake don't expect to cotton on to it overnight. And don't expect it to resemble any other system you've ever heard of or met. She adored this – the fluidity and grand evasiveness, the simultaneous slackness and tightness of organisation, like the US army pre all-round potheading. It seemed to her that she had always been destined for the Outfit, the way some were destined to be artists, snooker professionals or roofers. Could Iris have found another career where she and a colleague came across an old, disgustingly nosy journalist murdered at home, said nothing about it to Turkey or Link-Mite or the police or the world, and then tried to detect from what the journalist had written, or apparently written, who was trying to work some ploy through him and his paper? This was a truly grown up life. It brought obligations. Even if she'd had the beauty and shape to be a catwalk model, would the job provide such depth? And, despite the theology, she had never seriously thought of lady vicardom. She didn't mind the notion of sucking up to parishioners, poncily shaking hands in the porch, but knew she could never have done a marriage service: hell, the foul silk-style cravats bridegrooms wore these days.

Her eyes still stuck to the back of Kate's fair head, Iris had that idea about her again – driving 'like a fucking conqueror'. Yes, there was a confidence, even jauntiness, to the way she sat, hands on top of the wheel instead of at the recommended quarter to three spots: Kate followed the ready-for-anything, me-in-charge fashion, like kids of seventeen handling mummy's BMW. She seemed very still, or allowed herself a few economical movements when the driving needed it. No question, this damn smugness came because she thought she and Horton were due for a life of true distinction. The cow really believed in what they were doing. She'd convinced herself, the demented bitch, that three hundred pages of dirty blab was a fine notion, and too bad who gets hurt or killed as result. An Audi tried to push in ahead of Iris from a sidestreet. She accelerated to block the bugger out and offered a gorgeous smile to the driver as he did the finger. Then she readably mouthed to him, 'Wait, oh arsehole of arseholes.' Wasn't she part of an organisation with at least decades behind it of fouling up other people?

She couldn't tell whether Kate used the mirror much. Her head never bobbed about, the self-satisfied bit of wife. But, of course, her eyes could be upwards to it. If they were, they'd see a Volvo estate and a landscape gardener's van, and then maybe a glimpse of Iris in the Mazda. Kate wouldn't recognise her, even supposing she managed a look. She might get alert to a vehicle that stayed with her, though. Or perhaps she was so happy with the future she had no space for anxieties. Iris would give her some, but in due course.

Maybe a quarter of Iris's brain was on the tailing, the rest still preoccupied with Briers' newspaper report. She had sat with it for an age at home yesterday and earlier today, weighing, probing, guessing – what she'd have liked to call intuiting, but which she knew was only guessing. As she went over and over the piece then, and as she brought it back into her memory now, an impression returned that had come on her first reading: she did not think this always sounded like authentic newspaper writing. Of course, it would have gone through editors at *The Sunday Post* before making the page but, just the same, some of it seemed limply phrased. Perhaps Briers was such a star that people in the office were forbidden to change his prose. His? She returned to the paragraphs about Tate. *Police continue to regard the death as a road accident.* That was all right: factual, with main verbs full of message. *Other, less routine, explanations have been suggested.* This struck her as feeble and ironic, dismally unspecific, like something in an Oxbridge student paper.

Generally, the proper Press did not go in for irony. It could be misunderstood. They specified. They gave lists. So, tell us, *Post, what* explanations?

Then, *Was Tate deliberately removed?* Newspapers tried not to leave big questions like that trailing, didn't they? It was a kind of smear language – shifty, non-committed. *Look, we're not saying he was deliberately removed, are we, but what do* you *think, dear* Post *reader?* Although Iris Insole of course knew he had been deliberately removed, this was not thanks to nudges from *The Post*. She worked in the Outfit and had quickly come to realise that, despite no Berlin Wall, all things were still possible, many of them harsh and underhand. The ordinary *Post* subscriber would not have such insight. But one of the reasons Iris joined the security services was to be different from the ordinary *Post* subscriber and from most other folk. She prized special insights, had once thought theology might give her some. But theology turned out to be only earnest, big-word efforts to make architecture out of mist. Now, she needed to get knowledgeable about all the harsh and underhand ploys Outfit people and the enemies of Outfit people remained smart at. She needed to breathe this evil in full. After all, wasn't she a totally Outfit person herself? Vital to absorb the ethos. Getting themselves absorbed was what ethoses were for.

But, above all, she would have to try to give Simon Abelard some protection. *The Post* article fingered him. Briers, you malevolent dead twat. Obviously, Iris saw it might appear comically arrogant to imagine she could nanny Abelard. As the article said, he was formidable, and the idea that she might become in any style his minder would strike most people as absurd. So stuff most people. They would not know of it, anyway. She worried hardly at all about seeming arrogant. Although humility and meekness were important in some religions, they couldn't help much when you felt one very decent colleague had probably been targeted by an international drugs cartel and required a shield. Actually, of course, the article said Stanley Vermont was formidable. But Stanley Vermont *had* to be Simon Abelard. Nobody who knew recent Outfit folklore could doubt that.

The traffic had eased a little. They did seem to be making for Walworth. The Volvo and the van had gone and her cover now was an Escort estate and a Rover. She reckoned she'd brought it off, regardless of the training instructor's theories. She had such a hell of a lot to teach the Outfit. Iris felt comradeliness towards all its members, including Turkey and Link-Mite, and especially Abelard. There was advantage in being a noviate at this work. Perhaps she would see things more starkly than Simon, because they were strange to her and had to be assessed from new. Possibly this was the one plus from naïveté. Someone so used to feeling as 'formidable' as Abelard, might easily get smug. Yes, she must take care of him. Neither Turkey nor Roger Link-Mite was going to do it. Quite apart from their own secret aims, they'd probably consider it impudent to suggest bodyguards: a reflection on Abelard's ability to watch out for himself. Iris did not mind being thought impudent, and she doubted Abelard's ability to watch out for himself non-stop, if *The Post* article provoked all sorts into looking for the money. And it would.

In fact, they'd have been looking before the article. Briers would make them keener. Part of the keenness might have produced his death: an attempt to stop the sod inviting any more into the lovely, dollar-graced quest. Naturally, the other possible reason for Turkey and Roger not acting to preserve Abelard was that they actually *wanted* him removed. She did not know why this might be, but in an outfit like the Outfit you had to get used to such special thinking. Iris *would* get used to it, but this did not mean she'd always go along with it. She had her own special thinking. It involved feelings of rich comradeliness towards Abelard – just an aspect of what

belonging to the Outfit entailed. Comradeliness was priceless
and indispensable. Iris had heard of 'canteen culture' – the
term critics of the police used to describe their sometimes
obstructive team loyalty – and she meant to be part of the
Outfit's version. But she realised the feeling towards Abelard
was uniquely strong. She could not account for this, and was
almost certain it amounted *only* to comradeliness. As far as
she could tell, she felt no jealousy of this woman, Lynne
Martha Peterson, or, presumably, Lucy Mary McIver –
another name in Outfit folklore – wherever she was now, and
however much she might be worth. Iris did not consider it
naïve to believe there were more solid relationships than those
based on sex or money or sex *and* money. These could be to
do with making sure someone you worked with stayed safe.
Wasn't this just maturity? Of course, she would like to fuck
Abelard, but this did not necessarily suggest big, lasting
feelings. As St Paul never got round to mentioning in the
Epistles, fucking could be simply fucking.

According to the folklore and to Briers' article, there were
questionable sides to Abelard, but this only made Iris's
allegiance to him more powerful. No, no, not naïveté. She did
not think his colour made her even more intent on backing
him. It would be gross and utterly misplaced condescension,
and she was surely free of that? Surely. The suggestions that he
might be in on the loot, that he turned to Bowling's girl even
before Bowling's death – perhaps, anticipating she'd collect –
none of this troubled her too much. Were there hints in Briers
that Simon Abelard might actually have been active in the
execution of Bowling? Weasel questions in the article again:
*Did he have time to pass the money somehow to Lynne
Martha Peterson? Were she or Vermont or possibly both
somewhere near when he died?* And the paragraph that dealt
with the gunning down was skeletal, almost all omission:
Perhaps in search of Lynne Martha Peterson, Bowling later

came back to Britain himself. He appears to have been
detected very soon, then stalked and shot. Where was the
detail, the settings, the drama? These queries continued to
bother her, but she needed to give Kate a little more attention
now. She seemed to have reached wherever they were going.
Almost time to think of getting nearer, on foot.

Whatever had happened to Bowling, it could not disturb
Iris, nor deflect her from the resolve to keep Abelard intact. If
you picked a job from among all other jobs on offer you
accepted what it was like, and Abelard seemed to her to
symbolise this job all through and better than anyone else.
Damage him and you damaged a more or less worthwhile
trade, damaged passably true values, damaged a kind of
mystique. She felt certain he would understand why she had to
tail Kate. She felt certain he would feel proud of her for the
dogged skill in handling it. Iris liked to think of herself as
dogged – methodical, determined, undeterred – as well as
inspirational. She had to be all-round.

'Are you to do with the guy in the cape?'

'What guy in a cape?' Iris replied. 'I don't see any guy in a
cape.'

'Oh, come on,' Kate Horton said, 'he's here most days.'

'Buying jewellery?'

'Here. Doing an eye job.'

'I came alone.'

'Yes, maybe, but part of the same thing. Support and more
support.'

'Which?'

'Which what?' Kate asked.

'Which same thing?' Iris began to realise this was not going
to be a decorous little get-together, after all. Kate might not be
so easily squashable.

'It's kid's stuff, all this lurking,' Kate said. 'And now...
God... now they *actually* send a kid. But listen... yes...

listen... are you the one who did the alleged – I'll say *very* alleged – the alleged consumer survey on Oliver? He told me young, glasses. Your style of glasses.'

'Which?'

'They're fine... I mean, totally fine... nothing wrong with them at all... why should there be, for heaven's sake?... Or maybe they're just a ploy, anyway. Your game is full of ploys.'

'What ploy?'

'To make you look like... oh, I don't know... mild and otherworldly. Don't be upset. I mean, *nicely* mild and otherworldly. Like a lady vicar.'

'I might have become a lady vicar. Didn't go for it,' Iris replied.

'I don't suppose you're mild and otherworldly.'

'Which other world?'

'Oh, you know... like out of it all, above it all. Higher values. So, anyway, you bought the vicar-style specs. And you gaze about, all disarming and liberal.'

'I have to see.'

'What do you see?'

'Rotten trouble. No man in a cape, though,' Iris said.

'You think you'll squeeze me, do you – you, him, maybe others – all put the squeeze on me, and then you suppose I'll squeeze Oliver... make him go silent?'

'I think you could be more helpful than you have been to date.'

'Are you shagging Abelard now?' Kate replied.

'He's nice, isn't he?'

'I'd say you're frightened about something. You're frightened for Abelard? This is my impression... and yet, in a way, more than an impression... almost, in fact, a conviction. That's strong, but not too strong... in my view.'

'What did you mean, am I shagging him *now*? Were *you* shagging him previously?'

Iris had almost lost Kate when she parked her Focus and
walked to the Antiques Market building on the corner of
Sinclair Square in Walworth. Iris had to find parking, too,
and by the time she did Kate was out of sight. Iris had
scouted for a while, looking in shops, reading nameplates on
offices, in case she was mentioned there. When Iris decided
on the Market it was virtually a last shot. Wandering around
on the ground floor among the meat stalls, green grocery
stalls, novelties stalls, she had more or less bumped into a fat
man in a tan cape with a large imitation silver brooch up near
his ageing neck. He had on a white bobble cap which he
touched with one finger in a kind of salute when he
approached Iris and said, 'After Kate Horton?' He pointed
upstairs.

'What do you mean? How did you know?'

'Yes, upstairs.' He dodged off.

She had found Kate just opening the jewellery stall. Iris
waited, then went to fiddle with some of the stuff on show.
After about three minutes, Kate approached and came out
with the question about the cape man.

And Iris acted ignorant because the training said you never
gave an answer, a positive answer, to any question you could
not see the full purpose of, which meant pretty well all
questions: a bit like that advice for barristers in court which
said only put questions you already knew the answers to. Iris
had met the man in the cape, yes, and had been helped by the
man in the cape, but had no idea what he amounted to, nor
where he got his briefings.

Now, Iris said: with hefty, wrap-around foreboding: 'The
Briers death could be only the first.' They were standing on
each side of a junk jewellery case. Iris longed for almost all the
pieces. She doted on radiance, tasteful or cheap. It was the
halo stuff and stained glass that had drawn her to Theology
rather than Engineering.

'Were you part of that, the assassination?' Kate spoke quite conversationally.

'It's possible to see a likely future pattern in the violence.'

'You *are* shagging Abelard. You think he's next, don't you, because of the article? Pattern. Don't think I can't sympathise. Oh, I do, I do… but there are bigger issues. You're afraid Oliver will discover more about him and blow everything, dispensing with the stupid alias – Vermont?'

'As I see it, we should both be trying to get Olly to give up the book, Kate. Briers got killed because he wanted to write about things. Oliver wants to write about things. So—'

'Were you in on the Briers death?' Again, spoken almost throw-away.

'People are troubled by the written word.'

'Who sent you? Turkey? Link-Mite? Abelard himself? I've proposed a deal with him, you know. *Did* you know? But he doesn't like it, right? That it? Instead, he tells you to come and put the frighteners on me from behind those Billy Bunter specs.'

'What deal?' Iris replied.

'I'm allowed to talk to him in private.'

'What deal? A deal that says on your side Olly will chuck the book project? Does Olly listen to you on big topics like that, even though you were shagging Abelard? This was when you were already with Olly?'

'Oh, you know… a deal.'

'So, *were* you shagging him before?' Iris asked.

'But a deal that doesn't look as if it's on after all. I've got to admit that… well, I mean, would you be here if it was? I have to read the signs, haven't I?'

'Briers has said it all, hasn't he?' Iris replied. 'Why push on when it's so damn hairy?'

'Here's your friend in the cape.'

He went to a secondhand clothes stall opposite without

speaking to Iris or Kate. An old, very shiny tail suit seemed to capture him. He held the trousers against himself for length. The woman running the stall cried out, 'But it would enhance you, so – help you sum up an epoch.'

'Is it because Simon cornered so much of Bowling's wallet that you've changed feelings towards him now?' Iris asked. 'Supposing you *were* shagging him previously. But that's only envy, isn't it? Perhaps you're jealous of the girl Lucy. She's not around any more, honestly. Does Olly resent the money? And he reckons to catch up on some of it with the tale-telling? But even Stella Rimington's advance was only half a million for her book on the security services, they say, and she was head of MI5, really a star. You *can't* catch up on all those dollars, can you? Shagging him while you were with Olly?'

'If they're worried enough to send you and the cape man to Walworth it means, doesn't it... can't you see this, you child in a big scene... can't you see it, can't you?... it means they're sure Oliver's book is going to say something, doesn't it? They're scared of revelations. Why? Why – obviously because they have matters... precious, devilish, horrifying matters they want kept hidden. This makes Oliver and me even more conscious of our duty to publicise, a duty to ourselves, to the country and... yes, I'll not quibble at saying it... a duty to democracy.'

'How much the smaller, would-be diamond coronet?' Iris replied.

Chapter 16

'I want you to realise, my dear, how unsafe you are, how appallingly open. I say "My dear". Why do I say that? So damn phoney. Smarmy. Reeking. After all, you could be an enemy. You *are* an enemy. Are you?'

'Where did you get my address?'

'Well, exactly.'

Iris said: 'It's not in the phone book and the office wouldn't tell you.'

'No, I do appreciate that. Both. This is what I mean, isn't it – the availability? So easy to find you. You're young. Oh, I know you've completed courses and been taught self-preservation and awareness by people who have preserved themselves and are aware. But I'm not sure these things *can* be taught, you see. Perhaps they come only with actual practice, come in their fullness, that is. My son – he was in the same profession as you, yes, and quite a deal older when obliterated, yet even he did not have the experience to see all the hazards around him and cope with them. What chance for a novice like you if my masterful Julian failed? Has my husband been here sniffing? He'd be beautifully turned out – a suit from Agnew or Septimus Lake, most probably single-breasted yet plus waistcoat, plenty of mouth freshener.'

'Nobody has been here. Obviously. Nobody should have the address.'

'Philip possesses sharp, foul instincts,' Pamela Bowling said. 'Clearly, there must have been a time when he was lovable. I made my choice. Then came years to regret this in

various sites, seek relief. But to someone like you he might still
seem a possible. He has kept lean. In a hunt for money he
could assemble good charm and his palm and fingers in a
handshake are entirely unsweaty even into his seventies.'

'Someone like me in which sense?'

'What – he *has* been here, making you feel cherished? Sod
it. Perhaps this is why I said "My dear". I'm trying to reach
you, to compete. Phil had a fine singing voice, I'd never deny
that. Bach's *St Matthew's Passion*, roundelays. And he's kept
abreast. He'll chant the filthiest rap if called for. He wants
acceptance in general. Has he done some numbers for you?
I've heard him denounce as "absurdly negative" that Dorothy
Parker mot, "Men never make passes at girls who wear
glasses." For God's sake, we're talking about millions of
dollars here. A variable figure but always hefty. Phil, the
bonny old shit, would put his all into that, and nothing's
going to deter him, not glasses, dull complexion or rough hair.
Philip's single mindedness can be odious, can be admirable. I
think of him when younger wearing a greenish suit with a
waistcoat and there was undoubtedly presence. More than a
leprechaun. Possibly a buttonhole badge – something muted.
Philip is a man waistcoats are right for. What I'm saying, Iris,
is I have to recognise there would be nothing shameful a girl
like you going for him on a temporary basis, an interlude if
you were lonely. Please, has it happened? I think I'm entitled
to know this, so as to adjust my strategy.'

Pamela had arrived alone at Iris's front door in the
Peckham flat block about an hour ago. Under a man-style,
long, open beige trenchcoat, she wore a navy woollen suit
trimmed with purple at the lapels and around the square
jacket pockets. Her hat was navy and a cloche, one small
silver feather at the front. Iris had asked her in. Pamela shed
the trench coat and hat. They were in Iris's square living room
drinking cider. Pamela had methodically identified all the

framed prints on the walls: an Augustus John, a Sickert, two Tissots and a Chardin. 'Tissot's the lad for me,' she said. 'I'd give up fish and chips for Tissot.'

'I believe one of the real dangers in all this situation is directed at you, Pamela,' Iris said.

She nodded. 'Yes, it's a situation, isn't it? A mother accepts danger. I feel I have a duty to my dear, eliminated son to gather up his gains, and prevent them from further taint. They are tainted already, of course they are, but one does not want a *progression* of taint. This being my purpose, I know I must accept hazard for his sake. If Phil has been here, he'd probably extol some aspect of you that you've hardly considered, say forehead, ear lobe, shoulder symmetry, as if he, only he, can see your brilliance and that, therefore, to share all your knowledge, insights and so on with him would be merely natural. That's how the hardworking old strutter always operates. Our early years seemed so lovely – when Julian was small. Philip had such wit and sexuality, and his gorgeous flair for government assisted status as a factory owner. Credibility glowed in him then and makeshift honour. He could hold his smile without effort and there was no blatant catch in it. I would often write admiringly to my mother about him. These were pre-email days when a letter was truly a letter and one's sentiments took on the backing of fine stationery. I felt he merited that. You've heard of paper tigers? A watermark paper tiger, Phil was. Clearly, it would destroy me, I mean, physically destroy me – literally – if that fucking dreg cornered any more of Julian's filthy estate. This kind of shock at my age – it can't be just absorbed and forgotten about. I look well when all up together in these garments, but it's fragile. I must not fail my son. To a degree I still worship Phil, but not in any way intelligible to myself or other people – sane people.'

'These former business buddies of Julian would kill you or him without worrying, if they considered either of you, or both, an impediment,' Iris said. Part of settling with Julian.'

'Philip would be brave about such hazards. When I tell you he had a stupendous voice, plus humour, sexiness and a holy skill in fund-sucking from government, these are only some elements of his character. He had, has, courage, the bustling prick, and a scent of good money can always fill him with the most audacious evil. I would like him dead, clearly, but I'm certainly not going to ask a child like you in splatterable fourth form specs to see to that, and with hair still to find a shape. Nor ask your friends to see to it, as the damned Outfit saw to Julian. I think that when Phil's feeling sensible and balanced he would admit he has come to near the end and should move clear, so that those from a *true* relationship can take over. I'm referring, of course, to the relationship between self and Julian. All right, this is a relationship founded on memories now, but it *is* founded. Unhappily, though, these times of reasonableness do not continue very long in Phil and he's soon back to the toothsome quest for heavy coin. It's a continual, irresistible drive in him, like missionary endeavour for chapel folk, or the bowel movements of mice.'

'Does the cape man work for you?'

'I'd love to think Jules drew most of his crucial genes from me, yet I must acknowledge that Phil's treasure ethic may also have been passed on.'

Iris said: 'Cape man followed me from the jewellery stall, did he – and so my address? He must be good. I'm supposed to spot gumshoes, especially someone in that sort of gear.'

'I see it as not really to the point, your interest in Kate, or even Oliver. This is no route to the money. What I meant about your being young.'

'I might not be concerned about the money.'

'What I meant about your being young.'

'It's not necessarily naïve to think of other things than money,' Iris replied. 'I see life as a complexity. That's mature. I've an organisation to take care of. It needs me.'

'"Here am I; send me." Who said that?'

'Isaiah. You're shagging cape man in Portugal, are you, and he can help in other matters, too? So, if you don't think Kate and Olly matter why send cape man to watch her?'

'I look at you and am bound to recall Julian at the start of *his* career, aren't I? Pamela replied.

Iris split the last from the cider flagon between them. 'Wish Philip dead how?'

'Ah, I forget you're an expert and would wish to know method. I'll say this, Iris, I wouldn't approve any procedure against my Phil that Julian might not also have approved were he but here to be asked. When I hear Julian's voice now, it is the lisp of a child. There was a sweetness in Julian, not obvious to all, possibly, but a mother can sense these matters. I know Julian would want his daddy wiped out as much as I do, obviously, and wiped out decades ago, though most likely without unnecessary pain.' For a moment, she held up her hand with the glass in it, to repel objections. 'You, in your sharp, practical way, will say this begs important questions, such as, what's unnecessary? A fair cavil. Yes, yes, we have to take into account that he might have located the money, which probably means he has located Lucy McIver, or is in the process of that. This could explain why he hasn't visited you, if you're telling the truth and he hasn't. You would become an irrelevance, and Phil's intense about relevance when it's a cash matter. He is astonishingly clever and it would be within his range to find McIver solo. But the poignant thing about astonishingly clever people is they're always liable to discover information hidden from the rest of us, and then this has to be beaten or burned or enemad out of them by less astonishingly clever people, though in their own style gifted and resolute. In any study of torture – I mean purposeful torture, not just *jeux d'esprit* – yes, all these torture studies show that the proportion of astonishingly clever people given inhuman treatment is astronomical. They have things to say and have to be brought to saying them even though reluctant. You know, there are people who define an intellectual as someone *de factos* hit shit out of. Clearly, I wouldn't call Phil an intellectual any more than I'd call my vibrator intellectual, but he might be too bright for simple, painless extinction. Such a death could be a preposterous waste.'

'Do you like your pal to dress up when you have your fun sessions in Portugal?' Iris asked. 'There's the cape and that brooch. And he bought a really ancient style morning suit. He could play the adoring butler-chauffeur and you the flaking old star in *Sunset Boulevard*.'

'There's some sort of deal between Kate Horton and Abelard,' Pamela replied.

'That why you have your flunkey watching her?'

'Such as Abelard gives them all the deep detail for Olly's book of who did Julian and as reward Abelard is kept out of the grimmest stuff and might be able to hold on to his career and to a share of the funds. It could be a stout share, oh, yes. This is a set-up that's bound to concern me, concern me at the heart, isn't it, Iris? It's not only a matter of how the money is disposed and where. We are also talking about the details of my dear son's slaughter. This is a mother's agony, surely, not to know how her prized boy was annihilated and what happened to the exceptionally meaty funds he had so cheerily built up. Such feelings are exclusive to a mother, which is why I have to keep that slimy, invasive talent, my hubby, away from all possible roads to the gorgeous pension fund. Are you shagging Abelard? Was Kate previously shagging Abelard, or even now? I see life as very layered. As you said, complexity.'

'Cape man heard my little discussion with Kate, did he?'

'I don't see any inescapable reason why someone like Abelard couldn't find someone like you attractive enough,' Pamela Bowling said. 'No, definitely not inescapable.'

'What is someone like Abelard like? What is someone like me like?'

'Or are you playing the two of them along, Abelard and Philip, so you have a double chance of the pile? A woman's body can be adaptable and still stay this side of outright sluttishness.' She looked around Iris's flat, examining the furniture now, not the art. 'Often, I can tell when Phil has been in a room. I can't say how. It's not grey hair on a settee. I do believe in the communicativeness of place, don't you?'

Iris stood and went to the flat's front door. She was ground floor. When she opened up, she expected to see Cape man on duty somewhere outside, possibly in the morning suit. He was not there. From behind her, Pamela called: 'Who is it, damn you, Iris? You're expecting Philip? You want to head him off, don't you, because I'm here? What is it you're hatching? Oh, God, as if I didn't know.'

Chapter 17

Beyond Abelard and Turkey and Roger Link-Mite – that is, above them, commanding them – Iris knew there were, of course, the Minister and the Cabinet. Before this grubby, posturing level, though, and between it and Abelard, Turkey and Link-Mite came Judith Stewart.

Iris was asked to see her in an hour. The summons came face-to-face in Iris's room at the Outfit building, brought by one of Judith's assistants, Alfred Tom Tomes, a fair-quiffed, bonny boy from some ragamuffin school and university in the South West, as Iris had been told, and almost as young as herself. At the training depot while she was there he had still been a legend, for having sweetly measured his effort on all courses to within one or two marks of the pass. They reckoned this showed potential as an unwasteful administrator, and he had moved immediately on graduation to Judith's private office. Front line should have been all right for him, too: if he shot someone, a single bullet would do the job with thrift. He could talk a bit but people said this was all to a purpose, though you might not be able to spot it. Many conversations in the Outfit were like that: shaped to befog, but not pointless.

There were no tales yet that Judith had him, or none reaching Iris. However, on account of his famous ability to identify so accurately what was wanted and come up with precisely that, he might be providing some special closenesses, bed-sweat and verve for her, as well as his tight ship office skills. Quantity-controlled, unleisurely sex might not suit every woman, and especially not a woman like Judith, around fifty and with deep requirements, most probably, but she was certainly very busy on national duties and personal cover-up, so might need strictly to timetable her fucking. Alf Tom lived with his wife and baby girl called Alfreda in a flat in Uxbridge.

'What this proposed confab tells me, Iris, is that Judith may feel confident in you.'

'Well, I'd hope so.'

'Don't imagine trust is standard issue in the Outfit.' He frowned a good, programmed frown. 'Sorry, I'm Dutch-uncling you.'

No, she would not have expected trust to be standard issue, wouldn't have wanted it to be. That wasn't what she had joined for. Iris believed doubt equalled maturity, sophistication. But she said: 'Oh, why?'

The door to her room had been minutely ajar and Alfred Tom stepped in without knocking or even brushing his fingers across it as gesture to her privacy. He had a comradely smile in place, and sat down alongside her at the screen. She had been looking at summaries of the Tomlinson book and its Press coverage. 'Why? Oh, as ever, I suppose – factions,' he said.

'What factions?' She switched off the monitor.

'Conspiracy.'

'What conspiracy?'

'Good.'

'What's good?'

'Your ignorance of it. Apparent ignorance.'

'Which?'

'I'd say *real* ignorance of it. Eighty per cent of me feels your ignorance is true.'

'How much of Judith says it's true, though?'

'I'd guess at least similar, or would she invite you?'

'She might.'

'Well, yes, she might,' Alf Tom replied.

'What's the other twenty per cent?'

'Always there's going to be a margin of suspicion in the Outfit. It's only professional – no more than selfhood. Remember that line in the tv *Smiley's People* when Smiley meets Connie, the retired files room lady from the Service? He reminds her she used to say she wouldn't trust ex-boss Enderby further than she could throw his colleague, Lacon. It's normality.'

Yes, life signs. She was never going to argue. 'Who's conspiring, for God's sake?'

'Good,' Alf Tom replied, beaming. He had the teeth for it, neat, radiant, not horse-big.

'What's good?'

'The genuineness – in your voice. This genuineness sounds *really* genuine. OK, so you could be shagging Abelard. We only say *could* be. That doesn't mean you're inevitably part of a putsch, does it, even if you *are* shagging him?'

'Which we?'

'Judith, myself. Don't fret, we'd never offer it for general discussion among her staff.'

'Kind. She wants to interrogate me now, Alf?'

'I told you – she might think you're OK.'

'Might. I'm in a hazard area?'

'We believe the power of pillow talk can be exaggerated, as a matter of fact. You come into this job from student love affairs, bunk-ups with swap-about partners nightly in grim digs, so, naturally you're going to look for something more satisfactory once you're an Outfit staffer. But the fact you get this kind of enhanced relationship from Abelard—'

'I don't.'

'The fact you're into something grown-up with Abelard is no certain indication you'd scheme against Judith with the rest of them on account of Cadwallader, is it – because she got his job somehow?'

'What putsch?' Iris said. 'Look, Alf, has she got me marked? Judith's a rough lady, isn't she?'

'This with her could easily turn out to be a plus meeting for you, Iris. One way or the other.'

'Which?'

'Which what?'

'One way. Or the other,' Iris replied.

'I see it as in some senses routine, and yet sweetly tailored to you.'

'Tailored in which respect? Dangerous?'

'One-to-one and as far as I know no taping,' Alfred Tom replied. 'Private communion of souls.'

'How far *do* you know?'

'It's not for me to say whether she's got blood on her teeth from previous crises – Cadwallader, for instance – and, in any case, this is a wholly different era now.'

'You're gifted at spelling out what it's not for you to say, aren't you, Alf?'

'All right, so Verdun Cadwallader was great but greatness dims or is forcibly dimmed. Unavoidably forcibly dimmed. For heaven's sake, is it reasonable to upset everything now – I mean *now* – the truly now, the established, current, satisfactory and productive now, *our* now, Iris – can it be reasonable to upset all that because Cadwallader came to a due finale? I understand there was a pay-out to dependants, advantageously weighted, even though his corpse remains unfound. This was largesse. This was decency. In keeping.'

'Do we know who dimmed him?'

'Seminal issues she'd never discuss with me, obviously. That's not my role.'

'What *is*?'

'And yet I'm bound to pick up moods, flavours, tendencies.'

'What are they like, the ones around now? Are we talking about darkness? Will I be walking into it if I go to see her?'

'I like the way you think about every step. You've picked up the mode of the Outfit so fast, if I may say. Why I think this get-together could be an advance for you,' Alf Tom replied.

'Do you, personally, have meetings like this with her?'

'How?'

'One-to-one. Untaped. Tailored to you. Private communion of... well... souls.'

'Inevitably. In the nature of my role.'

'What *is* that?'

'She'll enjoy a talk with you – your bright, endless questions.'

'Which ones *are* the bright ones, Alf?'

'Judith loves being set back momentarily on her heels.'

'Some older women stay remarkably game, osteoporosis notwithstanding.'

'By a bright question. But she'll give at least as good as she gets, obviously.'

'How good *is* it?'

'What?'

'What she gets,' Iris replied.

'She's fond of the to-ing and fro-ing.'

'That right?'

'Of intellectual rejoinders.'

'How much?'

'What?' Alf said.

'To-ing and fro-ing, to-ing and fro-ing.'

'Until a recognisable and definite completion.'

'Ah.'

'The argument resolved.'

'Right. Who?'

'What?'

'Who's conspiring? Or whom does she *think* is conspiring? Are you saying Abelard? Turkey? Link-Mite? And, she suspects... half suspects... a quarter suspects... *me*? Conspiring about what? How? You think they've actually put up Olly to write the book and expose her – to set avengers on her? Or *one* of them has put him up to it? Who? Who do you think? Link-Mite? All the apparent efforts to stop Olly are only that – apparent? He's just a hired hack?'

'Good.'

'What is?'

'The bafflement in your voice. That sounds like *true* bafflement if I've ever heard true bafflement, and I have. Bafflement can be assumed and false, clearly, but your bafflement has the ring of *real* bafflement. Judith can sense something like that, even from her remoteness. The remoteness of leader. Yet a remoteness earned, a leadership earned, by an ability to read the authentic signs, such as, for the moment, your potential bafflement. Judith is eager to tackle the most hellish of puzzles. QED are among her favourite letters.'

'Which others, RIP?'

'She'll have an agenda,' Alfred Tom replied, 'though you might not perceive it.'

'Is there an agenda now, with *you*, Alf, though I can't perceive it? Yet, normally, if there's one thing I'm good at perceiving it's an agenda.'

'I know her mind could not be more open and undogmatic on the issue of whether you shag Abelard.'

'No.'

'She's hardly one to accept speculation from others, no matter how much there is of it, no matter how insistent.'

'Will this be agendad?' Iris replied.

'The possible shagging? As a topic? Her attitude to Abelard is variable.'

'Has he got the drop on her?'

'Drop?'

'Does he know something?' Iris asked.

'You're terrific on the *feel* of things here. She might have in-house blood on her teeth, she might not. Is there any Outfit figure with more than ten years' service one could not say this about? All right, in a few cases metaphorically only.'

'Why ten?'

'OK, four, then.'

'I've always thought of her as extremely genuine – from what I gathered,' Iris said.

'Exactly. Given her looks, could she possibly have made it to head of the Outfit without some roughhousing? You'll probably be the same in, say, twenty years.'

'What will *you* be?'

'So you'll ask, exactly *whose* blood on her teeth.'

'Yes, I will.'

'You're definitely not one easy to scare, Iris,' he replied.

She wanted to say, *Easier, much easier, than you fucking think,* but could not sacrifice her bit of image as cool Iris and kept quiet. Oh, Christ, was this the wrong job for her after all? The blasphemy in her head was only half a blasphemy. She felt suddenly keen on that vicarage career she'd walked away from to the Outfit, and she was *talking* to Christ, *asking* Christ, *praying* to Christ. Did she want to be got out of it?

Alf Tom said: 'My view is she'd be selective – no brutality without an aim. Judith is rightly known for balance. Although the past is not a big factor with her, she would definitely accept that it – that's the past – did occur in some describable though, naturally, debatable form. And in debate she's unbeatable. When she looks at the past she regards it as hers, to formulate as she likes. I'm pretty sure one of her hunches is that you and Abelard were first to find Briers snuffed. This is another of those factors that doesn't necessarily proclaim incontrovertibly you're shagging Abelard – not *necessarily*, not *incontrovertibly* – but you can see why she's alert. If you two are a pair it could be a *little* worrying for Judith. Stupid to deny that. Her degree's excellent, from one of those Scotch places quite a few people have heard of, and she doesn't believe in mental relaxation.'

'Can't you give her anything to provide diversions?'

'What sort of thing?' Alf Tom replied.

'And then she could go refreshed and jolly into a tough, big-wheel meeting, speaking to them with authority, cogently, unafraid. Semen's utterly odourless on the breath, talking of seminal issues. Who's she scared of? She anticipates some revenge thing, a cleansing? The Outfit's has always had its cleansings, hasn't it?'

'Revenge – so bloody romantic, so foreign. A cleansing would suggest Judith's tainted. This would be the damn past reaching out. This would be to give fucking Cadwallader a mythical, saintly status. That's mawkish and extreme. As I understand his character, if he were still about, he's someone who'd probably see the rightness in what happened to him. I don't say fairness or justice – those subjective, poncy terms – but rightness, in the sense of aptness, timeliness.' His eyes were very dark blue, not that Nordic, pale, unnerving, Gestapo shade Iris saw occasionally – Turkey's, for example – but Alf Tom's brightened and glowed now with delight, while he juggled the verbiage in a search for truth as he meant to sell it. Would he send her into Judith's den regardless?

'How *was* Cadwallader wiped out?' Iris said.

'Which is a tale in itself.'

'She's whispered it to you? Tell.'

'I wouldn't dispute there are people who can live all their Outfit career and never slip into an alliance with anyone.'

'I need allies?'

'And I'd never say that because someone is shagging

someone – no matter how heartily and often – I'd never say this is *ipso facto* evidence of a policy alliance. Gross simplification. These are discrete areas.'

'To remove Judith?'

'What?' Alf Tom replied.

'A conspiracy to remove Judith and I might be in it?'

'There's bound to be constant adjustments in an organisation like the Outfit. Judith would recognise that. Stasis is decay.'

'Remove in what sense?' Iris replied. 'Destroy her status through the book? Or more direct, more physical?'

'She certainly does not regard me as a bodyguard. I'm in an outer office, as you know, and do some basic screening, but that doesn't turn me into a bodyguard, for God's sake, does it?'

She's got other people for that? Cedric and his chums?'

'Secretarial wallah, that's me.'

'So, do you carry anything?'

'She sees survival as in some ways its own justification,' Alf Tom replied. 'In many ways. Doesn't it imply backing, approval? I'd certainly go along with this, myself. What's Darwin about if not that? There was a song my father used to sing to the *Auld Lang Syne* tune: "We're here because we're here because, we're here because we're here," and so on till drowsiness did him.'

When Iris arrived upstairs for the Judith Stewart meeting, Alfred Tom was back in the outer office, screening. He stood from his desk and pushed out both hands to show four pairs of fingers crossed for Iris: no other formalities. She'd had three pees since Alf Tom summoned her. She went in alone to talk to Judith. 'Iris! A treat to see you,' she cried. I want you to help me in a little thing, would you? Would you?'

'Well, certainly.'

'Wait to know what it is.'

'I know it will be fine,' Iris said.

'Brill. Eric Knotte, our number three in Operational Supplies, and on-site poet – piss poor poet, but on-site – is retiring. We need to give him a send-off do. Although he'll bring that creepy woman of his, we must show warmth. Can you help me organise things – flowers, a band, catering, that kind of carry-on?'

'Of course.'

'Grand.'

'Is that—?'

'Would you tell Alf Tom on the way out – crazy fucking name, yes? – like, *Monosyllabically yours* – would you tell him we've fixed everything together? At first, I was going to ask *him* to handle it with me, but he gets all blubbery and inept at partings, so I haven't spoken. This is the other side of his little coin. He can be so brilliantly controlled and shrewd in dealing with an organisation – any organisation, probably, but especially this one – yet if he has to witness some break-off from it – some abandonment of it, in his view – even when it's a lad full of years and tiredness like useless, versifying arsehole Eric – when this occurs, Alf Tom sees it as the potential collapse of the system he has learned to play so cleverly, and goes into bereft collapse himself, sad prick, feeling uncontexed, orphaned. Thanks, Iris. Not carnations. Those buggers are for wreaths.'

'Is that—?'

'Thanks, Iris.'

Chapter 18

This was a fucking nothing meeting, an insult, and being nothing and an insult, it transformed Iris. She must save the Outfit. Who else would, could? Yes, the Outfit *must* survive. She felt sure she could smell some vast, approaching international crisis which would make Intelligence agencies very necessary, even very fashionable again, not treated as obsolete cliques to be relegated, starved of money, ignored. She could not say where this feeling came from, but it was strong and she believed in it. That glib analysis Turkey spouted now and then – 'A man's enemies are the men of his own house' – that wasn't the whole tale, was it? There were *real* enemies about. Any day they might move.

Iris respected her hunches. In Theology she had felt a happy bond with the Old Testament prophets. They'd had their hunches, too. Why shouldn't prophesying powers still exist? For instance, she'd often get fierce intimations about the terrorism factor and its impact on the next few years. Months? Did the West worry enough? Oh, Britain knew about Northern Ireland violence, of course. But what about terrorism as a wider concept – global? Take the revival of kamikaze tactics – suicide attacks. Shouldn't we be more scared? At least two outrages already: US embassies in Nairobi and Dar es Salaam. What if they turned out to be comparatively miniature, sort of rehearsals only?

She might need a pistol to back her project, to make her project work, in fact. But use of a gun was a distant, distant possibility, surely. Surely. A possibility. A likelihood? As it happened, Eric Knotte ran the gun department. She would not get one officially from him, though. Iris had no statable reason for drawing one. In any case, she was not Firearms Authorised. Just the same, she would go down and see Eric. The leaving party provided an excuse, didn't it? Her sudden certainty that she had a unique, enormous task thrilled Iris, caused her to gasp. She must find *someone* to brief her on how to come by a piece. Newspapers said it was easy. In the Outfit you soon learned that not everything had to be official. Or not most things. Or not most things that mattered.

Is that all? At the idiotic, three-minute tête-à-tête-with Judith, Iris twice tried to complete her question when she heard why she'd been summoned. Each time, it was squashed. *Is that all, you dozy, contemptuous, autocratic bitch? Is that all?* Afterwards, telling Alf Tom in the outer office what Judith had wanted, Iris felt grossly shamed, even though this piffling job was supposed to put her one move up on him. He looked amazed at how fast Judith threw her out. If she was having him on a steady basis he might feel this earned him insights, the naïve prat. He obviously had had no hint of why Judith wanted to see her. Perhaps if the private session had been longer, he'd have suspected Iris was giving him some rapidly concocted, feeble cover tale, to hide the true orders. But she could tell he believed her, took it as shocking but absolutely credible, and this only plumped up her resentment. She had expected an inquisition about the deepest Outfit issues: her own integrity, Abelard's, the integrity of others. Instead, this sodding dogsbody catering chore. Flower-arranging duty. Didn't she rate as serious, as someone possibly damn dangerous, or as possibly a mighty bulwark, the Preserver, the seven Samurai in one? She *wasn't* a lady vicar, even if degrading, panicky moments came occasionally when she wanted to be. Aberrations. She kept the big-frame spectacles only to disguise electricity.

Always, Iris had regarded the obliqueness and evasiveness and dark subtleties of the Outfit as fascinating, and so admirably right for the work. Now, though, she felt they had been used against herself, forcibly, dismissively, and it enraged her. Judith must have known Iris was expecting something epic from this head-to-head, and handed her instead a silly fragment. It would have unnerved Iris as well as angered her, if she had allowed herself to be unnerved. She didn't hold with that, at least when she could prevent it. Of course, there were occasions earlier when she had been made to feel insignificant: a novice. But the humiliation today was so much worse than that rigmarole she'd been put through with the Olly Horton 'profile' – a profile nobody wanted. Ultimately, it could be handy, though. She'd picked up a lot about the Horton household and their habits, as well as the layout of the flat.

Iris knew she must assert herself, as she had asserted herself by tailing the Horton woman and focusing on Briers. Now, the compulsion was more powerful. She had come to sense that all the obliqueness and evasiveness and dark subtleties of the Outfit might be *too* damn subtle – subtle enough to strangle everyone if she didn't do some sorting out. Incredible, but splinters of that notorious, foolish British smugness from a *Rule Britannia* era lingered. Things went on – seemed to go on – as if they had a right to go on and always would. The Outfit preoccupied itself with the ducky, benign, routine affairs of... of the Outfit, never mind the world. Eric Knotte, a faded staffer was leaving, so let's call up tradition and give the old deadbeat a rave wave-off. Splendid! The right thing.

But outside there were Olly and Kate working away, scheming away, sniffing away, aiming to injure the Outfit, perhaps annihilate it, for money and kudos and sheer bloody career malevolence. Conceivably they had help from insiders. Conceivably they were only the instruments of insiders. *That* bit of the theory about a man's enemies being part of the household might be right. But the point was, this country needed the Outfit to continue, and continue as it was, unharmed, because of vast, diabolical enemies outside. *Iris* needed the Outfit to continue, and continue as it was, unharmed. She functioned here, could thrive here. It was her only milieu. Somebody had to protect it. Protecting it, she would protect herself.

She must get some introductory chit-chat ready to ease things along with Eric. Turn crafty. God, but the selection board who took her on had been smart to see this ex-theologian was the Outfit's future. She knew how she must have looked to them – like an amiable, woolly very kiddish kid, boringly encyclopaedic on the book of *Romans*, goofily mild behind what the Horton woman called Iris's Billy Bunter specs. They'd been able to spot potential, though. They saw loyalty, leadership, volcanic energy. Judith was on that board. So, why hadn't this smartness and perception continued? Didn't people like Judith realise now how near to catastrophe the Outfit was, either from political blindness and Treasury meanness, or the plain malice of its native enemies? Iris had not ditched Theology and consented to join this team to watch it die. If any dying was necessary, it would be outside the Outfit – perhaps... perhaps, someone who had once been *inside*, but no longer. This seemed to her an elementary proposition, yet who else understood it? What had the fuckers been eating or drinking or sniffing to dim them down like this? Eric Knotte had been on that selection panel, too.

However, definitely no chance of an armoury weapon, although Iris was range-trained and good at it. Eric would certainly refuse to supply Iris, never mind she was chief assistant – only assistant – on his valediction. And he would probably let it be known upwards that she had formally asked for something, if she was stupid and did. She wouldn't. Another area where she must act solo. All right. Initiative: hadn't they told her she'd need to show some?

Iris found that her instinct to offer protection, guardianship, was shifting from Abelard and towards the organisation Abelard belonged to, as she did. She yearned to believe they were more or less the same, Abelard and the Outfit: felt repelled by the notion he could be a destructive conspirator. Destroying Judith would probably be all right, but the Outfit might be brought down with her. This was how the Hortons' objective looked to her. And it was the Outfit that ranked highest now for Iris, as needing her brilliant care. Surely, Horton and his anarchic wife had to be stopped, really stopped. Some pistols were described bluntly like this in the handbooks: 'real stoppers'. Was Iris the only one to see that Olly, possibly both Hortons, might have to be fully neutralised in the long run? Kate could be the main, thinking, theorising, maverick source there, twisted, hellbent. How long was the long run?

Who, who, truly saw how things were, other than Iris, herself? This certainty of her uniqueness she did not regard as pride. Simply, she brought fresh perceptions, natural in someone young – a generational feature, nothing greater than that. And yet... yet... yes... great for its very ordinariness, for the spontaneous, bold, uncompromising strength of youth. She remembered a poem by Rupert Brooke that used to get mocked by people at university. Almost everything by Brooke got mocked at Oxford, and not just because he went to Cambridge: mocked for martial naffness and his versifier's mane. 'Now God be thanked who has matched us with His hour, And caught our youth, and wakened us from sleeping,' the first lines went, probably about the start of the Great War. She liked it as spot-on for her, today, though. Didn't it hit what she felt, except there was no 'us', no army, only Iris to be matched with the Outfit's bad hour. She could handle things, *would* handle things. Now and then it was uncomfortable to have such a totally clear idea of what had to be righted, and such an unwavering sense of destiny. But she must embrace these responsibilities, she knew that. They were her being. She gloried in them.

The feelings touched her hormones, and she was not surprised. As happened occasionally when something like inspiration jogged Iris, she found herself longing to make love in celebration: not make love with just anyone, though – just anyone ungrotesque, not too old and reasonably competent at it, and not Alf Tom. Sharing with Judith was out. While doing the Theology degree, Iris used to get these fine body surges occasionally if a slab of the Scriptures seemed all at once to speak right out to her, personally – for instance, something from the book of *Ruth* or especially *Romans*. Undergraduate friends used to describe this hotting up as 'Iris's divine afflalust.' Of course, there were a few ungrotesque, not too old and reasonably-competent-at-it men around her then, students and dons and locals in pubs. The Billy Bunter specs didn't put everyone off. Although Iris thought 'looseness' was not a charge that should be made against any woman in the current freed-up social and sexual era, if there had been such a category as loose woman nowadays, she would certainly never proclaim that her own looseness was a continuous, unmixed boon and OK for every woman regardless. But the point was, in Iris's case it could harmonise with other bright feelings and often helped round them off pleasantly. She did like to fix a pattern on to life and create a theme. Love-making seemed to contribute well to this if it could be got at just the right time and had quality.

Iris went downstairs to see Eric Knotte. Eric was nice, ungrotesque and possibly competent, though too old. Iris didn't feel pedantic about age but thought forty eight her top limit for the next two or three years. She had lately adjusted the figure up from forty because of the possibility of Abelard, if he *was* a possiblity. As she went towards thirty,

she would most probably come to regard early- or even mid-
fifties for men as OK. Not yet. Of course, the French said
about love, 'il n'y a pas d'âge, but go try and sell that in a
Rest Home. Approaching Eric's realm, Iris wondered
whether he knew he was leaving. In the Outfit under Judith
farewell parties were sometimes arranged ahead of
notification to their stars.

'Eric,' she said, 'wonderful, exactly the man I need.'

'You sure?'

'Sure. Two phrases, poetic, keep niggling me for
identification but I can't trace them, not even through the Net.
Then I thought, Eric will know, Eric poet and poetry scholar.
So, here they are: "wakened us from sleeping" and then the
rhyme, "into cleanness leaping."'

'Oh, Brooke.'

'Rupert?'

'There's another? What are you *really* here for, Iris?'

'Knowing it right off like that! You're marvellous.'

'I'm fifty-two, Iris.'

'Yes?'

'I hear you're helping Judith grease the slope for my exit.'

'But people here are always going to remember you, Eric.
Everyone admires the way you reorganised the armoury. Look
– a digression – i've often wondered what happens to weapons
that—'

He began to recite. Although physically slight and delicate-
featured, Eric had a voice grand in depth and passion and it
ricocheted around his little room off monitors and cabinets
and the corner wall safe. He had stood up.

'Now, God be thanked Who has matched us with His hour,
And caught our youth, and wakened us from sleeping,
With hand made sure, clear eye, and sharpened power,
To turn, as swimmers into cleanness leaping—'

'Spot on,' Iris said.

'Etcetera. Called *Peace*. Ironic. Written 1914, the year war's declared, and written *because* war's declared. Brooke believed he could only reach peace – spiritual peace – by being brave and noble and self-sacrificial on active service. He thinks he's going to leap into cleanness – ie, enlist – cleanness being for him the gallantry and fulfilment possible only in battle. Rugby school and others like it taught them this – that actual peace was an inferior state, akin to torpor and compliance. Classical, probably. But kamikazi pilots in the Second War and suicide attackers now – same belief. The poem finishes, "And the worst friend and enemy is but Death." See what I mean? You agree with her I must go?'

'You'll be glad to get clear of all the Outfit's episodes of stress and malice, Eric.'

'No.' After the poetry, his voice had fallen to normal, but it sounded very definite, very hurt, almost an injured snarl. The tone seemed wrong for his neat, friendly features. He had a small, fair, moustache, unwarrior-like, placatory. Of course, since Eliot and Larkin poets were inclined to look clerky, possibly even poets running arsenals.

'Don't want retirement? You can write more, read more,' she replied.

'I've still so much to do here. Iris, tell me, will I have to listen to that malign hag say in a speech how indispensable I've been, though stuck at Number Three – *oh, yes, absolutely invaluable and loyal and constructive, so cheerio, Eric. Piss off now, would you?*'

'I mean, your creation – your own creation – of a proper system for upgrading, updating, weapons. There must be many declared obsolete. A disposal problem? But that was such an achievement, the re-shaping. Before I arrived, yet I hear of it all the time. I gather things were almost chaotic previously.'

Moving across the room, he stood near the safe, as if ready

to defend it with full, puny might. He was in a brown tweed
suit and woven tie. He gave a little grunt. Eric was known for
grunts, when he disagreed with something. 'Elementary. It was
obvious what needed doing, but nobody had bothered. I've
not finished yet.'

Iris said: 'Yes, I do wonder sometimes what happens to all
the arms you declare outmoded. It must be a running
complication, Eric.'

He gave her a short stare. Iris sensed she had been wrong
to tack his name on the end. It made her sound as if she was
creeping to him. She didn't want that, because she was. 'Oh,
they're destroyed,' he replied. 'Things weren't always so, but I
insisted, made this a condition of staying on in Operational
Supplies.'

'All destroyed?'

'All. As I saw it, see it, you couldn't have weapons once
used by Outfit people circulating on the open market, for
heaven's sake – used either for training or operationally.
Consider if one of them were fired in a robbery and traced
back, the possible publicity complications. They used to be
sold off – to very reputable gun dealers, yes, but who could
tell what might happen to them after that? There was the
inconvenient prospect that anyone could go down to a
London villain pub – say the Page Dale or the Sauter – and
buy a gun that was once the Outfit's.'

'It's on account of changes like these you'll be remembered,
for as long as the Outfit exists.' Iris said.

'Only that long?' Grunt. 'I don't *want* to be remembered. I
want to be here. I'm fifty-two, fifty-two, not much older than
her. I've a *right* to be here. She decides no, I haven't – maybe
on account of some piece of politics or self-protection I don't
understand. How the hell could I harm her? Who can?'

'What kind of music?'

'What?'

'I've got to arrange a band.'

'Listen, a word, Iris. We're secure here. I've made sure this room's unbuggable, except by me. What you'd expect. But, yes, a word. Tell me, dear, you shagging Abelard? There's a buzz. She won't like that. It's not jealousy. I don't hear she's doing anything there herself. But she doesn't trust Abelard. Is scared of him. You could cop collateral damage if she acts, and she *does* act. Ask Verdun Cadwallader, except you're too late. You might not even get a leaving party. I worry for you.' He grunted again and sat down at one of the screens and seemed about to resume work. 'But possibly you realise all this. Of course you do. You see things. You'll know you have to look after yourself. Forgive me for intruding and for presuming to give advice. Is this why you're interested in a second hand weapon? Digression! All the lead-in poetry crap! Careful. The pub names are genuine. I considered you deserved that, in view of how things are. I know it's not you who's chucking me out. You can't countermand what she says, can you? Hardly. It might be a third- or fourth-hand gun. You never know where they've been, Iris. That's the first thing to learn about any used firearm. Sorry, I grow teachy again. Perhaps it's this tone of voice that's upset her. I could avoid it, honestly.' He sounded suddenly weepy, abject.

During training there had been test exercises which involved entering an unfamiliar pub and coming away before closing time with very detailed, very personal information jemmied and/or charmed out of one or two customers never encountered before. It had been tough but possible. In the Page Dale and later the Sauter she saw quickly that what she hoped to do was most likely *not* possible. Both places were crowded in the evenings, and she thought she could identify the villain clientele Eric had mentioned, but believed she saw a lot of ordinary local-boozer customers, also. Although there might be overlaps, Iris judged the two types to be pretty separate, and her problem was how to move from one group to the other. She, of course, was in the respectable, out-on-the-town-for-drinkies set. In each pub, what she took to be the heavies were notable for their good clothes – the men and the women – their heaviness – the men only – and their unpeacable faces – the men and the women. She had abandoned the Page Dale after a couple of solitary rum and blacks.

But in the Sauter at least one of these unpeacable faces looked attractive in its unpeacable way. As Eric and Rupert Brooke had said, peace was a variable item. Iris had the remains of two desires on the go and she wondered now if she could resurrect and combine them. He seemed to be of what she had decided was the crook style and yet stood at the bar alone, about twenty-eight, so nowhere near too old, exceptionally ungrotesque, and probably very competent. She put herself alongside him and said: 'Hi, you know, you might be able to help. I want to buy something.'

He glanced at her and gave a reasonably civil smile but didn't speak.

'You know? Buy something.'

'Buy what? A drink? Am I in your way?' He shifted a couple of inches along the bar, although there was plenty of space for her.

'I've got a drink,' Iris replied.

'Right.'

'But buy something.'

'What?'

'The fact is, I heard a whisper about this pub. Do you know what I mean when I say a whisper?'

'What are you – the police? I wouldn't push too hard in here, if I were you. It's a nice pub, but has its own... like... climate.'

'A whisper, and so I came to buy something.'

'What? I'm in terrazzo flooring.'

'Cement, terrazzo flooring, scrap metal – I know something like that's necessary as a—'

'Just terrazzo.'

'OK. But if I wanted to *buy* something – say something out of the ordinary, scarce? Cash, obviously. Something *out of the ordinary?*'

She considered winking but felt this would be crude.

'You shouldn't be in the Sauter with a load of cash on you, you know.'

'It's not something I could buy with a cheque, is it, or a credit card?'

A burly, cheery-looking man in waistcoat and dark trousers approached behind the bar. He might be the landlord, perhaps forty-eight or even forty-seven. She did not have any categorical feelings against waistcoats. 'Now, girl, I can't have you working here,' he said.

'Oh, I'm not working,' Iris replied.

'Love the enormous specs,' he said. 'That's original. You aim to look the studious kind? I don't mind a girl coming for a sit down and a drink, but I won't have you working the bar. You new? It bothers customers.'

'We're talking, that's all. Look, I want to buy something,' Iris said.

'Buy some terrazzo from Graham? What would you be doing with terrazzo, girl? Is business so good you've got a palace?'

'No, *buy* something,' she replied.

'Look, love, what's your name?' the landlord said. He angled his body to exclude terrazzo man for a minute, leaned forward and spoke quietly. 'Where do I find you after closing time, say about midnight? I get out for a bit of a change then. Yes, a bit of a change.'

She went and sat down at a table. The presumption she

was whoring knocked all the sex out of her for now, though she liked what he'd said about her glasses. The appetite for a gun was sinking, too. The difficulties had become too big. Perhaps the rum had begun to strangle her determination. A man said very sotto: 'Miss, excuse me for butting in, won't you, but I heard you might be searching for something.' She looked up and saw Eric Knotte. He sat down with her at the table, occasionally swigging direct from a bottle of beer. For a night out pubbing he was in a sports jacket and open-necked navy blue shirt. He looked like someone who usually wore a brown suit and rural enterprises tie but put on a sports jacket and open-necked navy blue shirt for pubbing, and drank straight from the bottle.

'Oh, God, Eric, you knew I'd be here?'

'Or at the Page Dale.'

'It's hopeless.'

'Of course it's hopeless. You need a few years' cred.'

'Have *you* got cred?'

'I've got a gun – a phased-out but perfect Walther automatic that was left over from one of the destruction programmes. Somehow, it happens occasionally, despite my exemplary vigilance. Unused. Not traceable. Not mentionable by me. I think you should have it.'

'Why?'

'I think you should. Perhaps you deserve it.'

'You're always telling me I deserve things. A proper deal, then. Payment.'

'Call it a deal: just inform and persuade the lady – persuade, persuade, please – persuade her that I want no bloody leaving do. I'll just go, disappear, like Captain Oates. Send on the re-dundough and pension papers and illuminated address.'

'But, Eric—'

'Inform and persuade her, all right? You can do it. You're the future.'

'But do they all realise that?'

With nearly authentic yobishness Eric tipped more ale into himself. 'Put you handbag under the table,' he said.

Soon afterwards he left, brisk in the jacket. Luckily, it must have good big pockets. Perhaps that was why he put it on, not just as a night out uniform. She liked the weight of her handbag now. This enhanced her. That gorgeous high-thigh excitement took hold of Iris again. She returned her rum glass to the bar. 'Left out of here and on the corner,' she told the landlord. 'What sort of car?'

'I knew you were an intellectual and would recognise another,' he said. 'Saab.'

Chapter 19

In line with her new cover role, Iris had to take £60 in unfolded tens from the landlord and a bottle of rum. The money felt like till cash, tightly packed, as if it had been under a spring clip not long ago. She did not say this because it might seem too observant for a standard girl about the place and footling, anyway: money for a bang was money and who cared where it came from? Iris had been trained to notice the seemingly incidental, even when it *was* incidental, and useless. The landlord would be remembered as the only man who asked her to keep her glasses on during, regardless of the bumping about. This was an intelligentsia screw. He ran his hands gently and lovingly over the arms and ear- fastenings of the spectacles as if they were sweet body nooks, or decent jewellery he meant to snatch. 'There,' he said, huff-and-puff concluding, 'Iris, you put up a damn first class show. You're a real credit to it.'

'To what?'

'A credit.'

'I don't know what you mean when you say "show".'

'As if you were gagging for it, not just crude business. I hardly had time to pull the thing on, girl. As I say, a credit to the game. You were smart to pick me instead of Graham. He's all coiffure.'

'What's crude about business? Pick? I don't pick, do I? I get picked. Instead of? Instead?' She gave this grand bewilderment.

After a couple of seconds he cottoned. 'God, you—?'

'I have to maximize tricks and takings, don't I? Basic to any evening out. Look, there was over an hour's wait before you appeared, sweetheart.' That much was right. She had sat by herself in the Mazda listening and re-listening to the four chapters of the book of *Ruth* on one of her Old Testament tapes for fifty minutes, keeping herself nicely intense and receptive.

'And you gave him the... the groans and scratching and wonderful love-me-do liveliness as well?' he said.

'Comes with the career, don't they?'

'Oh, do they? Protected?'

'I forget now. You're afraid Graham puts it about? I could have guessed he might. Definitely no novice.'

'Forget something like that?'

'You know how it can be.'

'How?'

'The way you said – wild.' She glanced at the nails of her right hand, as though looking for back skin under them.

'How wild?'

'Wild,' Iris replied. The landlord was pleasant enough but she thought some shag angst might give his character roundness.

He drove her back from the patch of riverside copse to the street corner, saying she would always be welcome in the pub as long as she kept things discreet, but not when his wife or Mrs WP Loxton was there. On the way, she opened her bag only minimally to put the money in, so as not to expose the Walther. 'Busy night. You'll have quite a treasure stack in there, then,' he said. Did he want some back to start health insurance?

'Quite a stack.' Her own momentary glimpse of the Walther's grey-blue barrel brought Iris true, satisfying peace. Rupert Brooke was not the only one to seek selfhood and fullness in cordite. Putting the bottle of rum in a shop doorway nearby, she hung about briefly after the landlord dropped her, like a resumption of touting: keep the charade active until he disappeared. From an Italian with exceptional English who said he worked in high-price shoe manufacture she received a very decent offer involving the rest of the night at his four star hotel and what he called "some quite safe, entirely mutually agreed addenda". But she did not want to bind herself for so long, although he was only in his mid-twenties, and pointed him on to another girl along the street a little.

After five minutes Iris picked up the rum and left. Just before reaching the Mazda she unstopped her bottle, paused and drank a short toast to Eric Knotte. Multiple blessings had come to her through him. A Saab of extremely recent registration was quite a prestige vehicle to fuck in the back of, and the surroundings had been urban-bosky and civilised, a tree branch occasionally stroking the window near her head when the breeze strengthened, like a would-be blessing. Location and environment could often set the tone of a rendezvous. This was a spot obviously well known to the landlord as discreet. But apart from these romantic boons, there was also the gun, the rum and the cash. Perhaps she'd get Eric a traditional skills tie out of the sixty, as well as trying to save his job and, in any case, kill the bloody farewell party.

From next evening for a few days, Iris went whenever convenient to watch the Hortons' flat at Paling Yard unobserved, or she hoped unobserved. A compulsion. It seemed to her that before she could act, really act, she had to know whether that terrifying, nauseating rumour, floated, half floated, by Alf Tom, about possible complicity with Olly's book from within the Outfit had anything to it: pointless to remove the Hortons if those controlling the Hortons continued, and possibly continued more powerful. It appalled Iris that Outfit people might co-operate with a project like

Olly's, even initiate it. For the sake of advancement, or malice, or vengeance, or money, or a stew of them all, they would risk the team's obliteration. Or obliteration in its present shape.

As she had told herself earlier, a plot against Judith could be understandable and even holy, but not one against the Outfit itself. Iris realised she might be into very chewy complexities here. If a leader turned out bad, and had in any case gained that leadership by dirty means, were subordinates entitled to get rid of her/him, even if this threatened the outfit/Outfit, s/he led? Was mutiny ever right? Ask Captain Bligh. Ask Captain Queeg of the US *Caine*. Or, come from the other direction and ask those German officers hanged on piano wire after the dud plot against Hitler. Judith wasn't at the top through divine right, as old kings claimed for themselves, but she did hold things together. Were there times when power was its own justification: getting it meant you deserved it? Didn't Kennedy say politics was power? Or was that Mao? *De facto* were a couple of the most ramparted, unarguable words ever. Iris knew she personally would most likely think so if she had a lot of power herself. She meant to have a lot ultimately, or sooner, and use it damn well, 'damn well' signifying, use it in a way to make sure she kept it. But not that only. She wanted to do good. You could not do good, though, unless you squashed the gang trying to push you out. Always there was a gang like that.

To have run an official, properly organised watch on the Horton flat would be easy. You rented somewhere nearby with good views of the property and did everything necessary from behind half closed curtains, with the best electronics for help, visual and aural. But once again Iris was not official. Official? Oh, come on. In fact, what Iris felt determined to expose, destined to expose, was itself perhaps official: the possible arrangement between Olly Horton and, say, Roger Link-Mite and/or Turkey Latham. Even between Olly Horton and Roger,

Turkey and/or Simon Abelard. But, no, Abelard must not be involved. No. No, not Si.

Of course, the training did tell you how to watch alone and without machinery, because one day you might be in a situation where no backup was available quickly enough, and where it would be insecure and possibly nuts to seek the co-operation of neighbours. The trouble was, Olly would know these gambits, too, and probably better, given his experience. For instance, surveillance from a car could be done through the rear window just as well as via the windscreen, and there were convincing statistics to show that a vehicle facing away from the target was less noticeable. Iris had been taught this. Likewise, Olly, though.

Just the same, she did it like that, once she could find street parking at all. Sink in the driving seat, angle the mirrors. Iris did not put *Ruth* on or *Romans* because, obviously, she did not need sexual stoking now. Besides, this was a reasonably quiet street and the sound might carry, especially the last verses of *Ruth* when the reader grew rhetorical with all the begats, leading up to Jesse and David himself. The OT could get OTT.

Last time Iris was here, she had needed to be non-stop ready to follow Kate. That urgency no longer applied. She was not waiting to tail. She wanted to see who called on the Hortons. If you smelled conspiracy, identify the conspirators. She'd brought the Walther. People could get hasty when protecting secrets, and Iris must think about defence. Eric had provided no loose ammunition but a full fifteen-round magazine. Perhaps he thought that handing her a box of bullets would have been too explicit, indelicate. Was it preposterous to think of shooting Turkey Latham or Roger Link-Mite, even to protect herself? Was it preposterous to think of shooting Simon Abelard, even to protect herself? Yes, oh, yes, it might be preposterous to think of shooting Simon Abelard, even to protect herself. Earlier, she had liked to think she felt only a kind of comradeship towards Abelard. That might be changing – *had* changed, hadn't it? She thought she could detect in herself, too, some creeping jealousy of Lucy McIver.

Of course, she realised that as surveillance her scheme was almost all holes. Who needed face-to-face? Anyone could contact the Hortons by phone or fax or email, and Iris wouldn't know. On a true Outfit operation those channels would be monitored. But – to ask again – how the hell could it be a true Outfit operation when the aim might be to nail grand Outfit cardinals? This spying was not continuous: Iris turned up only when her proper duties and the rest of her life allowed. Luckily, one of her duties was to help put Eric Knotte's kick-out party into shape, and she could at least pinch time by ignoring that.

As to the rest of Iris's life, her pub landlord had taken care of the sexual seething pretty well, and she could remain temporarily switched off and concentrate on work, although she did have an occasional curiosity about the Italian boot boy's so-said safe 'addenda'. In sexual things, good addenda, safe or not, could always get to Iris, and when the Italian promised mutual agreement as a condition of *his* addenda, he could not have realised how splendidly mutual Iris's agreement was in such addenda situations. But a complete night would have been too much from her timetable, no matter what the jubilant kinks, or the fee. Now that she had a gun and heartfelt project she needed to stock up energy through sleep. Iris knew about priorities, and sex dropped down the list sometimes – was probably never at the absolute top. Salvation of those in need always held that spot. To be committed to a mission was not always comfortable, yet she would accept, rejoice in it.

Although these sporadic hover sessions at Paling Yard might be inadequate, Iris knew no better tactics. She would have liked more vehicles to vary with her own, but the Outfit pool was extremely unavailable. If Horton came out and asked what she was doing here she might wind down the window and say she'd grown worried about him and decided on a bit of freelance minding. And she *had* grown worried about him. How could a capable brain slip to the extent his had? Perhaps when people were taught duplicity as the core of their trade duplicity became ingrained: a habit, and liable to go in all directions. Perhaps truth became unnatural to them, or merely one of several OK choices. Would Iris get like this eventually? Because she loathed and feared the notion, it had to be wiped out, and all who seemed to embody it. This, surely, was understandable, and helped power Iris's aim to become the Outfit's saviour. Only saviour. Her view was that we had all been born for something, but few had the skill or chance to get to it. She exulted in the way she had seen what was for her and had made the grab.

Iris put a description on to tape of anyone who walked the street while she watched, and especially anyone who called at the Hortons' place, in case… in case what? She was not clear about this and couldn't be. These were pedestrians and visitors on view whom she did not recognise and therefore unimportant for her conspiracy investigation. Or unimportant as far as she could tell. The Hortons would have friends, relations, neighbours, who might visit and know nothing of Olly's book, perhaps not even much about his previous occupation. As she spoke into her mike useless details of a woman with two small children who were admitted to the flat early on the first evening, Iris realised – well, she'd more or less realised it before now – anyway, she realised that this supposed surveillance concerned itself only with those three possible figures: Turkey, Roger, Simon Abelard. She could do nothing about anyone else – not stop them, identify them, interview them.

And what could she do if Turkey, Roger or Simon arrived, or any combination of them? She would work that out at the time, thank you very much. Iris saw her gifts as probably strongest on the impromptu side, though she certainly believed in training. It would be stupid to imagine you could kill someone with a Walther before he killed you, unless you had been on a small arms course and done well at it. Yes, but she recalled once more the part of training which actually and hearteningly said you needed sometimes to get yourself independent of training and act only from instinct – from the instant assessment of an unagendad situation, without cues from any manual or precedent. Great sectors of this career could never be charted in a textbook. Everyone recognised that. Which textbooks could conceivably have chapters on how to deal with stinking treachery by your own chiefs and suggest undetectable ways to annihilate them except, that is, textbooks used at a top-flight business school? Iris believed she knew how to deal with treachery, once she had proved its existence.

She had watched three evenings and into the nights. Twice the Hortons had gone out. She did not follow, convinced an experienced ex-spy like Olly would detect her instantly. Even Kate had presumably worked out she was tailed to the antiques market by Iris and would be alert to company. The Hortons were out together now. Iris saw them leave. They looked untroubled, almost relaxed, and joky and commanding. Perhaps an evening shopping trip. People with money to spend got like this, happy that sales assistants would soon be kow-towing to them and their funds. The Hortons left what looked like a table lamp on in the flat for security.

20.22 hours. Dark. Street lighting, no better than previous evenings. White male, 5' 10" to 11", and once again stuff the metrics. Thirty-five to forty, slim to thin, no hat, balding or close cut, three-buttoned jacket all done up, blue-grey single breasted, roll neck black shirt, navy or black trainers, black lace-up shoes. Approaching along pavement from in front of the Mazda. Other side of street. Observed during occasional glance through windscreen rather than rear window. Hair probably fair, if there were any. Light complexioned, face mildly aquiline, possibly blue eyes. Easy, brisk, maybe athletic walk – his most attractive feature. Doesn't anywhere near compensate for the rest. Missed where he appeared from. Possibly what could be black Omega, part-obscured by other parked vehicles. Passes the Mazda and does not seem to notice me. No?

Watching his back now through mirror. Enters apartment block porch and is soon hidden by mock doric fucking columns and masonry. What do you make of him, Iris? So use those prime and primed instincts. What? Who? Bric-a-brac dealer to see Kate? Drinking and football pal to see Olly? Was Olly into football? Didn't come up during the profile. Police? Doctor?

Iris stopped speaking to the tape and waited for the white male 5' 10" to 11" and stuff the metrics to reappear when he could not get a reply at the Hortons' door. More than one flat had a door in that porch? She didn't think so, but was not certain, and the columns and jutting side walls made it impossible to check, or for her to see white male 5' 10" to 11", if he were still outside. She timed him. After four minutes he had not reappeared.

Iris ran options. He was a commonplace burglar with lock and counter-alarm abilities who had watched Olly and Kate leave, like Iris, and was now among their gear. Or, a burglar, but not commonplace – rather someone with an interest in what Olly was writing, or sent by someone with an interest in what Olly was writing: she thought he looked more like wages than self-employed. Perhaps he had been commissioned to get a look at, take pix of, what Olly would publish. Or he might have been commissioned to lift it: improbable, not worth the risk, because there could be many copies – disk copies, typed copies. Or he could be in the flat waiting for the Hortons to return and catch them unprepared. What did that mean, 'catch'? Yes, what *did* it mean? He looked the sort who would like to catch people unprepared, and had caught people unprepared before this.

Should she get out of the car and stroll nearer, to see whether he was still hanging about, and to check whether after all there was a door to another flat, even other *doors* to other *flats*, that he might have entered? A passage to the rear of the building? Any of these could explain his disappearance. But would it be panic to leave the Mazda now – all that back window concealment abandoned? If the Hortons returned and found her in or about the porch, secrecy was finished. Perhaps no secrecy existed, anyway. Olly might have her and the Mazda noted. She couldn't be sure on this and had to hope the opposite. There would be no doubt she was rumbled, though, should the Hortons discover her on the doorstep.

She stayed in the car, still observing mainly via the mirror, but occasionally glancing forward in case the Hortons appeared from that direction. What would she do if they *did* show – let them go into the flat and face whatever was there to be faced, or decide then that she had to leave the car and give a warning? But she wanted them silenced, removed, didn't she? Why aid them? She thought a while about this. The shape of things had shifted momentarily, hadn't it? Suddenly, the man who might be in the flat was the enemy, the enemy because she did not know him or like how he looked. She felt a duty to take care of Olly. After all, he might have been a colleague. And, if she took care of Olly, she ought to take care of his woman as well. This sense of comradeship would pass, had to pass, but for now was decisive. So, if the Hortons arrived she'd probably do an interception, and insist

on entering with them, Walthered. The explaining afterwards
was likely to be painful. The operation – hers – would be over,
the pistol a waste, unless, of course, she had to use it when
they went in. She felt confused but formed one clear opinion:
it would be better if the Hortons did *not* come back until she
knew what went on.

And this slice of sketchy logic produced another. She saw
that she must go *now*, absolutely now, to find out who the
man in the flat was, and what he wanted. To sit here was a
kind of lazy dereliction. Iris carried the Walther at her waist in
a holster she had made from an old canvas duffle bag, with
loops to fix it on a leather belt. Handicraft she enjoyed and
would never regard as demeaning. She wore a three quarter
length navy reefer jacket to cover the armament. Iris believed
she had been supremely professional. To *buy* a holster for her
unrecorded pistol would be stupid. Gun shop people might
remember such a sale, especially such a sale to a woman. '*To
accommodate a 15-round Walther you say, madam? Certainly.
Just the holster? Madam already has the weapon?*' She
believed Eric when he told her the gun could not be traced.
And he would never be able to disclose its existence, because
he had culpably allowed it to survive. In any case, he had an
alliance with her. She would intercede with Judith, either
about Eric's job or the Get-lost-Eric party. This obsolescent
Walther was the *Quid Pro Quo* model, a binding little gift
between pals.

She put her hand on the door handle, ready to get out. As
she did, she had a last glance forward through the windscreen,
looking for the Hortons' car. No. She did see, though, another
man begin a walk down towards the Mazda and the flat. This
one unquestionably came from the Omega. When Iris first saw
him he was closing the front passenger door. She changed her
mind about getting out of the car and sank in her seat again.
Like the original man, the second would pass the Mazda on

the other side of the street, but she felt more conspicuous now
and kept her voice to a nervy whisper as she talked to the
tape. When she had watched and described the first man he
was just another pedestrian, like a dozen she'd word-painted,
including the woman and children. It was only when he made
for the apartment block porch he became special. This second
man she regarded as special from the start, because of the
Omega, and because Iris sensed immediately he would make
for the flat. She did not know anyone better at sensing than
herself. A gift – nothing else to say. Plus, the second, like the
first one, looked the part. Which part? Some kind of heavy
part which she could not define, but unfriendly to Olly and
Kate. And probably unfriendly to Iris, if he saw her now. She
wondered about lying down out of sight across the front seats.
Fine, as long as he hadn't already noticed her. If he had, any
attempt to hide would proclaim she was running some sort of
smart episode here. Trying to.

*Older. Less fit, but formidable. 200-210 lbs, 6'-6' 2". Say
48, possibly 50. Heavy, almost cumbersome walk. Long dark
overcoat, trilby probably grey, black fashion boots, square
faced, possible thin moustache – grey or mousy – big jaw. Less
fair skinned, maybe. Podgy nose? Broken? Could have a
complete missile defence system under that vast coat.
Mobiling – to/from pathfinder in flat? About Mazda and me?
Class villains, these two?*

But he went on past her car, not looking about very much,
or not seeming to look about very much. People who really
knew how to look about could look about without it ever
becoming noticeable they were looking about because they
never let the looking about get *too* much. He seemed old
enough and seasoned enough to have learned this skill. Iris
picked him up in the mirror. She wanted to pray that he would
keep on going, ignore the flat, as he seemed to have ignored
her, and so prove that he and the Omega were not items in an

operation – that, in fact, there might not be an operation, and even the disappearance of the first man was innocent. But she was against praying as an adjunct to this job. If you wanted prayer join the Church. She had opted for brilliant selfhood, and considered this did not mix with cries to God. Would God have made the second man walk on, if He'd been asked, and also given harmlessness to the first man? Would He?

Anyway, the second man did not walk on but turned into the apartment building porch and disappeared from Iris's view, like the first. Iris would have bet on this, with or without prayer. Bets sprang from judgement. She had it – judgement – and had picked the right career. Now, she felt sure the first man was the locks and alarms expert. He had been sent in to provide reasonably safe access for Brigadier-General Tepee-Overcoat. There was organisation here. Grand. She would take it on.

She left the Mazda. The pavement felt in tune with Iris, and compliant under her shoes. This was a winner walking. She knew it.

Chapter 20

And were they watching her – watching this winner – as she crossed the street from her Mazda towards the flats? And did *they* see a winner? She could understand when people failed to rate her right immediately, though not necessarily forgive it. She tried to look about without seeming to look about, the way *they* might have looked about without seeming to look about when she was in the car. She had two windows of the Horton's flat in her line of vision as she walked. One was lit by the security table lamp, the other dark, its curtains half drawn. She concentrated on this window and the gap in the middle, but hoped it seemed she was not concentrating on anything at all. If they were observing her, she wanted to appear simply like a young woman stepping from her ageing car and unhurriedly crossing the street to make an evening visit to a friend's sick sealyham or a fortune teller. Were they American, these two? Hell, where did that notion come from? She was mystified. Had she noticed something about the clothes or shoes or bearing, without realising it? What? Anyway, *were* they American?

She could have wished both windows were illuminated. She might have had a better chance of spotting anyone watching. But, did these two strike her as dim – dim enough to let themselves glint near a light? There was a fragment of her mind that would like to put, say, seven or eight shots from the Walther into the shady space between those curtains, leaving about half the magazine in case of later snags. Winners behaved like that. It was what made them winners. A blast would really amaze the sods, if they had time to think about it and get into amazement mode before they were mucking up the curtains and walls, and altogether setting up a memorable scene themselves for when the Hortons got home.

She still had that feeling of rightness and commendation coming up from the ground through her shoes. Iris could imagine herself, solid, poised, legs apart for balance, offering an irresistible fusillade to that fucking peep window, from a proper, two-handed grip on the Walther, arms out stiff in front. But this was a public street, for heaven's sake. She could not even walk with the Walther in her hand. Wasn't she playing someone harmless in big specs from an old Mazda? When she reached the porch she would undo the three-quarter-length coat, to make her holster and gun easy to get at. Some people spoke of the comfort of feeling a pistol on the hip, but to her now it seemed distant, not ready enough to meet whatever was concealed by Brigadier General Tepee-Overcoat's tepee overcoat, plus whatever Number One carried. There had been a strong US aspect to the Julian Bowling case, hadn't there: that other dead journalist?

She liked this – the international aspect, if there was one. It gave scope. It deserved her abilities. If silence had not been necessary she would have chuckled at any idea she could be limited to concocting a wave-off for some dear old dead-beat like Eric in a suit. She could not help feeling terrific. Although she still feared the Walther might be too enclosed by clothes – and naturally thought it even more as she came nearer to that window and the porch... all the same, the weight of it against her leg *was* lovely and belligerent, the weapon itself plus its stuffed box. Although the gun barrel stiffly cosseted her thigh, Iris's delight was not sexual, cliché sexual. Instead, she felt enhanced all through. No wonder the tarmac under her shoes gave a good message, said that everything indicated she would soon move to greatness. She must be getting close to Abelard in job aura. She knew this would not make him resentful and jealous, snarlingly unfuckable. He would have recognised from the start her astonishing flair and expect such career speed.

Iris's first recollections of the porch were right, and it contained only one front door. This confirmation set her up further. Her mind was behaving as it should and she had a state of things here she could manage. The door was pushed to, as if shut, but had been jemmied, and jemmied without starting Olly's alarms. There were three locks, including a mortise, and it would have taken even someone very gifted and with a bumper bunch of keys half an hour to get them open by subtlety. A jemmy worked faster. Where was it when Number One went past the Mazda? Up his sleeve? And was one of his pockets full of something electronic or granulated or syrupy to wipe out the alarm?

Iris had to assume now that nobody watched from the dark window. She was close and could make out something of the room behind. It would be a bedroom she thought. There was the shape of perhaps a chest of drawers to the left and further back an open built-in wardrobe, with clothes on hangers. Nothing moved. No head, no eyes, no gleam of metal. If they had seen Iris they would have stopped her, surely, when she paused half hidden from the street in the porch. They might have thought her harmless as she crossed from the Mazda, but by now would see her as an obvious menace. They would act, wouldn't they? She was aware this logic lacked something: they might not want to stop her until she came inside, so that whatever happened to her was completely invisible to passers-by and neighbours. This likelihood she had to ignore, or she would never enter the flat. There were times when logic equalled fright and inertia. Iris could not let herself get crushed like that: if she had wanted logic to run her she'd have become a philosopher. So, it was possible they had not seen her in the car, and it was possible they knew how long Olly and Kate would be away. No need for a sentry, then.

Ambushes: How to mount one; How to resist one; Disposition of forces; Suitable locales; Surprise as core factor. There was always a section headed something like this in terrorism and subversion handbooks Iris had been required to read in training. She wasn't concerned now with how to set one up but how to survive one laid by the enemy. A point made in all these manuals was that occasionally – and perhaps more often than that – occasionally, at least, it would be necessary to accept the risk of ambush if the potential gain seemed big enough. Thus, D-day. But, thus, also, Arnhem and thus, also, the charge of the Light Brigade.

Another decisive point made was, if you foresaw a possible ambush it had already lost its main quality – unexpectedness – and had therefore ceased to be an ambush in the full sense. In fact, if you knew an ambush was waiting and you prepared for it, you would have reversed the conditions and be able to profit from the conditions yourself. You could take over their ambush. It was an opening, an opportunity, a plus.

Yes, Iris would like to believe this, and so made herself believe it. That, also, was how to win. You fitted yourself up with lavish quantities of optimism and then induced the optimism to prove itself right. Ask any football coach. Think positive. Optimism turned itself into fact, sometimes. Slowly, she opened her coat, a kind of ceremonial unveiling of the Walther. She felt an increase in spiritual power, as if from religious ritual. For about twenty seconds, she put her hand on the butt of the gun. This added even more to her strength. She did not draw the pistol yet. Training said that if you flourished a gun you were possibly creating a gun scenario and might provoke unnecessary retaliation. British police used to believe this, though the theory was slipping, because so many villain guns existed that provocation had become unimportant. Anyway, Iris did just a bit of touchy-feely on the Walther, sucked what inspiration and magic she could from its metal, then pushed the ruined door back a couple of feet and edged around it into the flat's little hallway.

She had been here before, of course, for the profile visit. Kate, with her antiques knowledge, probably oversaw the furniture and décor. She seemed to like Edwardian. Against a wall just inside the front door was a delicate looking mahogany cabinet for sheet music. It stood on slender legs and the four drawers were each decorated with a string of painted flowers. Styles had lightened up towards the end of Victoria and become really airy and pretty in the first decade and more of the twentieth century. The cabinet would be from that period. It looked the kind of piece that could get irreparably ruptured in a rough house, the legs made with nice soirées in mind, not designed to prop some thug broken up by bullets collapsing on it. Iris had to think of others getting broken up by bullets, not herself, or she would have backed out through the front door and slunk to the Mazda. Nobody would know she had chickened. This was a private outing.

It would truly pain her to smash a sweet piece like the music cabinet while personally sagging down into death. Although she did not believe any death could ever be dignified, and especially not a violent death, she would regard it as total farce to squash and spread-eagle an elegant item around which people might once have sung fine hymns and madrigals on family evenings, while content with Edward VII or George V. There would be symbolism in that kind of destruction. She believed she was in a career meant to preserve excellent British creations, not fucking flatten them. Three vivid framed surreal prints hung in the hall, plenty of dots in valid, well-known colours, perhaps Pollock.

She stood near one of these pictures listening to the whole flat. The room where she talked to Olly last time was on the

left, its door closed. She was not given a tour when she called
then but thought one living-sitting-study room, two
bedrooms, kitchen, utility-room and laundry combined. A
door from the hall was open and she could see the stove,
fridge-freezer and sink unit of the kitchen. The door to the
living-sitting-study room was shut. She stepped quietly across
the hall and stood listening against this door, but very
focussed listening now. Although she picked up no voices she
did hear something – perhaps occasional wary movement,
perhaps things very carefully shifted: no ordinary burglary in
which rooms were trashed. She drew the Walther.

The appearance of this room was fairly strong in her mind:
oblong, about 25 feet by 18 with a bay at the main window
where they had a Pembroke table that served as work-station
for a 15 inch monitor, computer and printer. There were two
red leather chesterfields, a chiffonier-style sideboard and a
rosewood, round meal table with an ornamental fretwork
surround immediately below the dining surface. On the walls,
more modernistic art.

The drill for opening a door when you were armed, and
when you thought people inside might be, also, was to shove
it back hard, then stand out of sight on the side for a couple of
minutes, not framing yourself. Readjust to two hands on the
gun. After a few seconds, if there had been no firing from
inside, or even if there had, you jumped into full view, pistol
out in front, two hand grip again and ready to fire when you
seemed in the least threatened. The theory was that the enemy
would be re-loading or satisfied the threat had been dealt
with.

Well, Iris did not fancy this and never had, even in training.
Too many films and too many tv series showed entry to a
dicey room by such a method. The procedure was known,
known, known. People in a room attacked like that might
hold their fire, or just bang off a couple of token rounds, and

wait for the invader to pop out from the side with the classic two-handed grip, and knock her/him over before the classic two-handed grip could get any actual rounds moving. It always seemed to Iris that this approach chucked away the advantage gained by anticipating an ambush and plotting to up-end their surprise. She preferred the idea of opening the door very softly, uttering a word of warning or two, perhaps with the gun already aimed, and in the event of any disobedient movement, shoot. She considered that to fling the door open like a drug squad raid was theatrical, which might be why she saw so much of it on the screen. For herself, she would go for stealth and slyness always. With her left hand, she gripped the door knob, the Walther pointed ahead at shoulder height in her right.

In fact, the Overcoat had no weaponry at all under all that weighty cloth. This lack might have been what killed him. Iris did a proper, though 'Haste and basic', search of the body, expecting to find an armoury, but did not come across a gun, knife, cosh or even gas canister. Perhaps he was some kind of hired, artisan specialist and knew nothing about heavy work. All the same, he had tried some. In trying, he had got too close to Iris. It was not his role, not catered for. And so, he caught a bullet, caught two.

When she opened the door, she saw the first man, only the first man, on the other side of the room, and with his back to her. He seemed to be busy with three flip-over notebooks which must have lain near the computer or on the printer. It appeared he did not hear the door move. Iris was immediately anxious that she had located only half the crew. Without speaking her warning, she turned to look elsewhere in the room and it was then that the Overcoat came at her from the side, came at her with hands only – all he had – perhaps attempting to drag Iris into the room. His speciality, whatever it was, must have taken him at that stage to a spot in the room near the door and he presumably noticed it start to budge. Maybe he had been looking for a safe or a secret storage place on book shelves or behind pictures. His hands took her on the neck and shoulders and she was knocked askew, and her gun stance and the gun went askew as well.

Possibly the first man, Number One, was primed to react to the standard violent door shove as start of an assault and thought what he heard was it: not *thought*, behaved from instinct. He must have had a silenced pistol ready in front of him where he worked. He spun and fired twice, popping sounds, never expecting Overcoat to act like that, because Overcoat was not scripted to act like that. He was the safe-breaker or hidey-hole diviner, no battler. Overcoat, grappling with Iris, obscured her from the gun more or less completely and took two bullets. His body was hard against hers and she could smell authentic wool from the coat and fading mouthwash on his breath. Iris felt both impacts through his frame and thought afterwards, when she had time to mull, that she was lucky the rounds did not exit and get to her. This was almost point-blank and there'd be good initial velocity to the shots. No overcoat would slow them, best highland wool or not. They must have hit bone. As he fell, he was grabbing at her still, but now for support: no music cabinet in here to slow his tumble and give up the ghost under him as he gave up the ghost. Iris, already destabilised, was pulled down to her knees for a couple of seconds and the Walther knocked right out of her hand by the sinking body.

While she was neutralised like that the first man pushed past her to the door, a revolver in his hand, long barrelled because of the silencer, maybe a Colt, but pointed downwards to the floor, like a declaration of cease fire. He had had enough. Perhaps he thought she was with a party and he would be outnumbered. A girl in glasses on her own – impossible. Perhaps he had never met the Hortons and believed this was Kate and that Olly must be near. Perhaps he saw he had killed someone rare and distinguished, possibly a superior in whatever team they were from. At any rate, the pathfinder wanted escape fast.

By the time Iris had recovered herself and the Walther she heard Number One pull the front door to after him, as though to hinder pursuit, and then a sprint towards the street. Let him go. Her surveillance and intrusion here were private. She had blood on her clothes and possibly on her face and hair and did not want to be in a hue and cry out there, perhaps involving two handguns. She was sure she would look damn formidable, a gifted warrior, and consequently memorable.

She had brought a small flashlight and used it now, part covering the beam with her hand. Overcoat did not have much on him, or not much to be found in a 'Haste and basic' search. She had to get out of here. Olly and Kate might return. All clothing tags had been removed, and she was only guessing that the wool was best Scottish. The black lace-up shoes were Portuguese made. His trouser pockets had a mixture of British and US coins and a part-used packet of British aspirin. There was, of course, no specific identification in anything he carried and no engraving on his fine German watch. His wallet – high grade leather – contained seven hundred US dollars and eighty pounds in tens and twenties. He had no useful tattoos on arm, back, chest, or thigh, only tasteful portraits of old film goddesses: Betty Grable, Carole Landis, Carmen Miranda, with big, merry-making hat, Alice Faye. This must be a video person sold on *That Night In Rio*-type movies from the forties. She could give the flashlights full exposure when it was pointed into his mouth. His dentistry looked extremely good right to the very back. She had read about expensive work done in the USA on the teeth of Martin Amis, the writer, and thought this might be in that class, possibly New York's best.

One of the notebooks had fallen to the floor open during

the activity just now and she picked it up. Perhaps the page on view was what Number One had been studying. She saw and memorised a name, JJ Ovalle, with a Long Island address. Down the page was another name, but one she recognised, and some figures and letters she did not: Charles Tate 3172DL. This was the British journalist friend of Abelard mentioned in Briers' article and killed in an alleged New York road accident, wasn't it? Very alleged. The 3172DL did not look like part of an address, though some house numbering in the States went very high. And DL? Had Tate lived in a Duplex development, divided up according to alphabet letters? Would Tate have needed a work permit, and was this its coding? Mobile number? It obviously was not a conventional telephone listing. Another idea took a hold: cemetery plot? Had Tate been buried in the US? Did Olly mean to do a visit to the grave for some paragraphs in his book? And perhaps a pic.

Coolness was often a thing with Iris. She knew she ought to get out of the Horton flat now, but also knew she had seen one panic exit tonight and must guard against another herself. To get some ice-breaking chat under way on one-night-stands, tattoo lads would sometimes have personal matter – their names, the name of their cabin cruiser, or home town – needled on to their cocks. It was prestige, it was a giggle. She remembered a boy friend at Oxford who was so proud of being able to get the full name of his college, St Edmund Hall, inscribed. Because the search was 'Haste and basic', she had foregone this examination of Overcoat but felt she should do it now, if only to stop herself galloping away in a disgusting, scared rush. A dick scan of someone dead would settle her. She unzipped him and went close, in case any writing were fully plain only on arousal. She fiddled one handed with the skin folds, trying to finger as respectfully as she could, but could spot no message in the torch beam and eventually put him back together and shut the fly. She did not want Overcoat exposed when Kate and Olly got back because such a knowing search would suggest someone with a true professional background. She went to the kitchen and washed her hands. Iris's mother used to discuss all kinds of hygiene matters with her as she grew up.

Returning, she picked up the notebook again and went to the next page. She saw a simple genealogical diagram. It was headed OBITS.

Julian Bowling
d. Home Place, SW3, via Verdun Cadwallader??

who d. chemical vat? silage container? fuel tank?
via Judith Stewart???

to be continued...

There were further entries in this notebook but coded. During training, Iris had been pretty gifted at breaking ciphers, but could do nothing with this, not in the few minutes she allowed herself and with the limited light. Why was the material part in clear, part obscured? Perhaps he considered some of the information so well known that concealment would be idle. Was it?

It seemed mad to try for normality in the room when a man lay bloody there wearing a holed overcoat, but Iris did replace the notebooks. She wished either Overcoat or his partner had spoken, if only to say, 'What a fucking fuck up!' She could have confirmed the accent as US. Was one of them JJ Ovalle? Had they been sent by JJ Ovalle? Iris left. She pulled the broken front door closed, but it would not quite stick now there were no effective locks, and swung back slightly leaving a small gap. At least the Hortons would guess things might not be perfectly OK inside when they saw the torn timber, but were still sure to feel disgruntled on first entering the living room. Luckily, Olly would have been trained in disposals and sprucing up stained furnishings and walls.

BOOK THREE

Chapter 21

Naturally, it had occurred to Abelard that there would be people in the Government or on the back benches or weighty in think-tanks or in major Whitehall jobs who might actually *love* to see Olly Horton's book wreck the Outfit. Possibly they would even offer him help. *Feed our patsy.* Some of these people were suspicious of *all* intelligence gathering bodies and saw them as redundant, despite very unsettling terrorist incidents like the killing of Ahmed Shah Masood the other day, leader of the Afghan opposition. How long before these harsh bits of warfare were aimed against the homelands – that is, Western homelands: the United States, Europe, Britain? Wouldn't there be screams for good security and spying then?

As well as this political and Civil Service hostility, certain hard eminences actually within the Outfit possibly felt that Olly's book would not necessarily lead to the annihilation of the department but to its drastic rejig in which they might get gorgeous leg-ups, even to the very top. Perhaps Olly was getting aid from this direction, also. *Feed our patsy.* Like everyone in Intelligence, commerce and charity work, Abelard fretted and speculated more or less non-stop about conspiracies. His mother had spotted this in him not long ago and quoted those lines from the prophet Micah, her second favourite to Amos, lines also seminal for Turkey Latimer, of course: 'Trust ye not in a friend, put ye not confidence in a guide. A man's enemies are the men of his own house.'

For form's sake Abelard had tried to rebut this, though he was afraid she might be right. 'Ma, Dame Stella Rimington, ex-head of the whole MI5, not just a section, says in a newspaper interview that the only thing badly wrong in John le Carré spy novels was the idea that security services people fight one another, as well as the enemy,' Abelard told her.

'Well, her Dameness would say that, wouldn't she?'

Maybe she would. Abelard decided to drive down right away and do some unofficial night surveillance on the Hortons' flat at Paling Yard, and perhaps find whether they had significant callers: secret, distinguished bearers of bright, privileged advice and info for the book. The crappy deals Olly and Kate had proposed to Abelard perhaps showed that they *expected* special cooperation from within, might even be accustomed to it.

Of course, Abelard realised that to watch the Horton place like this was next to useless. All contact with the Hortons could be by phone, or email or fax. Because he would be acting solo, Abelard had no way to monitor these. Just the same, he would do a lurk. Generally, he detested operating alone, felt right only in a crew. Comradeship warmed him. That might date from childhood: Abelard's father would hymn the sanctities of teamwork. But Simon must do without this now. Occasionally a pavement stint did produce, and in this trade, *occasionally* added up to a very decent return rate.

He parked rear-on to the Horton apartment block and would watch it in the mirror. Surveillance training said this was the least obvious way to run a squint, but Olly would have had that surveillance training and might be sensitive to the backs of cars. Because this was a private jaunt, Abelard could not draw an Outfit vehicle and used his own Cleo. The little car was reasonably new and possibly Olly had never seen him in it. What seemed to be a table lamp shone in one of the windows. The rest of the flat visible to him was dark. He

began to wonder whether the Hortons were out and the lamp
on only to deter burglars. He would be able to see anyone
going in or leaving the flat, though the porch was part-
obscured by baby doric pillars.

Abelard found it easy to list those who wanted the
department obliterated or reconstituted. Many denied the
need today for a secret outfit of the Outfit's kind. The Outfit
was a Cold War item, and the Cold War had been gone so
long. Such hostility to its existence constantly surfaced,
despite Northern Ireland, despite the Middle East and
Afghanistan and Iraq. In any case, these areas required quite
a different kind of espionage and counter-terrorism, didn't
they? Government Ministers asked this kind of question,
MPs asked it, mandarins asked it, editors and leader writers
asked it, letters from St John's Wood and Accrington in the
Guardian asked it. What was this old-fashioned, expensive
network *for*? Even such voices had to concede, of course,
that the need for national security had certainly not
disappeared simply because the Eastern Bloc was no longer a
Bloc and a menace. But they insisted that the new, so called
'asymmetric' war threats – translation: terrorism – required a
different kind of resistance. The art of infiltration had
become impossible, hadn't it, when potential enemies were
so distant and disparate – so 'asymmetric'? What could the
Outfit actually *do*? Once, when gumshoeing was necessary, it
admittedly had some great gumshoes and general heavies.
Hadn't electronic snooping displaced those crude skills? In
democratic countries, shouldn't there be swifter, more
complete, movement towards openness? Weren't the Outfit
and several other Intelligence outfits really from the past,
preoccupied now with their own office wars?

Abelard could not discount these onslaughts as stupid.
Wasn't he here on a street stalk with Outfit colleagues as
potential targets? *A man's enemies are the men of his own*

house. These colleagues would certainly *not* have the same aim as politicians, thinksters and opinion-salesmen: to eliminate the Outfit. But they might long to reconstruct it with themselves in absolute control of the new version. This they would regard merely as natural selection. Change equalled progress as long as the change saw them all right. Turkey Latham and Roger Link-Mite shouted fierce loathing of Olly and his purpose, but – echo, echo – they would, wouldn't they? Abelard wondered about their real thinking. Horton's book might clear a route for one or both of them to more power. So, for the record they might cry: *Olly, you're a cancer.* As a hopeful aside, though, perhaps it was: *Olly, Your health!*

The trouble with surveillance from a car at night was that, although you had the vehicle back-on to the target, you were, of course, head-on and very evident through the windscreen to residents at the other end of the street. They might get uneasy about someone apparently casing the properties and call the police. To avoid this, it was important to drive around a couple of blocks occasionally and if possible find a different parking spot on return. Abelard made one of these little trips now. He arranged it to bring him back from the opposite direction, and for the few seconds available as he drove in front of the apartment block's porch had a fresh viewing angle to the front door. He was passing it now from the hinge side and looking towards the locks. Did he notice something wrong? He thought the door seemed closed, but not firmly closed, as if only casually pulled or pushed to. Wasn't it odd for Kate and Olly to be so careless, especially when they apparently left their guardian lamp burning? Almost anyone with security experience had a key-closed mortise as well as the automatic lock or locks on main doors and, if Kate and Horton were out, they would have engaged the mortise, with the door properly shut. Did Abelard glimpse splintered wood at two points? God, he might have been sitting so sweetly and discreetly in the street while hard things were already underway at the flat.

He parked and walked quickly back towards the porch. Naturally, he was unarmed. He would have had no disclosable, official reason to draw a weapon from Eric Knotte's emporium. Eric was probably still formally correct about such things, although the buzz said he would be ditched by the Outfit soon and felt resentful. When Abelard reached the porch, he stood there for a little while listening. He saw now that the door had been forced and could not be re-shut. Although noise from some of the other flats made it hard to be sure, he decided the Hortons' place was empty. Entering, he did not delay in the hall but went straight to the door leading to what he remembered as the sitting room. Without any safety rigmarole, he opened it. He felt convinced he was alone.

Iris Insole came to see him in his office next afternoon. 'Are we all right?' she asked.

'All right?'

She waved one hand slowly in a circle, pointing upwards. It meant, Room bug-free?

'Of course all right, Iris. Have you been reading Micah?'

'Micah was a good lad. Saw things before his time.'

'What prophets are for.'

'But badly obsessed about internal menace,' she replied and took a chair at the side of his desk. 'I need your help, Simon.'

'This is a team. We look after each other.'

'That right?'

'Have you been reading Micah?' he said.

'It's something really tricky and dark.'

'This is a team. We look after each other. Tricky and dark how?'

'Something that... well, something that just happened out of nowhere,' she said. 'Unexpected.'

'Big?' he asked.

'If not I wouldn't bother you.'

'Right.'

'Eric Knotte,' she said.

'Yes?'

'To be pushed out.'

'Yes, I heard. It's damn bad.'

'I knew you'd be upset, too.'

'You're really troubled about it?' Abelard replied.

'He's got so much to do here yet.'

'Yes, probably.'

'Look, if it wasn't for Eric, I wouldn't know about the Overcoat on Olly's floor.'

'What?'

'You know – the *Overcoat*.'

'Oh, the *Overcoat*.'

'That's it,' she said. 'I'm going to explain about all that. Later.'

'Good. You were peeping when I went to Olly's place last night?'

'Don't imagine *I* shot Overcoat, even if I have got a gun.'

'OK.'

'If you were to speak to Judith Stewart about Eric it would be stronger than coming from me,' she replied. 'I'm just a kid here.'

'Is he fucking you? That why you're bothered?'

'Eric?'

'He's got a way with him. Fetching moustache. Poets always do all right.'

'Too old.'

'Too old for the job?' Abelard asked.

'Not at all. Too old for fucking.'

'Well, yes, I suppose there have to be limits.'

'Not a hell of a lot too old, but too old at this juncture. I don't want to sound ageist,' she replied. 'And I'm not inflexible. Some older men are most likely fine. But not too *much* older.'

'Right.'

'Up in the forties, fine.'

'Right.'

'Listen Simon, I want the Outfit strong and good.'

'Eric got you a gun, did he, and you're grateful?' Abelard replied.

'Would I mention the Overcoat utterly unprompted if I'd shot him?'

'Another person was there, in the flat – but not Olly or Kate?'

'Someone has to be ready to do things for the Outfit,' she said.

'Right.'

'In a sense, to save it from itself. That's how I came to be near when the Overcoat got it. Very near.'

'"Save it from itself" how?'

'Oh, you know.'

'When you say "from itself" – what do—?'

'Or its ex-self,' she replied.

'Olly Horton?'

'Of course Olly Horton. And possibly people in the Outfit helping Olly Horton.'

'So you take a gun provided by Eric down to Olly's place? That it?'

'But unfired.'

'OK.'

'You could save Eric's job, probably, if you *really* spoke to Judith Stewart. You've got leverage there, haven't you? I don't mean sexual. *Leverage.*'

'The gun being – well, for what purpose?' Abelard replied.

'No, I definitely don't think you'd do anything sexual with Judith.' She glanced around the room again and mouthed the next words, no sound, just grand lip configurations: 'Definitely no bugging? You've checked – and checked? I mean, daily?'

'Definitely.'

'I can't see you having it away with Judith, but you could pressure her from what you know,' she said, using her voice again. 'Eric deserves that. In his way he guards the Outfit's soul. That's how I see it. He regards that as his duty.'

'How about you?'

'What?'

'It sounds as though *you'd* like to guard the Outfit's soul.'

'When I talk about people from inside helping Olly Horton, I've got to tell you I considered you,' she replied.

'This gun was for cleaning up, was it – Olly, anyone leaking to Olly? A mission.'

'I don't *want* to think you're part of that.'

'Thanks,' he said.

'If, for instance, you know what happened to Verdun Cadwallader, this means you could lean on her.'

Abelard said: 'Obviously, someone as clever as Eric can secretly save a gun or two from the destruction programme. What model is it?'

'I don't believe any longer that you're part of it – giving stuff to Olly, I mean. I don't *think* I believe that any longer.'

'Thanks.'

'Turkey Latham. Link-Mite. Clear possibles.'

'Plus ammunition?' Abelard replied.

'Do you think it's mad?'

'What?'

'The idea of quelling them.'

'Who?'

'The Hortons. How else to save the Outfit? Is this naïve? I mean, why were *you* there?'

'Where?'

'At the Hortons' place. If I see a car back-on to their porch with somebody aboard working the mirrors, of course I'm going to wonder who it is. I watched you do the circular tour and then go in. You'd noticed the door? Did you do the complete search? The tattoos? No line to identity in them, was there? Was there, Simon? Did I miss anything? I looked between all his toes. But maybe you recognised him. Is this JJ Ovalle? Listen Simon, if I'm on the spot when someone like that gets shot so the body's left on the living room floor – *living* room! – if I'm present for something like that I'm not going to just bugger off, am I? I get out, yes, but not run from the neighbourhood. So, I shift the Mazda off that street, naturally, and then come back and watch from someone's bit of front garden. I'm interested in what happens when the Hortons return. Or perhaps the accomplice will come back. Or there might be other callers. Such as you.'

'Did you wash your hands after messing about with him?' Abelard replied. 'I thought one of the drying up cloths felt as if it had been used not long before as a towel.'

'What about the coded pages? Could you do anything with them?'

'You'd better describe the other one.'

'Are these the same people as did your contact in New York and maybe Briers?' she said. 'They're scared they'll be fingered in the book?'

'I'm wondering whether it's too late to save Eric's job,' Abelard replied. 'I heard the leaving party was already planned.'

'No – no, it's *not* planned. I'm supposed to be in on that, and I'm bloody not doing it. It can all be stopped, Simon, can't it? Can't it? Couldn't you get Alf Tom Tomes in her outer office to threaten to withhold cock if she won't keep Eric? You know – the kind of thing men can have a little chat about and agree on in a decent cause.'

'Alf's the one who never does anything beyond the minimum, isn't he?'

'Get him to do less than the minimum for a while.' She had a document case with her and took a recorder from it. 'This was the one who did the Overcoat and who would have done me.' She ran the tape. Her voice came over, subdued and precise.

20.22 hours. Dark. Street lighting no better than previous evenings. White male, 5 feet 10 or 11 inches, and once again stuff the metrics. Thirty-five to forty, slim to thin, no hat, balding or close cut, three-buttoned jacket all done up, blue-grey single breasted, roll neck black shirt, navy or black trainers, black lace-up shoes. Approaching along pavement from in front of the Mazda. Other side of street. Observed during occasional glance through windscreen rather than rear window. Hair probably fair, if there were any. Light complexioned, face mildly aquiline, possibly blue eyes. Easy, brisk, maybe athletic walk – his most attractive feature. Doesn't anywhere compensate for the rest. Missed where he appeared from. Possibly what could be black Omega, part obscured by other parked vehicles. Passes the Mazda and does not seem to notice me. No?

'Know any white males, Simon?'

Chapter 22

Although, as far as Abelard could tell, Olly Horton did everything so radiantly right over losing the body he still got caught. In a way Abelard felt pleased he *was* caught, of course. It settled things – potentially vast things. But Abelard also sympathised a bit with him. Olly had the bleakest luck on this. Anyone would have been messed up by it, no matter how experienced and fly.

Abelard thought of Horton's behaviour as 'right' because, by the standards of advanced field training, it was. All officers considered liable to meet situations where an awkward corpse or corpses featured were routinely taught the classic procedures for 'Clean riddance' – also sometimes called 'Happy riddance'. Olly had picked one of these for the Overcoat. But the rightness in Olly's case was much more profound than this, wasn't it – more than just the method of deadman disposal? Surely, Oliver's decision to handle the whole thing himself had been wise, even though through dismal mischance he came unstuck. To call 999 merely because the Overcoat was dead on his carpet would have been panic – a contemptible slip from the psychological discipline and secrecy mode inculcated in him and Intelligence people generally: they had an identification now, but Abelard still thought of the body by Iris Insole's label.

The news on Olly started to emerge half an hour after she left Abelard's room following that conversation about Eric and the events at Paling Yard, bright, intrusive kid: had she told Abelard all she saw, though? Alf Tom Tomes came on the internal to say Judith Stewart required an immediate conference in her suite.

'Who's involved?' Abelard said.

'You, as Senior Principal (Personnel), Turkey as ADRC, Roger as fucking Roger, and one's self as water-pourer, note-taker, note-suppressor and time keeper,' Alf Tom replied. 'Plus a guest, I gather.'

'What guest?'

'Judith's pretty jubilant.'

'Will that mean unstinting, celebratory demands on you later, Alf? Jubilant about what?'

'Well, I don't want to anticipate, but I believe she thinks the Horton scare's over – the book and all that.'

'Why?'

'His status and credibility – apparently gone. Publishers and newspapers won't look at him from now on.'

This had been Roger Link-Mite's intent when proposing to, as he called it, *help* the police on Horton. For God's sake, he hadn't really tried that, had he?

'She believes Olly's destroyed himself, perhaps with clever assistance,' Alf Tom said.

The guest turned out to be someone pretty serious from Scotland Yard, though he had not come in response to Roger. This visitor was very slim, about middle height, his fair hair long, almost arty, his hands elegant. He did not look as if he would believe everything you told him, but you felt he would never guffaw outright or ostentatiously lip curl at statements he did *not* believe. He might have been an upper-echelon clairvoyant or a consultant physician with no convictions at all for molesting women *or* men patients. They sat around Judith's nice mahogany conference table. She introduced everyone and said: 'These are my people, Mr Templeton – the people who knew Oliver Horton best when he was with us.'

'Is Olly all right?' Abelard asked.

'Ah, still some comradeship there for you, Mr Abelard?' Templeton asked, his voice amiable.

'Is he all right?' Abelard replied.

Templeton said: 'Is it an advised means of unburdening yourselves of a nuisance cadaver to put it in a stolen car and torch the lot at some remote, hilly, rural spot?'

'When you say "yourselves," whom do you have in mind?' Judith asked.

'Oh, Intelligence units generally,' he replied. That's what I understand. A recognised drill. Can any of you confirm, please?'

'How do you mean, you *understand*?' Turkey asked.

'I've been briefed,' Templeton said.

'By?' Turkey replied.

'You really think we go about making bodies disappear and have an approved way of doing this?' Judith said.

'I wondered,' Templeton replied.

She turned away from him and spoke to the others: 'Oliver Horton and his wife were apparently taken at a wagon burn near a spot called Eglwys Ilan, overlooking Treforest in South Wales,' Judith said. 'Tom Jones country. Residents there are so pissed off by kids immolating stolen vehicles they have vigilante patrols. Olly and Kate were surprised by one of them before the Fiat they'd pinched for the purpose was properly alight.'

'I gather this form of removal is known to you folk as "pyre on wheels",' Templeton said.

It was another training course term.

Contempt seemed to dislocate Link-Mite's bony little face for several seconds so that he did not look like himself, nor like anyone else anyone else would want to look like. The framework appeared to have moved to the left, putting both his eyes over that side, as though they needed to be near each other in a crisis. 'The fucker couldn't get out of that?' he asked. 'Local amateurs and he's nobbled? My God, what kind of oafs are we recruiting now?'

'Mobile phones. There were twenty people there with baseball bats and metal piping within three minutes. Horton and his wife took a thumping,' Templeton said. 'It's dark. Then someone sees the burning car has a passenger on the floor in the back. They pull him out, get flashlights around the bullet holes and call emergency services.'

Link-Mite said: 'He gets taken by a fucking neighbourhood-fucking-watch posse? Thank God the fucker left. And he goes out working with his missus, like an office-cleaning team: *Oh, pass me the Heckler and Koch automatic, dear, would you?* – except he didn't have one. I take it he was unarmed, Templeton, not able to rout the sods? Ponce as he is.'

'Mr Templeton would be interested in anything we can tell him about dear Olly,' Judith said. 'He realises of course that some areas are sensitive.'

'I've got a murder here, Miss Stewart,' Templeton said. 'I can't be inhibited by supposed *sensitive areas*, can I? Attempted disposal of a body in that fashion – a fashion advocated by you people – am I to regard that as a *sensitive area?*'

'Oh, God, God, what would motivate Oliver to kill?' she replied, her voice giving a true shake. Judith's face always seemed to Abelard a lot too higher management, but she was able to soften it slightly now, make her eyes seem capable of tears, though not actually to produce some immediately.

'Mr Templeton, you believe Horton killed this man?' Abelard asked.

'What can he believe but this, Simon?' Judith asked.

'True,' Link-Mite said. 'Terrible.'

Judith would *want* Templeton to believe it, of course. Perhaps she believed it herself. This would really take Olly and his book out of the reckoning. Was that what Alf Tom had meant as basis for her joy? She disguised this joy superbly at present, but they might see some of it when Templeton left.

'No, I don't think Horton or his wife did him,' Templeton said.

'Why?' Link-Mite asked.

'Thank heaven,' Judith replied, relief aglow instantly in her. 'But who?'

'We've been to look at the Hortons' flat,' Templeton said. 'There's a possibility he was shot there. It had been cleaned up, but not absolutely.'

'This is terrible, terrible, for Olly,' Judith said. 'So damning – so damaging, I mean, even if, as you say, Mr Templeton, there is a chance he did not do it.'

'Terrible,' Link-Mite said.

'He claims the body was present when he and his wife returned from an evening out,' Templeton said.

'He blabs, the unprofessional fucker?' Link-Mite said. 'I suppose he told the local police where he used to work and where he lives? Is that how the case comes to the Yard?'

'Actually found in his flat?' Judith asked. 'How can this—?'

'We believe someone else, or more than one, might have been present,' Templeton said.

'How many more?' Judith said. 'You mean people in addition to Olly and Kate?'

'Horton could be telling the truth,' Templeton replied. 'They may genuinely have been out at the time. They are nicely alibied for part of the evening. We have to establish when the death happened.'

'But which people were present?' Judith said.

'Perhaps three – not all at once,' Templeton replied. 'In succession.'

'A break-in gang?' Judith asked.

'We don't know they were acting in concert,' Templeton said.

'Three unconnected people, all at the Horton place within... within what... an hour of each other? Less?' Turkey asked.

'It's possible,' Templeton said.

'Likely?' Turkey said.

'He has some drawing power, hasn't he?' Templeton replied.

'And you believe one of these three killed him?' Turkey asked.

'I know he was writing a book which could have frightened and angered all sorts,' Templeton said.

'The body identified from tattoos among other things,' Judith said. 'He's got Betty Grable in a dress on his back. In a dress! To nostalge about her at all is bad enough, but clothed? And he'd need two mirrors to look properly. Worth the effort?'

Turkey seemed to have gone back to an earlier part of the talk. 'Oh, those dark folklore tales about us do get around, Templeton. Same for you in the police, I expect. Is it really imaginable that we take our people with their fine degrees and general flair and impose a course in killing and cremation?'

Templeton did not answer this, but gave Turkey some special survey.

'An identification?' Abelard asked. 'So, who then? Who in the car? Do we know the steps – how Oliver came to be on a hillside like that with the body.'

Templeton switched the stare. 'Do we?' he replied.

'Alvan Charles Mindo,' Judith said, reading from a print-out. 'A considerable, middle-level New York villain, specialising in safes and counter surveillance.'

'US police say he was in the team of a JJ Ovalle,' Templeton said.

'We've heard of him, haven't we?' Abelard replied. 'Drugs?'

'Oliver worked direct to our RCV Latimer, Assistant

Director, Research and Co-ordination,' Judith said. 'He can tell you best about him.'

'A good officer,' Turkey said. 'Experienced, steady, loyal.'

'He left,' Templeton replied.

'Oliver had other ambitions,' Turkey said. 'We recruit multi-gifted folk. Occasionally, one of them will feel he or, indeed, she, would like to exercise a different batch of talents from those relevant to us.'

'Wounds where?' Abelard asked.

'Chest, both,' Templeton said.

'Do we know for certain where it happened?' Abelard said.

'Do we?' Templeton answered.

'You say *possibly* their flat,' Abelard said.

'Most likely.'

'This is Paling Yard?' Abelard asked.

'Door jemmied. Blood traces, despite the clean-up.'

'Jemmied?' Abelard said. 'My God, crude.'

'Spent rounds?' Turkey asked.

'Would possible revelations in his book upset JJ Ovalle?' Templeton said.

'Officers of Horton's calibre are encouraged to follow their own inquiry lines,' Turkey said. 'It's possible he ran across Ovalle and might have something about him in the book.'

'Wouldn't it be logged somewhere if he'd met Ovalle?' Templeton asked.

'Not unless Horton found something substantive, or potentially substantive,' Turkey said.

'And would a book like Horton's upset some of *you* people?' Templeton asked.

Judith said: 'I think we're rather used to them by now. We needn't fret.' She chuckled. 'No, I don't believe we can help you on motive in that respect, Mr Templeton. Oliver has gone from us, yes, but he would know the limits of disclosure. These scripts are submitted for vetting. And I'm sure his loyalties are still active. There are now plenty of comfortable precedents for such books. Dame Stella's reminiscences caused some pre-publication angst it's true, but I they turn out to be responsible, tactful – damn dull. I hear they're quite touching and extremely exhaustive about the agonies of single parenthood when having to turn up at the office or contact points every day.'

Alf Tom Tomes showed Templeton out. When Alf came back, Judith told him: 'I loved the way you did that. No triumphalism. An absolute absence of such grossness.'

He bowed a little to her, the movement seeming altogether free from jokiness or irony: 'Thank you, Judith. Triumphalism? I'd really like to think triumphalism would never taint my behaviour.'

'This was a supremely beautiful operation against Olly,' Judith replied. 'I don't know which of you originated it, or in what combination, and I don't wish to. Subtle. Devastating. Opportunist in the most delightful sense. Olly could see some jail. Where's his research then? More than that – where's his status now? In the media when this comes out he's going to appear as a possible killer who tries to destroy a body.'

'And fucks it up,' Link-Mite said.

'Do you think Olly *did* kill him?' Abelard asked.

'Of course not, of course not,' Judith replied. 'That would be to diminish you lads, wouldn't it – at least one or some of you. I regard this as a wonderful piece of in-house scheming. I can see you possibly carrying it out, Simon, or you Alf, or you Turkey, or you, Roger. Or any permutation of you. Brill. One of you, two of you, three of you, all four of you, saw to Mindo's death, yes? He was turning out a nuisance to one of you, two of you, three of you, four of you, was he? *You'd* have a particular grievance against Ovalle and his followers, wouldn't you, Simon? I won't dig further, though. So, at any rate, remove Mindo. Fine. Necessary, perhaps. But after that comes the act of genius – dump the body on Oliver to fuck him up in a style he can never recover from. This was a lovely, considerate act, with the preservation and enhancement of the Outfit given magnificent urgency.'

Turkey, Roger and Alf stayed pretty well blank faced, but Abelard guessed they must be wondering which of them had done all this, if Judith's interpretation of things held water. Abelard knew, of course, that it was nowhere near right, but it might do, or do for now. He said: 'Like you, Judith, I don't want to get too deeply into the detail of this interesting coup, but I'd guess there must be a convenient, untraceable weapon involved.'

'You actually *know* this from your own... well, your own inspired activities... don't you, oh, don't you, Simon? Judith cried, clapping her hands silently twice. 'It was you? Alone?'

So, Link-Mite's project for discrediting and disabling Olly had happened without Link-Mite's participation. Link-Mite would not even understand how it *did* happen. 'As I see things, a perfect weapon like that must have come from one source only,' Abelard said.

'"One source." "One source."' Judith acted out some heavy thinking for a couple of seconds: 'Ah, a pro-Eric lobby?' she said. 'I'd heard there was resentment at my decision to accept Eric's early retirement.'

'He'd be a loss,' Abelard said.

Now, Judith let pain invade her face. 'My arm's being twisted.'

'Eric's a grand lad,' Abelard said.

'Did he *really* help you in this, Simon?' she asked. 'Crucially?'

'He's a grand lad,' Abelard replied.

She pondered. 'Well, perhaps he is. I've got his leaving party scheduled and in preparation but I don't believe that know-all slapper, Iris, has done a thing about it.'

'Iris is a grand girl,' Abelard said.

'Is Eric shagging her?' Judith replied. 'Has she asked you to intercede? Are *you* shagging her?'

'Her wish to benefit the Outfit is unsurpassed,' Abelard said.

She sighed – a pastiche of defeat. 'All right. I'll think about Eric.'

Chapter 23

Among the comparatively small results of the September 11 attacks on the World Trade Centre and the Pentagon was confirmation that Eric Knotte could keep his job. When Abelard was called to watch the disasters on an Outfit tv set in the Press Relations office, he had been re-reading a *Times* second leader about the death of that Afghan dissenting figure, Ahmed Shah Masood, in a suicide bomb attack which the paper said 'bore all the hallmarks of Osama bin Laden.' Abelard did not have any space in his head while staring at the screen to think about implications, except for those in the buildings.

But in a day or two other implications sprouted. Everyone began talking about the failures of Intelligence and the crying need for immediate, future Intelligence, and declaring how wrong – culpably, even treasonously wrong – how wrong and idiotic it had been to run the Service down. Eric and anyone else with a bit of knowledge and nous was needed. K7, the Middle-East Section, disbanded under Dame Stella, would be restored in some form. Judith reckoned the Outfit would also do all right. 'Didn't we show we could protect ourselves when all about us and some among us were blaming things on us? Goodbye Olly. Goodbye your evil tome – a chicken feed item now, but a true menace yesterday. People will deduce that if we can look after our private interests so deftly we can look after the big scene just as well. Naturally, the Foreign Office, Defence and Number 10 are terrified of letting any Section decline now.'

Change. Sameness. Despite all the rough and agonising developments, Abelard found he remained nominally the owner of half of whatever was left of £13m. Lucy reckoned this amounted to about $10m, which was earning interest – very poor, almost laughable interest, but even very poor, almost laughable interest on $5m would have been a nice afternoon out in Harrods, or quite a few queue-jumped hip replacements should he come to need them. Naturally, it had been a stupendous, lovely shock to meet Lucy like that again and get a swift, constructive talk: nothing more, in the circumstances. The circumstances were the location and the fact that she did not seem to want any more than swift, constructive talk now, and he felt this would have been so whatever the location. She did tell him she was at present 'what I guess you'd call "on terms"' with someone else she had met somewhere sometime lately and this was turning out wonderful so far. No, he probably would *not* have called it "on terms". He would have called it fucking someone else and/or living with someone else.

At this stage he would not touch the money. Lucy was the same. They could do no ostentatious spending or people might ask where the cash came from. On top of that, he knew his mother would still grow enraged and despise him if she thought Abelard were drawing on what she would regard as exclusively Lucy's funds. Abelard had suggested to Lucy the other night, when they met so unexpectedly at the Hortons' flat, that Pamela and even Philip Bowling could possibly be given a little more of their boy's gains, but this had infuriated her as much as Mrs Abelard would have been infuriated if she thought Abelard was helping himself to Lucy's treasure, as she would see it.

'That fucking greed-prince, Philip, was trying to track me, you know,' Lucy had said. 'And getting close.'

'He's gifted like that. Where were you?

'Not gifted enough, but a nuisance, anyway.'

'Pam said he'd search. Where were you?'

'We paid them off once, and once will do. He doesn't need it, except as macho proof that he can get whatever he decides he wants. And Pamela – I hear she's got an ex-pat in Portugal, a retired mobster, full of saved loot from all sorts of rackets.'

'Does he wear a cape?' Abelard replied: yes, such a treat to talk to Lucy again, even in conditions bound to give some strain. There had been a time when he thought of her face as slightly beaky. Not now – birdlike, maybe, but a pleasant and beautiful bird, utterly knowing, psychic about where to catch the worms, early or late, and uncageable. Her clothes that night were the usual dazzling mix of style and cost: battered desert boots, a silk blue jacket, unarseflattering and undesigner label jeans.

Almost at once, Lucy said she thought she recognised the Overcoat, even without much light. 'JJ Ovalle's entourage?' She had an idea she remembered him either through file pictures or surveillance. 'That near-Hapsburg jaw and the widespread nose.' Lucy no longer pretended to be an ordinary government clerk with no access to classified notes.

'Isn't this the guy with Betty Grable on his back?' Lucy asked. 'Yea, I think the records say so. Betty Grable in a dress! My God, is that... well, perverse? Yes. Have you had a good look at him?'

'Fairly good.'

'But no definite identification?' Lucy said.

'Grable, Veronica Lake, Alice Faye, Carole Landis, not him.'

'As I recall it, no dong tattoo. Sometimes a name or nick-name there.'

'How do you mean, as you recall it?' Abelard replied.

'Profile notes, Dumbo.'

'Right.'

'You think I fuck moustached crooks?'

'What about the others? Anyway, does it matter now, Lucy?'

'Right. Look, I'd say, Alvan Charles Mindo. Big, status-wise. And, as you can see, just big. Your friend, Oliver, and his wife will have trouble moving him.'

'On their own.'

'You think we should wait and assist?'

'It seems shitty to leave something like this as finale to a pleasant night out.'

'How do you know? They might have been collecting more rough stuff about us.' She gave a little, theatrical groan and looked for a while at the bulk of Mindo again. 'I don't understand why, but, all right, we wait.'

'How don't understand?'

'My information is, you and the rest of the Outfit want to fuck Horton up so he can't write a book that might damage you, them, and me, too. Oh, yes, me, too. Mindo found here would fuck him up big, wouldn't he? But you'd like to be gallant and help them.'

'Yes, it's a bit strange. I used to work with Olly, that's all.'

'So?'

Abelard said: 'I knew it was you – before you spoke, before I saw you.'

'How? I'm not wearing scent.'

'I knew, that's all.' He had just reached a coded page in one of the notebooks when he grew certain someone had entered the flat. And it was true that he'd never considered it might be Olly and Kate. There would surely have been crisis whispers when they saw the state of the front door. Or possibly not. Possibly they would have kept silence, in case whoever did the door was still inside. But whether or not they'd have given themselves away was irrelevant. He had sensed, intuited, known it was Lucy: not a matter of sound, absence of sound, smell, absence of smell, but something mystical. One-way mystical. He could see she was not interested any longer in such things between her and him. This was September 10 2001, and since their grand time together in 1997 Lucy had progressed, if you wanted to describe it like that, and Abelard did not.

She said: 'Yes, I heard Horton will be throwing some shit about in the book. Not all cleaned up and harmless like your Stella Rimington's. Have you seen that pap serialisation of her in the *Guardian*, for Chrissake? And not lame like the final *Post* article by Briers, either. What happened there?'

'Maybe his paper got scared and re-wrote – an editorial committee re-wrote. It had that sort of evasiveness, wooziness.'

'Re-write Carl Briers?'

'If they were scared enough,' Abelard replied.

'I decided I'd like to talk with Horton, you know? So, I came.'

'From where?'

'I don't want to stay long.'

'Just to talk?'

'Only talk. I mean, Simon, am I armed?'

'I don't know, Lucy, are you?'

'And, naturally, you're not.'

'Social visit.'

'Possibly, as well as the talk, I thought I'd offer him some of the money for silence,' she said. 'From my own share only. Don't get anxious.' She and Abelard had sat in easy chairs on different sides of the room, talking across Mindo and the overcoat's thick acres. Minor light from street lamps came in through the uncurtained windows.

'I'm not anxious,' Abelard replied. 'Not about the money, at least. I think it should all be yours, anyway.'

'No you don't. You're not mad. You like it.'

'Well, yes, of course.'

'But?'

'But it can't be used. And my mother—'

'How is she?' Lucy asked. She and Mrs Abelard had got on well for a while when things between Lucy and him were good and full.

'Great but damned honourable,' Abelard said. 'She's usually very sound on money and what's proper. I can't defy her.'

Lucy lay down on the floor alongside the Overcoat, face almost against face. 'Yes, yes, I recall profile shots. It's Mindo. Nose broken or is that mess just congenital?' She stayed there, her head near Abelard's shoes. When she spoke to him some of the volume went up his trouser legs. 'OK, OK, so we leave most of the money banked for the present. Time will help us. Memories thin out. But a payment to Olly now wouldn't draw attention. He's not going to yell about it, is he?'

'He's probably unbribable. Principled.'

'Principled and he wants to piss over former friends?'

'He sees a powerful duty to expose what he thinks are wrongs. And he yearns for a writing career.'

'I hear his wife's got a business head, though,' Lucy said.

'She's a hotchpotch, like us all. There's a lot of large theme thinking there, too. It's possible she motivated Olly.'

'If there's a hotchpotch we can manage, Simon. That means persuadable, as long as the fee's right.' Lucy stood up and went back to her chair.

'Not sure,' Abelard said. 'She's convinced him he has a grail to get. I imagine *she* pressured him to leave the Outfit.'

Lucy said: 'She sells imitation jewellery from a fucking market stall, doesn't she? We're supposed to bow down to *her* integrity as well as *his* principles?'

'He'll need a career. That would be important to Olly, as important as cash. He's—'

She had held up one hand then. He stopped talking and heard, as she must have heard a moment earlier, very careful footsteps in the porch. Then, after a few seconds, the sounds came closer, were in the hall. Lucy had left the sitting room door slightly ajar. Abelard took a few steps and pulled it wide. 'Kate, Olly,' he said, giving it large affability, 'this will look bad for us, I know, but we didn't hit him, believe me. If you can. Lucy McIver and I stayed on only to help. I expect you've run across Lucy's name in your research, Olly. I thought I could make it out a few times in that bloody Boer War code you're still using.'

Horton and Kate stood near the body, staring down. 'What is this, a ploy?' Olly asked. 'Fuck you, Simon.'

'What ploy?' Abelard replied.

'You kill him here, or more likely bring him here, to destroy me,' Olly said.

'I don't think that,' Kate said. 'Who is he?'

'I knew you'd see things like they are,' Lucy replied.

'He works for Ovalle,' Abelard said. 'JJ. *He's* in your notebooks, too, isn't he, Olly? You've been very good. I think you're close on Cadwallader – that diagram, and the possible death setting.' He *knew* Horton was close. Abelard had seen pictures. 'But it's not going to matter, is it?'

'So why dead, how dead?' Kate had asked. Her voice was good, despite the sharp surprise, and better than Olly's. He seemed to Abelard near seize-up. Lucy went to the window and pulled the curtains to, then turned on the lights.

'We don't know why dead or how,' Abelard replied. 'Internal war?'

'Why here?' Kate said.

'It means things grow perilous,' Lucy said.

'We expected them to grow perilous,' Kate answered. 'Are you two fucking? We're up against a cosy cabal, are we?'

'You're up against a *few* cabals,' Lucy said. 'None of them cosy.'

'You two worked this out in bed?' Kate replied, 'as a change from the sweet talk and gasps?'

'I wouldn't want any change from the sweet talk and gasps if the sweet talk and gasps were available,' Abelard said.

'This won't stop us,' Olly said. 'I know about disposals.'

'Of course you do,' Abelard replied.

'We clean up the place, do a happy riddance and it's finished,' Olly said. 'Unless you two talk.'

'I told you, we stayed to give a hand,' Abelard replied.

'Is that part of it?' Olly asked.

'What?' Abelard said.

'The ploy. You fix it to get us caught disposing,' Olly answered.

'We could have made it known you have a shot corpse in your sitting room,' Lucy said.

'But not as good as *in flagrante* disposing, is it?' Olly replied. 'We're alibied tonight. No weapon present, is there?'

Abelard said: 'We'll help clean up the place and get you on your way with the body.'

'Why?' Olly had asked.

'He's like that,' Lucy said. 'Always was.'

'I don't want you ruined by this sort of thing,' Abelard said. 'Put it down to the old comrades bit if you like. Of course, I'd like to stop you publishing – my own sake, Lucy's, the Outfit's. But not that way.'

'It's rot,' Kate said. 'Bogus bonding.'

'Great phrase,' Lucy said.

'You want us to love you for your generous spirit and respect for the past,' Kate said, 'and so abandon the book. Not, *not* fucking on.'

'There's money as well as all the brilliant male gush,' Lucy said.

'Of course there's money,' Olly said. 'About $13m, give or take. Did you spot in the coded bits that I'd found out about

that, too, Simon? Lucy McIver came in for all Julian Bowling's
gains. That's very dangerous, very illegal money. Once we
took any bit of that you'd have us tied up for ever, wouldn't
you?'

'If you took it it would be because you'd agreed not to
publish,' Lucy replied. 'That's the only tying up we want.'

'Not, *not* fucking on,' Kate said.

'Ditch the past,' Lucy had replied.

'But one element from that past is a now matter, a today
matter, isn't it?' Olly replied. 'It put Judith Stewart at the top
through the destruction of Verdun Cadwallader. And she's still
in place.'

'Yes, it's tough,' Lucy said. 'This work can be like that,
can't it?'

They had cleaned the flat pretty thoroughly. Then the two
men lifted the Overcoat on to his feet between them and held
him up, gripping his arm pits through the cloth. They took
him out of the flat in a semblance of a walk like this, Lucy and
Kate ahead to obscure the view of him by passers-by and
neighbours. It was a very short distance to the side of the
apartment block and underground car park for residents.
Down there, they put the Overcoat flat in the back.

'Somewhere distant and remote,' Abelard said. 'Get
another car. Transfer him. Torch it. Well, obviously. You know
all that, Olly.'

Horton said: 'Thanks, Simon. Thanks Lucy.' For a second,
he had looked as though he would shake hands with both of
them, but seemed to think again.

'I'm really sorry we couldn't get an agreement,' Lucy said.

'What's that mean?' Kate asked.

'I'm really sorry we couldn't get an agreement,' Lucy
replied.

'A threat?' Kate said. 'This car is tailable, is it?'

'Not by me or Lucy,' Abelard said.

'By friends of yours?' Kate said.

'Somewhere distant and remote,' Abelard replied.

'So there's plenty of time and space to tail,' Kate said.

'We're finished, aren't we, if we're caught?' Olly said.

'Of course you are,' Lucy replied.

'You'll arrange it?' Kate asked.

'I don't know how,' Abelard said.

'No?' Kate had replied.

Chapter 24

Abelard was going through some personnel files of recently retired people who might be asked back for the emergency when Iris Insole dropped in at his room to thank him for looking after Eric. She said orders for the leaving party had been withdrawn. Iris seemed sure Abelard had said something effective.

'She changed her mind, that's all,' he said. It's the situation since September 11. All good men and experienced are needed now. And women. I'm trying to find more.'

'The *Outfit* is needed.'

'Absolutely.'

'Lucky in a way what happened to Olly – from that point of view, I mean,' Iris said.

'Which?'

'Continuance of the Outfit.'

'Tough for him. And, really, it became irrelevant after the 11th. Makes everything else look trivial, doesn't it?' Abelard said. 'Iris, you were still watching the other night, were you, when we brought the Overcoat out? You didn't mention it last time, but I suppose you were somewhere outside. You'd hardly leave after what you'd found.'

'No, I didn't say. It would have seemed like... like, I don't know... like leaning on you, pressuring you. Who was the second woman – not Kate? I had to drive around the block for a little tour. It's recommended, you know.'

'I heard.'

'She must have gone into the flat while I was away. Maybe

that drill is not so smart. Who?' Iris asked. 'Old suede boots. The famed Lucy?'

'She's good with entrances, and even better with exits. We needed two of us to keep him upright and the women to provide a sort of veil.'

'And did you let someone know they were travelling with the body,' she said. 'Tailed, and then a local South Wales action group tipped off there was to be another car blaze?'

'No, no. God, I'd never do that.'

'It would be so damn clever, but not too damn clever to be beyond *you*, Simon. I'd love to think you choreographed that.'

'Olly Horton was a friend.'

She sat back in her chair, hit a pose that was almost parental – turned vastly oracular. 'I didn't come out of theology to be hamstrung by supposed ethics and decency, Simon, did I? Oh, of course, they have their place. *Only* a place. They must not get pervasive. I've always thought it absolutely obvious there were times when the end vastly justifies the means. That with Olly was one, no question. And then, wouldn't they have shot down those Boston planes if they'd known what was going to happen – planes full of ordinary customers and crew? At times, morality's only survival and, or arithmetic.'

'I would have liked to get Olly out of that particular bit of farce with the body,' Abelard replied.

'The Outfit needs people at the top who can see past transient concerns with fellowship and manly pity.'

'I'm not *at* the top.'

'One day. Eric says you, then me. We ought to celebrate – celebrate Eric's survival. He's promised me he won't do a poem about the WTC and Pentagon. You wouldn't want to celebrate the wipe-out of Olly, I know. It would be a gloat and however much you'd like to gloat you wouldn't. Would you? No. But the salvation of Eric – that's because of you,

not events. This was personal power. This was goodness. Say
a drink one night?'

FICTION/CRIME & MYSTERY

Safe As Houses
Carol Anne Davis

'A terse and compulsive thriller that rivals Barbara Vine's fiction in its dark hues'
The Scotsman

Women are vanishing from the streets of Edinburgh and only one
man knows the answers. David is a sadist with a double life. He
divides his time between the marital home – shared with devoted
wife, Jeanette and young son – and his Secret House.
The Secret House is where fantasies become horrible reality and
where screams go unheard. Slowly Jeanette begins to realise that
all is not well...

NEW EDITION – with an introduction from the author

'Sexually violent, brutal, and disturbing psychological thriller that lays bare the
twisted soul of a psychopathic killer.' Booklist
BLOODLINES

B-format paperback
ISBN 1-904316-10-7 £6.99
Extent: 256 pages
Fiction/Crime & Mystery
NEW EDITION

FICTION/BRITISH NOIR

Grief
John B Spencer

'GRIEF is a speed-freak's cocktail, one part Leonard and one part Ellroy, that goes right to the head.' George P Pelecanos

Simon likes to think of himself as a hard man and he's not about to stand by and watch his mum get ripped off by a smooth estate agent. Nor is he going to lose the love of his life – even if she happens to be his best mate's woman – without a fight.

The mate, Ollie, is too busy collecting debts and milking muddled old J W Morgan for money to 'dispose of' his ex-wife's new husband (a perverted German surveillance expert called Rolph) to notice.

And Lucy the journalist oscillates between a snide lesbian colleague, her evil junky brother and her married estate agent lover. Who, in turn, is trying to get Simon's mother to sell her house...

When these disparate individuals collide, it's Grief. John B Spencer died in 2002, aged just 57. This is his final and greatest novel.

'Spencer writes the tightest dialogue this side of Elmore Leonard, so bring on the blood, sweat and beers!' Ian Rankin

Casebound
ISBN 1-904316-11-5 £15
C-paperback
ISBN 1-904316-17-4 £7.99
Extent: 256 pages

FICTION/CRIME & MYSTERY

No One Gets Hurt
Russell James

No One Gets Hurt is a hard-bitten, multi-layered underworld thriller of frightening
intensity from 'the best of Britain's darker crime writers' (The Times).

When a young woman is gruesomely murdered, her friend and fellow reporter
Kirsty Rice feels bound to investigate. Just as Kirsty enters the murky world of
call-girls, porn and Internet sex, she discovers that she is pregnant. Despite his
unconvincing denials, Kirsty is shocked to discover that the father of her unborn
child is involved with the pornographers. Did he know about the killing? And how far was he mixed up with London's
infamous Miller family?
No One Gets Hurt is a tense and powerful thriller, hurtling from a truly
shocking opening to an even more shattering climax.

'One of the UK's finest genre writers' – Booklist
BLOODLINES

Casebound edition
ISBN 1-904316-06-9 £15
B-paperback
ISBN 1-904316-07-7 £6.99
Extent: 402 pages

LITERATURE

The Indispensable
Julian Rathbone

'Julian Rathbone's characters live; he writes with elegance, with wit and with conviction' Books & Bookmen

At last! The collected work of one of Britain's most successful and accomplished literarists, chosen by the author himself.' The Indispensable...' contains rare essays, shorts stories, reviews and even the complete novel, 'Lying In State'. Julian Rathbone has published over 30 novels in 16 languages, been shortlisted (twice) for the Booker, won a CWA dagger and his thrillers have won prestigious prizes in Germany and Denmark. Reviewers have compared him – to his advantage – with Graham Greene, Eric Ambler, John Updike, Charles Dickens, William Thackeray, John le Carré and William Burroughs. On top of that, he's an accomplished reviewer and essayist, has written successfully filmed screenplays, and much, much more.

'One of the best storytellers around' Daily Telegraph

With an introduction by Mike Phillips

Casebound
ISBN 1-904316-12-3 £17.99
C-paperback
ISBN 1-904316-13-1 £9.50
Extent: 468 pages
Rights: World

The Do-Not Press
Fiercely   Independent   Publishing

Keep in touch with what's happening at the cutting edge of
independent British publishing.

Simply send your name and address to:
The Do-Not Press (AME)
16 The Woodlands, London SE13 6TY (UK)

or email us: ame@thedonotpress.com

There is no obligation to purchase
(although we'd certainly like you to!)
and no salesman will call.

Visit our regularly-updated web sites:
www.thedonotpress.com
www.bangbangbooks.com

Mail Order

All our titles are available from good bookshops, or (in case of difficulty)
direct from The Do-Not Press at the address above. There is no charge for
post and packing for orders to the UK and Europe.

(NB: A post-person may call.)

The Concise Guide to
Baby Knits

Knit stunning clothes, toys and accessories

Contents

Introduction

Knitting for babies is a particular favourite with knitters of all levels, not just because of the small and sweet designs, but because of the inherently personal quality that comes with a lovingly woven hand-knit item. Baby knits are the perfect way to commemorate the arrival of a precious new-born, whether you're knitting for your own baby or for a family member or friend. Imagine receiving such an affectionately crafted gift for your child, to be worn and played with, and cherished for years to come. Baby knits are a joy to receive, a joy to knit, and are highly rewarding little projects.

This book presents an adorable range of knits for babies, including cute garments, cosy cot blankets and cuddly toys. From little cardigans and smocks for girls, to sailor sets and soft shorts for boys, there are over thirty lovely patterns to knit for any baby. With traditional knits and vintage inspired outfits, these baby knits are classic and irresistible, and will make unique hand-me-downs for future generations of babies.

Knit a family of rabbits or create delightfully fruity hats and cutie booties for colder days and nights. With cute clothing, home accessories and toys, this charming collection of baby knits will inspire knitters of all abilities to create something small but beautiful.

Each pattern is illustrated with adorable photographs, alongside clear instructions and charts and diagrams where necessary. The helpful introduction provides an illustrated guide to basic stitches and knitting skills for new knitters, with a concise introduction to the essentials in knitting tools and terminology. This guide contains everything you will need to create gorgeous, soft and truly special baby knits.

Learn to knit:
Knitting Essentials

Learning the lingo, understanding needle sizes and being able to change colours are essentials that every keen knitter should know.

Knitting is an enjoyable and rewarding hobby, but sometimes it can be daunting. It may look like a world of meaningless letters and confusing numbers but by learning the lingo and becoming familiar with the tools and techniques, it will all make sense. Knitting abbreviations are one of the trickiest elements of the knitting world, but 'k2tog' does actually mean something. The list opposite will decipher the code and it will soon be second nature. Needles come in a wide variety of sizes.

They are your most vital tool so it is important that you know your 6s from your 6mm. Thin needles are required for small and fine projects whereas larger needles are used for chunkier tasks.

The chart opposite will help you chose the right needle for your project. We will also guide you through the basics of changing colour for when you are ready to move on.

Needle Conversion Chart

mm	UK	US
2.0 mm	14	0
2.25 mm	13	1
2.5 mm	12	
2.75 mm	12	2
3.0 mm	11	3
3.25 mm	10	3
3.5 mm	9	4
3.75 mm	9	5
4.0 mm	8	6
4.5 mm	7	7
5.0 mm	6	8
5.5 mm	5	9
6.0 mm	4	10
6.5 mm	3	10½
7.0 mm	2	
7.5 mm	1	
8.0 mm	0	11
9.0 mm	00	13
10 mm	000	15

Changing Colour

Changing colour to create stripes is most easily done at the end of a row. First, knit all the rows that you need to, with your first colour.

When you are ready to change colour, drop the old colour. Pick up the new colour by threading the beginning of the new colour through the back of the last stitch and pulling the old colour tightly, trapping the new colour.

Hold both the start of the new colour and the end of the old colour together and resume knitting as normal, using the new colour. After every row, pull the end of the new colour to keep it tight, but ensure that the tension is kept even. Cut the old colour, leaving a 15cm/6in tail. Use a tapestry needle to weave the loose ends in.

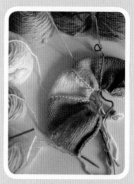

Abbreviations

alt	alternate	**m1**	make one*	**sl1**	slip 1 st
approx.	approximately	**m1l**	make one left	**skpo**	sl1, k1, pass sl st over
beg	beginning	**m1r**	make one right	**sm**	slip marker
CC	contrast colour	**m1p**	make one purl	**ssk**	slip first st, slip second st, then knit both together off right-hand needle
cont	continue	**MC**	main colour		
dec	decrease(ing)	**N1/N2**	needle 1/needle 2		
DPN	double-pointed needle	**p**	purl	**st(s)**	stitch(es)
foll	following	**p2tog**	purl 2 together	**st st**	stocking stitch
folls	follows	**patt**	pattern	**tbl**	through back loop
g st	garter stitch	**pm**	place marker	**tog**	together
inc	increase(ing)	**psso**	pass slipped st over	**w&t**	wrap and turn
k	knit	**pwise**	purlwise	**wyif**	with yarn in front
k2tog	knit 2 together	**rem**	remain(ing)	**WS**	wrong side
kfb	knit into front and back of stitch	**rep**	repeat	**yf**	yarn forward
KTS	knit the steek st	**rnd**	round	**yo**	yarn over
kwise	knitwise	**RH**	right hand	**yon**	yarn over needle
LH	left hand	**RS**	right side	**yrn**	yarn round needle

*make one by lifting the bar between sts, placing it onto the LH needle and knitting into the back of the lifted bar

Learn to knit:
The Basic Stitches

The following pages contain the basic stitches that you will need to begin knitting. Each how-to section covers a different stitch, with comprehensive step-by-step explanation and accompanying images.

Slipknot

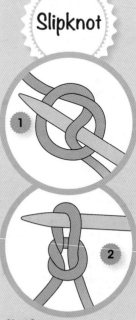

Long-tail cast on

This uses a single needle and produces an elastic knitted edge like a row of garter stitch.

Step 1

Leaving an end about three times the length of the required cast-on, put a slipknot on the needle. Holding the yarn end in the left hand, take the left thumb under the yarn and upwards. Insert the needle in the loop just made on the thumb.

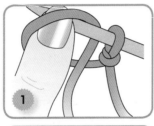

Step 2

Use the ball end of the yarn to make a knit stitch, slipping the loop off the thumb. Pull the yarn end to close the stitch up to the needle. Continue making stitches in this way.

Chain cast off

A simple knit stitch cast off is used in most of these projects. Knit two stitches. * With the left needle, lift the first stitch over the second. Knit the next stitch. Repeat from * until one stitch remains. Break the yarn, take the end through this stitch and tighten.

Step 1

A slipknot is the first stage of any cast on. Loop the yarn around two fingers of the left hand, the ball end on top. Dip the needle into the loop, catch the ball end of the yarn and pull it through the loop.

Step 2

Pull the ends of the yarn to tighten the knot. Tighten the ball end to bring the knot up to the needle.

Ends

The end of yarn left after casting on should be a reasonable length of approx 10-30cm/4-12in so that it can be used for sewing up. The same applies to the end left after casting off.

Knit Stitch (K)

Choose to hold the yarn and needles in whichever way you feel most comfortable. To create tension in the yarn – that is, to keep it moving evenly – you will need to twist it through some fingers of the hand holding the yarn, and maybe even take it around your little finger. Continuous ows of knit stitch produce garter stitch. It does take some practice to get the stitches even so don't be discouraged, keep on practising.

Step 1

Insert the right needle into the first stitch on the left needle. Make sure it goes from left to right into the front of the stitch.

Step 2

Taking the yarn behind, bring it up and around the right needle.

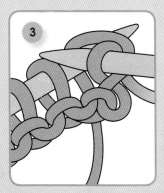

Step 3

Using the tip of the right needle, draw a loop of yarn through the stitch.

Step 4

Slip the stitch off the left needle. There is now a new stitch on the right needle.

Purl Stitch (P)

Step 1

Insert the right needle into the first stitch on the left needle. Make sure it goes into the stitch from right to left.

Step 2

Lower the tip of the right needle, taking it away from you to draw a loop of yarn through the stitch.

Step 3

Taking the yarn to the front, loop it around the right needle.

Step 4

Slip the stitch off the left needle. There is now a new stitch on the right needle.

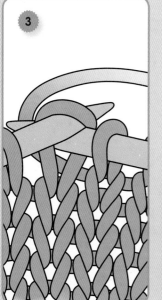

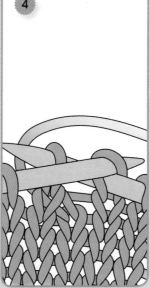

Decreases

Decreases have two basic functions. They can be used to reduce the number of stitches in a row, as in armholes and necklines, and combined with increases, they can create stitch patterns.

Right slanting single decreases (k2tog)

Knitting two stitches together makes a smooth shaping, with the second stitch lying on top of the first.

Step 1

Insert the right needle through the front of the first two stitches on the left needle, then take the yarn around the needle.

Step 2

Draw the loop through and drop the two stitches off the left needle.

Left slanting double decreases (sk2po)

For a double decrease that slants to the left, worked on a right-side row, you'll need to take the first stitch over a single decrease. For a similar-looking decrease worked on a wrong-side row, purl three together through the back of the loops (p3tog tbl).

Step 1

Insert the right needle knitwise through the front of the first stitch on the left needle, and slip it onto the right needle.

Step 2

Knit the next two stitches together, then lift the first stitch over as shown. To make a right-slanting double decrease, simply knit three stitches together (k3tog).

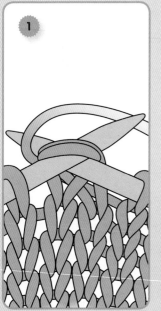

Yarn Over (yo)

It's essential to take the yarn over the needle so that the strand lies in the same direction as the other stitches. Working into this strand on the next row makes a hole, but if the strand is twisted, the hole will close up.

When the stitch before a yarn over is purl, the yarn will already be at the front, ready to go over the needle.

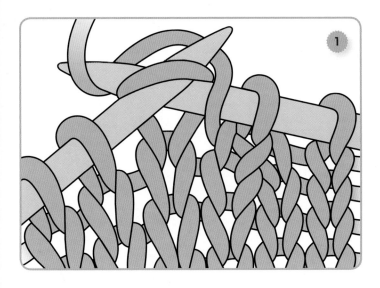

Step 1

To make a yarn over between knit stitches, bring the yarn to the front as if to purl, then take it over the needle to knit the next stitch.

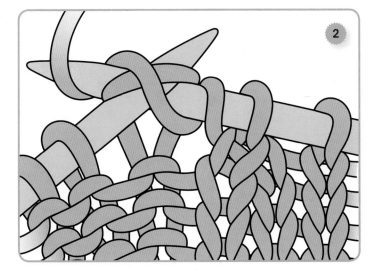

Step 2

To make a yarn over between a knit and a purl, bring the yarn to the front as if to purl, take it over the needle and bring it to the front again, ready to purl.

Increases

Here are two of the most basic methods of increasing a single stitch – bar increase and lifted strand increase.

Bar increase on a knit row (kfb)

Knitting into the front and the back of a stitch is the most common increase. It's a neat, firm increase, which makes a little bar on the right side of the work at the base of the new stitch. This makes it easy to count rows between shapings and doesn't leave a hole.

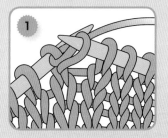

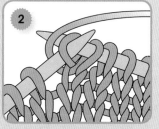

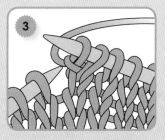

Step 1

Knit into the front of the stitch and pull the loop through, but leave the stitch on the left needle.

Step 2

Knit into the back of the stitch on the left needle.

Step 3

Slip the stitch off the left needle, making two stitches on the right needle. Note that the bar of the new stitch lies on the left.

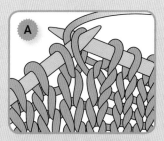

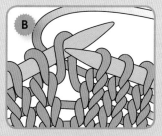

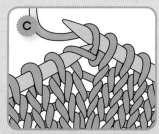

Lifted strand increase to the left (ml or mIL)

Making a stitch from the strand between stitches is a very neat way to increase.

Picture A

From the front, insert the left needle under the strand between stitches. Make sure the strand lies on the needle in the same direction as the other stitches, then knit into the back of it.

Lifted strand increase to the right (mIR)

This right-slanting increase balances exactly the lifted strand increase to the left.

Picture B

From the back, insert the left needle under the strand between the stitches. It will not lie in the same direction as the other stitches, so knit into the front of it.

Double increase

This is one of the simplest ways to make three stitches out of one.

Picture C

Knit one stitch without slipping it off, take the yarn over the right needle from front to back then knit the same stitch again. A small but decorative hole is left in the fabric.

Twists

Twisting stitches is working two or three stitches out of sequence, but without using a cable needle. This is an easy way to create patterns where lines of stitches travel over the surface of the knitting.

Left twist (t2L)

This twist is worked on a right-side row. As the stitches change place, the first stitch lies on top and slants to the left, while the stitch behind is worked through the back of the loop.

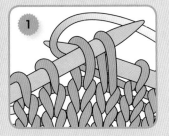
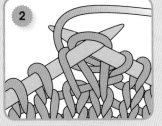
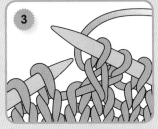

Step 1
Knit into the back of the second stitch.

Step 2
Knit into the front of the first stitch.

Step 3
Slip both stitches off the left needle together.

Right twist (t2R)

In this right-sided row twist, the second stitch lies on top and slants to the right, while the stitch behind is worked through the back of the loop.

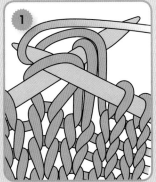
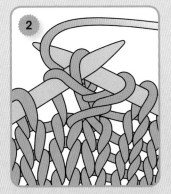
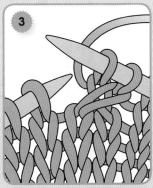

Step 1
Knit into the front of the second stitch.

Step 2
Knit into the back of first stitch.

Step 3
Slip both stitches off the left needle together.

Learn to knit:
Fair Isle

Fair Isle or stranded knitting is a really popular technique and it's easy when you know how.

Traditional Fair Isle may use many colours in the design. However, only two colours are typically used in a row, which makes it less complex to work than it seems. Patterns are worked in stocking stitch from charts, using colours or symbols to indicate each different colour. Charts are read from the bottom, starting at the right-hand side. Each square represents a stitch, each row of squares a row of knitting.

In flat knitting, right side rows are normally worked from right to left, wrong side rows from left to right. Odd numbered rows will usually be knit, even rows purl. In circular knitting, all rows are read from right to left and, as a rule with Fair Isle, all rows will be knit as the right side of the work is always facing you.

Yarn

For good pattern definition, a fine Shetland wool is traditionally used, being warm, light and durable. Other wool will work well and Fair Isle patterns can be found on a wide range of projects from fine socks through to heavier sweaters and jackets.

Try swatching non-wool yarns for handle and appearance. Some yarns, especially cottons, can be slippery, which can make maintaining even tension more difficult.

Colour changing

When changing colours the yarn not in use (the 'float' or 'float yarn') is carried across the wrong side of the work by stranding or weaving in to avoid constantly breaking off and rejoining the yarn.

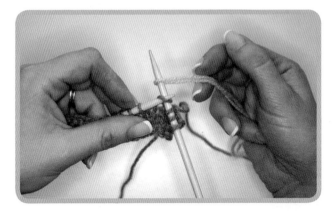

Knit row

1. To work the chart shown, starting at the bottom right and working from right to left, knit in colour A (dark blue) until the first colour change. Make the next stitch by joining in colour B (light blue) as normal. Leave a tail of B for darning in later and don't cut off A.

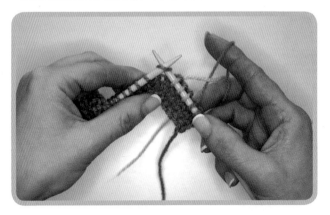

2. Knit in B to the next colour change. Lift yarn A from beneath, under B, and knit with A until the next colour change. Repeat for each colour change, lifting the new yarn from under the working yarn.

Repeat this process, changing yarn according to the chart until the end of the row. At the end of the row check that when the fabric is slightly stretched, the floats are not pulling the fabric in.

Stranding

This method works well where colour changes are frequent (no more than four or five stitches apart). It gives a less dense, lighter fabric and uses less yarn than weaving in.

Weaving in

Weaving in avoids loose floats across the back of the work and the two colours in the row are neatly entwined or woven together at each stitch.

Both techniques have their place. Stranding is ideal for areas with frequent colour changes within the row and where a lighter, less dense fabric is required.

For firmer fabrics, where the floats would be too long or where even short floats would be likely to snag, weaving in may be preferable. With socks or gloves, the floats may catch on rings or between toes. This can be annoying and may spoil your knitting so weaving in may be the better method here for changing colours within the row.

Purl row

1. Work the next row of the chart from right to left in purl. As with the knit row, lift the new colour from beneath the working yarn at each colour change so the old yarn lies in front of the new yarn as it faces you.

Weaving in: Knit Row, using B.

1. To work a stitch in yarn B (light blue), A (dark blue) is woven in. Insert RH needle to begin a k st as normal. Take A over the top of B and wrap round RH needle as if to knit. Take B around RH needle as if to k. A sits behind B on RH needle.

2. Before completing the k st, bring A back around the RH needle. Note how A now lies over B. Leaving A over B, k the next st as normal in B.

Sometimes there's a long run of stitches in a single colour. In this case, it's possible to catch in the second colour every three or four stitches using the weaving-in method (below). This differs from the full weaving-in technique because the yarn is only woven in every few stitches rather than every single stitch. This technique may combine better with stranding as it's less dense and better matches the feel and density of a stranded fabric.

The best way to decide which method to use is by swatching. Test each section of the pattern, bearing in mind the type of garment or accessory you're making. Where will the pattern be? Will it get lots of wear? Is it likely to be in an area prone to snagging?

Can the techniques be combined?
Yes – in fact, with some patterns it may be unavoidable, but you need to swatch carefully. With properly worked swatches, there shouldn't be any difference in tension, but be aware of the feel of the fabric. Be sure to include some rows of single-colour knitting in your swatches if they feature in the pattern as these may also feel slightly different to the coloured sections.

Learn to knit:
Double Knitting

Many of us love colourwork but are frustrated by the messy wrong side – this clever technique creates a completely reversible fabric.

Double knitting is a fascinating technique that can be used in a variety of ways. This section looks at using double knitting to create reversible, double-faced fabric where both sides of the fabric are permanently interlocked and joined together.

This kind of double knitting can be worked flat or in the round and colourwork looks stunning. With double knitting, a red star on a white background on one side magically transforms into a white star on a red background when viewed from the other side, and no one will know how you did it!

How double knitting works

While there's no problem simply following the instructions and accepting that the pattern does what it says on the tin, you may find it helpful when following charts to understand how the technique works. A knit stitch is smooth on the side facing you and has a bump on the reverse. Purl stitches on the other hand show a bump on the front as it faces you but are smooth on the side facing away from you.

The nature of this knitting technique means that the bumps are trapped between the smooth knit stitches and therefore can't be seen. This leaves only the smooth (right) sides visible on both outer faces of the fabric.

Terminology

As both sides of the work are effectively the right side, you may find it easier to think of the two sides as A and B. Each yarn will be both main (background) and contrasting (foreground) yarn, so if yarn X is the main colour (MC) on side A, it will be the contrasting colour (CC) on side B.

Yarn Y will then be the CC on side A but the MC on side B. The colours may also be referred to in patterns as MC1 and MC2.

Casting on

Double knitting patterns normally specify a cast on. If not, you can use any cast on, working with both yarns at the same time. Note that you will cast on twice as many stitches as there are squares in your chart as each square represents two stitches.

Before you begin knitting, make sure that the stitches are in pairs in the same order – for example, all the pairs should be XY. Using both colours will create a two-colour cast-on edge. For a single colour edge, a provisional cast on such as tubular cast on can be used.

Knitting two fabrics that interlock
(one side is a negative image of the other)

Reading double knitting charts

Double knitting patterns are usually charted. Unlike in regular knitting, in double knitting each square on the chart represents two stitches.

Depending on the colour of the square, this will determine which colour yarn is knitted and which yarn is purled.

As the two fabrics form a reversible pattern, a stitch knitted on side A in yarn X will give a visible stitch in X on side A. If a stitch is purled using yarn X on side A, this stitch will not be seen on side A but will be visible on side B.

As with other charts, charts for flat knitting read right to left then left to right. For knitting in the round, all rows read right to left.

 Start knitting here

□ Odd rows (side A knit in X (MC1), purl in Y (MC2)
Even rows (side B knit in Y (MC2), purl in X (MC1)

[•] Odd rows (side A knit in Y (MC1), purl in X (MC2)
Even rows (side B knit in X (MC1), purl in Y (MC2)

Flat & circular knitting

Step 1

Below the contrasting yarn you will see a series of bumps made in the main yarn (X).

These bumps are picked up in this row, increasing the stitches and forming the stitches for one face of the fabric (side A). The existing stitches form the other face (B).

Need to know

Tubular cast on

Using a piece of smooth contrasting waste yarn, cast on half the total number of stitches needed plus one extra stitch (You can use the backwards loop method as this is easier to unpick later).

For our sample chart (see page 15), cast on 15 stitches (total stitches = 28, halved = 14, plus 1 = 15).

Set up rows

Knitting in the round

Join work into circle, checking that there are no twisted stitches.

Change to yarn X.

Set Up Row 1: P2, p2tog, p to end

Set Up Row 2: Purl.

Change to yarn Y.

Set Up Row 3: Purl.

Set Up Row 4: Purl. Purl side should be facing you.

Flat knitting

Change to yarn X.

Set Up Row 1: P2, p2tog, p to end.

Set Up Row 2: Knit.

Change to yarn Y.

Set Up Row 3: Purl.

Set Up Row 4: Knit. Purl side should be facing you.

Step 2

Chart Row 1 (Side A): *With RH needle, lift bump of main yarn (X) below contrasting yarn, place on LH needle and ktbl. Bring both yarns X (MC1) and Y (MC2) to front of work and p next stitch using just yarn Y. Repeat from * to last stitch.

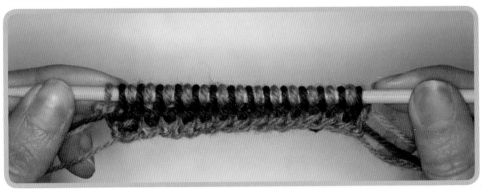

Step 3

Check you have the correct number of stitches before proceeding. The final stitch should be a purl to maintain the pairing of stitches. For flat knitting, turn to work side B (chart row 2). For knitting in the round, place a marker and continue knitting round 2 (chart row 2) without turning the work. Note that you will have twice the number of stitches as squares shown in the chart (28 sts, 14 squares on the chart). This is because each square represents two stitches. The waste yarn can be carefully removed after several rows have been worked.

Flat knitting

Step 4

Hold both yarns to the back of the work, but knit the next stitch in just yarn Y.

Step 5

Bring both yarns to front of work. Keeping both yarns at the front, but using yarn X (MC1) only, purl next stitch. The first chart square is now completed.

Finishing a row (flat knitting only)

When working flat/straight (as opposed to knitting in the round), you will need to make a neat finish to the edges. For a tidy edge with a neat, solid line of each colour running up the sides, try the following technique:

Step 6

Repeat steps 4 and 5 to last square on chart. Two stitches on LH needle. Keeping both yarns at back of work, slip next stitch purlwise (as if to purl).

Step 7

Bring yarn that is the same colour as the final stitch (X in this case), to the front of work. (One yarn either side of work). Keeping just this one yarn to the front, slip final stitch purlwise.

The side facing you (B) will have a row of smooth stitches in colour Y (MC2), the side facing away from you (A) will have a row of smooth stitches in colour X (MC1). Purl stitches worked in X (MC1) produce a barely visible bump on side B facing you but are visible and smooth when viewed on side A.

Step 8

Turn the work. One yarn (Y in this case) is in front, facing you and one is at the back, away from you (X). Knit first stitch in the same colour as the final stitch of the last row (X in this case).

Hints & tips

You may be working an X colour stitch over a Y colour stitch, even though you are working a block of a single colour (see steps 11 and 12). Don't worry – if you are following the pattern it will turn out correctly! Focus on which is the MC and which is the CC for the side you are on and not the colour of the next stitch on the LH needle.

Remember that, irrespective of the colours being used, stitch pairings are always knit, purl. You shouldn't have any knit (or purl) stitches together.

The chart should have a clearly explained key but it may help to write out the key with your choice of colours written on to keep you on track.

Step 9

Bring X (MC1) to the front. Both yarns are now together at the front of the work. Purl next stitch with just yarn Y (MC2).

Step 10

Take both yarns to back and continue to work rest of row, knitting in X (MC1), purling in Y (MC2). By working in this way at the end of each row, after several rows you will see a neat row of chain stitches up each side of the work.

Knitting in the round

Repeat steps 4 and 5 following chart (see page 15), but, because you are always working with side A facing you, work knit stitches in X (MC1) and purls in Y (MC2), still with two stitches for each square on chart. Mark end of round with a stitch marker.

The side facing you (A) will have a row of smooth stitches in colour X (MC1), the side facing away from you (B) will have a row of smooth stitches in colour Y (MC2). Purl stitches worked in Y (MC2) produce a barely visible bump on side A facing you but are visible and smooth when viewed on side B.

Hints & tips

Some patterns will specify a cast on, in which case it is advisable to use the specified method. If no method is specified, the tubular cast on worked in a single colour, will give a neat edge to match the slipped stitch side edges

Practise working with both yarns over your finger as this helps to keep the tension even and also makes it easier to ensure that you always bring both yarns back and forwards together

If you spot a stray bar across a stitch this means you have left a yarn behind when moving front to back or vice versa and the work will need to be taken back to the appropriate point

Step 11

The next pair of stitches need to produce a visible stitch in CC (Y on this row). To produce a visible stitch we need to knit it, so if we want a visible stitch in Y we have to knit the next stitch in Y.

Step 12

We don't want to see the next stitch on this side of the work so it is purled using X.

Step 13

Repeat this process for each CC square on the chart. When a square is shown in MC, work these stitches by knitting in X and purling in Y. Note that we are still working knit, purl, but we will have two same-colour stitches next to one another at each colour change.

Need to know

Working patterns and motifs

When you reach the first pattern row for the motif, it helps if you think in terms of main colour (MC) and contrast colour (CC). Unlike other colourwork, there are no solid runs of a single colour since every chart square is worked twice and every square will always be worked once in each colour. What changes is not the order of knit and purl (this always stays the same) but which colour of the pair you use to knit with and which colour you purl with.

Looking at Row 6 in our chart, whether you are working flat or in the round, the motif begins with side A facing you. The knit stitches on this side (A) were worked in yarn X, so X is our MC for this face of the work. Yarn Y is therefore the CC. Work as above, working the knit stitches in X and purling the paired stitches in Y until you reach the colour change.

26

Casting off

Step 14

For a neat cast off, grafting (kitchener stitch) is a great choice. For this, you will need two double-pointed needles (DPNs) in the same size as your main knitting. Work to within one row of the end of the pattern. Holding 2 DPNs parallel in your RH, slip knit stitches onto front needle and purl stitches onto back needle. To avoid a stepped finish, work one row of purl on just the stitches on the back needle. Don't turn the work but slide the knitting back to the RH end of the DPNs. Graft the two edges together as normal. Whereas on side B the heart is in yarn X with the background in Y, when viewed from side A, the heart is in yarn Y with the background in X.

Need to know

Flat knitting

At the end of the row, follow the steps for finishing a row as above, then work side B. As side B has Y as the MC, X is the CC, so work all MC squares with the knit stitch in Y and the purl stitch in X. Work CC squares with X as the knit stitch and Y as the purl stitch.

Note: Remember that in flat knitting, rows on a chart are worked right to left then left to right.

Knitting in the round

When knitting projects in the round, there will be no edge stitches so no need to perform any slipped stitch manoeuvres at the end of the round and you can ignore the section for finishing a row (above).

Charts for knitting in the round are always worked from right to left so you will always have side A facing you. This makes things easier as the MC and CC will remain the same throughout.

Learn to knit:
Cable Knitting

Knitting groups of stitches out of sequence creates exciting stitch patterns. Cables can be worked with two or more stitches and crossed to the front or the back.

For rich texture and dramatic shape it is impossible to ignore cables. In their simplest terms, cables are essentially combinations of knit and purl stitches worked out of sequence.

Cables can be worked in an endless variety of sizes and combinations. Stitches are transferred to a short needle (a cable needle) and these stitches are then held either at the front or the back of the knitting.

A number of stitches are then knitted from the main needle. To complete the sequence, the stitches from the cable needle are then knitted.

This has the effect of creating a crossed fabric. Where stitches are held at the back the cross will be to the right. Stitches held at the front will create a cross moving to the left.

What are cables?

Cables are usually worked in knit stitches on a reverse stocking stitch background.

The contrast between the smooth knit stitches and the bumpy, dense purl side of the reverse stocking stitch allows the cable pattern to stand out clearly.

Cables can be simple, single braids or complex combinations of braids, honeycombs and plaits.

Hints & tips

Cable needles come in straight versions, straight with a kink in the middle or occasionally hooked which can prevent stitches sliding off. Choose whichever works best for you If you don't have a cable needle handy, use a short DPN.

Step 1

For a simple six-stitch cable that crosses to the left, purl to where the cable begins. Take a cable needle in the same (or slightly smaller) size as the main needles. Hold it in the RH, slightly above and parallel to the RH needle. Slip the next three stitches onto the cable needle as if you were going to purl them (p-wise).

Step 2

Slide the slipped stitches (these will be worked later) along to the centre of the cable needle and hold the cable needle with stitches on to the front of the work. The cable needle can be supported in the RH as you work the next stitches or left loose at the front of the work. Alternatively, you can carefully poke it into the fabric but care should be taken not to split the yarn or snag the fabric.

Step 3

Knit the next three stitches from LH main needle as normal. Avoid a hole at the crossover point by drawing up the yarn quite firmly after the first stitch. These stitches may feel tight and quite difficult to work. Don't worry, this is normal!

Step 4

Next, work the stitches on the cable needle. Leave LH main needle at back of work. With cable needle in LH in front of the LH main needle, slide the stitches to the RH end of the cable needle. Be careful to keep the stitches in the same order and make sure you don't twist the stitches when lifting the needle.

Step 5

This completes the LH-twisted cable. This type of cable may also be referred to in some patterns as a left cross, LH or front-cross cable.

Step 6

For a cable that twists to the right, purl up to the point where the cable is to be made. Slip the next three stitches onto a cable needle. This time, hold the cable needle to the back of the work. Again, if it is easier, poke the needle through the knitted fabric, but being careful to avoid 'pulls'.

Step 7

Knit the next three stitches from the LH main needle.

Step 8

Now bring the cable needle to the front of the work, taking the LH main needle to the back. Be careful not to twist the stitches. Knit the three stitches from the cable needle in their original order.

Step 9

This completes the right-twist cable (also referred to as a right cross, RH or back-cross cable). Depending on the pattern a number of 'plain' rows (rows with just knit and purl and no cabled or crossed stitches) may now be worked before the next cable row.

Step 10

In this swatch a left-twist cable is combined with a right-twist cable to create a wave effect. Two cables are also worked at either end of the swatch. Each cable is separated by purl stitches and a purl band is worked at each edge to make the cables stand out. There is lots of fun to be had playing with cable combinations.

Baby Clothes

Knitters love baby clothes because they're so quick and easy to knit, and they're a great way to practice all the techniques you need before you start making adult garments.

Tadpole Romper & Booties

2

Intermediate

This cute little set is so snuggly and soft, it's the perfect way to show your little ones you love them – and in neutral colours, it's great for girls as well as boys.

The yarn we chose for this pattern is silky-smooth and machine-washable, as well as being surprisingly hard-wearing – so it's absolutely perfect for baby knits!

Romper

CAST ON

Using shorter circular needle and MC, cast on 58 (64, 72, 74, 76, 76, 84) sts.

Row 1 (WS): P9 (9, 10, 10, 11, 11, 11), pm, p10 (12, 14, 14, 14, 14, 16), pm, p20 (22, 24, 26, 26, 26, 30), pm, p10 (12, 14, 14, 14, 14, 16), pm, p to end.

Row 2: [K to st before marker, m1, k1, sm,k1, m1] four times, k to end.

Row 3: Purl.

Rep these last two rows 1 (0, 1, 0, 1,2, 0) more times. 74 (72, 88, 82, 92,100, 92) sts.

Next row: K1, m1, [k to st before marker, m1, k1, sm, k1, m1] four times, k to lastst, m1, k1.

Next row: Purl.

Rep these last 2 rows 1 (2, 2, 3, 2, 2, 4) more times. 94 (102, 118, 122, 122, 130, 142) sts.

Tie a piece of waste yarn at beg and end of previous row to mark it for when working button bands.

Keeping raglan incs correct (i.e. either side of each marker), work front shaping as follows:

Row 1: K1, m1, work to last 3 sts, ssk, k1.

Row 2: Purl.

Rep these two rows 9 (9, 10, 11, 11, 12, 12) more times, then rep Row 1 every 4th row 3 (4, 4, 4, 4, 5) times..

Special Instructions

w&t (wrap and turn): Wyif, sl next st, bring yarn to back, sl st back to LN, turn work to beg next row.

Backwards loop cast on: Place thumb behind yarn; turn thumb so it is pointing up and yarn is wound counterclockwise around thumb; push tip of needle from bottom to top under yarn on thumb; remove thumb, leaving yarn on needle; pull gently to snug the loop on the needle; repeat for as many sts as required.

About this pattern

Sizing
Newborn (3, 6, 9, 12, 18, 24 months) to fit actual chest measurement of 38 (40.5, 43, 45.5, 48, 50.5, 53) cm

Yarn
Artesano Superwash Merino
For romper: 5 (6, 6, 7, 7, 8, 9) balls in Biscuit (MC)
1 ball in Cocoa (CC)
For booties: 1 ball each in MC and CC

About the yarn
DK; 112m per 50g ball; 100% Merino wool

Needles
4mm circular, 60cm
4mm circular, 120-150cm
4mm DPNs

Tension
Measured over St st:

Other supplies
4 stitch markers
For romper: 8 (9, 10, 11, 12, 12, 12) buttons (12mm)
For booties: 4 buttons
Waste yarn or stitch holder

At the same time

When there are 52 (56, 58, 62, 64, 66, 70) sts between the 2nd and 3rd markers (i.e. the back of the garment), remove sleeve stsas follows:

Next Row (RS): [Work to marker, sm, slip next 42 (46, 48, 50, 52, 54, 56) sts onto waste yarn, rm] twice, work to end. 106 (114, 118, 126, 130, 134, 142) sts.

After front shaping rows have been completed, cont in St st until body measures approx 21 (21.5, 22.5, 23.5, 25,26, 26) cm from back neck.

Continue shaping front.

Row 1: K1, k2tog, k to last st, m1, k1.

Rows 2-4: Work 3 rows in St st.

Repeat these four rows 2 (3, 3, 3, 3, 3, 4) more times, then repeat Row 1 every 2nd row until crotch gusset is completed.

At the same time

When body measures approx 22 (23.5, 25,24, 25.5, 26.5, 28) cm from back neck,beg short row shaping as follows:

Row 1 (RS): Work to marker, sm, k to 5 sts before marker, w&t.

Row 2 (WS): P to 5 sts before marker, w&t.

Row 3: K to end, lifting and knitting wrap tog with st as it is passed.

Row 4: P to end, lifting and knitting wrap tog with st as it is passed.

Work 4 (4, 4, 6, 6, 6, 6) rows in St st, keeping front shaping correct.

Rep from Row 1 twice more, then work two rows in St st, keeping front shaping correct.

Keeping front shaping correct, work crotch gusset as follows:

Row 1 (RS): Work to marker, rm, k26 (28, 29, 31, 32, 33, 35), pm, m1, pm, k to marker, rm, k26 (28, 29, 31, 32, 33, 35), pm, m1, pm, work to end.

Row 2: [P to marker, sm, m1p, p to marker, m1p, sm] twice, p to end.

Row 3: [Work to marker, sm, m1, k to marker, m1, sm] twice, work to end.

Rep these last two rows 2 (2, 3, 3, 4, 4, 5) more times.

NEWBORN (6, 12, 24 MONTHS) SIZES ONLY

Next Row: Purl. 132 (152, 172, 192) sts.

3 (9, 18) MONTHS SIZES ONLY

Next Row: As for Row 2. 142 (162, 178) sts.

Keeping front shaping correct, k across next row to second marker, slip next 52 (56, 58, 62, 64, 66, 70) sts onto DPNs to be worked next. Break yarn, leaving a long tail, and graft both gussets together, removing markers. Slip rem sts onto waste yarn.

Right leg

Rejoin yarn to rear gusset and, using DPNs, k around to front gusset, pu 4 sts along edge of gusset, pm to mark beg of rnd. 56 (60, 62, 66, 68, 70, 74) sts.

Work in St st until work measures approx 48.5 (52.5, 57, 60.5, 65, 69.5, 73) cm from neckline. [Leg measures approx 11 (12.5, 16, 19, 22, 25, 33) cm from crotch.]

Change to CC.

Work 5 rnds in G st.

Cast off p-wise.

Left leg

Using smaller circular needle and MC, rejoin yarn to front gusset, pm, pu 4 sts along edge of gusset, remove waste yarn, placing live stitches onto LH needle, k to last st, m1, k1. 58 (62, 64, 68, 70, 72, 76) sts

Row 1 (WS): Purl.

Row 2: K1, k2tog, k to last st, m1, k1.

Rep these two rows until there are 9 (9, 8, 9, 10, 10, 11) sts between marker and end of row, then rep Row 2 every 4th row 2 (2, 2, 3, 3, 3, 3) times.

Cont in St st until left leg measures the same as right leg before G st.

Change to CC.

Work 5 rows in G st.

Cast off k-wise.

Sleeves (make 2)

Using DPNs and MC, rejoin yarn to underarm, pu 2 sts, pm to mark beg of rnd, pu 2 sts, remove waste yarn, placing live sts onto LH needle, k to end. 46 (50, 52, 54, 56, 58, 60) sts.

Work 12 rnds in St st.

Dec Rnd: K2tog, k to last 2 sts, ssk.

Rep Dec Rnd every 12th rnd 2 (2, 3, 3, 4, 4, 5) more times. 40 (44, 44, 46, 46, 48, 48) sts.

Cont to work even in St st until sleeve measures 24 (26.5, 29, 32, 34.5, 37, 39.5) cm from top of shoulder.

Change to CC.

Work 5 rnds in G st.

Cast off p-wise.

Hood

Using smaller circular needle and MC and with RS of garment facing, pu and k58 (64, 72, 74, 76, 76, 84) sts along neckline.

Row 1 (WS): P24 (26, 30, 30, 31, 31, 34), pm, p10 (12, 12, 14, 14, 14, 16), pm, p to end.

Row 2: K1, k2tog, k to last 3 sts, ssk, k1.

Row 3 & all WS rows: Purl.

Row 4: K1, k2tog, k to marker, m1, sm, k to marker, sm, m1, k to last 3 sts, ssk, k1.

Rows 6-9: Rep Rows 2-5.

Row 10: Knit.

Row 12: As for Row 4.

Rows 14-17: Rep Rows 10-13. 54 (60, 68, 70, 72, 72, 80) sts.

Row 18: K to marker, m1, sm, k to marker, sm, m1, k to end.

Rep Row 18 every 6th row 3 (3, 3, 3, 3, 4, 4) more times. 62 (68, 76, 78, 80, 82, 90) sts K to marker, rm, k5 (6, 6, 7, 7, 7, 8), pm, k to marker, rm, k to end.

Cont in St st until hood measures 19.5 (19.5, 19.5, 20.5, 20.5, 21, 21.5) cm from beg.

Dec Row (RS): K to 2 sts before marker, ssk, sm, k2tog, k to end.

Rep dec row every 4th row 2 (3, 3, 3, 4, 4, 4) more times, then every 2nd row 5 (5, 6, 6, 6, 6, 7) times. 46 (50, 56, 58, 58, 60, 66) sts.

Next Row (WS): P to marker, rm. Graft hood sts together.

The button bands and hood edging are worked as follows:

Using long circular needle and CC, with RS facing, pu sts at a ratio of 2 sts for every 3 rows, starting at base of inside left leg and working up the left side to waste yarn marker at neck, pm, pu sts along hood to waste yarn marker at neck, pm, pu 93 (104, 105, 115, 125, 137, 137) sts down right front to base of leg.

NOTE: An exact st count is only necessary for the button loop side.

Row 1 (WS): Knit.

Row 2 (RS): K to st before marker, kfb, sm, kfb, k to end.

Rep these two rows once more.

Button Loop Row: K to st before marker, kfb, sm, kfb, k to marker, sm, k2, *using backwards loop method, cast on 4 sts, k11 (11, 10, 10, 10, 11, 11); rep from * to last 3 sts, using backwards loop method, cast on 4 sts, k3. 8 (9, 10, 11, 12, 12, 12) button loops made.

Cast off k-wise.

Overlapping front bands by approx 2cm, sew buttons (placed approx 1.5cm from edge) to correspond with button loops, weave in all ends and block to finished measurements.

Booties (both boots)

With CC, cast on 30 (34, 38) sts. Join to work in the rnd, being careful not to twist.

Pm to mark beg of rnd.

Rnd 1: *K1, p1; rep from * to end.

Rnd 2: P1, m1, [k1, p1] six (seven, eight) times, k1, m1, p1, k1, m1, [p1, k1] six (seven, eight) times, p1, m1, k1. 34 (38, 42) sts.

Rnd 3: *P1, k1; rep from * to end.

Rnd 4: K1, m1, [p1, k1] seven (eight, nine) times, p1, m1, k1, p1, m1, [k1, p1] seven (eight, nine) times, k1, m1, p1. 38 (42, 46) sts.

Rnd 5: As for Rnd 1.

Rnd 6: P1, m1, [k1, p1] eight (nine, ten) times, k1, m1, p1, k1, m1, [p1, k1]

eight (nine, ten) times, p1, m1, k1. 42 (46, 50) sts.

Rnd 7: As for Rnd 3.

SIZES 6-9 & 12-18 MONTHS ONLY

Rnd 8: K1, m1, [p1, k1] ten (eleven) times, p1, m1, k1, p1, m1, [k1, p1] ten (eleven) times, k1, m1, p1. 50 (54) sts.

Rnd 9: As for Rnd 1.

SIZE 12-18 MONTHS ONLY

Rnd 10: P1, m1, [k1, p1] twelve times, k1, m1, p1, k1, m1, [p1, k1] twelve times, p1, m1, k1. 58 sts.

Rnd 11: As for Rnd 3.

ALL SIZES

Change to MC.

Next Rnd: Purl.

Knit 6 (8, 10) rnds.

Shape instep

Row 1: K23 (28, 33), ssk, turn.

Row 2: Sl1, p4 (6, 8), p2tog, turn.

Row 3: Sl1, k4 (6, 8), ssk, turn.

Row 4: As for Row 2.

Rep these last 2 rows 5 (8, 10) more times.

Next Row: Sl1, k4 (6, 8), ssk, k to end. 27 (29, 33) sts.

Right boot

Row 1: K10 (10, 11), k2tog, k7 (9, 11), kfb, turn.

Row 2: P26 (28, 32), rm as it is passed, pfb. 28 (30, 34) sts.

Row 3: Knit.

Row 4: Purl.

Rep these last 2 rows 5 (6, 7) times.

Break yarn, leaving sts on needle.

With CC and starting at the base of opening on heel side, with RS facing, pu 10 (11, 12) sts evenly to top of boot, pm, k across 28 (30, 34) sts on needle, pm, pu 10 (11, 12) sts evenly to base of opening.

Row 1 (WS): Knit.

Row 2: K to st before marker, kfb, sm, kfb, k to 2 sts before marker, kfb, kfb, sm, k to end.

Row 3: As for Row 1.

Row 4: K to st before marker, kfb, sm, kfb, k to 3 sts before marker, kfb, kfb, k1, sm, cast on 4 sts, k6 (7, 8), cast on 4 sts, k to end.

Cast off k-wise.

Left boot

Next Rnd: K10 (10, 11), k2tog, k to end.

Row 1: K6 (6, 7), kfb, turn.

Row 2: P26 (28, 32), rm as it is passed, pfb. 28 (30, 34) sts.

Row 3: Knit.

Row 4: Purl.

Rep these last 2 rows 5 (6, 7) times.

Break yarn, leaving sts on needle.

With CC and starting at the base of opening on toe side, with RS facing, pu 10 (11, 12) sts evenly to top of boot, pm, k across 28 (30, 34) sts on needle, pm, pu 10 (11, 12) sts evenly to base of opening.

Row 1 (WS): Knit.

Row 2: K to st before marker, kfb, sm, kfb, k to 2 sts before marker, kfb, kfb, sm, k to end.

Row 3: As for Row 1.

Row 4: K4, cast on 4 sts, k6 (7, 8), cast on 4 sts, kfb, sm, kfb, k to 3 sts before marker, kfb, kfb, k1, sm, k to end.

Cast off k-wise.

Finishing: Sew sole seam. Overlap button bands by approx 2cm and sew in place at base. Sew buttons (placed approx 1.5cm from edge) to correspond with button loops and weave in all ends.

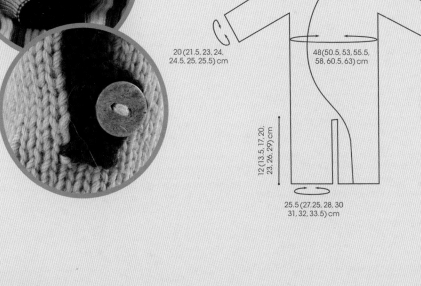

7.5 (10, 12.5) cm

25 (27.5, 30, 33, 35.5, 38, 40.5) cm

20 (21.5, 23, 24, 24.5, 25, 25.5) cm

48 (50.5, 53, 55.5, 58, 60.5, 63) cm

49.5 (53.5, 58, 61.5, 66, 70.5, 74) cm

12 (13.5, 17, 20, 23, 26, 29) cm

25.5 (27.25, 28, 30, 31, 32, 33.5) cm

Little Snowflake Cardigan

2
Intermediate

This scaled-down Scandinavian design will make a great gift for the smallest people in your life. You won't find a cuter way to keep out the chills this winter.

About this pattern

Sizing
Cardigan: 0-6mths (6-12mths, 1-2yrs, 2-3yrs). See schematic for measurements

Yarn
Patons Diploma Gold DK
Cardigan: 3 (4, 5, 5) balls in Red 06151; 1 (2, 2, 2) ball in Cream 06142

About the yarn
DK weight; 120m per 50g ball; 55% wool, 25% acrylic, 20% nylon

Needles
3.25mm and 4mm straight 30cm long

Tension
Measured over St st using 4mm needles:

10 cm

10 cm

30 rows

22 sts

Other supplies
Tapestry needle
5 (5, 6, 7) buttons

Cardigan

CAST ON

Back and fronts
(worked in one piece to armholes)
Using 3.25mm needles and MC, cast on 102 (112, 124, 132) sts.

Row 1 (RS): *K2, p2; rep from * to end.

Row 2: *P2, k2; rep from * to end.

These 2 rows form k2 p2 ribbing. Work 6 more rows in rib patt.

Change to 4mm needles. Work 4 rows in St st, starting with a knit row.

Next row: K1 (1, 1, 0), join in CC and then rep chart 9 (10, 11, 12) times, k2 (1, 2, 0).

Continue in pattern for another 8 rows, working chart as appropriate.

Break off CC and continue in St st with MC only until work measures 13 (14.5, 16, 17) cm, ending with a WS row.

Divide for armholes

Next row (RS): K25 (28, 31, 33), turn.

Next row: Cast off 2 sts, purl to end. 23 (26, 29, 31) sts.

Decrease for raglan shaping

Next row: K to last 2 sts, k2tog. 22 (25, 28, 30) sts.

Work 1 (3, 1, 3) rows in St st.

Next row: K to last 2 sts, k2tog. 21 (24, 27, 29) sts.

Next row: Purl.

Rep these 2 rows 7 (8, 9, 11) more times. 14 (16, 18, 18) sts.

Neck shaping

Next row: Cast off 2 sts, k to last 2 sts, k2tog.

Next row: P to last 2 sts, p2tog. 10 (12, 14, 14) sts.

Continue to dec on every RS row at raglan edge as before, and dec at neck edge on next 3 (6, 6, 6) rows, and then next 2 (1, 2, 2) RS rows, ending with a WS row.

Break yarn and pull through rem st(s) to fasten off. Rejoin yarn to rem sts, with RS facing. Cast off 2 sts, k until there are 50 (54, 60, 64) sts on R hand needle, turn.

Next row: Cast off 2 sts, p to end. 48 (52, 58, 62) sts.

Decrease for raglan shaping

Next row: SSK, k to last 2 sts, k2tog.

Work 1 (3, 1, 3) rows in St st.

Next row: SSK, k to last 2 sts, k2tog.

Next row: Purl.

Continue to dec in this way until 18 (20, 22, 24) sts remain, ending with a WS row. Cast off.

Hints & tips

When doing the neck shaping on the fronts, keep a note of how many rows you have worked. It can be confusing trying to keep track of neck and raglan shaping at the same time!

Rejoin yarn to rem 25 (28, 31, 33) sts with RS facing.

Next row: Cast off 2 sts, k to end.

Next row: P to end. 23 (26, 29, 31) sts.

Decrease for raglan shaping

Next row: SSK, knit to end.

Work 1 (3, 1, 3) rows in St st.

Next row: SSK, knit to end. 21 (23, 27, 29) sts.

Next row: Purl.

Rep these 2 rows 7 (8, 9, 11) more times. 14 (16, 18, 18) sts.

Next row: K2tog tbl, k to end.

Next row: Cast off 2 sts, purl to last 2 sts, p2tog. 11 (13, 15, 15) sts.

Continue to dec on every RS row at raglan edge as before, and dec at neck edge on next 3 (6, 6, 6) rows, and then next 2 (1, 2, 2) RS rows, ending with a WS row.

Purl 1 row.

Break yarn and pull through rem st(s) to fasten off.

Sleeves

Using 3.25mm needles and MC, cast on 30 (34, 38, 38) sts. Work 8 rows in k2 p2 rib, starting with k2.

Change to 4mm needles. 62 Knit.

Next row: K1, m1, k to last st, m1, k1.

Work 3 rows St st, beginning with a purl row. Inc in this way at each end of next row then every 4th row 5 (2, 2, 3) times, then every 6th row 1 (3, 5, 5) times, then every 8th row 0 (1, 0, 0) times. 46 (50, 56, 58) sts.

Purl 1 row.

Work 8 rows in St st, starting with a knit row.

Next row: Cast off 2 sts, k to end.

Next row: Cast off 2 sts, p to end. 42 (46, 52, 54) sts.

Decrease for raglan shaping

Next row: SSK, k to last 2 sts, k2tog.

Work 1 (3, 1, 3) rows in St st.

Next row: SSK, k to last 2 sts, k2tog.

Next row: Purl.

Rep these last 2 rows until 12 (14, 16, 16) sts remain. Cast off.

Button band

Using 3.25mm needles and MC, PU and k46 (54, 58, 66) sts along left front edge.

Work 6 rows in k2 p2 rib, starting with p2. Cast off.

Buttonhole band

Using 3.25mm needles and MC, PU and k46 (54, 58, 66) sts along right front edge.

Work 3 rows in k2 p2 rib, starting p2.

SIZES 1 & 3 ONLY

Next row: K2, *p2, yo, k2tog, [p2, k2] twice, rep from * 2 (3) more times, p2, yo, k2tog, p2, k2.

SIZES 2 & 4 ONLY

Next row: K2, *yo, p2tog, k2, [p2, k2] twice, rep from * 3 (4) more times, yo, p2tog, k2.

ALL SIZES

Work 2 more rows in k2 p2 rib.

Cast off.

Neckband

Sew raglan sleeve seams and sleeve seams.

Using 3.25mm needles and MC, PU and k14 (15, 16, 17) sts over right front band and up slope of neck, 12 (14, 16, 16) sts over cast off sts for sleeve, 18 (20, 22, 24) sts at back of neck, 12 (14, 16, 16) sts over cast off sts for sleeve, 14 (15, 16, 17) sts down left front neck and over left front band.

Work 3 rows k2 p2 rib, starting with p2.

Next row (RS): K2, yo, p2tog, k2, rib to end.

Work 2 more rows in rib. Cast off.

Finishing: Sew on buttons.

Schematic

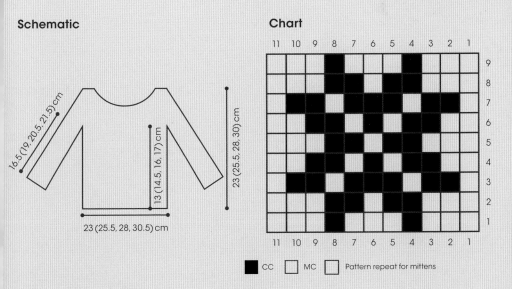

16.5 (19, 20.5, 21.5) cm

13 (14.5, 16, 17) cm

23 (25.5, 28, 30) cm

23 (25.5, 28, 30.5) cm

Chart

11	10	9	8	7	6	5	4	3	2	1	
											9
											8
											7
											6
											5
											4
											3
											2
											1

11 10 9 8 7 6 5 4 3 2 1

■ CC   ☐ MC   ☐ Pattern repeat for mittens

45

Vintage Baby Set

2
Intermediate

Now you know how to knit Fair Isle patterns, it's time to put your skills to good use with this adorable baby set.

This is a classic pattern, which will no doubt be loved and cherished for years to come. If you fancy experimenting with different yarns, this is a great project to do it. Sport-weight yarns are sometimes listed as a light DK and include popular yarns like Debbie Bliss Baby Cashmerino, among others. There are plenty of lighter DK yarns that will knit nicely to this tension, so have a rummage through your box of oddments.

Cardigan

CAST ON

With MC, cast on 121 (133, 145, 157, 169) sts.

Work in G st for 2.5cm, ending after a WS row.

Row 1 (RS): K6, pm, work Row 1 of chart, working pattern rep 9 (10, 11, 12, 13) times, work last st in chart, pm, k6.

Row 2 (WS): K6, sm, work next row of chart to last 6 sts, sm, k6.

Cont until all rows of chart have been worked. With MC only, work for 1.5cm in G st, ending after a WS row.

Row 1 (RS): Knit.

Row 2 (WS): K6, p to last 6 sts, k6.

Rep last 2 rows until work measures 15 (20, 19.5, 21.5, 24.5) cm from cast-on edge.

Set up for twisted rib bodice and buttonholes

Row 1 (RS – buttonhole): K2, k2tog, yo, k2, *k1tbl, p3; rep from * to last 7 sts, k1tbl, k6.

Row 2 (WS): K6, *p1tbl, k3; rep from * to last 7 sts, p1tbl, k6.

Continue in rib as set for 2 (0, 8, 6, 4) more rows.

About this pattern

Sizing
3 (6, 12, 18, 24) months, designed to fit with 5cm positive ease

Yarn
Yarn Love Marianne Dashwood

1 skein in Allure (MC), 16 (16, 16, 20, 20) yds each in Shiny Penny (CC1) and Martini (CC2)

About the yarn
Sport/5-ply; 302m per 100g skein; 100% Merino wool

Needles
3mm circular, 40cm
2 3mm DPNs (for gusset grafting)

Tension
Measured over St st:

10 cm

10 cm   32 rows

24 sts

Other supplies
2 stitch markers
1cm buttons (3, 3, 4, 4, 4)
Safety pin
Stitch holders
Waste yarn
Tapestry needle

Special Instructions
The cardigan is worked seamlessly and flat on straight needles. Sleeves are worked flat and then seamed and sewn into place.

The leggings are worked seamlessly, in the round, with short rows along the backside to adequately cover behind. Waistband in stockinette that folds over and an i-cord tie is threaded through.

Hints & tips

When working the Fair Isle pattern flat, catch each CC into the garter stitch border for a few stitches. This helps the Fair Isle pattern to lay flat.

You will now separate into front/back/sleeves. While working the right front at the same time rep buttonhole every 12th row for a total of 3 (3, 4, 4, 4) buttonholes.

Separate for fronts and sleeves

Next Row (RS): K6, *cont in rib as set for 21 (24, 27, 30, 33) sts, cast off 12 sts, continue in rib over next 42 (48, 54, 60, 66) sts, cast off next 12 sts, continue in rib to last 6 sts, k6.

Cont on left front (last 27 (30, 33, 36, 39) sts) and leave back and right front sts on waste yarn or stitch holders.

Left front

Next Row (WS): K6, work in rib to end.

Row 1 (RS): Work in rib to last 6 sts, k6.

Row 2: K6, work in rib to end.

Rep these last 2 rows 9 (10, 11, 13, 14) more times.

Neck and shoulder shaping

Row 1 (RS): Work in rib to last 6 sts, k6.

Row 2 (WS): Cast off 6 sts, work in rib to end. 21 (24, 27, 30, 33) sts.

Rows 3, 5, 7 & 9: Work in rib as established.

Row 4: Cast off 3 (3, 3, 4, 4) sts, work in rib to end. 18 (21, 24, 26, 29) sts

Rows 6 & 8: Cast off 2 (3, 3, 4, 4) sts, workin rib to end. 14 (15, 18, 18, 21) sts.

Row 10: Cast off 1 (2, 3, 3, 3) sts, work in rib to end. 13 (13, 15, 15, 18) sts.

Row 11: Cast off 6 (6, 7, 7, 8) sts, work in rib to end. 7 (7, 8, 8, 10) sts.

Row 12: Cast off 1 (1, 1, 1, 2) sts, work in rib to end. 6 (6, 7, 7, 8) sts.

Cast off rem sts.

Back

With WS of work facing, place back sts onto needle and attach yarn.

Next Row (WS): Work in rib to end of row.

Cont in rib for 26 (30, 32, 36, 38) more rows.

Neck & shoulder shaping

Cast off 6 (6, 7, 7, 8) sts at beg of next 4 rows. 19 (25, 27, 33, 35) sts.

Cast off all sts.

Right front

With WS of work facing, place right front sts back onto needle and attach yarn.

Next Row (WS): Work in rib to last 6 sts, k6.

Next Row (RS): K6, work in rib to end.

Rep these last 2 rows until work measures 11.5 (12, 12.5, 13, 13.5) cm from beg of rib and last buttonhole has been worked.

Work 1 more WS row.

Note: Cont working buttonholes, as previously instructed, every 12th row.

Neck shaping

Row 1 (RS): Cast off 6 sts, work in rib to end. 21 (24, 27, 30, 33) sts.

Row 2, 4, 6 & 8 (WS): Work in rib as established.

Row 3: Cast off 3 (3, 3, 4, 4) sts, work in rib to end. 18 (21, 24, 26, 29) sts.

Row 5 & 7: Cast off 2 (3, 3, 4, 4) sts, work in rib to end. 14 (15,18,18,21) sts.

Row 9: Cast off 1 (2, 3, 3, 3) sts, work in rib to end. 13 (13,15,15,18) sts.

Row 10: Cast off 6 (6, 7, 7, 8) sts, work in rib to end. 7 (7, 8, 8, 10) sts.

Row 11: Cast off 1 (1, 1, 1, 2) sts, work in rib to end. 6 (6, 7, 7, 8) sts.

Cast off rem sts.

Sleeves (make 2)

With MC, cast on 50 (52, 54, 56, 58) sts. Beg with a RS row work in G st for 2cm, ending after a WS row.

Beg working in St st and work 2 rows.

Beg incs as follows:

Row 1 (RS): K1, m1, k to last st, m1, k1. 52 (54, 56, 58, 60) sts.

Rep this inc row every 6 (6, 8, 8, 10th) row four more times. 60 (62, 64, 66, 68) sts.

Cont in St st until sleeve measures 18 (19, 21.5, 23, 24) cm from cast on, ending after a WS row.

Cast off all sts.

Finishing: Sew shoulder seams, then sleeve seams, leaving 2.5cm unseamed at the armpit. Sew sleeves onto armhole edges, opening and sewing the unseamed sleeve section onto the underarm cast off on bodice of cardigan.Sew buttons onto left front edge to correspond with buttonholes.

With straight (or circular) needles, MC and RS of work facing, pu and k21 (24, 25, 28, 29) sts along right front neck edge, 19 (25, 27, 33, 35) sts along back and (24, 25, 28, 29) sts along left front neck edge. 61 (73, 77, 89, 93) sts.

Knit 2 rows, cast off all sts k-wise on the WS. Weave in all ends.

Leggings

Waistband

With circular needles and MC, cast on 96 (120, 124, 140, 144) sts. Join to work in the rnd, being careful not to twist. Pm for beg of rnd.

Work in St st for 9 rnds, then purl 1 rnd (turning row), then cont in St st for another 4 rnds.

Eyelet Rnd: K45 (57, 59, 67, 69) sts, k2tog, yo, k2, yo, ssk, k to end of rnd.

Cont in St st for 4 rnds.

Stitch marker set up

Next Rnd: K25 (31, 31, 37, 37), pm, k46 (58, 58, 70, 70), pm, k to end of rnd.

Schematics

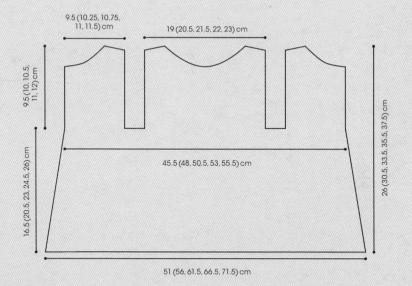

9.5 (10.25, 10.75, 11, 11.5) cm

19 (20.5, 21.5, 22, 23) cm

9.5 (10, 10.5, 11, 12) cm

45.5 (48, 50.5, 53, 55.5) cm

26 (30.5, 33.5, 35.5, 37.5) cm

16.5 (20.5, 23, 24.5, 26) cm

51 (56, 61.5, 66.5, 71.5) cm

Cardigan body

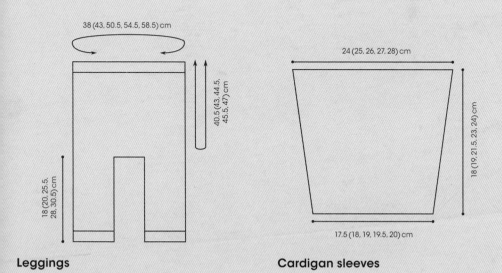

38 (43, 50.5, 54.5, 58.5) cm

40.5 (43, 44.5, 45.5, 47) cm

18 (20, 25.5, 28, 30.5) cm

Leggings

24 (25, 26, 27, 28) cm

18 (19, 21.5, 23, 24) cm

17.5 (18, 19, 19.5, 20) cm

Cardigan sleeves

Short rows

Short Row Rnd: K to 1 st before marker, w&t, sl1, p47 (59, 59, 71, 71), w&t, sl1 p-wise, k to end of rnd working wraps as you come to them.

Cont in St st and work Short Row Rnd every 8th rnd. Cont until work measures 15 (16, 16, 16, 17) cm from purled edge, measuring on the front side, removing markers on last rnd.

Gusset

Next Rnd: K2 (2, 3, 1, 2), pm (this is the new beg of rnd), k44 (56, 56, 68, 68), pm, m1, k4 (4, 6, 2, 4), m1, pm, k44 (56, 56, 68, 68), pm, m1, k2 (2, 3, 1, 2), m1, k to end of rnd. 100 (124, 128, 144, 148) sts.

Rnd 1: Knit.

Rnd 2: *K to marker, sm, m1, k to marker, m1, sm; rep from * once more, k to end of rnd. 104 (128, 132, 148, 152) sts.

Rep these last 2 rnds 4 (5, 6, 7, 7) more times. 120 (148, 156, 176, 180) sts.

Separate for legs

Next Rnd: *K to marker and remove, place next 16 (18, 22, 20, 22) sts onto DPN, remove marker; rep from * once more.

Cut yarn 40cm in length.

Holding gusset WS tog, DPNs parallel, use tapestry needle and graft these sts tog using kitchener Stitch.

Legs (make 2)

Place one set of leg sts onto waste yarn and beg with other set on needle. *Attach MC and pu and k4 sts along gusset edge, pm. 48 (60, 60, 72, 72) sts.

Beg working in the rnd, in St st until leg measures 9 (11.5, 17, 19.5, 22) cm from gusset.

Work in G st for 1.5cm, ending after a p rnd.

Beg Row 1 of chart, work pattern rep 4 (5, 5, 6, 6) times per rnd.

Cont until all rows of chart have been worked. With MC only, work in g st for 2.5cm, ending after a K row.

Cast off all sts purl-wise.

For 2nd leg, rep from *.

i-cord tie

With DPNs and MC, cast on 4 sts.

i-cord row: *K4. Do NOT turn. Slide all sts to other end of needle. Rep from * until tie measures 70 (75, 85, 90, 95) cm. Cast off all sts.

Finishing: With tapestry needle, weave in all yarn ends. Fold waistband to the inside and slip-stitch in place.

With safety pin attached to one end of icord tie, thread tie through eyelet opening at front waistband edge and thread through waistband, to other eyelet opening. Tie a knot in each end of tie.

Chart

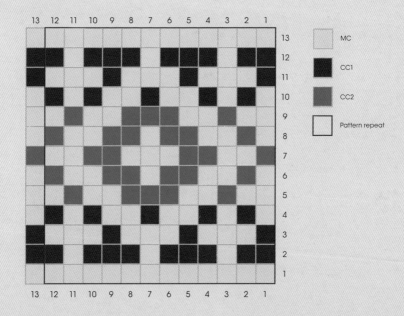

Bloomer Loaf & Cheesy Top

1

Beginner

The warmer weather doesn't mean that you can't still knit for your children. This cute set is comfy and practical, perfect for little mischief makers.

Top

CAST ON

Cast on 72 (78, 84, 84, 96, 96) sts. Join to work in the rnd, being careful not to twist.

PM to mark beg of rnd.

Work in 1x1 rib for 2.5cm.

Work in patt (see over) until work measures 15 (18,19,20,21.5,22.5) cm.

[K31 (33, 36, 36, 41, 41) in patt, cast off next 5 (6, 6, 6, 7, 7) sts] twice.

Note: From now on knit first and last st of every row, maintain rest of sts in patt.

Front

Work 31 (33, 36, 36, 41, 41) sts flat in patt for 4.5 (5, 5, 5, 5.5, 5.5) cm.

Next Row: Work 10 (10, 11, 11, 13, 13) sts in patt, cast off next 11 (13, 14, 14, 15, 15) sts, work in patt to end of row.

Right front shoulder

**Dec 1 st at neck edge on next two WS rows. 8 (8, 9, 9, 11, 11) sts.

Work even in patt until work measures 9 (9.5, 10, 11, 12, 13.5) cm from armhole cast off.

Knit 4 rows.

Cast off.**

Left front shoulder

With WS facing, join yarn to remaining front sts.

Rep from ** to **.

Back

With WS facing, join yarn to back sts. 31 (33, 36, 36, 41, 41) sts.

Work in patt for 7 (7.5, 7.5, 8.5, 9, 10) cm.

Row: Work 10 (10, 11, 11, 13, 13) sts in patt, cast off next 11 (13, 14, 14, 15, 15) sts, work in pattern to end of row.

Left back shoulder

Dec 1 st at neck edge on next two WS rows. 8 (8, 9, 9, 11, 11) sts.

Work even in patt until work measures 9 (9.5, 10, 11, 12, 13.5) cm from armhole cast off.

Knit 2 rows.

Next Row: K2, yo, k2tog, knit to last 3 sts, yo, k2tog, k1.

Knit 3 rows.

Cast off.

Right back shoulder

With WS facing, join yarn to remaining back sts.

About this pattern

Sizing

Top: 0-3 (3-6, 6-12,12-18, 18-24, 24-36) months
Bloomers: 0-3 (3-6, 6-12, 12-18, 18-36) months

Yarn

Knit Picks Shine Worsted
Top: 2 (2, 3, 3, 3, 3) skeins in Citrine (baby sample) or Platinum (toddler sample)
Bloomers: 2 (3, 3, 4, 4) skeins in Macaw (baby sample) or Pageant and Platinum (toddler sample)

About the yarn

Aran/worsted; 68m per 50g ball; 60% Pima Cotton, 40% Modal natural beech wood fibre

Needles

4mm circular, 30cm
4mm DPNs, 30cm for bloomers

Tension

Measured over St st:

10 cm

10 cm

28 (29, 29) rows

19 (18, 16) sts

Other supplies

Waste yarn or stitch holders
Tapestry needle
15mm buttons (for top)
5 stitch markers, all different colours

Hints & tips

For stripes you'll need 1 (2, 2, 2, 2) skeins of each colour. Change colours every 10 rnds (apart from waistband and cuffs which were worked in one colour) If substituting yarn, check the yardage. The yarn used is very dense and you don't get a lot in 50g compared to other aran weight yarns.

Dec 1 st at neck edge on next two WS rows. 8 (8, 9, 9, 11, 11) sts.

Work even in patt until work measures 9 (9.5, 10, 11, 12, 13.5) cm from armhole.

Knit 6 rows.

Cast off.

Finishing: Sew right back shoulder to right front shoulder by overlapping garter stitch band.

Sew buttons onto left front shoulder.

Weave in ends.

Bloomers

Cast on 72 (80, 88, 96, 104) sts. Join to work in the rnd, being careful not to twist.

Pm to mark beg of rnd.

Waistband

Work in 2x2 rib for 2.5cm.

Next Rnd: *K2tog, yo, p2; rep from * to end of rnd.

Work in 2x2 rib until waistband measures 5cm total.

Body

Next Rnd: K36 (40, 44, 48, 52), PM, knit to end of rnd.

Short row section

Note: Always pick up and work wraps as you come to them.

**Work in St st for 6 rnds.

Next Rnd: [K1, M1, knit to 1 st before marker, M1, k1] twice.

Next Rnd: Knit to 1 st before marker, w&t, purl to 1 st before marker, w&t, knit to end of rnd.**

Repeat from ** to ** twice more. 84 (92, 100, 108, 116) sts.

Work in St st until work measures 15 (18, 20.5, 23, 25.5) cm measuring along shorter side (the side with no short rows).

Gusset increases

Next Rnd: K17 (19, 21, 23, 25), PMA, k8, PMB, k34 (38, 42, 46, 50), PMC, k8, PMD, knit to end.

Next Rnd: Knit to marker A, M1, sm, k8, sm, M1, k to marker C, M1, sm, k8, sm, M1, knit to end.

Next Rnd: Knit.

Rep these last 2 rnds three more times. 100 (108, 116, 124, 132) sts.

Next Rnd: Knit to marker D, place sts between marker D and marker A on spare yarn or stitch holder.

Cut yarn leaving a long tail (30-45 cm) and graft previous 8 sts together with the next available 8 sts (those btw markers A and B) using Kitchener stitch.

Legs

First leg: The stitches that are left on the needles are the first leg sts. Divide them evenly among DPNs then pu and knit 2 sts from the side of the gap left by the crotch. Pm after the first of these picked up sts to mark beg of rnd. Join to work in the rnd. 44 (48, 52, 56, 60) sts.

**Work in St st for 3 rnds.

Next Rnd: K1, m1, knit to 1 st before end of rnd, m1, k1.**

Rep from ** to ** twice more. 50 (54, 58, 62, 66) sts.

Work even in St st until leg measures 5 (6, 7.5, 9, 10) cm.

SIZES 0-3 (-, -, 12-18, -) MONTHS ONLY

Next Rnd: *K2tog, p1; rep from * to last 2 sts, k1, p1. 34 (-, -, 42, -) sts.

SIZES (3-6, -, -, 18-24) MONTHS ONLY

Next Rnd: *K2tog, p1; rep from * to end. - (36, -, -, 44) sts.

SIZES (-, 6-12, -, -) MONTHS ONLY

Next Rnd: *K2tog, p1; rep from * to last 4 sts, k2tog, p2tog. - (-, 38, -, -) sts.

Stitch pattern: In the round

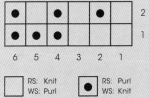

Stitch pattern: Worked flat

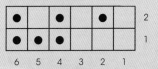

Instructions

Pattern Stitch: Pattern is worked the same in the round and flat.

Row/Rnd 1: *K3, p3; rep from * to end of rnd.

Row/Rnd 2: *K1, p1; rep from * to end of rnd.

These two rows/rnds form pattern.

ALL SIZES

Work in 1x1 rib for 2.5cm.

Cast off in pattern.

Second leg: Place stitches that are on spare yarn or holder on DPNs, distribute sts evenly and work as for first leg.

Finishing: Weave in ends. Make an i-cord of appropriate length for the drawstring and thread through.

Schematics

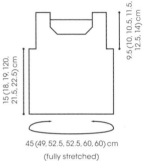

9.5 (10, 10.5, 11.5, 12.5, 14) cm

15 (18, 19, 120, 21.5, 22.5) cm

45 (49, 52.5, 52.5, 60, 60) cm
(fully stretched)

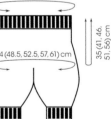

37.5 (42, 46, 50.5, 54.5) cm

44 (48.5, 52.5, 57, 61) cm

35 (41, 46, 51, 56) cm

7.5 (8.5, 10, 11.5, 12.5) cm

Rice Pudding Cardigan

2
Intermediate

This yarn is beautifully soft against your skin, so it's absolutely perfect for keeping babies nice and warm, and the textured stitches make it even warmer.

This little cardigan in rich green will look great with little jeans and the leaf- shaped buttons are the perfect finishing touch.

CAST ON

Body

Using circular needles, cast on 74 (78, 82,86, 90, 94) sts.

Row 1: Sl1, k1, *p2, k2; rep from* to end.

Row 2: Sl1, p1, *k2, p2; rep from* to end.

Rep these 2 rows five times more or until work measures 5cm, ending with WS row.

Next row (RS): Sl1, p to last st, k1.

Next row: Sl1, p to end.

Row 1 (RS): Sl1, k3 (3, 4, 4, 5, 5), p2, k6,p2, knit to last 14 (14, 15, 15, 16, 16) sts, p2, k6, p2, k to end.

Row 2 (and all WS rows): Sl1, p3 (3, 4, 4, 5, 5), k2, p6, k2, purl to last 14(14, 15, 15, 16, 16) sts, k2, p6, k2, p to end.

Row 3: Sl1, k3 (3, 4, 4, 5, 5), p2, C4F, k2, p2, knit to last 14 (14, 15, 15, 16, 16) sts, p2, C4F, k2, p2, k to end.

Row 5: As Row 1.

Row 7: Sl1, k3 (3, 4, 4, 5, 5), p2, k2, C4B, p2, knit to last 14 (14, 15, 15, 16, 16) sts, p2, k2, C4B, p2, k to end.

Rows 1-8 form Cable pattern. Continue working in pattern as set until work measures 15 (17.5, 19, 20.5, 21.5, 22.5) cm from cast on edge, ending with a WS row.

Next row (RS): Sl1, p to last st, k1.

Next row: Sl1, p to end.Break yarn and place body aside.

About this pattern

Sizing
Newborn (0-3, 3-6, 6-12, 12-18, 18-24 months)

Yarn
Colinette Skye – 1 (2, 2, 2, 2, 2) x 100g hank(s) in Velvet Leaf (113)

About the yarn
DK; 150m per 100g; 100% wool

Needles
4.5mm circular, 60cm long
4.5mm DPNs

Tension
Measured over St st:

Other supplies
4 (4, 5, 5, 5, 6) buttons (roughly 20mm should do)
Stitch markers
Cable needle

Special Instructions

C4F: Sl2 to CN, hold to front, k2, k2 from CN.
C4B: Sl2 to CN, hold to back, k2, k2 from CN.
Moss stitch
(over an even number of sts):
Row1: *K1, p1; rep from * to end of row.
Row 2: *P1; k1; rep from * to end of row.
Rep these two rows to form pattern.
Moss stitch
(over an odd number of sts):
Row 1: *K1, p1; rep from * to last st, k1.
Rep this row to form pattern.

Hints & tips

To help keep the edges smooth, I slip the first st of every row. On RS rows knit the last st of every row, and on WS rows purl the last st of every row.

Sleeves (make two)

Using DPNs, cast on 24 (24, 28, 28, 28,32) sts. Join to work in the rnd, beingcareful not to twist.

Work in 2x2 ribbing for 12 rows or untilwork measures 5cm.

Next Rnd: Purl.

Next Rnd: Knit, increasing 0 (2, 0, 2, 2, 0)sts evenly across rnd. 24 (26,28, 30, 30, 32) sts.

Rnds 1 and 2: K7 (8, 9, 10, 10, 11), p2,k6, p2, k to end of rnd.

Rnd 3: K7 (8, 9, 10, 10, 11), p2, C4F,K2, p2, k to end of rnd.

Rnds 4-6: As Rnd 1.

Rnd 7: K7 (8, 9, 10, 10, 11), p2, k2,C4B, p2, k to end of rnd.

Rnd 8: As Rnd 1.

Rnds 1-8 form pattern. Continue in pattern as set until work measures 11.5 (13, 15, 18, 20.5, 23) cm, ending on an even rnd. On last rnd, don't knit the last 3 sts.

Place these 3 unworked sts, as well as the first 3 sts of rnd, on waste yarn. Place remaining sleeve sts on holder.

Yoke

Return to the body sts, and with RS facing:

Next row: Sl1, k14 (15, 16, 17, 18, 19), PM, place next 6 sts onto waste yarn, knit first sleeve sts fromholder onto needle continuing to work them in cable pattern, PM, k32 (34, 36, 38, 40, 42), PM, place next 6 sts onto waste yarn, knit second sleeve sts onto needle as for first, PM, k to end.

The sts on the needle should be as follows: 15 (16, 17, 18, 19, 20) sts for Right Front, to be worked in moss st.

18 (20, 22, 24, 24, 26) sts for Right Sleeve, to be worked in Cable pattern.

32 (34, 36, 38, 40, 42) sts for Back to be worked in moss st.

18 (20, 22, 24, 24, 26) sts for Left Sleeve, to be worked in Cable pattern.

15 (16, 17, 18, 19, 20) sts for Left Front, to be worked in moss st.

Work in pattern as set (slipping first st of each row) for 6 (6.5, 6.5, 7, 7.5, 8) cm, ending with WS row. Then work first set ofdecreases as follows:

NEWBORN:

Sl1, k2tog, [p1, k2tog] to marker, *[ssk] twice, p2tog, work 6 cable sts, p2tog, [k2tog] twice*, p1, [k2tog, p1] to 1 st before marker, k1, rep from * to *, [p1, k2tog] to end. 54 sts.

0-3 MONTHS:

Sl1, [k2tog, p1] to marker, *ssk, sk2p, p2, work 6 cable sts, p2, k3tog, k2tog*, p1, [k2tog, p1] to marker, rep from * to *, [p1, k2tog] to last st, k1. 59 sts.

3-6 MONTHS:

Sl1, k1, [p1, k2tog] to marker, *[ssk] three times, p2, work 6 cable sts, p2, [k2tog] 3times*, [p1, k2tog] to marker, rep from * to*, [p1, k2tog] to last 2 sts, p1, k1. 64 sts.

6-12 MONTHS:

Sl1, k2tog, [p1, k2tog] to marker, *[ssk] twice, sk2p, p2, work 6 cable sts, p2, k3tog, [k2tog] twice*, p1, [k2tog, p1] to 1st before marker, k1, rep from * to *, [p1, k2tog] to end. 66 sts.

Cable pattern

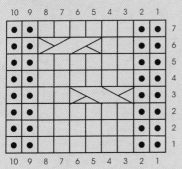

Instructions

Cable pattern (worked flat):

Row 1 (RS): P2, k6, p2.

Row 2 and all WS rows: K2, p6, k2.

Row 3: P2, C4F, k2, p2.

Row 5: As Row 1.

Row 7: P2, k2, C4B, p2.

Cable pattern (worked in the round):

Rnds 1 and 2: P2, k6, p2.

Rnd 3: P2, C4F, k2, p2.

Rnds 4-6: As Rnd 1.

Rnd 7: P2, k2, C4B, p2.

Rnd 8: As Rnd 1

12-18 MONTHS:

Sl1, [k2tog, p1] to marker, *[ssk] twice, sk2p, p2, work 6 cable sts, p2, k3tog, [k2tog] twice*, p1, [k2tog, p1] to marker, rep from* to *, [p1, k2tog] to last st, k1. 69 sts.

18-24 MONTHS:

Sl1, k1, [p1, k2tog] to marker, *[ssk] four times, p2, work 6 cable sts, p2, [k2tog] four times*, [p1, k2tog] to marker, rep from * to*, [p1, k2tog] to last 2 sts, p1, k1. 74 sts.

Work in new pattern as set for 3(3, 3.5, 3.5, 3.5, 3.5) cm, ending with a WS row. Cable pattern should be maintained on sleeves (newborn size will now have a p1 on either side of cable instead of a p2) and moss stitch on fronts and back. The new moss st pattern should be easy to pick up – the stitches which were k2tog will be knit on WS and the stitches which were purled will also be purled on WS. Remember to slip the first st of every row.

Then work second set of decreases as follows:

NEWBORN:

Sl1, [k2tog, p1] to marker, *ssk, p2tog, work 6 cable sts, p2tog, k2tog*, k1, [p1, k2tog] to marker, k1, rep from * to *, [p1, k2tog] to last st, k1. 37 sts.

0-3 MONTHS:

Sl1, k1, [p1, k2tog] to marker, *ssk, p2tog, work 6 cable sts, p2tog, k2tog*, [p1, k2tog] to marker, rep from * to *, p1, [k2tog, p1] to last st, k1. 42 sts.

3-6 MONTHS:

Sl1, k2tog, [p1, k2tog] to marker, *ssk, k1, p2tog, work 6 cable sts, p2tog, k1, k2tog*, [p1, k2tog] to marker, rep from * to *, [p1, k2tog] to end. 44 sts.

6-12 MONTHS:

Sl1, k2tog, [p1, k2tog] to marker, *ssk, k1, p2tog, work 6 cable sts, p2tog, k1, k2tog*,p1, [k2tog, p1] to 1 st before marker, k1, rep from * to *, [p1, k2tog] to end. 46 sts.

12-18 MONTHS:

Sl1, [k2tog, p1] to marker, *ssk, k1, p2tog, work 6 cable sts, p2tog, k1, k2tog*, [k2tog, p1] to marker, rep from * to *,[k2tog, p1] to last st, k1. 48 sts.

18-24 MONTHS:

Sl1, k1, [p1, k2tog] to marker, *[ssk] twice, p2tog, work 6 cable sts, p2tog, [k2tog] twice*, p1, [k2tog, p1] to marker, rep from * to *, [k2tog, p1] to last st, k1.51 sts.

Work in new pattern as set for 3 (3, 3.5, 3.5, 3.5, 3.5) cm, ending with a WS row. Again, cable pattern should be maintained on sleeves (all sizes will now have a p1 on either side of cable instead of a p2) and moss stitch on fronts and back. Remember to slip the first st of every row.

Then work third set of decreases as follows:

Next Row: Sl1, k2tog 0 (1, 0, 0, 1, 1) times,*k1, k2tog; rep from * to last 0(0, 1, 0, 0, 0) st, k0 (0, 1, 0, 0, 0). 25 (28, 30, 31, 32, 34) sts.

Knit 4 (4, 4, 6, 6, 6) rows, slipping first stof every row. Cast off.

Button bands

Note: You shouldn't have a problem getting the button band to lie flat, as it has a lot of knit to end horizontal and vertical stretch. But if your tension is a lot tighter in garter stitch, simply use a larger needle to work button bands.

Right button band

With RS facing, starting at bottom edge, PU and k1 in every slipped st along body. Knit 8 rows. Cast off.

Left button band

With RS facing, starting at top edge, PU 1st and k1 in every slipped st. Knit 4 rows.

Next row (buttonhole):
[K4, yo twice, cdd] four (four, five, five, five, six) times, k to end.

Knit 3 rows. Cast off.

Finishing: Graft armholes together. Weave in ends. Sew on buttons. Block if desired.

Schematic

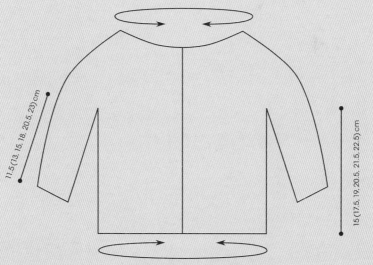

15.5 (17.5, 18.5, 19.5, 20, 21) cm

11.5 (13, 15, 18, 20.5, 23) cm

15 (17.5, 19, 20.5, 21.5, 22.5) cm

43 (48, 53, 56.5, 57, 58.5) cm

Buster Baby Jacket

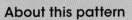

2
Intermediate

Lots of us love the vintage look for ourselves, but here's a little something to prove that vintage knits aren't just for grown ups!

Back

With single strand of MC, cast on 108 sts.

CAST ON

Work 4 rows in St st.

Next Row: K2, *yo, k2tog; rep from * to end of row.

Next Row: Purl.

Work 4 rows in St st.

Continue in St st and follow the chart for Rows 1-52.

Continue in MC only.**

Next Row: Knit.

Next Row: P6, *p2tog; rep from * to last 6 sts, p6.

Continue using 2 strands of MC held together.

Knit 6 rows.

Yoke

Row 1: *P3, k1; rep from * to end of row.

Row 2: *P1, k3; rep from * to end of row.

Row 3: *P3, k1; rep from * to end of row.

Row 4: *P1, k3; rep from * to end of row.

Row 5: Purl.

Row 6: *P1, k3; rep from * to end of row.

Row 7: *P3, k1; rep from * to end of row.

Row 8: *P1, k3; rep from* to end of row.

Row 9: *P3, k1; rep from * to end of row.

Row 10: Knit.

Shape armhole

Keeping continuity of rib pattern, cast off 3 sts at beg of the next 2 rows.

Work Rows 3 -10 of rib pattern, then Rows 1-10, then Rows 1-8.

Cast off 18 sts at beg of the next 2 rows.

Cast off remaining sts.

Left front

With single strand of MC, cast on 54 sts.

Work as for back to **.

Next Row: Knit.

Next Row: P10, *p2tog; rep from * to end of row. 32 sts.

Continue using 2 strands of MC held together.

Knit 6 rows.

About this pattern

Size
12-24 months

Yarn
Excelana wool 4ply –
4 x 50g balls in Cornflower Blue (MC); 1 x 50g balls each in Powdered Egg (CC1); Nile Green (CC2); Persian Grey (CC3); Alabaster (CC4) and Ruby Red (CC5)

About the yarn
4-ply; 165m per 50g; 100% wool

Needles
3mm straight, 30cm long

Tension
Measured over St st with yarn held double:

Other supplies
9 buttons
Tapestry needle

Yoke

Row 1: *P3, k1; rep from * to end of row.
Row 2: *P1, k3; rep from * to end of row.
Row 3: *P3, k1; rep from * to end of row.
Row 4: *P1, k3; rep from * to end of row.
Row 5: Purl.
Row 6: *P1, k3; rep from * to end of row.
Row 7: *P3, k1; rep from * to end of row.
Row 8: *P1, k3; rep from * to end of row.
Row 9: *P3, k1; rep from * to end of row.
Row 10: Knit.

Shape armhole

Keeping continuity of rib pattern, cast off 3 sts at armhole edge. 29 sts.

Continue to Row 10 of rib pattern, then work Rows 1-10 once more.

Shape neck

Cast off 5 sts at neck edge. 24 sts.

Continue in rib pattern and dec 1 st at neck edge on every row until 18 sts rem. Cast off.

Right front

With single strand of MC, cast on 54 sts. Work as for back to **.

Next Row: Knit.

Next Row: *P2tog; rep from * to last 10 sts, p10. 32 sts.

Continue using 2 strands of MC held together. Knit 6 rows.

Yoke

Row 1: *P3, k1; rep from * to end of row.
Row 2: *P1, k3; rep from * to end of row.
Row 3: *P3, k1; rep ffrom * to end of row.
Row 4: *P1, k3; rep from * to end of row.
Row 5: Purl.
Row 6: *P1, k3; rep from * to end of row.
Row 7: *P3, k1; rep from * to end of row.
Row 8: *P1, k3; rep from * to end of row.
Row 9: *P3, k1; rep from * to end of row.
Row 10: Knit.

Shape armhole

Keeping continuity of rib pattern, cast off 3 sts at armhole edge. 29 sts.

Continue to Row 10 of rib pattern, then work Rows 1-10 once more.

Shape neck

Cast off 5 sts at neck edge. 24 sts.

Continue in rib pattern and dec 1 st at neck edge on every row until 18 sts rem. Cast off.

Sleeves (make 2)

With single strand of MC, cast on 38 sts. Work 4 rows in St st.

Next Row: K2, *yo, k2tog; rep from * to end of row.

Next Row: Purl.

Work 4 rows in St st.

Continue in St st using 2 strands of yarn held together, following stripe pattern as follows:

CC1: 4 rows
CC2: 4 rows
CC3: 4 rows
CC4: 4 rows
CC5: 4 rows
MC: 4 rows

AT THE SAME TIME:

Inc 1 st at each end of next row and every following 7th row until there are 48 sts.

Continue in St st and stripe pattern until work measures 20cm from eyelet row. Dec 1 st at each end of next and every following row until 20 sts rem. Cast off.

Buttonhole band

With MC and with RS facing, begin at lower edge of Right Front and PU and k88 sts.

Next Row: Purl.

Next Row: Knit.

Next Row: Purl.

Next Row: K4, *yo, k2tog, k8; rep from * to last 4 sts, yo, k2tog, k2.

Next Row: Purl.

Next Row: Knit.

Next Row: Purl.

Next Row: K2, *yo, k2tog; rep from * to end of row.

Next Row: Purl.

Next Row: Knit.

Next Row: Purl.

Next Row: K4, *yo, k2tog, k8; rep from * to last 4 sts, yo, k2tog, k2.

Next Row: Purl.

Next Row: Knit.

Next Row: Purl.

Cast off.

Schematic

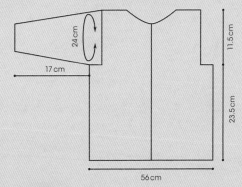

64

Button band

With MC and with RS facing, begin at upper edge of Left Front and PU and k88 sts.

Next Row: Purl.

Work 6 rows in St st.

Next Row: K2, *yo, k2tog; rep from * to end of row.

Next Row: Purl.

Work 6 rows in St st.

Cast off.

Fold in picot hems on bands and stitch in place.

Collar

With MC, cast on 90 sts.

Work 4 rows in St st.

Next Row: K2, *yo, k2tog; rep from * to end of row.

Next Row: Purl.

Work 8 rows in St st.

Next Row: K2, *k2tog, k5; rep from * to last 4 sts, k2tog, k2. 77 sts.

Work 3 rows in St st.

Next Row: K3, *k2tog, k5; rep from * to last 4 sts, k2tog, k2. 66 sts.

Next Row: Purl.

Cast off.

Finishing: Fold in all picot hems and stitch in place.

Sew shoulder seams.

Sew sleeve tops in place.

Sew side and sleeve seams.

Sew collar to neck edge.

Sew buttons to match buttonholes.

To smock yoke: Join adjacent ribs at 'purl' bumps with a few straight stitches in contrast yarn to form diamond shapes (see picture for guide).

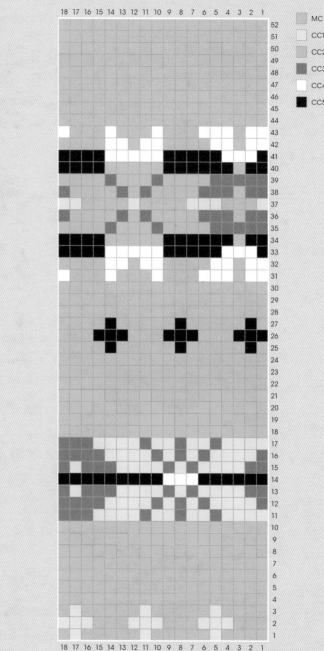

Phoebe Pinafore

This yarn is spun from the fleece of British sheep – even the dyes are homegrown.

Back and front
Work two the same

Cast on 73 sts.

Row 1: K1, *[k2tog] three times, [yo, k1] five times, yo, [k2tog] three times, k1; rep from * to end.

Row 2: Knit.

Row 3: Knit.

Row 4: K1, p to last st, k1.

Rep Rows 1-4 twice more.

Next row (decrease row): K2, ssk, k to last 4 sts, k2tog, k2.

Continue in St st and dec 1 st at each end of every following fourth row until there are 63 sts, then on every alternate row until there are 43 sts.

Next Row: Purl.

Knit 2 rows.

Next Row: K1, *yo, k2tog; rep from * to end.

Next Row: Knit. Work 6 rows in St st.

Shape neck

Next Row: K14. You will now work over these sts only. Turn work so WS is facing.

Next Row: Purl.

Dec 1 st at neck edge on next and every alternate row until 7 sts rem.

Next Row: Purl. Cast off loosely.

Place centre 15 sts on stitch holder and rejoin yarn to remaining sts with RS facing.

Next Row: Knit.

Next Row: Purl.

Dec 1 st at neck edge of next and every alternate row until 7 sts rem.

Next Row: Purl. Cast off loosely.

Sleeves

Cast on 55 sts.

Row 1: K1, *[k2tog] three times, [yo, k1] five times, yo, [k2tog] three times, k1; rep from * to end.

Row 2: Knit.

Row 3: Knit.

Row 4: K1, p to last st, k1.

Rep Rows 1-4 twice more.

Next Row: K1, *k2tog; rep from * to end. 28 sts.

Next Row: Purl. Cast off loosely.

Making up

Join shoulder seams. With RS facing and beginning at top left edge, PU and k16 down Left Front, k15 from Centre Front stitch holder, PU and k16 up Right Front, pu and k16 down Right Back, k15 from Centre Back stitch holder, PU and k16 up Left Back. 94 sts.

Purl 1 row. Cast off.

Sew up underarm seam of sleeve. Thread ribbon through eyelets and tie in a bow at centre front.

Finishing: Weave in ends and block.

About this pattern
Sizing
One size fits baby-toddler
See schematic for finished measurements
Yarn
Natural Dye Studio Dazzle DK – 1 skein in Sugar
About the yarn
DK weight; 240m per 100g skein; 100% British Bluefaced Leicester wool
Needles
4mm straight, 30cm long
4mm circular, 80cm long
Tension
Measured over St st:

Other supplies
1m narrow ribbon
Stitch holders
Tapestry needle

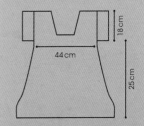

This popover
pinafore will fit from
newborn to 18 months – the
ribbon tie can be pulled in
to fit – so it'll make a great
gift. As it only uses one skein,
it is an ideal way to make
a little something
luxurious for baby.

English Rose Set

2
Intermediate

This pretty cardigan and matching booties with the simple lace detail and pretty colour will make a lovely gift for a little girl.

We love quick knits for babies and tots – it can feel silly to spend weeks or months on something that might only fit for a couple of months. This cardigan, knitted in lovely aran-weight lambswool, fits the bill perfectly. The body is knit flat, but we recommend using a circular needle to give you a bit more flexibility and help keep your tension even. However, if you only have straight needles to hand, they will do the trick.

Cardigan
Yoke

CAST ON

With straight or circular needles, cast on 3 sts.

Set-up Row: *Kfb, k2, sl3 sts p-wise back onto LH needle; rep from * until there are 15 (15, 18, 18) sts in total. (12, 12, 15, 15 sts on RH needle, 3 sts on LH needle.

Place these 3 sts on holder).

Turn work so WS is facing:

Row 1 (WS): Sl1, k5 (5, 6, 6), yo, ssk, k4 (4, 6, 6). 12 (12, 15, 15) sts.

Row 2 and all RS rows: Knit.

Row 3: Sl1, k7 (7, 9, 9), w&t.

Row 5: Sl1, k3 (3, 4, 4), w&t.

Row 7: Sl1, k to end working all wraps tog with their adjacent sts.

Rep Rows 2-7 a further 33 (36, 41, 47) more times.

Next row (RS): Cast on 3 sts onto LH needle, *k2, ssk, sl3 p-wise onto LH needle; rep from * until 4 sts rem, k2, ssk.

Special Instructions
Rosebud chart

Row 1 (RS): K1, k2tog, yo, k, yo, ssk, k1.

Row 2 and all WS rows: Purl.

Row 3: K2tog, yo, k3, yo, ssk.

Row 5: K1, yo, ssk, yo, k3tog, yo, k1.

Row 7: K2, yo, sk2p, yo, k2.

Row 8: Purl.m pattern.

About this pattern
Sizing
Newborn (6m, 9m, 12m), worn with no ease (cardigan)/ 2.5cm negative ease (bootees)

See schematic for finished measurements

Yarn
JC Rennie Chunky Aran Lambswool 2 (2, 3, 3) balls in Couture 1464

About the yarn
Aran; 95m per 50g ball; 100% lambswool

Needles
5mm straight, 30cm or circular, 60cm
5mm DPNs, 20cm

Tension
Measured over St st (G st):

10 cm
10 cm
24 (32) rows
17 (17) sts

Other supplies
3 (3, 4, 4) buttons or Velcro
2 stitch holders or scrap yarn
darning needle

Body

Turn yoke so slipped st edge is uppermost, 3 live sts rem on RH needle.

Row 1 (RS): PU and ktbl 103 (112, 127, 144) sts along slipped st edge, k3 from holder. 109 (118, 133, 150) sts.

Row 2 (Buttonhole row): Sl3 p-wise wyif, p1, yo, ssp, p to end.

Row 3: Sl3 p-wise wyib, k7 (9, 10, 12), *m1, k15 (19, 18, 24); rep from * to last 9 (11, 12, 15) sts, m1, k9 (11, 12, 15). 116 (124, 140, 156) sts.

Row 4 and all non-buttonhole WS rows: Sl3 p-wise wyif, p to end.

Row 5: Sl3 p-wise wyib, k16 (17, 19, 21), place 22 (24, 28, 32) sts on holder, k34 (36, 40, 44), place 22 (24, 28, 32) sts on 2nd holder, k to end. 72 (76, 84, 92) sts.

Row 7: Sl3 p-wise wyib, k11 (11, 13, 14), [m1, k22 (24, 26, 29)] twice, m1, k to end. 75 (79, 87, 95) sts.

Work 7 (9, 11, 13) rows in St st, starting with a purl row and slipping the first 3 sts of each row as set, working a buttonhole row, as described above, on the 7th (7th, 9th, 9th) row.

Next row: Sl3 p-wise wyib, k12 (13, 20, 15), [m1, k23 (24, 41, 30)] twice (twice, once, twice), m1, k to end. 78 (82, 89, 98) sts.

Work 7 (9, 11, 13) rows in St st, starting with a purl row and slipping the first 3 sts of each row as set, working a buttonhole row, as described above, on the 0th (9th, 11th, 9th) row.

Lace border

Row 1 (RS): Sl3 p-wise wyib, p to last 3 sts, k3.

Row 2 (WS): Sl3 p-wise wyif, p to end.

Row 3: Sl3 p-wise wyib, k1 (3, 3, 4), [work Rosebud Chart, k2 (2, 3, 4)] seven (eight, eight, eight) times, work Rosebud Chart once more for newborn size only, k to end.

Row 4: Sl3 p-wise wyif, p to end.

Rep Rows 3 & 4 until Rosebud Chart is complete, working an additional buttonhole on the final rep of Row 4 for Newborn, 9m & 12m sizes. Rep Rows 1 & 2 to complete border.

Keeping WS facing, cast-off as follows: *sl4 sts p-wise onto LH needle, p2tog, p2; rep from * until 6 sts rem.

Divide these sts in half and graft tog using Kitchener st.

Sleeves (both the same)

With DPNs, PU and k3 sts from base of armhole, k sts from holder, k1 from underarm again. Join to work in the rnd. PM to mark beg of rnd. 25 (27, 31, 35) sts.

Rnd 1: K1, k2tog, k to last 2 sts, ssk. 23 (25, 29, 33) sts.

Work in St st for 18 (20, 22, 26) rnds.

Work in garter st for 10 (12, 14, 16) rnds. Cast-off p-wise.

Finishing: Soak in a tepid wool wash and block to dimensions given. Weave in ends. Sew on buttons.

Booties (both the same)

With straight or circular needles, cast on 7 (8, 9, 10) sts.

Knit 22 (24, 26, 28) rows.

This forms the sole.

Next 2 rows: Cast on 10 (12, 14, 16) sts, k to end. 27 (32, 37, 42) sts.

Knit 9 (9, 11, 11) rows.

Short-rows: K to last 3 sts, turn, work back to last 3 sts, turn.

Rep the short-rows three (four, four, five) times in total decreasing by an additional 3 sts each time. On the last row you should have worked 9 (8, 13, 12) sts before the final turn. K to end. Cast-off all sts k-wise.

Leave a 40-45cm yarn tail for seaming.

Finishing: Lay bootie 'T' RS face up with cast on at the bottom. For right bootie, fold left wing diagonally so that its cast on edge is directly above the left edge of the sole.

Fold right wing diagonally so that its cast on edge is directly above the right edge of the sole. Using the yarn tail and a running stitch, seam top of boot to sole on three sides. For left bootie, fold the right wing down first and proceed as with right bootie. Turn booties inside out and fold down cuff 1-2cm. With a spare piece of yarn pop a few sts through the top of the instep, just under the cuff, to hold the sides together and keep the ankle well fitting.

Schematic

5.5 (5.5, 7.7) cm

7.5 (8, 8.5, 9) cm

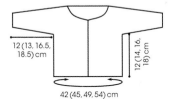

12 (13, 16.5, 18.5) cm

12 (14, 16, 18) cm

42 (45, 49, 54) cm

Rosebud Chart

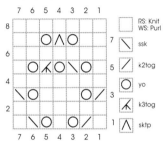

	RS: Knit / WS: Purl
╲	ssk
╱	k2tog
O	yo
⅄	k3tog
∧	sktp

Little Sailor

2
Intermediate

Add a nautical twist to any simple outfit with this cute set.

Sailor suits are smart and traditional, but they can be fun too. The collar can also double as a bib for messy babies – but we'd recommend reversing the colours!

Collar

Using cream, cast on 200 sts.

CAST ON

Row 1: Sl1, p24, pm, [p50, pm] three times, p25.

Row 2: Sl1, [k to 3 sts before marker, k2tog, k1, sm, k1, ssk] four times, k to end. 8 sts decreased

Row 3: Sl1, purl to end.

Rep Rows 2-3 once more in cream, once in blue, twice in cream, once in blue and then cont in cream until 64 sts rem.

Slide work to end of needle and hold in left hand, with RS facing. With blue, cast 3 sts onto LH needle, work i-cord for 10cm, slide collar back to tip of needle, *k2, k2tog tbl (one st from needle, one st from cord), slide sts back to LH needle; rep from * until all neck sts have been worked, work i-cord for 10cm, cast off.

About this pattern

Sizing
6-12 months, see schematic for finished measurements

Yarn
Betty and Belle DK
Hat: 1 ball Vanilla Slice, Part-ball Blueberry Muffin
Collar: 1 ball Vanilla Slice, Partball Blueberry Muffin
Both can be knit with 2 balls of cream and 1 ball of blue

About the yarn
DK; 75m per 25g ball; 100% acrylic

Needles
4mm straight

Tension
Measured over St st:

10 cm
10 cm
28 rows
24 sts

Other supplies
Darning needle
4 stitch markers

Collar Schematic

12.75 cm

Outer cicumference: 84.5 cm

Neck circumference: 26.5cm

Hat

Cast on 82 sts in cream.

Rows 1 & 3 (WS): Sl1, p to end.

Rows 2 & 4: Sl1, k to end.
Switch to Blue.

Row 5: Sl1, p to end.

Rows 6, 8 & 10: Sl1, *p1, k1; rep from * to last st, p1.

Rows 7 & 9: Sl1, *p1, k1; rep from * to last st, k1.

Switch to cream.

Row 11 and all WS rows: Sl1, p to end.

Row 12: Sl1, k4, [m1, k8] nine times, m1, k5. 92 sts.

Row 14: Sl1, k5, [m1, k9] nine times, m1, k5. 102 sts.

Row 16: Sl1, k6, [m1, k10] nine times, m1, k5. 112 sts.

Row 18 & 20: Sl1, k to end.

Row 22: Sl1, [ssk, k9] ten times, k1. 102 sts.

Row 24: Sl1, [ssk, k8] ten times, k1. 92 sts.

Row 26: Sl1, [ssk, k7] ten times, k1. 82 sts.

Row 28: Sl1, [ssk, k6] ten times, k1. 72 sts.

Row 30: Sl1, [ssk, k5] ten times, k1. 62 sts.

Row 32: Sl1, [ssk, k4] ten times, k1. 52 sts.

Row 34: Sl1, [ssk, k3] ten times, k1. 42 sts.

Row 36: Sl1, [ssk, k2] ten times, k1. 32 sts.

Row 38: Sl1, [ssk, k1] ten times, k1. 22 sts.

Row 40: Sl1, [ssk] ten times, k1. 12 sts.

Row 41: [P2tog] six times. 6 sts.

Break yarn, slip through rem sts and pull tight to fasten.

Finishing: Sew up back seam with mattress st.

Hat Schematic

14.5cm

14.5cm

Talaitha Smock

1
Beginner

The designer of this top chose the name Talaitha, which is Romany for 'little girl' – and we can't think of a sweeter gift for a little princess.

Whether you're a new mum knitting for your own baby, or there's a new niece or goddaughter in the picture, you'll love knitting this quick and easy smock top. Most of it is knit in plain stocking stitch, with simple shaping and clever smocking detail around the middle.

CAST ON

With MC, cast on 98 (105, 112) sts.

Row 1: K1, kfb, k to end. 99 (106, 113) sts.

Row 2: K to last 6 sts, cast off 3 sts, k to end. 96 (103, 110) sts.

Row 3: K3, cast on 3 sts, k to end. 99 (106, 113) sts.

Row 4: K to last 6 sts, [ktbl] three times, k2tog, k1. 98 (105, 112) sts.

Row 5: Cast off 7 sts, k to end. 91 (98, 105) sts.

Row 6 and all even rows: Purl.

Row 7: K5 (9, 12), [k4, m1, k4] ten times, k to end. 101 (108, 115) sts.

Row 9: K5 (9, 12), [k5 m1, k4] ten times, k to end. 111 (118, 125) sts.

Row 11: K5 (9, 12), [k5, m1, k5] ten times, k to end. 121 (128, 135) sts.

Row 13: K5 (9, 12), [k6, m1, k5] ten times, k to end. 131 (138, 145) sts.

Join to work in the rnd, being careful not to twist. Pm to mark beg of rnd.

Rnd 14 and all even rnds: Knit.

Rnd 15: K5 (9, 12), [k6, m1, k6] ten times, k to end. 141 (148, 155) sts.

Rnd 17: K5 (9, 12) [k7, m1, k6] ten times, k to end. 151 (158, 165) sts.

Rnd 19: K8 (11, 15) [k4, m1, k5] fifteen times, k to end. 166 (173, 180) sts.

Rnd 21: K8 (11, 15), [k5, m1, k5] fifteen times, k to end. 181 (188, 195) sts.

Rnd 23: K8 (11, 15) [k6, m1, k5] fifteen times, k to end. 196 (203, 210) sts.

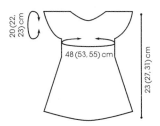

20 (22, 23) cm

48 (53, 55) cm

23 (27, 31) cm

About this pattern

Sizing
0-6m (6-12m, 12-18m)
See schematic for finished measurements

Yarn
Debbie Bliss Rialto 4-ply – 1 (1, 1) l ball in Purple 022 (MC),
1 (1, 2) balls in Cerise 020 (CC)

About the yarn
4-ply; 180m per 50g ball;
100% Merino wool

Needles
3.25mm circular, 40cm long

Tension
Measured over St st:

10 cm

10 cm

32 rows

26 sts

Other supplies
Stitch marker
Button, 1 cm in diameter
Sewing needle & thread

Rnd 25: K8 (11, 15) [k6, m1, k6] fifteen times, k to end. 211 (218, 225) sts.

Rnd 27: K8 (11, 15), [k7, m1, k6] fifteen times, k to end. 226 (233, 240) sts.

Rnd 29: K29 (32, 36), [k14, m1, k14] six times, k to end. 232 (239, 246) sts.

6-12M SIZE ONLY

Rnd 30: Knit.

Rnd 31: K43, [k7, m1, k7] eleven times, k to end. 250 sts.

12-18M SIZE ONLY

Rnd 30: Knit.

Rnd 31: K15 [k7, m1, k7] fifteen times, k to end. 261 sts.

Rnd 32: Knit.

Rnd 33: K15 [k35, m1, k35] three times, k to end. 264 sts.

ALL SIZES

Rnd 30 (32, 34): K32 (35, 36), p53 (56, 60), k62 (68, 72), p53 (56, 60), k to end. 232 (250, 264) sts.

Rnd 31 (33, 35): Knit.

Rnd 32 (34, 36): K32 (35, 36), p53 (56, 60), k62 (68, 72), p53 (56, 60), k to end. 232 (250, 264) sts.

Rnd 33 (35, 37): K32 (35, 36), cast off 53 (56, 60) sts, k61 (67, 71) sts, cast off 53 (56, 60) sts, k to end. 126 (138, 144) sts.

Rnd 34 (36, 38): Purl.

Rnd 35 (37, 39): Knit.

Start sl pattern.

Change to CC.

Rnd 1: *Sl2 wyif, k1, sl3 wyif; rep from * to end. Break off CC and loosely knot the yarn ends in front.

Change to MC.

Rnds 2-3: Knit.

Change to CC.

Rnd 4: *Sl5 wyif, pu strand from Rnd 1 and knit together with next st; rep from * to end. Break off CC and loosely knot the yarn ends in front.

Change to MC.

Rnds 5-6: Knit.

Change to CC.

Rnd 7: *Sl2 wyif, pu strand from Rnd 4 and knit together with next st, sl3 wyif; rep from * to end. Break off CC and loosely knot the yarn ends in front.

Rep Rnds 1-7 three more times.

Change to MC and knit 2 rnds.

Change to CC.

Next Rnd: *Sl5 wyib, pu strand from three rnds below and knit together with next st; rep from * to end.

Change to MC and knit 1 rnd. Purl 1 rnd.

Break MC.

Change to CC.

Next Rnd: *Kfb, k2; rep from * to end. 168 (184, 192) sts.

Knit until the top measures 22 (26, 30) cm from back of neck to hem.

Work 5 rnds in G st, starting with a purl row. Cast off.

Finishing: Undo knots on the sl st pattern and weave in all yarn ends. Block lightly. Line up button to buttonhole and sew on securely.

Hints & tips

When slipping stitches with the yarn held in front (wyif), allow the yarn to fall loosely, especially at the start and end of the round. It has to be gathered three rows up and you don't want it to pucker. Yarn held to the back of the work should be held loosely enough to allow the knitting to retain its stretch.

Accessories

Here are some adorable little accessories for your beloved babies. They're quick to make, so they make ideal last-minute gifts.

Darling Bonnet & Booties

2

Intermediate

This pretty little set makes a great gift for newborns and you only need one ball for the whole set!

It's surprising how much further your yarn goes when you're knitting a lace pattern and this design is proof of that. Note that our little model is accidentally wearing the bonnet backwards (whoops!) but hopefully you'll still get a good idea of how it should look.

Bonnet

CAST ON

Cast on 54 (60, 66) sts.

Knit 11 rows.

Next row (inc row): K6, p8 (11, 11), [pfb] 25 (25, 31) times, p9 (12, 12), k6. 79 (85, 97) sts.

Begin Lace pattern:

Row 1 (RS): K7, *yo, ssk, k1, k2tog, yo, k1; rep from * to last 6 sts, k6.

Row 2 and even rows: K6, p to last 6 sts, k6.

Row 3: K7, *k1, yo, sk2po, yo, k2; rep from * to last 6 sts, k6.

Row 5: K7, *k2tog, yo, k1, yo, ssk, k1; rep from * to last 6 sts, k6.

Row 7: K6, k2tog, yo, *k3, yo, sk2po, yo; rep from * to last 11 sts, k3, yo, ssk, k6.

Row 8: As for Row 2.

These 8 rows form patt.

Cont in patt until work measures 10 (11, 12) cm from beg of lace patt, ending with Row 1 or 5.

Shape crown:

Row 1 (WS): K6, p to last 12 sts and turn.

Row 2 (RS): Sl1, patt to last 12 sts and turn.

Row 3: Sl1, p to last 18 sts and turn.

Row 4: Sl1, patt to last 18 sts and turn.

Row 5: Sl1, p to last 24 sts and turn.

Row 6: Sl1, patt to last 24 sts and turn.

Row 7: Sl1, p to end. 79 (85, 97) sts.

Dec row: K10 (7, 9), *sk2po, k1; rep from * to last 9 (6, 8) sts, k to end. 49 (49, 57) sts.

Knit 1 row.

12m size only:

Dec row: K6, k2tog, k8, *k3tog, k8; rep from * to last 8 sts, k2tog, k6. 49 sts.

Knit 1 row.

All sizes:

Dec row 1: K6, k2tog, k6, *k3tog, k6; rep from * to last 8 sts, k2tog, k6. 41 sts.

Knit 1 row.

Dec row 2: K6, k2tog, k4, *k3tog, k4; rep from * to last 8 sts, k2tog, k6. 33 sts.

Knit 1 row.

About this pattern

Sizing
Newborn (6 months, 12 months)
To fit head 30 (35, 40) cm
To fit foot length 7 (8, 10) cm

Yarn
Betty and Belle DK
1 ball each in Vanilla Slice

About the yarn
DK; 75m per 25g ball; 100% acrylic

Needles
4mm straight

Tension
Measured over St st:

10 cm

10 cm

28 rows

24 sts

Other supplies
50cm of 6mm ribbon for bonnet
80cm of 3mm ribbon for booties
Stitch holder
Tapestry needle

Dec row 3: K6, k2tog, k2, *k3tog, k2; rep from * to last 8 sts, k2tog, k6. 25 sts.

Knit 1 row.

Dec row 4: K6, k2tog, *k3tog; rep from * to last 8 sts, k2tog, k6. 17 sts.

Knit 1 row.

Dec row 5: K5, k2tog, k3tog, k2tog, k5. 13 sts.

Dec row 6: K5, k2tog, k6. 12 sts.

Cast off.

Fold cast-off sts in half and sew to create back seam.

Cut ribbon in half and attach at each side of neck.

Finishing: Block gently by steaming bonnet to shape, without allowing the iron to touch the fabric.

Booties

Cast on 25 (31, 37) sts.

Knit 2 rows.

Begin Lace patt:

Row 1 (RS): K1, *yo, ssk, k1, k2tog, yo, k1; rep from * to end.

Row 2 and even rows: Purl.

Row 3: K1, *k1, yo, sk2po, yo, k2; rep from * to end.

Row 5: K1, *k2tog, yo, k1, yo, ssk, k1; rep from * to end.

Row 7: K2tog, yo, *k3, yo, sk2po, yo; rep from * to last 5 sts, k3, yo, ssk.

Row 8: As for Row 2.

These 8 rows form patt.

Work 8 (8, 12) more rows in patt.

NEWBORN SIZE ONLY:

Knit to last 2 sts, M1, knit to end. 26 sts.

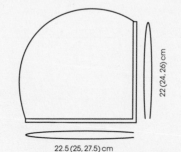

22.5 (25, 27.5) cm

22 (24, 26) cm

10 (13, 15) cm

7 (8, 10) cm

6M AND 12M SIZES ONLY:

Knit to last 2 sts, k2tog. 30 (36) sts.

Purl 1 row.

Eyelet row: K2, *yo, k2tog, rep from * to last 2 sts, k2.

Purl 1 row.

Shape instep:

Next row: K18 (20, 24), turn.

Leave foll 8 (10, 12) sts on holder.

Next row: P10 (10, 12), turn. Leave foll 8 (10, 12) sts on holder.

Working on the 10 (10, 12) sts on the needles only, work 12 (14, 16) rows in St st. Break off yarn.

With RS facing, rejoin yarn to first stitch holder on RH side of instep and k8 (10, 12), pu and k9 (11, 13) sts up side edge of instep, k10 (10, 12) sts from instep, pu and k9 (11, 13) sts evenly down side edge of instep and k8 (10, 12) sts from second stitch holder. 44 (52, 62) sts.

Knit 11 (13, 15) rows.

Shape foot:

Dec row 1: K1, k2tog, k14 (18, 23), k2tog, k6, k2tog, k14 (18, 23), k2tog, k1. 40 (48, 58) sts.

Knit 1 row.

Dec row 2: K1, k2tog, k13 (17, 22), k2tog, k4, k2tog, k13 (17, 22), k2tog, k1. 36 (44, 54) sts.

Knit 1 row.

Dec row 3: K1, k2tog, k12 (16, 21), k2tog, k2, k2tog, k12 (16, 21), k2tog, k1. 32 (40, 50) sts.

Knit 1 row.

6M AND 12M SIZES ONLY:

Dec row 4: K1, k2tog, k(15, 20), [k2tog] twice, k(15, 20), k2tog, k1. 36 (46) sts. Knit 1 row.

ALL SIZES:

Cast off.

Join leg and foot seam.

Cut ribbon in half and thread through eyelet row, tie in a bow at front of bootie.

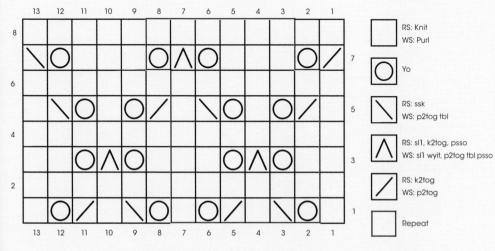

	RS: Knit WS: Purl
O	Yo
\	RS: ssk WS: p2tog tbl
∧	RS: sl1, k2tog, psso WS: sl1 wyit, p2tog tbl psso
/	RS: k2tog WS: p2tog
	Repeat

Little Snowflake Hat & Mitts

2
Intermediate

This cute little snowflake hat and mitts set will add a certain spark to your baby's outfit during the winter season.

Hat

CAST ON

Using 3.25mm needles and MC, cast on 82 (90, 102) sts.

Work 8 (10, 10) rows in k2 p2 rib, starting with k2.

Change to 4mm needles.

Work 4 rows in St st, starting with a knit row, and dec 1 st at end of 1st row.

For 1st size only.

Next row (place chart): K2 (1, 2), work chart to last 2 (1, 1) sts, k2 (1, 1).

Cont in working chart and then in St st until hat measures 9 (10, 11) cm from cast on edge, ending with a WS row.

Decrease for top of hat

Row 1 (RS): K0 (0, 2), *k7, k2tog; rep from * 8 (9, 10) more times, k0 (0, 1). (72, 80, 91) sts.

Row 2 (and every alt row): Purl.

Row 3: K0 (0, 2), *k6, k2tog; rep from * 8 (9, 10) more times, k0 (0, 1). 63 (70, 80) sts.

Row 5: K0 (0, 2), *k5, k2tog; rep from * 8 (9, 10) more times, k0 (0, 1). 54 (60, 69) sts.

Row 7: K0 (0, 2), *k4, k2tog; rep from * 8 (9, 10) more times, k0 (0, 1). 45 (50, 58) sts.

Row 9: K0 (0, 2), *k3, k2tog; rep from * 8 (9, 10) more times, k0 (0, 1). 36 (40, 47) sts.

Row 11: K0 (0, 2), *k2, k2tog; rep from * 8 (9, 10) more times, k0 (0, 1). 27 (30, 36) sts.

Row 13: K0 (0, 2), *k1, k2tog; rep from * 8 (9, 10) more times, k0 (0, 1). 18 (20, 25) sts.

Row 15: K0 (0, 2), *k2tog; rep from * 8 (9, 10) more times, k0 (0, 1). 9 (10, 13) sts.

Break yarn, leaving a long tail, and pull through rem sts. Sew side seam.

Mitts

Using 3.25mm needles and MC, cast on 30 (34, 34) sts.

Work 8 (8, 10) rows in k2 p2 rib, starting with k2.

Change to 4mm needles and work 2 (4, 2) rows in St st.

SIZES 1 & 2

Chart placement row (RS).

For right mitt: K3 (4), k9 from chart, k to end.

About this pattern

Sizing
Hat and mitts: 0-6mths (6-12mths, 1-3yrs)

Yarn
Patons Diploma Gold DK

Hats and Mitts: 1 (2, 2, 2) x 50g in Red 06151; 1 x 50g in Cream 06142

About the yarn
DK weight; 120m per 50g ball; 55% wool, 25% acrylic, 20% nylon

Needles
3.25mm and 4mm straight 30cm long

Tension
Measured over St st using 4mm needles:

10 cm

10 cm · 30 rows

22 sts

Other supplies
Tapestry needle
5 (5, 6, 7) buttons

For left mitt: K to last 12 (13) sts, k9 from chart, k to end.

Continue in St st, working remaining 8 rows of chart, then work 1 (3) rows plain, ending with a WS row.

Decrease for top of mitt

**Row 1: K1, ssk, k10 (12), k2tog, ssk, k10 (12), k2tog, k1. 26 (30) sts.

Row 2 (and every alt row): Purl.

Row 3: K1, ssk, k8 (10), k2tog, ssk, k8 (10), k2tog, k1. 22 (26) sts.

Continue to dec in this way on next 2 (3) RS rows, ending with a WS row. 14 (18) sts.

Cast off, dec as before on cast off row. Sew seam

SIZE 3

Next row: K16, kfb twice, k16. 36sts.

Next row: Purl.

Chart placement row (RS)

For right mitt: K3, k9 from chart, k4, kfb, k2, kfb, k16. 38 sts.

For left mitt: K16, kfb, k2, kfb, k4, k9 from chart, k3. 38 sts.

Next row (and every WS row): P to end, continuing to work chart where appropriate.

Next row: Work 16sts, kfb, k4, kfb, work to end. 40sts.

Continue to inc in this way on every RS row, and working chart on all rows where appropriate, until there are 44 sts, ending with a WS row.

Next row: Work 28sts (working chart if appropriate), turn.

Next row: Cast on 1 st, p11, turn.

Next row: Cast on 1 st, k12. 13sts.

Work 5 rows in St st on these 13 sts for thumb, ending with a WS row.

Next row: K2tog 3 times, k1, k2tog 3 times. 7 sts.

Break yarn, thread through rem sts and fasten off. Sew thumb seam.

Rejoin yarn to base of thumb, and pick up and knit 1st from 2sts cast on at base, work to end (working chart if appropriate). 34sts.

Work 7 rows st st, starting with a WS row.

Dec as for second size mitten, from ** onwards.

Schematic

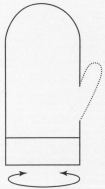 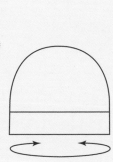

13.5 (15.5, 16) cm
Thumb only on largest size

36 (40, 45) cm

Chart

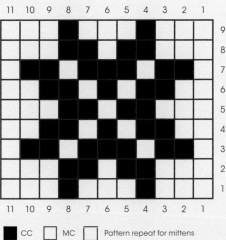

 CC   ☐ MC   ☐ Pattern repeat for mittens

Vintage Baby Bonnet

This beautiful bonnet is perfect for vintage enthusiasts and will brighten up any outfit!

2
Intermediate

About this pattern

Sizing

3 (6, 12, 18, 24) months, designed to fit with 5cm positive ease

Yarn

Yarn Love Marianne Dashwood
1 skein in Allure (MC), 16 (16, 16, 20, 20) yds each in Shiny Penny (CC1) and Martini (CC2)

About the yarn

Sport/5-ply; 302m per 100g skein; 100% Merino wool

Needles

3mm circular, 40cm
2 3mm DPNs (for gusset grafting)

Tension

Measured over St st:

10 cm

10 cm / 32 rows

24 sts

Other supplies

2 stitch markers
1cm buttons (3, 3, 4, 4, 4)
Safety pin
Stitch holders
Waste yarn
Tapestry needle

Bonnet

CAST ON

With MC, cast on 65 (69, 73, 77, 81) sts.

Work in G st for 2.5cm, ending after a WS row.

Row 1 (RS): K8 (4, 6, 8, 4), pm, work Row 1 of chart, working repeat 4 (5, 5, 5, 6) times, then work last st on chart, pm, k0 (4, 6, 8, 4).

Row 2 (WS): K8 (4, 6, 8, 4), work chart as set to end, k8 (4, 6, 8, 4).

Cont until all rows of chart have been worked. With MC only, work in G st for 1.5cm, ending after a WS row.

Row 1 (RS): Knit.

Row 2 (WS): K8 (4, 6, 8, 4), p to marker, k8 (4, 6, 8, 4).

Rep last 2 rows until bonnet measures 14 (15, 16, 17, 18) cm from cast-on edge, ending after a WS row.

Dec 1 (5, 1, 5, 1) sts evenly over next RS row. 64 (64, 72, 72, 80) sts.

Knit 1 row.

Crown

Row 1 (RS): *K6 (6, 7, 7, 8), k2tog, rep from * to end. 56 (56, 64, 64, 72) sts.

Row 2 & all WS Rows: Purl.

Row 3: *K5 (5, 6, 6, 7), k2tog, rep from * to end. 48 (48, 56, 56, 64) sts.

Row 5: *K4 (4, 5, 5, 6), k2tog, rep from * to end. 40 (40, 48, 48, 56) sts.

Cont dec'ing in the same manner as above until 8 sts remain.

Knit 1 row.

Next Row (RS): *K2tog; rep from * to end. 4 sts.

Cut yarn, leaving a 30cm tail. With tapestry needle, thread tail through rem sts and close up seam along crown.

Chin strap

With RS bottom front corner of bonnet facing, use MC, pu and k6 sts. Work in G st for 9 (10, 11, 12, 13) cm, ending after a WS row.

Next Row (RS): K2, k2tog, yo, k2.

Work in G st for 4 more rows.

Cast off.

Finishing: With tapestry needle, weave in all yarn ends. Sew button onto left front bottom edge to correspond with buttonhole.

Special instructions

Bonnet is worked from the forehead to the crown and decreased at the back of the head. A garter stitch chin strap is knit on after.

Twisted Rib 1x3

Row 1: K1tbl, p3

Row 2: K3, p1tbl

Chart

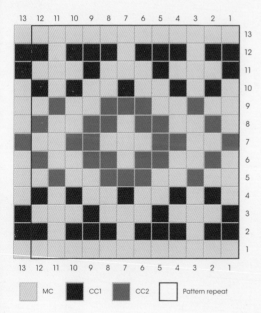

| | MC | | CC1 | | CC2 | | Pattern repeat |

Schematic

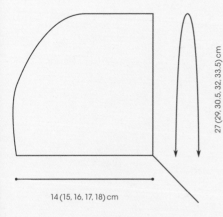

14 (15, 16, 17, 18) cm

27 (29, 30.5, 32, 33.5) cm

90

Fruity Beanies

These adorable little blueberry and strawberry hats are fun and easy to knit.

These hats are designed to sit low on the head, pulled right down over the ears for warmth. Practise with the Blueberry beanie, then move on to the Strawberry, which comes with a little stranded colourwork.

Strawberry

CAST ON

Cast on 74 (82, 90) sts.

Rows 1-8: Sl1, k to end.

Row 9: Sl1, p to end.

Row 10: Sl1, k to end.

Rows 9-10 establish St st.

Work - (4, 8) rows in St st and then begin working from chart, starting with Row 13 (7, 1) and working the 8-st repeat section a total of 9 (10, 11) times across the row.

After chart has been completed, 11 (12, 13) sts rem. Continue working in CC2.

Next row: Sl1, k2tog 4 (5, 6) times, k2 (1, -). 7 sts.

Next row: P2tog 3 times, p1. 4 sts.

Next row (i-cord): Knit. Slip all sts back to LH needle.

Work i-cord row 4 more times.

Cut yarn, thread through rem sts and pull tight to fasten.

Blueberry

Cast on 74 (82, 90) sts.

Rows 1-8: Sl1, k to end.

Row 9: Sl1, p to end.

Row 10: Sl1, k to end.

Rows 9-10 establish St st.

Work in St st for 13 (19, 25) more rows and then begin crown decreases.

Crown decreases

Row 1: Sl1, *k6, k2tog; rep from * to last st, k1. 65 (72, 79) sts.

Row 2 and all even rnds: Sl1, p to end.

Row 3: Sl1, *k5, k2tog; rep from * to last st, k1. 56 (62, 68) sts.

Row 5: Sl1, *k4, k2tog; rep from * to last st, k1. 47 (52, 57) sts.

Row 7: Sl1, *k3, k2tog; rep from * to last st, k1. 38 (42, 46) sts.

Row 9: Sl1, *k2, k2tog; rep from * to last st, k1. 29 (32, 35) sts.

Switch to CC.

About this pattern

2 Intermediate

Sizing
Newborn (6 months, 12 months)

Shown in 6 months size

Yarn
Blueberry beanie: 1 ball Blueberry Muffin (MC), small scrap Peppermint Green (CC)

Strawberry beanie: 1 ball Strawberry Fool (MC), small scraps Vanilla Slice (CC1) and Peppermint Green (CC2)

About the yarn
Betty and Belle DK; DK; 75m per 25g ball; 100% acrylic

Needles
4mm straight

Tension
Measured over St st:

Other supplies
Darning needle

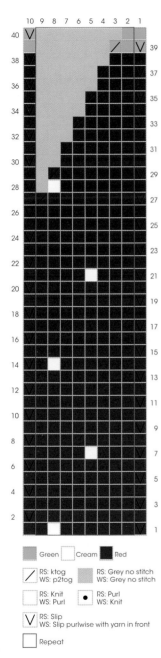

Row 11: Sl1, *k1, k2tog; rep from * to last st, k1. 20 (22, 24) sts.

Row 13: Sl1, *k2tog; rep from * to last st, k1. 11 (12, 13) sts.

Row 15: Sl1, k2tog 4 (5, 6) times, k2 (1, -). 7 sts.

Row 16: P2tog 3 times, p1. 4 sts.

Next row (i-cord): Knit. Slip all sts back to LH needle.

Work i-cord row 4 more times. Cut yarn, thread through rem sts and pull tight to fasten.

Finishing (both): Sew the seam using mattress st. Weave in ends. To even up the stitches, block gently by pinning out and using steam. Do not over-steam and do not allow the iron to touch the fabric.

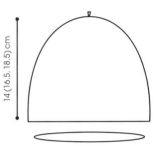

14 (16.5, 18.5) cm

31 (34, 38) cm

	Green		Cream		Red

/ RS: ktog / WS: p2tog   RS: Grey no stitch / WS: Grey no stitch

RS: Knit / WS: Purl   • RS: Purl / WS: Knit

V RS: Slip / WS: Slip purlwise with yarn in front

Repeat

93

Elfine Hood

1
Beginner

This simple hood was inspired by the designer's love of vintage knitting patterns, but it looks as good today as it would've done fifty years ago.

Most of us love knitting for babies and children, but it can be frustrating when they grow out of their lovingly knitted gifts so soon. The beauty of a hood like this is that it will last a little while longer than a jumper or a pair of booties, so you'll get the maximum out of this gorgeous yarn.

Border

Cast on 30 (37, 44) sts.

CAST ON

Row 1 (WS): P 0(1,0), *k1tbl, p1; rep from * to end.

Row 2: Knit.

Row 3: K 0(1,0) tbl, *p1, k1tbl; rep from * to end.

Row 4: Knit.

Rep these four rows once more, then rep

Row 1.

Body

Row 1 (RS): K9 (9, 9), *k3, yo, k2tog, k2; rep from * to end.

Row 2: [P3, yo, p2tog, p2] 3 (4, 5) times, [p1, k1tbl] 4 times, p1.

Row 3: As for Row 1 of body section.

Row 4: [P3, yo, p2tog, p2] 3 (4, 5) times, [k1tbl, p1] 4 times, k1tbl.

Rep these four rows until work measures 96 (121, 126) cm from cast on edge, ending with Row 3.

Border

Row 1: K 0(1,0) tbl, *p1, k1tbl; rep from * to end.

Row 2: Knit.

Row 3: P 0(1,0), *k1tbl, p1; rep from * to end.

Row 4: Knit.

Rep these four rows once more, then rep Row 1.

Cast off.

Finishing: Fold scarf in half lengthways with WS together. Make hood by joining back edges together and using mattress stitch form a seam 12 (15, 18) cm long from fold. Wash and block.

Schematic

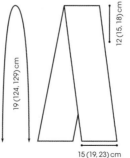

15 (19, 23) cm

19 (124, 129) cm

12 (15, 18) cm

About this pattern

Sizing
Baby (Toddler, Child)

Yarn
Lion Brand Superwash Merino Cashmere – 2 (3, 4) x 40g balls in Blossom

About the yarn
Aran weight; 80m per 40g; 72% Superwash Merino wool, 15% nylon, 13% cashmere

Needles
5mm straight

Tension
Measured St st:

10 cm

10 cm

24 rows

20 sts

Other supplies
Tapestry needle

Home
Accessories

Beautify the nursery with these adorable blankets
and cushions. All these patterns use standard
weight yarns so it'll be easy to substitute for yarns
which match your colour scheme.

Play & Learn Cushions

2
Intermediate

These cushions look great on the nursery floor, but they can also be used to aid learning.

If you haven't tried Swiss darning (also known as duplicate stitch) before, these cushions are a great way to practise a new technique.

CAST ON

Front and back
(make 2 – both designs)

Using cream yarn, cast on 50 sts. Work in st st for 54 rows.

Cast off loosely.

Finishing (both designs)

Using a tapestry needle, carefully sew the front and back together using mattress stitch, leaving an 8cm hole. Stuff the cushion until filled but still fairly soft and sew the hole closed.

Using blue, and beginning at the bottom-right corner, embroider a zigzag pattern around the edge of the cushion, following the seam. When working up and down the sides of the cushion, insert the needle under one strand of yarn 1½ sts away from the seam line. *Move up 3 rows, then insert the needle under one strand of yarn 1½ sts away from the other side of the seam line. Rep from * until the corner is reached.

When working across the top and bottom of the cushions, insert the needle under both strands of the stitch 2 rows away from the seam line. *Move along 2 sts, then insert the needle under both strands of the st 2 rows away from the other side of the seam line. Rep from * until the corner is reached.

Embroidery – shapes

Right side

The shapes pattern is applied using duplicate stitch (see Special Instructions box). Each shape – square, triangle, diamond – is represented as a chart. The charts are placed into a 3x3 grid on the cushion, beginning 2 rows below the embroidered edging as follows: Top Row: square (blue); triangle (red); diamond (green). Middle Row: diamond (red); square (green); triangle (blue). Bottom Row: triangle (green); diamond (blue); square (red).

About this pattern

Yarn
3 balls in Vanilla Slice, 1 ball each in Strawberry Fool, Blueberry Slice and Peppermint Green

Needles
4mm straight

Tension
Measured over St st:

10 cm

10 cm

28 rows

24 sts

Other supplies
Darning needle
Tapestry needle
Toy stuffing

Schematic

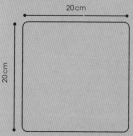

20 cm

20 cm

Embroidery – numbers

The numbers pattern is applied using duplicate stitch (see Special Instructions opposite).

The number side of the cushion is represented as a chart. The chart begins 3 rows below the embroidered edging and 3 sts away from the embroidered edging at each side.

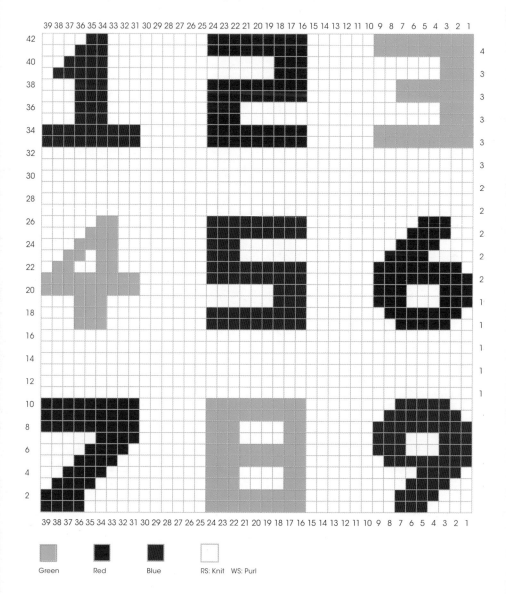

Green   Red   Blue   RS: Knit   WS: Purl

Special instructions

Duplicate stitch: This form of embroidery replicates the appearance of intarsia, or stranded knitting, without the need to use both yarns while knitting the item itself. Each stitch in knitting is comprised of a loop that travels up, across and back down the stitch. The up and down legs of the stitch form the 'V' that is visible on the right side of stocking stitch. Duplicate stitch uses a darning needle to trace the path of the knitted yarn through the stitch, and when worked from the right side sits above the knitted yarn, obscuring it.

Diamond

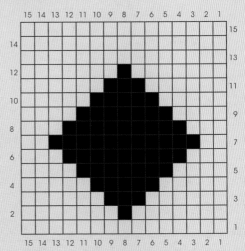

Triangle

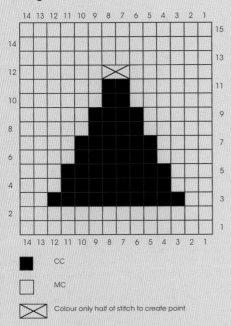

Square

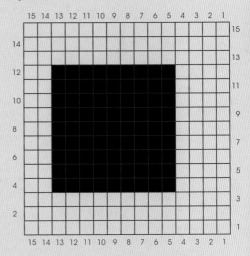

■ CC

☐ MC

⊠ Colour only half of stitch to create point

101

Stippling Blanket

2
Intermediate

Now you've learned how to do double knitting, practise your skills with this snuggly baby blanket.

This blanket makes use of the double layer created in double knitting to create a super soft, snuggly blanket that babies will love – and so will parents, since the yarn is machine washable! You will be beginning with 632 stitches. This will probably require using all three circular needles at once. As you gradually reduce the number of stitches on the needles, you can use fewer circular needles, and eventually use a single circular needle, switching to the smaller-length circulars as you continue to decrease stitches. Switch to DPNs once the stitches will no longer fit on the smallest circular.

CAST ON

Loosely cast on 632 sts using the double knitting cast-on (see Special Instructions box), starting with a stitch of MC2 (ie MC1 on your thumb during the cast on). Join to work in the rnd, being careful not to twist. pm to mark beg of rnd.

Set-up Rnd: *K1 MC2 wyib, p1 MC1 wyif; rep from * to end.

Rnd 1: Sm, [work Row 1 of Chart A, pm] three times, work Row 1 of Chart A.

Rnd 2 and all even rnds: Sm, sl1 p-wise wyib, sl1 p-wise wyif, [work next row of Chart A as set] four times. 616 sts.

Rnd 3 and all odd rnds: [Sm, work next row of Chart A as set] four times.

Cont patt as set until all 25 rows of Chart A have been worked. 440 sts.

Rnd 26: Sm, sl1 p-wise wyib, sl1 p-wise wyif, [work Row 1 of Chart B] four times. 424 sts.

Rnd 27 and all odd rnds: [Sm, work next row of Chart B as set] four times.

Rnd 28 and all even rnds: Sm, sl1 p-wise wyib, sl1 p-wise wyif, [work next row of Chart B as set] four times. 408 sts.

Cont patt as set until all 53 rows of Chart B have been worked. 8 sts.

Break yarns.

Removing markers as you come to them, thread the tail of MC2 through the rem four MC2 stitches; and then thread the tail of MC1 through the remaining four MC1 stitches.

Weave in all ends as invisibly as possible between the two layers of the blanket.

About this pattern

Yarn
Crystal Palace Mochi Plus/ Solid 4 balls each in Intense Rainbow 551 (MC) and Ecru 1500 (CC)
Note: the sample used very close to 200g of each yarn, you may like to buy 5 balls to be on the safe side.

About the yarn
Aran; 87m per 50g ball; 80% Merino wool, 20% nylon

Needles
6mm circular, 150cm
6mm circular, 80cm
6mm circular, 40cm
6mm DPNs

Tension
Measured over double knitted St st:

10 cm
10 cm
22 rows
26 sts (13 per side)

Other supplies
3 stitch markers
1 round marker (noticeably different from the stitch markers)
Cable needle

Special instructions

This blanket uses a slightly different cast-on to the one recommended.

We've put step-by-step instructions from Kathleen on our website www.knitnowmag.co.uk

Reading charts: All chart rows should be read from right to left.

Cdd: (Sl st onto CN and hold in front, sl1 p-wise) twice, rm, sl st onto CN and hold in front, transfer 2 sts from RH needle back to LH needle, transfer 3 sts from CN back to LH

needle, wyib sl2 as if to k2tog, k1 MC2, pass slipped sts over, wyif sl2 as if to p2tog-tbl, p1 MC1, pass slipped sts over, pm.

Chart A

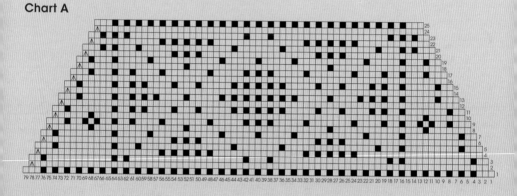

Schematic

67 cm

67 cm

Chart B

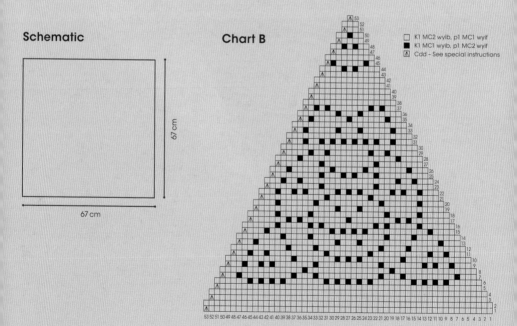

☐ K1 MC2 wyib, p1 MC1 wyif
■ K1 MC1 wyib, p1 MC2 wyif
⚠ Cdd – See special instructions

Corner to Corner Blanket

2
Intermediate

This cute blanket is an easy introduction to lace and it's perfect for using up odds and ends of yarn.

It's always good to have a lovely snuggly blanket to hand for baby. This one is fun to knit and easily adaptable to whatever yarn you have available, so feel free to experiment and try out different yarn.

Starting corner

CAST ON

With red yarn, cast on 3 sts.

Row 1 (RS): Knit.

Row 2 and all WS rows: K1, p to last st, k1.

Row 3: K1, yo, k1, yo, k1.

Row 5: K1, yo, k3, yo, k1.

Row 6: K1, p to last st, k1.

Main body

Still using red, work Rows 1-8 of Inc Lace Pattern seven times.

Change to cream and work Rows 1-8 of Inc Lace Pattern six times.

Change to blue and work Rows 1-8 of Inc Lace Pattern four times.

Change to cream and work Rows 1-8 of Inc Lace Pattern twice.

Still using cream, work Rows 1-8 of Dec Lace Pattern twice.

Change to green and work Rows 1-8 of Dec Lace Pattern four times.

Change to cream and work Rows 1-8 of Dec Lace Pattern six times.

Change to red and work Rows 1-8 of Dec Lace Pattern seven times.

Ending corner

Cont in red.

Row 1: K1, yo, sssk, k1, p1, yo, sk2p, yo, p1, k1, k3tog, yo, k1.

Row 2 and all WS rows: K1, p to last st, k1.

Row 3: K1, yo, sssk, p1, yo, sk2p, yo, p1, k3tog, yo, k1.

Row 5: K1, yo, sssk, yo, sk2p, yo, k3tog, yo, k1.

Row 7: K1, yo, sssk, k1, k3tog, yo, k1.

Row 9: K1, yo, sk2p, yo, k1.

Row 11: K3.

Cast off.

About this pattern

Yarn
1 ball each in Blueberry Muffin, Peppermint Green, Strawberry Fool, 3 balls in Vanilla Slice

Needles
4mm straight

Tension
Measured over St st

10 cm	
10 cm	28 rows
	24 sts

Other supplies
Darning needle

Hints & tips
If you're using the charts, please note that only RS rows are shown and they are read from right to left. For the WS rows, on every row you should work as follows: **k1, p to last st, k1**

Inc Lace Pattern

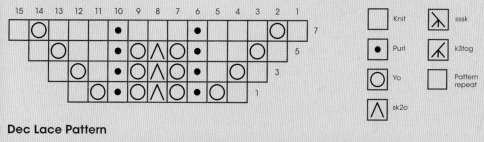

15 14 13 12 11 10 9 8 7 6 5 4 3 2 1

Symbol	Meaning	Symbol	Meaning
☐	Knit	sssk	sssk
•	Purl	k3tog	k3tog
◯	Yo	☐	Pattern repeat
∧	sk2o		

Dec Lace Pattern

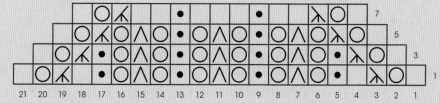

21 20 19 18 17 16 15 14 13 12 11 10 9 8 7 6 5 4 3 2 1

Special instructions

Inc Lace Pattern

Row 1 (RS): K1, yo, *p1, yo, sk2p, yo; rep from * to last 2 sts, p1, yo, k1.

Rows 2, 4, 6 and 8 (WS): K1, p to last st, k1.

Row 3: K1, yo, k1, *p1, yo, sk2p, yo; rep from * to last 3 sts, p1, k1, yo, k1.

Row 5: K1, yo, k2, *p1, yo, sk2p, yo; rep from * to last 4 sts, p1, k2, yo, k1.

Row 7: K1, yo, k3, *p1, k3; rep from * to last 5 sts, p1, k3, yo, k1.

Dec Lace Pattern

Row 1 (RS): K1, yo, sssk, k1, *p1, yo, sk2p, yo; rep from * to last 6 sts, p1, k1, k3tog, yo, k1.

Rows 2, 4, 6 and 8 (WS): K1, p to last st, k1.

Row 3: K1, yo, sssk, *p1, yo, sk2p, yo; rep from * to last 5 sts, p1, k3tog, yo, k1.

Row 5: K1, yo, sssk, yo, sk2p, yo, *p1, yo, sk2p, yo; rep from * to last 4 sts, k3tog, yo, k1.

Row 7: K1, yo, sssk, k2, *p1, k3; rep from * to last 7 sts, p1, k2, k3tog, yo, k1.

Toys

A cuddly toy can be a friend for life, and hand-knitted ones are already full of love in every stitch. These little sweeties are sure to be a big hit with your little ones.

Drawstring Bag & Pouch

2
Intermediate

These little knitted pouches are great for adding a splash of colour to your baby kit.

Simple stripes are fun to knit and we love the way these colours play together in stripes. If you have scraps of DK yarn in your stash, this would be an ideal pattern for using them all up.

Drawstring bag

CAST ON

Using blue yarn, cast on 77 sts.

Work in St st in stripes as follows:

6 rows blue, then **6 rows green, 2 rows cream, 2 rows red, 6 rows blue, 2 rows green, 6 rows cream, 6 rows red** then 2 rows blue. Rep from ** to ** once more.

Break off all yarn except blue and cont in blue only.

Knit 1 row.

Dec row: K2, k2tog, *k6, k2tog; rep from * to last st, k1. 67 sts.

Knit 10 rows.

Eyelet row: K4, k2tog, yo, *k6, k2tog, yo; rep from * to last 5 sts, k5.

Knit 12 rows.

Cast off k-wise.

i-cord

Using green, cast on 2 sts.

Work i-cord for 55cm.

Cast off.

Sew in ends. Join side seams. Placing seam at centre back, join bottom seam.

Thread i-cord through eyelets and tie in a bow.

About this pattern

Yarn
1 ball each in Blueberry Muffin, Peppermint Green, Vanilla Slice and Strawberry Fool

This is enough to knit both the bag and the pouch

About the Yarn
Betty and Belle DK; DK; 75m per 25g ball; 100% acrylic

Needles
4mm straight

Tension
Measured over St st:

10 cm

10 cm

28 rows

24 sts

Other supplies
Tapestry needle
Yarn bobbin (optional)

i-cord

K all sts on DPN. Without turning, slide sts to other end of needle. Rep until cord reaches desired length.

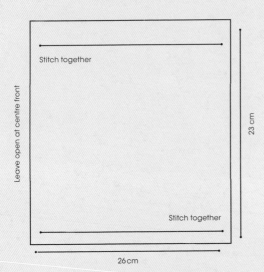

Stitch together

Leave open at centre front

Stitch together

23 cm

26cm

30 cm

30cm

Pouch

Before you start, wind off a small amount of green into a second ball or bobbin.

Using the main ball of green, cast on 63 sts.

**Row 1 (RS): Using green, knit.

Row 2: Using green, k6, p to last 6 sts, k6.

Row 3: K6 green, k51 blue, k6 green using smaller ball/bobbin.

Row 4: K6 green, p51 blue, k6 green.

Keeping 6 sts at each end in green and G st, work centre 51 sts in St st stripes of 6 rows in red, 2 rows in cream, 6 rows in green, 2 rows in blue, 6 rows in red, 2 rows in cream** then 8 rows in green, and finally rep from ** to ** but reversing the order of stripes.

Cast off.

i-cords (make 2)

Using red, cast on 2 sts.

Work i-cord for 20cm.

Cast off.

Sew in ends.

Wth WS facing, join side seams for approximately 5cm at each end. Placing open seam at centre front, join side seams. Turn pouch inside out.

Sew i-cords across G st at each side of gap and tie in a bow.

Special instructions

i-cord can be knitted on two needles as follows:

Cast on 2 sts.

Row 1: K2,*sl these 2 sts back onto left-hand needle, k2, rep from * until work measures required length.

Cast off.

Changing colours: twist yarns together at back of work to prevent a hole forming.

Fuzzy Bear

1
Beginner

A beloved teddy is a friend for life – but he needn't take that long to knit! Using simple shaping techniques, you can make this little guy in a few days.

The yarn is what makes this project absolutely perfect – the mohair content in Rowan Kid Classic gives Fuzzy Bear his name. He's quite an easy make, but if you want to make an even easier bear, skip the change of colour on his belly. The teddy is knit from the bottom up, and the body and head are knit in one piece.

Body and head

CAST ON

With MC, cast on 10 sts.

Row 1 (and all WS rows unless otherwise noted): Purl.

Row 2 (RS): K1, [kfb] nine times. 19 sts.

Row 4: K1, [kfb, k2] six times. 25 sts.

Row 6: K1, [kfb, k3] six times. 31 sts.

Row 8: K1, [kfb, k4] six times. 37 sts.

Row 10: K1, [kfb, k5] six times. 43 sts.

Row 12: K1, [kfb, k6] six times. 49 sts.

Row 13: P18, join CC and p12, join another ball of MC and purl to end.

Row 14: With MC k1, [kfb, k7] twice, kfb; with CC k7, kfb, k6; with MC k1, [kfb, k7] twice. 55 sts.

Row 15: With MC p18; with CC p17; with MC p20.

Row 16: With MC k20; with CC k17; with MC k18.

Rep Rows 15 and 16 five times more, then Row 15 once more.

Row 28: With MC [k8, k2tog] twice, k1; with CC k7, k2tog, k6; with MC k2, k2tog, k15. 51 sts.

Row 29: With MC p14, p2tog, p3; with CC p4, p2tog, p6; with MC p1, p2tog, p7, p2tog, p8. 47 sts.

Row 30: With MC k8, k2tog, k6, k2tog, k1; with CC k5, k2tog, k2; with MC k4, k2tog, k13. 43 sts.

Row 31: With MC p19; with CC p6; with MC p18.

Break CC (and extra MC) and continue in MC only.

Row 32: K1, [k2tog, k5] six times. 37 sts.

Row 34: K1, [k2tog, k4] six times. 31 sts.

Row 36: K1, [k2tog, k3] six times. 25 sts.

Row 38: K1, [kfb, k3] six times. 31 sts.

Row 39: [P4, pfb] six times, p1. 37 sts.

Row 40: K1, [kfb, k5] six times. 43 sts.

Row 42: K1, [kfb, k6] six times. 49 sts.

Row 44: K1, [kfb, k7] six times. 55 sts.

Row 46: K1, [kfb, k8] six times. 61 sts.

Rows 48, 50, 52, 54: Knit.

Row 56: K1, [k2tog, k8] six times. 55 sts.

Row 58: K1, [k2tog, k7] six times. 49 sts.

About this pattern

Yarn
Rowan Kid Classic – 1 x 50g ball in Bear 817 (MC) and 1 x 50g ball in Straw 851 (CC)

About the yarn
DK weight; 140m per 50g ball;
70% lambswool, 26% mohair, 4% nylon

Needles
3.75mm straight

Tension
Measured over St st:

10 cm

10 cm — 32 rows

24 sts

Other supplies
Tapestry needle
Polyester fibrefill
9mm safety eyes
15mm safety nose

Special instructions
Pfb: Purl through the front and then through the back of the same stitch.

Row 60: K1, [k2tog, k6] six times. 43 sts.

Row 62: K1, [k2tog, k5] six times. 37 sts.

Row 64: K1, [k2tog, k4] six times. 31 sts.

Row 66: K1, [k2tog, k3] six times. 25 sts.

Row 67: [P2, p2tog] six times, p1. 19 sts.

Row 68: K1, [k2tog, k1] six times. 13 sts.

Break yarn and draw tail through rem sts, pull tight, and fasten.

Using mattress stitch, seam the body, leaving a hole at the bottom open.

Ears (make 2)

With MC, cast on 22 sts.

Rows 1, 3, 5 (RS): With MC k11; with CC k11.

Rows 2, 4, 6: With CC p11; with MC p11.

Row 7: With MC k1, [k2tog] five times; with CC [k2tog] five times, k1. 12 sts.

Row 8: With CC [p2tog] three times; with MC [p2tog] three times. 6 sts.

Cut CC and fasten on the WS. Break MC, leaving long tail. Draw tail through rem sts, pull tight, and fasten.

Fold the ear with the wrong sides facing. Seam down the side.

Muzzle

With CC, cast on 25 sts.

Row 1 (RS): Knit.

Row 2 and all WS rows: Purl.

Row 3: As Row 1.

Row 5: K1, [k2tog, k1] eight times. 17 sts.

Row 7: K1, [k2tog] eight times. 9 sts.

Row 9: K1, [k2tog] four times. 5 sts.

Break yarn, leaving long tail. Draw

tail through rem sts, pull tight, and fasten. Seam down the side. Attach safety nose or embroider nose to middle of muzzle.

Arms (make 2)

With MC, cast on 10 sts.

Row 1 and all WS rows (WS): Purl.

Row 2: K1, [kfb k2] three times. 13 sts.

Row 4: K1, [kfb, k3] three times. 16 sts.

Row 6: K1, [kfb, k4] three times. 19 sts.

Rows 8, 10, 12, 14, 16: Knit.

Row 18: K1, [k2tog, k1] six times. 13 sts.

Row 20: K1, [k2tog] six times. 7 sts.

Break yarn, leaving long tail. Draw tail through rem sts, pull tight, and fasten. Fold the arm with the wrong sides facing. Using mattress stitch, seam down the side. Stuff and seam across the top.

Legs (make 2)

With MC, cast on 16 sts.

Beginning with a knit row, work in St st for 20 rows.

Row 21: K5, [kfb] seven times, k4. 23 sts.

Row 22: Purl.

Work in St st for 4 rows.

Row 27: K5, [k2tog] seven times, k4. 16 sts.

Row 28: [P2tog] eight times. 8 sts.

Break yarn, leaving long tail. Draw tail through rem sts, pull tight, and fasten. Fold the leg with the wrong sides facing. Using mattress stitch, seam down the side. Stuff. If you want your bear to be able to sit, seam across the top of the leg, with the foot facing you.

Finishing: Stuff body. Using mattress stitch, attach the muzzle to the centre of the face. Stuff the muzzle before it is fully attached. Add the safety eyes, or embroider eyes, about 4 sts up from the muzzle and 3 sts apart. Attach ears to the side of the head, with the bottom of the ears level with the eyes. Seam up the hole at the bottom of body and attach arms and legs to sides and base of body.

Schematic

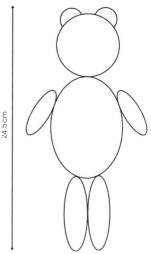

24.5cm

Hints & tips

When working the intarsia part for the tummy, remember to twist the yarn together at the colour changes so you do not get a hole. Before you start knitting, wind some of the main colour into a separate ball so you have a ball for either side of the colour change.

Barnyard Pals

1
Beginner

The ideal size for little hands, this trio of friendly toys will give the lucky recipient as much pleasure at playtime as you'll get from knitting them.

This cow, sheep and donkey are just bursting with character, and we know you'll love bringing them to life. With one ball of each colour, you can make the sheep and the donkey or the cow – with two balls of each colour, you can make all three.

Cow

Legs (make 4)

Leg starts from the top of the leg.

With MC1, cast on 20 sts.

Work in St st for 6 rows.

Change to MC2 and work in St st for 4 rows.

Purl 2 rows.

Row 13: *K1, k2tog, k1; rep from * to end. 15 sts.

Row 14: *P1, p2tog; rep from * to end. 10 sts.

Row 15: *K2tog; rep from * to end. 5 sts.

Break yarn and draw tail through rem sts, pull tight, and fasten.

Body (make 1)

Body starts from neck.

With MC1, cast on 10 sts.

Row 1: *Kfb; rep from * to end. 20 sts.

Row 2: Purl.

Row 3: *Kfb, k1; rep from * to end. 30 sts.

Row 4: Purl.

Row 5: *K1, kfb, k1; rep from * to end. 40 sts.

Row 6: Purl.

Row 7: *K1, kfb, k2; rep from * to end. 50 sts.

Work in St st for 15 rows.

Row 23: *K1, k2tog, k2; rep from * to end. 40 sts.

Row 24: Purl.

Row 25: *K1, k2tog, k1; rep from * to end. 30 sts.

Row 26: Purl.

Row 27: *K1, k2tog; rep from * to end. 20 sts.

Row 28: Purl.

CAST ON

About this pattern

Yarn

Lion Brand Superwash Merino Cashmere – 1-2 x 40g balls in Blossom (MC1) and 1-2 x 40g in Wine (MC2)

About the Yarn

Aran; 80m per 40g ball; 72% Merino wool, 15% nylon, 13% cashmere

Needles

5 mm, straight

Tension

Measured over St st:

10 cm

10 cm | 25 rows

17 sts

Other supplies

Tapestry needle
Toy stuffing
Crochet hook to add hair

Hints & tips

Pin the pieces of your animal together before sewing, just in case you find one ear is slightly out of place or if your animal topples over when you stand him up. To give your animal a flatter foot cut out small cardboard circles and insert them in the leg before stuffing

Row 29: *K2tog; rep from
* to end. 10 sts.

Row 30: *P2tog; rep from
* to end. 5 sts.

Break yarn and draw tail through
rem sts, pull tight, and fasten.

Head (make 1)

Head starts from top of head.

With MC1, cast on 12 sts.

Row 1: K1, [kfb] 4 times, k2, [kfb]
4 times, k1. 20 sts.

Row 2: Purl.

Row 3: K2, [kfb] 6 times, k4, [kfb] 6
times, k2. 32 sts.

Work in St st for 3 rows.

Row 7: K6, [kfb] 4 times, k12, [kfb] 4
times, k6. 40 sts.

Work in St st for 11 rows.

Change to MC2 and work in St st
for 6 rows.

Row 25: K6, [k2tog] 4 times, k12,
[k2tog] 4 times, k6. 32 sts.

Row 26: Purl.

Row 27: K2, [k2tog] 6 times, k4,
[k2tog] 6 times, k2. 20 sts.

Row 28:   Purl.

Row 29: K1, [k2tog] 4 times, k2,
[k2tog] 4 times, k1. 12 sts.

Cast off.

Ears (make 2)

Ears start from bottom of ears.

With MC2, cast on 10 sts.

Row 1: K1, [kfb] twice, k4, [kfb]
twice, k1. 14 sts.

Work in St st for 3 rows.

Row 5: K1, k2tog, k1, k2tog, k2,
k2tog, k1, k2tog, k1. 10 sts.

Row 6: P1, [p2tog] 4 times, p1. 6 sts.

Row 7: K1, [k2tog] twice, k1. 4 sts.

Row 8: [P2tog] twice. 2 sts.

Cast off.

Horns (make 2)

With MC2, cast on 10 sts.

Row 1: K2tog, k2, [kfb] twice,
k2, k2tog.

Row 2: Purl.

Row 3: [K2tog] twice, [kfb] twice,
[k2tog] twice. 8 sts.

Row 4: Purl.

Row 5: K2tog, k1, [kfb] twice,
k1, k2tog.

Row 6: Purl.

Row 7: *K2tog; rep from
* to end. 4 sts.

Row 8: Purl.

Row 9: [K2tog] twice. 2 sts.

Cast off.

Patch 1

With MC2, cast on 6 sts.

Row 1: Cast on 1 st, k7. 7 sts.

Row 2: Cast on 1 st, p8. 8 sts.

Row 3: Cast on 3 sts, k11. 11 sts.

Row 4: Cast on 1 st, p12. 12 sts.

Work in St st for 2 rows.

Row 7: Cast off 4 sts, k7. 8 sts.

Row 8: Purl.

Row 9: Cast off 1 st, k6. 7 sts.

Row 10: Cast off 1 st, p5. 6 sts.

Row 11: Cast off 1 st, k4. 5 sts.

Row 12: Cast off 1 st, p3. 4 sts.

Cast off.

Patch 2

With MC2, cast on 6 sts.

Row 1: Purl.

Row 2: Cast on 2 sts, k8. 8 sts.

Row 3: Cast on 2 sts, p10. 10 sts.

Work in St st for 3 rows.

Row 7: Cast off 5 sts, k5. 5 sts.

Row 8: Purl.

Cast off.

Tail

With MC1, cast on 10 sts.

Work in St st for 3 rows.

Cast off.

Sheep

CAST ON

Legs (make 4)

Leg starts at top of leg.

With MC2, cast on 16 sts.

Work in St st for 8 rows.

Row 9: Purl.

Row 10: *P1, p2tog, p1; rep from * to end. 12 sts.

Row 11: *K1, k2tog; rep from * to end. 8 sts.

Row 12: *P2tog; rep from * to end. 4 sts.

Break yarn and draw tail through rem sts, pull tight, and fasten.

Body

Body starts at top of neck.

With MC1, cast on 10 sts.

Row 1: *Kfb; rep from * to end. 20 sts.

Row 2: Purl.

Row 3: *Kfb, loop st; rep from * to end. 30 sts.

Row 4: Purl.

Row 5: *Loop st, kfb, k1; rep from * to end. 40 sts.

Row 6: Purl.

Row 7: *Loop st, k1; rep from * to end.

Row 8: Purl.

Row 9: *K1, loop st; rep from * to end.

Rep Rows 6-9 once, then rep Rows 6-8 once more.

Row 17: *K1, k2tog, loop st; rep from * to end. 30 sts.

Row 18: Purl.

Row 19: *K2tog, loop st; rep from * to end. 20 sts.

Row 20: Purl.

Row 21: *K2tog; rep from * to end. 10 sts.

Row 22: *P2tog; rep from * to end. 5 sts.

Break yarn and draw tail through rem sts, pull tight, and fasten.

Head

Head starts at top of head.

With MC2, cast on 8 sts.

Row 1: K1, [kfb] twice, k2, [kfb] twice, k1. 12sts.

Row 2: Purl.

Row 3: K1, [kfb] 3 times, k4, [kfb] 3 times, k1. 18 sts.

Row 4: Purl.

Row 5: K3, [kfb] 3 times, k6, [kfb] 3 times, k3. 24 sts.

Row 6: Purl.

Row 7: K4, [kfb] 4 times, k8, [kfb] 4 times, k4. 32 sts.

Work in St st for 9 rows.

Row 17: K4, [k2tog] 4 times, k8, [k2tog] 4 times, k4. 24 sts.

Row 18: Purl.

Row 19: K3, [k2tog] 3 times, k6, [k2tog] 3 times, k3. 18 sts.

Row 20: Purl.

Row 21: K1, [k2tog] 3 times, k4, [k2tog] 3 times, k1.12 sts.

Row 22: Purl.

Row 23: K1, [k2tog] twice, k2, [k2tog] twice, k1. 8 sts.

Break yarn and draw tail through rem sts, pull tight, and fasten.

Ears (make 2)

Ears start at bottom of ears.

With MC2, cast on 10 sts.

Row 1: Purl.

Row 2: K1, [kfb] twice, k4, [kfb] twice, k1. 14 sts.

Row 3: Purl.

Row 4: K1, [k2tog] twice, k4, [k2tog] twice, k1. 10 sts.

Row 5: P1, [p2tog] 4 times, p1. 6 sts.

Row 6: K1, [k2tog] twice, k1. 4 sts.

Row 7: [P2tog] twice. 2 sts.

Cast off.

Hair

With MC1, cast on 8 sts.

Row 1: Purl.

Row 2: [Loop st, k1] 4 times.

Row 3: Purl.

Row 4: [K1, loop st] 4 times.

Cast off.

Donkey

CAST ON

Legs (make 4)

Work as for cow, casting on with MC2 then changing to MC1.

Body

Body starts at neck.

With MC2, cast on 8 sts.

Row 1: *Kfb; rep from * to end. 16 sts.

Row 2: Purl.

Row 3: *K1, kfb; rep from * to end. 24 sts.

Row 4: Purl.

Row 5: *K1, kfb, k1; rep from * to end. 32 sts.

Row 6: Purl.

Row 7: *K1, kfb, k2; rep from * to end. 40 sts.

Work in St st for 15 rows.

Row 23: *K1, k2tog, k2; rep from * to end. 32 sts.

Row 24: Purl.

Row 25: *K1, k2tog, k1; rep from * to end. 24 sts.

Row 26: Purl.

Row 27: *K1, k2tog; rep from * to end. 16 sts.

Row 28: Purl.

Row 29: *K2tog; rep from * to end. 8 sts.

Row 30: *P2tog; rep from * to end. 4 sts.

Break yarn and draw tail through rem sts, pull tight, and fasten.

Head

Head starts at top of head.

With MC2, cast on 10 sts.

Row 1: Purl.

Row 2: *K1, kfb; rep from * to end. 15 sts.

Work in St st for 3 rows.

Row 6: *K1, kfb, k1; rep from * to end. 20 sts.

Row 7: Purl.

Row 8: *K1, kfb, k2; rep from * to end. 25 sts.

Row 9: Purl.

Row 10: *K2, kfb, k2; rep from * to end. 30 sts.

Row 11: Purl.

Change to MC1.

Row 12: *K5, kfb ; rep from * to end. 35 sts.

Row 13 and all odd rows: Purl.

Row 14: *K3, kfb, k3; rep from * to end. 40 sts.

Row 16: *K2, kfb, k1; rep from * to end. 50 sts.

Row 18: *K4, k2tog, k4; rep from * to end. 45 sts.

Row 20: *K2, k2tog, k1; rep from * to end. 36 sts.

Row 22: *K1, k2tog, k1; rep from * to end. 27 sts.

Row 24: *K1, k2tog; rep from * to end. 18 sts.

Row 26: *K2tog; rep from * to end. 9 sts.

Break yarn and draw tail through rem sts, pull tight, and fasten.

Tail

Work as for cow.

Ears (make 2)

Work as for cow.

Schematics

Cow

Floor to top of horns: 13 cm

Nose to tail: Approx. 20 cm

Sheep

Floor to top of ears: 9 cm

Nose to bottom: Approx. 11 cm

Donkey

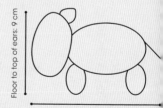

Floor to top of ears: 9 cm

Nose to tail: Approx. 18 cm

Making up

For all animals sew up the seam of the head, leaving a gap for stuffing and attaching eyes. For a neat result use mattress stitch.

To make the eyes make a French knot and attach it in place. Check that both eyes are level.

Stuff and sew along the seam of the body. Stuff the legs and attach these to the body using pins.

Attach the head with pins and check the animal stands without support. Now sew the pieces together.

Secure the tail to the cow and the donkey's backside and add some strands of hair by cutting lengths of yarn that are twice as long as you want the finished hair to be plus maybe little bit more, to allow for the knot and a final trim.

Insert a crochet hook into the back of the tail and put a folded strand of yarn on the hook.

Pull the loop through and then take the two ends of yarn and pull them through the loop to create a knot.

Repeat a few more times and trim the tail.

Repeat the same technique to the top of the donkey's head to give him his mane and trim to your desire.

For the sheep sew the loopy hair piece to the top of his head.

To create the horns and ears, fold these in half and sew along the seam. Attach to the head using the cast on seam. Add the patches to the cow.

Your barnyard pals are now ready to wreak havoc in your home!

Special instructions

Loop stitch:

To make a loop, knit one stitch like normal but instead of dropping the yarn off the left needle like a normal knit stitch, leave on LH needle. Bring the yarn from back to front in between needles and loop it around your thumb. Bring the yarn tail back between the needles and knit the stitch off the LH needle. You now have 2 sts on RH needle and a loop in between. Now pass the first st over the second st to secure the loop.

Bunny Family Picnic

1

Beginner

Mummy, Daddy and Baby bunny are so cute – and just the right size for tiny hands. They even have their own little picnic blanket to sit on!

This set uses gorgeous yarns from Blacker Yarns, which are spun at its specialist wool mill at Launceston on the Devon/Cornwall border using the fleece of British sheep. If you want to make these characters 100% wool, you can also buy carded wool that you can use for stuffing.

Mummy

(Repeat for Daddy, they are both alike)

Bunnies are worked on 3.75mm needles.

CAST ON

Head (make 1 in MC)

Work begins at back of head.

Cast on 3 sts.

Row 1 (WS): Purl.

Row 2: K1, *m1, k1; rep from * to end. 5 sts.

Row 3: Purl.

Row 4: K1, *m1, k1; rep from * to end. 9 sts.

Row 5: Purl.

Row 6: [K1, m1] three times, k3, [m1, k1] three times. 15 sts.

Work in St st for 7 rows.

Row 14: [K1, ssk] twice, k3, [k2tog, k1] twice. 11 sts.

Row 15: Purl.

Row 16: K1, [ssk] twice, k1, [k2tog] twice, k1. 7 sts.

Row 17: Purl.

Row 18: K1, [k2tog] three times.

Break yarn and draw tail through rem sts, pull tight, and fasten.

Body (make 2 in MC)

Cast on 7 sts.

Row 1 (WS): Purl.

Row 2: K1, m1, k5, m1, k1. 9 sts.

Work in St st for 3 rows.

Row 6: K1, m1, k7, m1, k1. 11 sts.

Work in St st 3 rows.

Row 10: K1, m1, k9, m1, k1. 13 sts.

Work in St st for 9 rows.

Cast off.

Leg (make 2 in MC)

Cast on 9 sts.

Starting with a purl row, work in St st for 13 rows.

Row 14: K1, ssk, k3, k2tog, k1. 7 sts.

Row 15: Purl.

Row 16: K1, ssk, k1, k2tog, k1. 5 sts.

Break yarn and draw tail through rem sts, pull tight, and fasten.

About this pattern

Yarn

Blacker Yarns pure British wool – 2 balls Shetland DK in Katmogit (MC), 1 ball Romney Guernsey in Natural (CC1), 1 ball Isles of Scilly Jacob Guernsey in Navy (CC2), 1 ball Romney Guernsey in Oxblood (CC3)

About the yarn

Shetland: DK; 110m per 50g ball; 100% Shetland wool

Guernsey: 5-ply; 116m per 50g ball; 100% British wool (Romney or Jacob)

Needles

3.25mm straight
3.75mm straight
4mm straight

Tension

Measured over stocking stitch using 3.75mm needles:

10 cm

10 cm

26 rows

18 sts

Other supplies

2 small shirt buttons
Toy stuffing
Small length of black yarn for facial features

Hints & tips

It is important to use the yarns stated to achieve the correct results. The Guernsey DK yarn is thinner than average DK, and the clothes are designed to fit the bunnies using this yarn only.

Arm (make 2 in CC1)

Cast on 7 sts.

Starting with a purl row, work in St st for 9 rows.

Row 10: K1, ssk, k1, k2tog, k1. 5 sts.

Row 11: Purl.

Row 12: Ssk, k1, k2tog. 3 sts.

Break yarn and draw tail through rem sts, pull tight, and fasten.

Ears (make 2 in MC and 2 in CC1)

Cast on 3 sts.

Row 1: Purl.

Row 2: [K1, m1] twice, k1. 5 sts.

Row 3: Purl.

Row 4: Knit.

Row 5: P2tog, p1, p2tog.

Row 6: Knit.

Row 7: P1, p2tog, pass the first st over the second stitch.

Break yarn and draw tail through rem st, pull tight, and fasten.

Baby

Head (make 1 in MC)

Cast on 3 sts.

Beginning at back of head, p one row.

Row 2: K1, *m1, k1; rep from * to end. 5 sts.

Row 3: Purl.

Row 4: K1, *m1, k1; rep from * to end. 9 sts.

Row 5: Purl.

Row 6: [K1, m1] three times, k3, [m1, k1] three times. 15 sts.

Work St st for 5 rows.

Row 12: [K1, ssk] twice, k3, [k2tog, k1] twice. 11 sts.

Row 13: Purl.

Row 14: K1, [ssk] twice, k1, [k2tog] twice, k1. 7 sts.

Row 15: Purl.

Daddy bunny

Row 16: K1, [K2tog] three times. 4 sts.

Break yarn and draw tail through rem sts, pull tight, and fasten.

Body (make 2 in MC)

Cast on 7 sts.

Row 1: Purl.

Row 2: K1, m1, k5, m1, k1. 9 sts.

Work in St st for 3 rows.

Row 6: K1, m1, K7, m1, k1. 11 sts.

Work in St st for 11 rows.

Cast off.

Arms (make 2 in MC)

Cast on 7 sts.

Starting with a purl row, work in St st for 5 rows.

Row 6: K1, ssk, k1, k2tog, k1. 5 sts.

Row 7: Purl.

Row 8: Ssk, k1, k2tog. 3 sts.

Break yarn and draw tail through rem sts, pull tight, and fasten.

Legs (make 2 in MC)

Cast on 8 sts.

Starting with a purl row, work in St st for 10 rows.

Row 11: K1, ssk, k2, k2tog, k1. 6 sts.

Row 12: Purl.

Row 13: K1, ssk, k2tog, k1. 4 sts.

Break yarn and draw tail through rem sts, pull tight, and fasten.

Ears (make 2 in MC and 2 in CC1)

Cast on 3 sts.

Row 1: Purl.

Row 2: [K1, m1] twice, k1. 5 sts.

Row 3: Purl.

Row 4: Knit.

Row 5: P2tog, p1, p2tog.

Row 6: Knit.

Row 7: P1, p2tog, pass the first st over the second stitch.

Break yarn and draw tail through rem st, pull tight, and fasten.

Making up

Head

Starting at the nose (cast off) end, sew the head seam together, stuffing as you go. Use small pieces of stuffing to achieve a good shape. Sew the ears together in pairs of one MC and one CC1, all around the edges. Attach the ears to the head towards the back. For the Baby Bunny, attach the ears facing downwards. Embroider two eyes and a nose in black yarn.

Body

Join the bottom and side seams of the body pieces and stuff. (The wider part of the body is the bottom edge.) Join the shoulder seams. Sew the head to the body.

Legs

Join the back seam for the leg using mattress stitch, stuffing as you go. At the top of the leg, flatten the top, with the seam at the centre back of leg, and stitch across the top. Sew the legs to the body.

Arms

Join the back seam for the arm using mattress stitch, stuffing as you go. At the top of the arm, flatten the top, with the seam at the centre back of arm, and stitch across the top. Sew the arms to the body.

Mummy's dress (make 2 in CC3)

On 3.25mm needles, cast on 24 sts.

Knit 2 rows.

Begin pattern

Row 1: Knit.

Row 2: Purl.

Row 3: *K3, p1; rep from * to end.

Row 4: Purl.

Row 5: Knit.

Row 6: Purl.

Row 7: K1, P1, *K3, P1; rep to last 2 sts, K2.

Row 8: Purl.

These 8 rows form pattern.

Complete 3 repetitions of the pattern in total.

Begin waist decreases:

Row 27:   K2, ssk, k4, ssk, k4, K2tog, k4, K2tog, k2. 20sts.

Row 28: Knit.

Work in 1 x 1 ribbing for 2 rows.

Row 31: Keeping continuity of rib, dec 1 st at each end of this and following 2 alternate rows. 14 sts.

Row 36: 1 x 1 rib.

Split for neck

Work 4 sts 1x1 rib, turn and work 3 more rows in 1x1 rib on these 4 sts.

Cast off.

Rejoin yarn and pick up 1 st at the base of the first shoulder strap. Cast off 7 sts,

1x1 rib to end of row.

Work 3 more rows in 1x1 rib on the remaining 4 sts.

Cast off.

Sew dress together at shoulders and from ribbed bodice to hem on sides.

Daddy's trousers
(make 2 in CC2)

On 3.25mm needles, cast on 20 sts.

Knit 2 rows.

St st 10 rows.

Cast off 2 sts at beginning of next 2 rows. 16 sts.

St st 6 rows.

Work 1x1 rib for 2 rows.

Cast off in rib.

Braces
(make 2 in CC3)

On 3.25mm needles, cast on 3 sts.

Row 1: K1, p1, k1.

Row 2: P1, k1, p1.

Cont until each brace strap measures 12cm.

Cast off.

Join the back of the trousers to the front and join the leg seams. Attach one brace strap to each side of the front waistband, and attach the other end to the back waistband, crossing the braces at the back. Sew a button to the front braces at the waistband.

Baby's dress
(make 2 in CC1)

On 3.25mm needles, cast on 20 sts.

Knit 2 rows.

Begin pattern

Row 1: Knit.

Row 2: Purl.

Row 3: *K3, p1; rep from * to end.

Row 4: Purl.

Row 5: Knit.

Row 6: Purl.

Row 7: K1, p1, *k3, p1; rep from * to last 2 sts, k2.

Row 8: Purl.

These 8 rows form pattern.

Complete one more repetition of the pattern.

Begin waist decreases:

Row 19: K1, ssk, k14, ssk, k2tog, k1. 18 sts.

Row 20: Knit.

Row 21 and 22: *K1, p1; rep from * to end.

Row 23: Ssk, *k1, p1; rep from * to last 2 sts, k2tog. 16 sts.

Row 24: K1, *k1, p1; rep from * to last st, k1.

Row 25: Ssk, *p1, k1; rep from * to last 3 sts, p1, k2tog. 14 sts.

Rows 26-29: *K1, p1; rep from * to end.

Cast off in rib.

Schematic

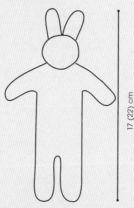

8 (8) cm
Baby (Mummy/Daddy) Bunny

17 (22) cm

Mummy bunny

Join the shoulders with a few stitches at the outside edge of each shoulder. Join the side seams from the ribbed bodice to the hem.

Flower for Baby's dress
(make 1 in CC3)

On 3.25mm needles, cast on 3 sts.

Next Row: *Kfb; rep from * to end. 6 sts.

Next Row: *Kfb; rep from * to end. 12 sts.

Cast off loosely.

Form the flower into a ring and sew the side edges together. Sew to the front of the dress.

Flower for Baby's head
(make 1 in CC3)

Cast on 2 sts.

Next Row: *Kfb; rep from * to end. 4 sts.

Next Row: *Kfb; rep from * to end. 8 sts.

Cast off loosely.

Form the flower into a ring and sew the side edges together. Sew to the head between the ears.

Flowers for Mummy's dress
(make 6 in CC1)

Cast on 2 sts.

Next Row: *Kfb; rep from
* to end. 4 sts.

Next Row: *Kfb; rep from
* to end. 8 sts.

Cast off loosely.

Form the flower into a ring and
sew the side edges together. Sew
around the bottom of the dress.

Picnic blanket

Using all the yarn held double
throughout and 4mm needles,
cast on 32 sts in CC3.

Knit 2 rows in CC3.

The blanket has a border in CC3. Use
separate balls of yarn at each side
for the border, do not carry the yarn

across the back of the blanket.

Begin blanket:

Row 1: K2 CC3, k28 CC1,
k2 CC3.

Row 2: K2 CC3, p28 CC1,
k2 CC3.

These 2 rows form the
pattern. Continue the stripe
sequence in this pattern
as follows:

4 rows CC2, 2 Rows CC3,
4 Rows CC2, 2 rows CC1.

Repeat this sequence
twice more.

Work 4 rows CC2

Row 43 and 44: K32 in CC3.

Cast off.

Sew in all ends and block the
blanket to flatten it.

Baby
bunny